# THE BOY IN THE SNOW

## BY THE SAME AUTHOR

*White Heat*

Nonfiction as Melanie McGrath

*The Long Exile: A Tale of Inuit Betrayal and Survival
in the High Arctic*

*Silvertown: An East End Family Memoir*

*Motel Nirvana*

# THE BOY
## IN
# THE SNOW

M. J. McGrath

VIKING

VIKING
Published by the Penguin Group
Penguin Group (USA) Inc., 375 Hudson Street,
New York, New York 10014, U.S.A.
Penguin Group (Canada), 90 Eglinton Avenue East, Suite 700,
Toronto, Ontario, Canada M4P 2Y3
(a division of Pearson Penguin Canada Inc.)
Penguin Books Ltd, 80 Strand, London WC2R 0RL, England
Penguin Ireland, 25 St. Stephen's Green, Dublin 2, Ireland
(a division of Penguin Books Ltd)
Penguin Books Australia Ltd, 250 Camberwell Road, Camberwell,
Victoria 3124, Australia
(a division of Pearson Australia Group Pty Ltd)
Penguin Books India Pvt Ltd, 11 Community Centre, Panchsheel Park,
New Delhi – 110 017, India
Penguin Group (NZ), 67 Apollo Drive, Rosedale, Auckland 0632,
New Zealand (a division of Pearson New Zealand Ltd)
Penguin Books (South Africa) (Pty) Ltd, 24 Sturdee Avenue,
Rosebank, Johannesburg 2196, South Africa

Penguin Books Ltd, Registered Offices:
80 Strand, London WC2R 0RL, England

First published in 2012 by Viking Penguin,
a member of Penguin Group (USA) Inc.

10  9  8  7  6  5  4  3  2  1

Publisher's Note
This is a work of fiction. Names, characters, places, and incidents either are the product
of the author's imagination or are used fictitiously, and any resemblance to actual persons,
living or dead, business establishments, events, or locales is entirely coincidental.

LIBRARY OF CONGRESS CATALOGING IN PUBLICATION DATA

McGrath, M. J.
  The boy in the snow : an Edie Kiglatuk mystery / M. J. McGrath.
  p.  cm.
  ISBN 978-0-670-02369-1 (hardback)
  1. Inuit women—Alaska—Fiction.  2. Iditarod (Race)—Fiction.  3. Boys—Crimes against—
Fiction.  4. Christian sects—Fiction.  I. Title.
  PR6113.C4775B69 2012
  823'.92—dc23
  2012015038

Printed in the United States of America
Set in Warnock Pro
Designed by Alissa Amell

**For Peter and Margaret**

# THE BOY IN THE SNOW

# 1

Edie Kiglatuk had no way of knowing how long the bear had been looking at her. His eyes, brown and beady, were like dark stars in a summer sky, set in clouds of fur. He raised his nose and snuffled, scenting her out, his huge body framed by the snow-laden spruce of the Alaska forest.

She had spent enough of her life around polar bears to be sure that, despite its colour, the animal standing before her wasn't one. Ice bears had longer heads, sharper snouts and smaller ears. This creature was different, snub-snouted and raggedy, the size of a black bear. Only not black. And, with its brown eyes, no albino either.

On the long flight over from her home in Autisaq in High Arctic Canada, Edie had passed the time reading guides to Alaskan flora and fauna and it now occurred to her that the animal was a spirit bear. *Qalunaat,* white folk, called them Kermode bears but the native people, the Gitga'at, knew them as *mooksgm'ol,* and never hunted them. They said the bears were outsider animals, creatures with the power to pass messages across the invisible portals between the living and the dead.

Something in her felt compelled to get closer. Swinging from her snowmobile she landed with a dull thud in the snow. Alarmed, the animal gave a short bark and rose on his hind legs. He was about six feet tall but his stance wasn't so much aggressive as . . . *As what?*

Edie had been around bears all her life, but there was something about this one she couldn't read.

For a moment the animal continued to face her, his nostrils flaring, small eyes brown and shiny as rain-soaked rock, then he dropped back down and slowly began to tromp away among the trees, turning his head from time to time to make sure she was not following.

Or maybe to make sure she was.

The animal reached a patch of sunlight between two spruce, stopped and turned around. Then he stood, making little coughing sounds, his breath fogging the air.

Waiting.

She moved towards him, slowly at first, then with more confidence. For a few moments he stood fast, then he turned and began to lumber further into the forest. She continued forward, sure now that the bear was leading her somewhere, that he had sought her out.

Glancing at her watch, she saw it was just past 9 a.m. In two hours from now Sammy Inukpuk would be pulling into the official start of the Iditarod dogsled race at Willow, expecting to see his ex-wife among the backup crews. It was her job to make sure he had all the supplies he needed and to offer moral support at the start of what were bound to be two of the most challenging weeks of Sammy's life as he raced sixteen dogs 1150 miles through some of the toughest terrain on the planet. From then on, she'd remain in Anchorage, organizing supplies and being on hand to receive any dogs that might get injured en route, while her old friend and ally, Derek Palliser, provided logistics support and managed communications up at the race finish in the northwestern town of Nome.

Edie walked on, the bear maybe fifty feet ahead, through stands of white spruce then out into clumps of quaking aspen, wading through deep snow, her heart thudding in her throat. It seemed as though they had been travelling a long time when, all of a sudden, the bear stopped and swivelled about. He was a long distance away now, his body visible through the trees like a patch of mist in the dark. He watched her heading closer for a while, then raised his head and smelled the air, turned and cantered away.

Edie looked about. For the first time in her adult life, she realized that she was lost. Glancing back at her footprints, she could already see that the bear had led her round in circles, jumbling the prints into a series of long switchbacks. Now she found herself in a dank world full of shifting shadows and strange, whispering sounds, like something from a childhood dream, with absolutely no sense of where to turn next. She felt her throat tighten and her palms begin to sweat.

She took in a deep, calming breath and stood listening, absorbing the sounds of the forest and trying to take some meaning from them. Where Edie came from, up on Ellesmere Island, just shy of the North Pole, there weren't any trees, only raw, rocky tundra. On a clear day you could see the earth's curve. The unfamiliarity of the landscape was just one more thing about Alaska she hadn't really thought about when she'd agreed to step in to help Sammy after his one surviving son, Willa, broke his arm. Now the wind picked up and began snaking along the forest floor, bothering the snow into little fountains of flakes. The trunks of the spruces all around her creaked very softly and a drift of accumulated powder snow swept from the branches and tumbled to earth. If she'd been in Alaska any longer than two days she might already know where the prevailing winds blew from, but even of that she was ignorant. She looked up but could not see the sun through the canopy. No chance of knowing which direction she was going in.

Far away, a few ravens chattered, a nearby twig snapped, and there was the rustle of something low to the ground, a fox perhaps.

It had been crazy irresponsible to come out here without so much as a rifle, the kind of thing she'd had a habit of doing when she'd been drinking. The kind of habit she hoped she had kicked.

A thin rumble came to her, more a vibration than a sound, then it deepened and grew louder until it resolved into the deep whine of an engine and she felt a hollowing sense of relief. The vehicle drew closer and before too long a snowmobile came into sight. She grinned and waved and waited but when the vehicle carried on without even slowing, she ran into its path, shouting and waving her hands, bewildered. The driver opened his visor and a pair of eyes almost lost in a furze of salt and pepper facial hair looked out. A female passenger in silver fox mitts sat impassively behind him. Under their down parkas, they both appeared to be wearing long, billowing tunics and matching trousers. The couple had obviously been doing the week's grocery shopping. There were bags hanging off the snowmobile's every surface.

'Hey, didn't you see me waving?' She felt irritated. Did people have no manners down here? 'I'm lost. I need to get back to the Hatcher Pass.'

The man shrugged. 'You're on Old Believer land,' he said simply.

She wanted to say that right now she didn't care if she was on Kiss-My-Ass land, but held back. 'I need directions to my vehicle.'

The man looked momentarily surprised, but then he flipped his head in the direction he and his companion had just come from. 'If you can't make out your own tracks, then follow ours,' he said. 'Was that your snowmachine down there on the track?'

Snowmachines. That's what they called them down here in the south, in Alaska. Where Edie was from, you saw a snowmobile with no one on it, you didn't just ride by, you stopped to make sure no one was in trouble.

'You always this helpful?'

The man sucked his teeth disapprovingly. 'The concerns of the worldly are no concerns of ours,' he said, then glancing back at the woman sitting behind him he seemed to relent a little. 'We don't appreciate outsiders trespassing on our land is all. If I were you, I wouldn't be fixing to come up this way again any time soon.'

With that, he let go of the brake, flipped his visor and swung on the throttle. The snowmobile began sliding forward and Edie watched the two travellers disappear into the gloom of the forest, then she turned and followed the man's instructions, keeping their snowmobile tracks in view to her left. A while later a gap in the trees signalled the position of the road back into town and in the distance she caught a glimpse of her vehicle.

Relieved, she began to walk towards it. Where the tracks finally gave out onto the packed snow of the path, not far from the snowmobile, she spotted a bright yellow object lying at the base of a spruce, protected from the snowfall by the tree's branches, slightly to one side of the pass itself. The thought occurred to her that something had been thrown from the couple's snowmobile. Straying from the track a little, she wandered over to take a look.

Closer up she was surprised to see that the yellow object was a tiny wood-plank house of the sort you might make for a small dog, about a yard long and half as wide, with a sloping roof and solid sides. The front was decorated with ornate shapes, and there was a door, fastened shut with a crude wooden lever.

Edie looked around. A very thin layer of snow had collected on the roof, but there was none banked up against the sides, suggesting that the house had been there since the last snowfall, but most likely not much longer. There were no animal or human tracks either around or leading up to it. The little house sat as though it had always been there in the snow, as though it belonged to some other reality and there were tiny fairies living inside.

All thoughts of getting back for the Iditarod had gone from her head. She called out, having no sense of who or what might answer, but there was only silence. Reaching the house, she crouched down and with her right hand turned the lever on the little door. She could see something inside, though it was too dark to see what. Her first thought was to draw out whatever it was, but something stopped her. The spirit bear came to mind, the power of its quiet, ghostly pallor. She was struck suddenly by the realization that it was the bear who had led her here, that the spirits had sent their messenger to draw her to this very place.

She went back to the snowmobile, took her flashlight out of the pannier, trudged back to the house and opened the door once more. The light revealed a package, wrapped in a very elaborately embroidered red cloth. Edie reached out carefully and touched it. The cloth itself was crisp without being frozen hard. Since it was probably −25, even in the relative shelter of the forest, it was unlikely to have lain there for very long, she thought. She opened the door wide, reached in and pulled at the object. It was unattached and came away quite easily. The cloth was exquisite, satin she guessed, and embroidered all over with a pattern of flowers and tendrils. In places there were ribbon ties. Whatever was inside was very hard, something long frozen. She stood up with the package in her hand, moved over to the snowmobile, and rested it on the saddle so she could take a better look. Tucked in under the ornate fabric, she saw now, was a square of white linen-like cloth. She pinched it between her finger and thumb. Almost instantly, the cloth came away and as it did so, it seemed to dislodge the ties around the parcel, exposing what lay inside.

In an instant, her breath left her and a burning, tightening sensation shot up her spine. She blinked, trying to make the terrible thing go away, but when she opened her eyes it was still there. She felt herself lurch away. Her legs no longer held her and she reached out and grabbed the nearest tree. She felt faint, then wanted to throw up, but did neither. Clasping her arms around her chest, she closed her eyes and squeezed hard until the pain calmed her. When her breath returned, irregular, gasping, she eased herself back towards the horror she had released from its tiny yellow house.

There, lying on the saddle of the snowmobile, was the body of a baby boy, a month or maybe two in age, lying on his belly, dead and hard frozen. The boy's arms were raised, the hands balled into tiny fists, the legs angled down from the body as if in repose, his skin glittering with ice crystals. The skin on one shoulder was puckered with what looked like an ice burn but there was nothing to suggest how he had died, or when.

Reaching out with the utmost caution, she clasped the body at the shoulders with her mittened hands and slowly turned the boy over. His face was veiled with ice, the eyes were closed and he wore an expression of softness and calm. He looked so waxen, so distant from life, that, for the tiniest instant, Edie convinced herself he was a doll even as she knew that she was looking at a corpse.

Onto the delicate new skin of the boy's body someone had smeared grease and what looked like charcoal, or maybe ashes, in an elaborate, inverted cross.

# 2

**A**nchorage Mayor Chuck Hillingberg helped his wife Marsha out of the official vehicle at the Iditarod HQ near Willow, just outside of Wasilla, and beamed for the waiting cameras. His colleague at Wasilla City Hall, J. G. Dillard, the only mayor in Alaska to sport a comb-over, came striding over, hand outstretched, pulling his mouse of a wife behind him, eager to join in the picture-taking. Chuck had no interest in the man – unlike Chuck, who had thrown his hat into the ring for the upcoming race for Alaska governor, Mayor Dillard wasn't going anywhere – but today was all about playing nice.

'We're sure glad to see you both up here,' Dillard said. 'Thought all that time in the big city, maybe you both forgot your Wasilla roots.' It was said with bonhomie, one mayor to another, but there was an edge to it. On the drive up (Chuck had wanted to take the mayoral 'copter but Marsha had dissuaded him on the grounds that it would look too fancy, and in this, as in so many other things, she'd been right), he'd decided to make this section of his day all about loyalty. He'd not been on the ground for five minutes and Dillard was already questioning his hometown identity. It pissed him off.

'Never forget home, JG,' Chuck said, pumping the hand offered to him. That much was true, at least. Chuck never had forgotten home, which, for him, was Jersey City, New Jersey, a place he'd left at the age of four and still felt an almost painful nostalgia towards. As for Wasilla, he loathed the place with an unholy passion. People went on about the spectacular setting of the town, bounded by verdant valleys to the south, the Chugach Mountains to the east, the Talkeetnas to the north. They rattled away about its clear water, its homey Christian values and community spirit. People like J. G. Dillard. All Chuck could recall of his years in Wasilla were the godawful winters he'd spent cooped up in his tiny bedroom in the family cabin on the Willow side of the town, not ten minutes' drive from where they were now, listening to his hippy dropout parents taking out their disappointments on each other, and longing to be somewhere, anywhere, but the self-proclaimed Duct Tape Capital of America.

From the bank of cameras, Dillard led them to an OB truck parked just shy of the race starting line. Already knots of people had gathered on either side, stamping off the cold and chattering excitedly about who they were tipping to win the race. Chuck's director of communications, Andy Foulsham, had reminded him over breakfast that he and Marsha were scheduled to do a joint interview on KTMS, the local TV station. At the door to the truck Chuck stopped and waved Marsha in before him. Over the long years of their marriage, he thought, they'd really got the public affection thing off to a fine art. It made his heart sing to think how good they'd got. Who would believe that they hadn't actually kissed and meant it since they were college students together at U of Alaska? In the world of municipal and state politics they were a roaring success, their marriage often referred to as one of the most stable partnerships around—and in a way it was. All kinds of things held marriages together. Among them, secrets.

He'd already got the most challenging part of the day over, giving a speech at the soft start of the Iditarod race down in Anchorage early that morning, timed to make the breakfast news shows. Unlike the official start, this earlier, soft start in Anchorage was all about family. Parents got to take their kids to pat the dogs and ride with the competitors' sleds for a while. His speech then had been all about Alaska's rugged community spirit, how the Iditarod, a race whose proud origins in an epic emergency medical run to get supplies of diphtheria vaccine to the remote settlement of Nome, epitomized Alaskan grit and generosity. The speech had gone well, he'd been able to harness the positive energy of the morning whilst subtly allying himself with the courage and tenacity of those original sledders. The message he hoped he'd left in Anchorage was that a vote for Chuck Hillingberg in the upcoming gubernatorial race was a vote for the spirit of the Iditarod.

As the Hillingbergs clambered onto the truck, Chuck decided to let Marsha do most of the talking. He listened to his wife charming the interviewer with a few of the downhome huntin' and shootin' stories of her youth. In fact, she'd not been hunting very much, certainly not as much as Chuck, who'd spent a great deal of his adolescene taking out his rage on everything from muskrat to moose, but Marsha always made a great job of playing up her rugged, homestead raising and, since she was an only child and both her adoptive parents were dead, there was no one left to contradict her. Unlike him, she didn't have to fake her enthusiasm for the state. She'd always said to him that there weren't many places in America where you could do more or less as you pleased and get away with it. Living in the frontier state really was like the tourist brochures suggested, 'Beyond Your Dreams, Within Your Reach'. The trick, Marsha always said, was to ensure that nothing was beyond your dreams.

He had first noticed her as a bright, determined sixteen-year-old during her campaign for Prom President at Wasilla High. She was beautiful then, he thought, her long, chestnut hair thick and glossy, the slim waist unspoiled by age, but it wasn't her looks which attracted him so much as the streak of ruthlessness he detected in her smile. The story of her adoption moved him because he could see how absolutely determined she was to fit in, to change the circumstances of her birth: to become an Alaskan. From that first meeting at the Prom President stump, he knew she was going places and she wasn't going to let anyone stop her.

They'd split up briefly when he'd got the intern job at the Washington offices of Steven Horowitz, the Republican junior senator from South Carolina, but she'd taken him back when he returned, broken, carrying the burden of his own hickness. He and Marsha had got married later that year. It wasn't a marriage of convenience so much as a confluence of mutual interest.

For the last year, this interest had been focused on the gubernatorial contest. Up to a few weeks ago, the incumbent, Tom Shippon, had been looking pretty invincible. The Shippons were Alaska royalty, a genuine 'sourdough' family, Alaskans before Alaska officially became a state in 1958. Tom's father, Scoot, had been closely involved in Alaska politics since before then. The Shippons had fingers in every pie from the salmon fishery through timber to oil and gas exploration. About the only enterprise they weren't directly involved in was tourism and leisure. Pussy business, Tom Shippon called it, though only ever in private.

Chuck had neither the advantages of incumbency nor the kind of pedigree which automatically got you where you wanted to go in state politics. It was hard for a boy from New Jersey to go against that and hope to win. Other outsiders had tried but few had succeeded and they'd usually been blocked from taking up top positions. He looked too much like a *cheechako*, a greenhorn. In the early stages of the campaign, there were those who had even accused him of abandoning Alaska by going Outside to Washington, which, given that it was twenty years ago, was just ridiculous. But Alaskans did persist in thinking of themselves as separate and apart. You were either for them or against them, which was why the episode in Washington was seen by some blowhards as an act of treachery even now.

Over the past year, he'd had to work twice as hard to convince them that he was Alaskan at heart, which was all the more difficult given that it wasn't true. As councilman, then Mayor of Anchorage, it wasn't all that difficult for his opponents to set him up as a big city man, remote from the concerns of real Alaskans. Which was where Marsha had come in. Her genuine enthusiasm for the state had helped make him look like more of an all-state kind of a guy. The image uplift had assisted him in tangible ways, not least of which was in campaign funding. He was aware that no amount of schmoozing or reassuring patter about the depth of his devotion to the forty-ninth state would encourage the wealthy sourdoughs of Alaska to put their hands in their pockets for his gubernatorial campaign to the degree to which they had done almost automatically for Shippon, but he'd been able to raise enough to at least present a challenge. Until last week his campaign team would have said, even on the most optimistic forecasts, that the chances of him ousting Shippon were pretty low, but that was before the unemployment figures came out and the polls showed Shippon's popularity starting to go south. Somewhere in all those stats was an opportunity, the biggest opportunity of Chuck Hillingberg's life. But the campaign needed money to be able to push it through, which was why, after he'd fired the Iditarod starting gun, he was heading directly to a $10,000-a-plate luncheon back at the Sheraton in downtown Anchorage. He'd already given his fundraising speech dozens of times. The message was the one business people and entrepreneurs always wanted to hear. Alaska needed to rein back state spending and find new and innovative ways for private enterprise to grow and develop. But now there was a new energy to it, fuelled by the belief that he just might win. Over breakfast, Marsha, his communications director Andy Foulsham and himself had decided that his lunchtime speech needed to reflect the campaign's new confidence. He was intending to say that the Alaska state motto, North to the Future, meant North to a future only Chuck Hillingberg, as governor, could deliver.

He climbed down the steps of the OB unit back out into the cold sun of the Alaskan March morning. In the fifteen minutes that he and Marsha had been in the mobile studio, the crowd had swelled considerably and he was pleased to see a bank of TV cameras in the press enclosure. Walking from the unit along the barricade, he was flattered to observe friendly and familiar faces pressing forward to say hi or shake his hand, until he remembered that Andy had fixed it that way. Well, never mind. The TV crews didn't know the difference.

The fact that the race soft-started in Anchorage gave Chuck one of his few advantages over Tom Shippon and he meant to make the most of it. As mayor of the city, it was easy for him to take ownership of the race, even when it moved to its official start in Wasilla, and there was nothing that Shippon, stuck in the governor's residence way down in Juneau, could do about it. The race was huge statewise, but it also had considerable national and international reach. The Iditarod may not be the only dog race on the planet, but it was the one with the richest provenance and in many people's eyes the only one that really counted. Folk who had no interest at all in dog races had heard of the Great Race of Mercy, the heroic five-and-a-half-day trek during the fierce winter of 1925, when 20 mushers and 150 dogs rushed to bring diphtheria antitoxin

675 miles across the Alaskan ice to the remote gold-rush town of Nome and thereby prevent an epidemic. And even if people didn't know the details of the event, many had seen Balto, the lead dog in the final relay team, immortalized in bronze in New York's Central Park. Since the first race commemorating the Great Race of Mercy in 1973, the Iditarod had grown enormously in terms of the number of competitors and, more significantly for Chuck, in terms of its profile. Back in the twenties, live news of the epic journey was broadcast on the new medium of radio. Now, TV crews flew in from all over world and, with the twenty-four-hour news cycle, they had plenty of time to fill. Within minutes of the start of the race, clips would be all over the Internet and he, Chuck, hoped to figure in at least some of them. Wasn't Andy always telling him that maintaining a healthy Internet profile was as critical to electoral success in the twenty-first century as cross-country stump tours had been for politicians in the nineteenth and twentieth, a cheap and dynamic platform from which the Hillingberg campaign could spin blogs and tweets non-stop from now until election day. Take command of the blogosphere and the twittersphere and you were already halfway there. Wasn't that how Obama had done it?

Mayor Dillard led them over to inspect the dog teams and to talk to a couple of the big hitters: Steve Nicols, the favorite and last year's winner, and the challenger, Duncan Wright. While Chuck busied himself with the two frontrunners, Dillard's mousy wife took Marsha to connect with one or two of the stragglers whom Andy Foulsham had previously identified as having some kind of news potential, one a widow whose husband had been killed in a rig accident up on the North Slope oilfield, another a native man who'd come all the way from High Arctic Canada and was running the race in tribute to his dead son.

That done, Chuck and Marsha made their way up to the podium

by the starting line. The crowd was roaring now, eyes fixed on the line-up of dogs and sleds and the heroic sledders who were about to set off on their epic, two-week, 1150-mile journey through mountain ranges and ice fields, through the rocky scree of the Farewell Burn, along the great ice ribbon of the Yukon River and through the shifting pan of Norton Sound to the finish at Nome, knowing that of the ninety-seven teams in the race, somewhere between twenty and forty would be forced to drop out.

Dillard climbed the steps onto the podium and began the introductions. Someone flipped on the rousing music and on a signal from Andy Foulsham, Chuck and Marsha followed Dillard up the steps hand in hand, Chuck grinning and nodding in acknowledgement, Marsha smiling mutely by his side. As the dog handlers began bringing out the teams, Chuck moved to the microphone and said his piece, then he raised the starting gun and fired into the air. A tremendous chorus of shouts from the mushers and howls from the dogs came up from the track, followed by the whoosh of sled runners on compacted snow. As the sleds flashed by, the dogs straining at their harnesses and picking up speed as they spun further into the distance, the crowd went crazy.

Chuck stood back and was so absorbed in the furore he didn't notice the tiny, good-looking native woman in a sealskin parka pushing her way through the crowd, frantically waving her arms and shouting, until she was almost on him.

# 3

**A** woman brandishing a clipboard emerged from a door at the back of the Anchorage Police Department offices in downtown and called for 'Edith Kiglake'.

Edie swung her head round, nodded, then slung her parka over her arm and stood. It was 8 p.m., and she'd been waiting in the public area of the building since just after midday. The find in the woods had shaken her up, but she hadn't yet felt the full force of what had happened. It was like being wounded. Even when you knew you should be hurting like crazy, the adrenaline numbed the pain. Right now, her predominant sensations were those of tiredness and hunger and above all else the sense of being assailed by heat and noise. Her study of Alaska's wildlife hadn't prepared her for the thrum and muddle of its urban jungle. There was a perpetual churn of human noise down here which made her feel crowded out and irritable. For eight hours she'd been at the mercy of the treble of the vending machines, the PA system, the swooshing of the automatic doors and the congregation of drunks and hookers who flowed in and out like a restless tide.

'Ms Kiglake?' The woman's gaze was narrow and impatient. She was plump and native, not Inuit – the nose was too prominent for that – and her dismissive air was that of a person who'd been eating hard times for breakfast and had forgotten there was any other kind.

'It's Kiglatuk,' Edie said.

The woman checked her clipboard, nodded and waved Edie through. On the other side was an open-plan office studded with workstations where men and women were talking on the phone or gazing at their screens, a few typing. A handful of uniformed officers stood among them, deep in conversation.

The woman led her past the cubicles to a room at the back. Here a balding man of about fifty sat at a single table studying a file. His face hinted at a kind of conservative intelligence, Edie thought, the lines and folds of skin like a frozen sea swell, indicative of a narrow range of facial reactions. Used to keeping his feelings to himself, she thought. He stood up, held out a hand, introduced himself as Detective Bob Truro and motioned Edie to sit.

'Can Kathy here get you anything?' the detective said casually. 'Coffee? A soda?'

'I'm guessing you don't have any sealmeat soup, or maybe a roast flipper?' Edie asked, though she already knew the answer to this. Inexplicably, Alaskans seemed to think of themselves as northerners, but from everything she'd seen, Alaska was a southern place, rimed here and there with Northern frost, but southern at its core. The look Truro shot his colleague only confirmed her suspicions. Already they thought of her as slightly mad.

'We can probably find you a hamburger,' he said drily.

Edie scoped out the room, feeling weird now, anaesthetized, spaced out. A few hours ago she'd been following a spirit bear who'd led her to a dead boy lying in a yellow house in the snow.

'Let me explain to you why you're here,' Truro continued, as though it wasn't obvious. He went on. Wasilla came under the auspices of the Anchorage metropolitan district and since this was a serious case, the APD had taken over the investigation from the Wasilla police and it was this that in part explained the delay in interviewing her. Truro had read the notes from that morning and there were a few things he needed to clarify. He took out some papers from an embossed leather binder, and then flipped the cover closed. The embossing read 'Paradise Gospel Church of the Holy . . .' The rest was too faded to make out.

'The man and woman on the snowmachine . . .'

' . . . mobile, it was a snowmobile.'

He looked tired. His voice was impatient. 'In Alaska we call them snowmachines.' He ran a hand around the back of his neck. 'So, these Old Believers . . .'

Edie leaned forward in her seat. 'They didn't tell me they were Old Believers.'

Truro wiped his neck again.

'The notes say that, once he'd pulled you off Mayor Hillingberg, for which, incidentally, the mayor has been kind enough not to press charges, you told Trooper Wilde that the couple on the snowmachine were Old Believers.'

Edie shrugged. 'The man on the snowmobile said something about being on Old Believer land, but I don't even know what that means.'

Truro bit his lip.

The door sprang open and Kathy came in carrying a tray. On it were two burgers wrapped in yellow waxed paper.

Detective Truro allowed Edie a moment to eat, watching her slide the meat out from under its doughy parka, pushing everything that wasn't meat back inside the wrapper. The burgers brought Edie back to earth a little, so that instead of feeling spacey, she now felt a rush of horror at her find in the forest.

'OK,' Truro said. 'Let's start again.' He turned on a camera. 'Why are you here, Miss Kiglatuk?'

'Because my stepson broke his finger.' She bit into the second burger. The satisfying, fatty meatiness soon gave way to a revolting tang of chemicals. She spat it back out onto the bun and pushed it away. 'My ex-stepson if you want to be completely accurate. Which I'm sure you do, detective. My ex-stepson, Willa, broke his finger, so I had to step in.'

'I meant, what's the purpose of your visit?'

She turned to him. His gaze came back at her, calm, without emotion.

'It's like I told the trooper. I came for the Iditarod, as backup to Sammy Inukpuk. Officially he's my ex too . . .'

The detective gave her a pained look and held up his hand.

'If you could just answer my questions.' His tone was not altogether kind. Edie felt the bile rising.

'Listen, detective, I was born in Autisaq on Ellesmere Island. Seventy people live in Autisaq. Before this trip, I'd left Ellesmere twice, once to go to Iqaluit, the second time to go to Greenland. I watch TV, I teach at the school, but your world, this world, is hot and crowded and noisy and you eat stuff that doesn't even resemble food and I found a dead baby and then had to wait outside in your corridor for eight hours.'

Truro sighed but looked chastened.

'I'll try to bear that in mind.'

There was a pause.

'You know who the mother is yet?' Edie said. Suddenly it seemed important to tell the woman how peaceful her baby had looked, how it seemed he hadn't suffered.

'We're tracing her right now.'

'I'd like to talk to her.'

'Miss Kiglatuk,' Truro sighed, as though commanding infinite reserves of patience. 'First off, this is a police investigation into a possible homicide. Second, I need you to answer my questions. I do not need you to make demands.'

Detective Truro consulted his notes. He was wearing a pin in the shape of a fish in the lapel of his jacket, she noticed. A Christian, then. Evangelical, she guessed from the name of the church on the leather folder. *Qalunaat* evangelicals appeared every so often at home, on Ellesmere Island. Missionary work. Only in the summer though. Most of the villagers were happily Anglican or Catholic, or, like her, they stuck to the old beliefs, but the evangelicals usually made a convert or two. Edie guessed that was why they kept coming back.

'The man you spoke to, he have an accent at all?'

'An accent compared to what?' Edie allowed herself to feel offended because, for an instant, it gave her the upper hand. Truro's brow wrinkled, as though he was waiting for some addendum. Edie thought of the little boy in the snow and relented.

'Some kind of accent, yes.'

Truro nodded and went on.

'The clothes the two were wearing, the long robes. The man's facial hair. Are you aware that what you described is typical of the Old Believers?'

'Since I already told you I don't know what that means, I guess the answer's no.'

Detective Truro began to stroke his tie. He caught her eye and looked away. Then he reached out and turned off the camera.

'Miss Kiglatuk, I have to ask you, why did you pick up the body?'

Why had she? It was hard to say. At that moment, her thoughts had been swirling around in a blizzard in her mind.

'I didn't know what was in the parcel when I picked it up. And then, when I did, I guess I wanted to try to comfort him.' She thought about the ghosts of people she'd loved and lost.

Truro lifted his eyes from the desk and cut her an icy look.

'You make a habit of comforting the dead, Miss Kiglatuk? You realize you could have seriously compromised our investigation?'

She didn't answer.

Truro continued to look at her, his gaze fading away to a scowl. She held it. They sat like this for a moment.

'The Old Believers are a religious cult. Are you familiar with that term?'

She blew air down her nose. 'I'm Inuit, not an idiot.'

'Of course.' His eye flipped across a typewritten page. 'Your people here call themselves Eskimos, by the way.'

'I'm guessing they call themselves Alaskans too,' she said, 'which, by the way, technically makes them your people.'

'You believe in God, Miss Kiglatuk?' Truro looked put out.

She looked at the badge on his lapel.

'Not in the way you do.'

'In evil then.'

'You mean, the Devil?' She thought about the little boy lying frozen in the woods. If he'd asked whether she believed in devilishness, she'd have said, oh yeah, seen plenty of that, but a red guy with a forked tail? She shook her head.

A look of frustration or maybe disappointment spread across Detective Truro's face.

'Let me tell you something about these people you ran into, the Old Believers. They're not regular folk, like you and me.'

She had to pinch herself to stop herself talking back. Regular folk? What did that mean?

Truro didn't appear to notice her expression and continued. 'Originally, they came from Russia. People here still call them Russians though they haven't actually lived there since they broke away from the Russian Orthodox Church hundreds of years ago and started wandering across the globe. They've been here in Alaska forty years and some of 'em still don't even speak English. They're closed people, they stick with their own, they call folk like us "worldly" and do their best to avoid us,' he said. 'We don't know much about them, but we don't much like what we do know.'

He picked up a pen, see-sawed it about between his fingers.

'You remember the cross, the one marked on the body?'

She looked at him, aghast. How could he imagine she would forget it?

'That silk stuff wrapped around the body of the little boy you found? The Believers use that for their religious ceremonies. The little house is a spirit house. It's an Athabascan native tradition.'

He turned the camera back on and Edie wondered if anything he had said amounted to much more than supposition, prejudice even.

'Now, let's go back to when you saw the two Old Believers on the snowmachine.'

She wanted to tell him about how little snow drift there had been around the house, about the absence of footprint or tracks leading up to it and what all that said about when the house had been left. She wanted to explain about how the ice crystals had broken where they had touched the frozen corpse, how she didn't understand what it meant though she was sure it was significant, but she no longer had any confidence that he'd listen.

It was about 10 p.m. as she made her way down Fourth Avenue after the interview. The weather was clear but street lights formed a ceiling of brightness just over her head, obscuring her view of the stars. The contrast between the stifling heat of the APD building and the cold March night brought on a thrumming jaw ache. She passed by some souvenir stores selling cheap native crafts, tacky bits of fake mammoth-tooth carving, furs inexplicably sewn into miniature copies of the fur-bearing creature they first came from, moose-shit novelties, trash of all kinds. A couple were bent over the glass, window-shopping. Beside her, on the street, trucks rumbled by, leaving a wake of diesel fumes.

She made her way up to the cheap studio she'd rented for the duration of the Iditarod and, not for the first time since she'd opened the grisly package in the forest, was struck with a powerful desire to drink herself into oblivion. Not that drinking was any solution to anything, except the pain of the moment, but the pain of the moment held her so powerfully that she had to say the words out loud in order to make herself commit to them: *I will not drink.*

Instead, she went to the kitchenette and put on the kettle for a mug up. On either side of her, through the drywall, she could hear the sounds of her neighbours' bedtime routines: the burble of TVs, the coughs and sighs of men and women settling down for the night. When she'd first arrived two days ago, she'd knocked on the doors on her floor, intending to introduce herself, but hardly anyone answered and she could tell from the bewildered and wary expressions of those who did that they suspected her of being crazy. She didn't tell them what she really thought, that they were living like cliff birds, wedged into their tiny little fortresses, puffing up their feathers and pecking away all comers, wary of any motives that were not their own.

Going over to the single window, she flipped the blind to block out the thin light coming in from a fluorescent tube in the walkway outside. Then, with a mug of hot tea in one hand, she went over to the phone and dialled the number Derek had given her for his digs in Nome, the finishing point for the Iditarod. An unfamiliar voice answered and asked her to wait, then came Derek's soft, familiar tone.

'Edie, hi. I was waiting for you to call.'

'Who was that picked up?'

'Zach Barefoot. The friend from the Native Police Association I told you about? I'm staying in his spare room.'

Derek was right, he had told her. She felt relieved, slightly foolish. Over the course of the day she'd almost forgotten what she was doing in Alaska in the first place. Still, she wanted to keep what had happened as private as possible till they'd had time to talk it through.

'Zach still there?'

'No, why?' Derek's voice sounded alarmed. Without waiting for an answer, he said, 'Sammy set off OK?'

'Yeah. At least, I think so. I wasn't there.'

'I thought we agreed you were going to see him off.' Derek sounded peeved.

She told him everything that had happened. 'The thing that freaked me out, it seemed like Truro had an angle, like he just wanted me to say that these Old Believer people had done it.' She knew Derek would understand her reservations about religious nuts of all kinds. It was missionaries and zealots who'd told them that the old customs were evil, even though in some cases, like when the brother of a dead hunter took the widow for his second wife, they saved lives. But it was mostly their absolute moral intransigence which bothered her. You were either with them or against them. You were one of the saved, or you were the Devil's work.

Derek heard her out and was sympathetic. He tried to get her to come up to Nome for a couple of days. 'I don't like the thought of you being alone.'

She let out a dry laugh.

'I know,' he said. 'The lone wolf. Even lone wolves have to return to the pack sometime.'

'Is that what you are, Derek, the pack?'

'Don't be ridiculous, Edie.' He sounded irritated. 'I'm your friend.'

The rebuke stung her a little, but she knew it was deserved. She took a pause to signal that she'd taken it in.

'Then do me a favour, as my friend. Don't mention any of this to Sammy, OK?' She'd already decided not to speak to her ex for the duration of the race unless there was no way to avoid it. As she understood her role, there would be no particular need to speak to him unless something happened in the race which required her assistance in Anchorage. His more routine communications would be routed through Derek at the Iditarod HQ in Nome. She didn't trust herself not to be selfish and tell Sammy the whole story.

'If you think that's for the best,' Derek said, unconvinced.

'It's just that he's been wanting to run the Iditarod ever since I've known him. It was all he used to talk about when we were married. If he gets wind of what's happening down here, he's gonna be on the first plane to Anchorage, thinking he can rescue me.'

'I understand,' Derek said simply.

Edie smiled to herself. In her experience, most men shared certain rescue fantasies, particularly when it came to women.

'But you know, Edie, I really think this is a matter for the police department. Why don't you come up here?'

'I'll think about it,' she said, to humour him. She liked Derek, admired him even. At the same time she knew there were things about her he'd never understand.

Later, in bed, she tried to get the image of the dead baby out of her mind.

'Why me?' she asked herself, as though her heart didn't already know the answer.

# 4

Derek Palliser was woken by an unfamiliar sound. At first he thought it was the doorbell of the police detachment at home in Kuujuaq, then he remembered he was at his friend Zach Barefoot's house in Nome, on the northwest coast of Alaska. An instant later he also recalled what he was doing there. Edie Kiglatuk had suckered him into taking annual leave to come over to Alaska to help Sammy Inukpuk's bid at the Iditarod on the grounds that he knew dogs and didn't have any other kind of a life. He'd agreed on condition that he base himself at the Iditarod finish line in Nome, leaving Edie down in Anchorage. Derek's role would be to remain in Nome and act as principal communications liaison with Sammy. All Sammy's supplies – dog food, dog booties, spare clothes, dog harness and sled tracks and the like – had been shipped up to the appropriate checkpoints prior to the start of the race and unless something went badly wrong, Derek didn't anticipate being called on until the end. Sammy wouldn't want the distraction of having people he knew turn up at the checkpoints.

He yawned and glanced at the window. Thin threads of deep grey light hung like ribbons from the blinds. He looked around, then, with a sinking feeling, recalled his late-night phone conversation. Why had he been dumb enough to more or less insist that Edie join him in Nome? It wasn't that he didn't like her. On the contrary, he liked her so much that he sometimes wondered whether there wasn't more to it than just liking, but the woman also drove him completely crazy. On the other hand, he couldn't help but feel protective towards her and he didn't trust her not to get herself into some kind of scrape. Edie seemed to be attracted to trouble in the way that foxes were attracted to bait traps.

He heard voices speaking softly, then there was a knock on the door and Zach called his name.

'Aileen Logan, the Iditarod boss, is here to see you. I'll get coffee.'

Zach and Derek had met at the annual conference of the Native Police Association in Yellowknife a few years back and kept in touch. They both shared a laid-back approach to law enforcement. Zach worked out of Nome as a brownshirt, an Alaska Wildlife Trooper. His job mostly involved enforcing hunting and fishing regulations, and in the navigation season he worked closely with the coastguard monitoring shipping across the Bering Strait. It was a police household. When she wasn't on maternity leave, Zach's wife Megan Avuluq worked as a Village Public Safety Officer, the first responder covering the area from the Safety roadhouse a few miles east of Nome to the Inupiaq village of White Mountain.

Stumbling out of the put-up bed, Derek pulled on yesterday's shirt and pants and went into Zach's living room.

A plump woman with a cloud of dirty blonde hair sat on the sofa. In front of her was a mug of coffee.

'Rise and shine.' She had the voice of a musk ox in rut.

Derek rubbed his eyes, yawned and checked his watch again. 5.30 a.m. He'd only been in bed a couple of hours.

Aileen gave a little hoot of laughter. 'You Iditarod rookies make me roll about,' she said. 'Fella, up here 5.30 a.m. is what counts as a lie-in.'

Zach came through with more coffee. Derek sat with his mug,

heating himself up before moving too fast. Mornings never had been his strong suit.

'Listen,' Aileen said, 'I heard about your friend down in Anchorage. That's too bad what happened.'

She saw the look of surprise on Derek's face.

'Welcome to Alaska, the biggest small town in the world.' She let out another hoot. 'But, listen, I didn't disturb your beauty sleep just to commiserate about your friend,' she went on. 'Your man got a little problem.'

A call had come in on the radio from the Yentna checkpoint, only 66 miles from Wasilla, to say that Sammy was giving up his lead dog.

'Not Bonehead?' Derek said. After two of Sammy's team tore their pads on a patch of candle ice during practice, Sammy had borrowed Bonehead from Edie. The dog was bombproof.

'You tell me,' Aileen said. 'Cut paw. His bootie fell off and there was a piece of glass ice.' The stewards at Yentna would hold the dog until one of the bush planes that plied the route during the course of the race – the self-styled Iditarod Air – could take him back to Anchorage.

'You'll have to pick him up from the Pen.' The warden at the Women's Correctional Facility in Anchorage had set up a rehab programme for women prisoners at the end of their sentences, giving them sick or injured dogs to look after until their owners could pick them up. It was in the handbook Derek had read rather too hastily on the flight over. 'They'll keep him a couple of days if you need 'em to, but you got that friend of yours taking care of things down there, don't you? Needs something to take her mind off all that trouble with the kid.'

# 5

From the moment Edie turned out the light, the face of the dead baby appeared in her mind, as though someone had engraved it there. Eventually, she abandoned any idea of sleeping. Rising early, she took a shower and while braiding her hair tried to turn her thoughts to Sammy. Her ex had probably travelled just over a hundred miles by now. In a few days he'd reach the high peaks of the Alaska Range. Beyond those lay the Kuskokwims, after which there would be 150 miles of hard, bumpy, dangerous sledding along the ice of the Yukon River before he reached the ice pack of Norton Sound.

Sammy had no thought of winning and not much prospect of it either, but that wasn't the point. He needed this race as much as he'd needed anything in his life. Certainly as much as he'd ever needed her. He'd begun seriously talking about entering about three months after Joe died and he'd kept on talking about it. He had this burning need to do something difficult, to push himself in ways he'd never dared before. Once he'd made up his mind to run, he'd put all of his energies into fixing his sled, training up his team and raising the money. All that activity had helped keep him sane. A year on, he still hadn't forgiven himself for his son's death. For Sammy the Iditarod was the perfect displacement activity, but it was more than that. Running the race was a chance to heal his wounded pride, to convince himself that, in spite of the fact that he had failed to protect his son, he was a man still, and capable of the kinds of things men were put on this earth to be able to do.

It was a long time since Edie had relied on Sammy, but knowing he was so far away increased her sense of aloneness and being awake in the early hours of the morning only added to her isolation. She had the feeling of being sucked into something she did not understand but had no power to stop. Emotions she had kept at bay for years had begun creeping back into her consciousness, like some kind of muscle memory starting to stir, the boy in the snow dragging her back to a time she wanted to forget. Some feelings got to be like parts of the body, she thought. You could ignore them for years, and then, one day, they started playing up and it became impossible to think about much else.

Pulling on her outerwear, she left the studio and trudging through hard packed snow still crusted with the night's ice, made her way down K Street to the Snowy Owl Café, the only place she'd found in Anchorage so far serving something approaching real food. The early shift waitress, Stacey, came bundling up to show her to a table. She and Stacey had already bonded over the hassles of long hair – the brushing and drying and tying it demanded – and now the waitress was admiring the rickrack Edie had just braided into her plaits. Not that Stacey was the kind of girl to go in for rickrack. She thought of herself, she told Edie, as a Northern Goth and had the tattooed skulls on her wrists to prove it.

'My grandma was tattooed,' Edie said, and Stacey's eyes said she wanted to hear the rest of that story. 'It was a right of passage. They tattooed on little blue rays, and whiskers inking out from here.' She wiped a finger along her upper lip. 'It was kind of a tribute to the *ugjuq*, the bearded seal, which kept us alive back in the day. They don't do it any more.'

Stacey had made a long face. 'I guess you have other things keeping you alive these days.'

Edie laughed. 'Sometimes I wonder.' Stacey was *qalunaat*, of course, and so belonged to another world, but there was something about her sparky energy and hungry, angry eyes which reminded Edie of her younger self and for a moment she longed to tell Stacey about the spirit bear and what she'd found in the forest and why she hadn't slept all night. But the door swung open and another customer came in and the moment passed.

To kill time while she waited for breakfast, Edie leafed through the Sunday edition of the Anchorage *Courier*. The front page was dominated by Iditarod news. Steve Nicols, the favorite to win the race, had already pulled ahead, passing the checkpoint at Yentna as the paper went to press. By now, he'd be heading into the foothills of the Alaska Range. Below that was a piece about some newly published stats on sexual assault and rape in the city reaching twice the national average. Way down at the foot of the page was a small single column piece noting that the opening ceremony had brought a surprise when a 'distressed native' had launched herself at Anchorage Mayor Chuck Hillingberg. At the foot of the piece was a link to the leader inside, which was titled 'Hillingberg a Breath of Fresh Air', but Edie couldn't be bothered to stick with the article long enough to find out why. Instead she flipped back through the pages looking for something about the discovery of the dead baby and found it in a single paragraph, at the bottom of page 4 beside the fold edge.

The body of Lucas Littlefish, four-month-old son of Homer native TaniaLee Littlefish, was found by a passer-by in forest north of Wasilla on Saturday. The body was wrapped in ornate ceremonial cloth and hidden in a traditional spirit house. A spokesman for the Anchorage Police Department confirmed that they are treating the death as suspicious and are questioning a 54-year-old man believed to be from the Old Believer community near Meadow Lake.

They got his age wrong. The baby wasn't four months. Edie rolled his name around her tongue, felt the sounds catching in her throat. Lucas Littlefish. It wasn't the kind of name you easily forget. Knowing it made his case more pressing to her. She thought about his spirit, roaming the forest, stuck halfway between the worlds of the living and the dead with only a bear the colour of old smoke for comfort and company.

After breakfast she walked back to an Internet cafe a couple of blocks away, paid for an hour of surfing time and sat down to find out what she could about the Old Believers. Others, she knew, *qalunaat* certainly, but Inuit too, would think she'd gone a little crazy. But she didn't feel crazy. She felt driven.

It wasn't as easy as she'd imagined to pin down a complete story. There were dozens of websites on the Old Believers but they all appeared to vary in the details. From what she could gather by patching together the numerous partial accounts, the group had fallen out with the mainstream Russian Orthodox Church in the mid-seventeenth century over what seemed to Edie to be arcane details about the shape of the Orthodox Cross. The Old Believers worshipped before a cross with a footrest and a head bar, which they claimed was the only true representation of the cross on which Jesus was crucified. By contrast, the Orthodox Church held that the original cross carried only a head bar. There were other differences too. The Old Believers had abolished the priesthood, preferring to confer religious authority on community elders on a rotating basis. Unsurprisingly, the Orthodox Church didn't think much of that, and the Old Believers had found themselves shunned.

Eventually they felt they had no choice but to quit Russia altogether for some part of the world where they would be free to practise what they regarded as their purer, more ancient version of the Orthodoxy. So far as Edie could tell, they'd been wandering across the globe ever since.

From time to time groups had broken away eager to find somewhere even more removed from what they increasingly saw as the polluting effects of modern society, which they called the Outside. One such group had left Alberta in the 1970s and seemed to have found the peace and separateness they craved in Alaska.

Until now.

Edie was about to log off, when a pop-up appeared enclosing a website address. Clicking the link produced a dark screen which then automatically redirected her to the website of an organization calling itself SpiritCleanse. There, embedded in what seemed to be a list of links to websites offering exorcism services, were the hyperlinked words 'Old Believers'. Following the link took Edie to a blog headlined *Old or Dark?* She scanned the piece. The text seemed to be suggesting that a group calling itself the Dark Believers had splintered off from the main sect a few years before. Among the questionable practices of this new group, so the blogger said, were animal sacrifice and a number of unspecified satanic rituals.

Nut job. Edie closed the page and was just about to get up from her chair when some lingering curiosity caused her to turn back to the screen and google the words Dark Believers. A stream of URLs for blogs and discussion threads instantly scrolled up the screen. The Dark Believers, it seemed, were more than the paranoid fantasies of a single blogger. She clicked on a few links. The discussions were vague and, without exception, conspiratorial in tone. A few were accompanied by images of texts written on what looked like animal skin, strange configurations of Russian script and symbols variously deciphered, and by ancient-looking Russian icons. Others incorporated images of the Old Believers in their outlandish costumes. She was in the middle of reading, clicking between the various versions, when the administrator, a solemn-looking man in his early twenties with yellow, fox eyes, came over. Edie checked her watch. There were ten minutes left on her hour.

'I'm sorry, man, but I'm gonna have to ask you to, like, leave.'

'What?' She felt floored.

Fox eyes shrugged sheepishly. 'Look, man, if it was me, I'd be, like, cool with whatever, but my boss freaks out about this kind of thing.' He reached across her and closed down the website. 'Yeah, see, all that Dark Believer satanist stuff? My boss goes ape about that.'

She returned his shrug with one of her own and, trying not to sound as rattled as she was, she said it was OK, she'd done with looking at the stuff anyway, but the young man hovered over her, rubbing his palms together, a look of profound unease on his face that indicated he wasn't done.

'I'm cool about refunding your minutes, but I just gotta ask you to leave.'

She stood up and moved towards the entrance. At the door he nodded to her obligingly. As she turned onto the street she saw him bend down and pull the computer plug.

Sensitive topic, this Dark Believers thing.

Edie made her way back to the studio. There was a message on the answering machine from Derek, asking her to call. She dialled his number and he picked up right away.

'How you doing?'

'OK,' she lied.

'Zach told me they got a suspect, some guy called Peter Galloway, the fella you saw on the snowbie.'

'Yeah,' she said. 'It was in the paper.'

'Zach's sources say they'll want to formally arrest him and put the whole thing to bed soon as they can. Eyes of the world on Alaska right now and all.'

Edie's heart sank. She felt bad that she hadn't mentioned the lack of footprints around the house and the unexplained crust of broken ice crystals on the body to Detective Truro. On the other hand, who was to say that it would have made any difference? Truro would almost certainly know things she didn't. He'd have had his reasons for thinking the Galloway fella was involved.

She mentioned what she'd found in the Internet cafe and the reaction of the clerk to it. Derek sounded wary.

'It was me, I'd stay away from that stuff, Edie.'

'But it isn't you.'

'No.' He paused sufficiently long to make his disapproval clear, then moved the discussion on to the news about Bonehead. It was particularly disappointing because Edie knew that the old dog probably didn't have many races left in him. Once he started slowing down, she'd have to let him go. She laughed to herself at the euphemism. A *qalunaat* habit, that. Maybe something she'd picked up early on from Peter, her *qalunaat* father. What would actually happen was that, once Bonehead stopped being able to pull his weight on the sled, she'd have no choice but to shoot him.

One of the bush pilots had volunteered to bring the dog to Anchorage in mid-afternoon along with some supplies. The race administrators would take him directly from the airport to the Anchorage Women's Correctional Facility. Edie would need to go and fetch him when she could but there was no hurry about it. They'd keep him at the centre for a day or two.

'Why don't you come up to Nome for a coupla days, meet the race folks up here?'

'Thanks,' she said. 'But I got stuff to do.'

'Like what?' he said.

'Like picking up Bonehead.'

'Did you hear what I just said? They'll keep the dog.' There was a pause. 'Edie, tell me you're not gonna get yourself wrapped up any more in this dead baby case.'

She felt a sudden stab of irritation and hurt, the feeling of being ridden roughshod over by someone who preferred to close his eyes. 'Don't you think it's too late to be asking me that?' Her voice sounded strained and angry but so what, it was an accurate reflection of how she was feeling. 'Given how I found the kid's body and all. Or maybe you'd forgotten?'

He sighed but said nothing. There was nothing more to be said.

She sat in the studio awhile just staring into the middle distance then decided that wasn't going to get her anywhere. There was something depressing about the low ceiling and cheap, bland fittings, the constant buzz of sound coming from the studios on either side. Right now, she had a need for distraction.

Remembering an advertisement for a silent film festival she'd seen earlier in the *Courier*, she made her way out and onto K Street towards the downtown picture house. At the box office she pushed a ten-dollar bill through the gap in the glass and asked for one adult. The cashier, a young woman with a pierced tongue, handed her a ticket then pointed down a dark corridor.

'Screen two.'

The theatre was empty but for three or four people and she realized that, in her distracted state, she'd forgotten to ask which movie was showing, but the lights went down and it felt warm and so she settled in.

Edie's experience of the movies had been out of the ordinary, even for a girl growing up on the most northerly landmass on the planet. Back in the day, her father, Peter, had set up a film club in what was then the tiny community centre in Autisaq. This was before video or DVDs, when all movies came in aluminium cans and had to be spooled through projectors. She didn't know how her father came by the films, except in so far as he was *qalunaat*, a white man, and so had access to these things, but the movies he showed were almost always the classic silent comedies. Whether that was a reflection of his taste or simply what he could get his hands on, she didn't know.

Once a month, everyone in the village who wasn't out hunting would turn up with their mugs, help themselves to sweet hot tea and a few hard-boiled ptarmigan eggs and find a space on caribou skins on the floor, the children perching on their parents' laps, rapt expressions on their faces. One of her few memories of her father was of sitting in the warmth of his lap, the taste of sugar in her mouth and the rapture of the flickering images on the screen. These days, when she wanted to feel accompanied, she had only to put a Harold Lloyd or Charlie Chaplin movie on her DVD player and those golden moments of her childhood all came flooding back.

Up on the screen, the title faded up.

Charlie Chaplin in *The Kid*.

A thin bolt of shock shot up from her feet and settled in her chest, winding up her heart like the key turned on a clockwork toy. It seemed too much to imagine that the one film she'd been drawn to see, the story of an abandoned baby and his distraught mother, was nothing more than a coincidence. The spirits sent messages, she believed that.

An hour or so later, she was back out on the street. The sunshine had been replaced by low cloud and it was warmer, maybe even warm enough to snow. Pulling off her sealskin parka, she wrapped it around her waist then stopped and closed her eyes for a moment, drinking in the cool air. When she opened them she noticed a young woman sitting on a bench on the other side of the road whose face seemed oddly familiar. She had a mass of dark blonde hair pulled into braids and she was heavily pregnant. Her face, which was moon-like and searching, and entirely without make-up, was as pale as a winter fox but there were crescents of deep purple under her eyes. Edie tried to place her, then remembered. It was the same woman who had been hanging around in the foyer of the cinema when Edie came in. They'd made eye contact for a brief moment and the young woman had turned away. Now, Edie had the strong impression that the young woman wanted to talk with her.

Edie reached the edge of the sidewalk, and swung her head, remembering that in the city you had to watch out for the traffic. An ice truck swooshed by, klaxon hooting; tyre chains clicking on the salty blacktop. By the time it had passed, the young woman had left the bench on the opposite side of the sidewalk and was making her way down the road. Edie called out 'Hey!' but the girl just kept on walking, so she crossed the road and for a moment made to follow her, but the girl stepped up her pace and the moment was lost.

Back at the studio Edie heated up some hot, sugary tea and thought about the movie and the young woman. Maybe she'd been wrong about her. About the movie, about spirit guides, about everything. Still, the whole day had rattled her somehow. She felt disorientated, unsafe, as though she was stuck in a dream from which she couldn't wake. Finally, she punched in Derek's number in Nome. The voicemail came on. She checked her watch.

'Police, it's me.' She opened her mouth, then closed it again. 'You know what? Just forget I called, OK?'

# 6

Derek Palliser strode past the massed ranks of hacks tapping away at their laptops and into the support team area at the Iditarod's Nome HQ. He took in the still, stale air, which, like the air of hotel conference rooms everywhere, smelled of cleaning fluids. The atmosphere was anything but still. Teams of men and women, even children, hovered over the screens on which the various positions of the competitors were plotted.

Derek sat at one of the terminals, entered Sammy's race number and keyed in a password. Immediately, his location popped up on a map of the race route, along with his average speed – 3.87 miles per hour – and the time and number of minutes he'd been stopped at each checkpoint. A pop-up window gave the various meteorological details at his current location.

Derek closed the window. The stats were useful in themselves but naturally they said nothing about what running the race was really like. Derek wondered if knowing he was being tracked somehow dimmed Sammy's experience. From his own perspective, it would, he thought. One of the joys of the spring patrols he was required to undertake as part of his duties as Ellesmere Island Police Sergeant and Chief Wildlife Officer, was the liberating sense of being out of touch with everyone for days at a time. There were moments, when he was being plagued by the usually petty demands of small town policing, when he could transport himself back to the days and nights out on the remotest corners of his territory and experience again the intensity of being alone in nature.

He got up from his station and went over to the coffee machine. The race director, Aileen Logan, came up beside him and winked. He lifted the cup from the machine and passed it over to her.

'I'm guessing you need this more than me right now.' She smiled and took the cup.

'Ha, it is kinda crazy. We got some Japanese film crew whose interpreter's got sick.' She took a sip of the coffee and looked soothed for a moment, then asked, ruefully, 'I don't guess you know anyone round here speaks passable Japanese?'

Derek saw her scan his name badge, reminding herself of his name.

'You guys got off to a rough start.' Her face bore an expression of sympathy. 'I heard your teammate has been helping the PD down in Anchorage. That poor baby. Some bad shit going down there.' She waited till Derek slid his coffee cup from the machine then went on, 'You ask me, Alaska's the greatest place on earth, but we got our fair share of kooks. Maybe more than most.' She leaned in, her breath moist and coffee-scented, and lowered her voice. 'Folks around here don't like those Old Believer types much. Been rumours about them for years.'

Derek was about to ask her to expand when a woman in her mid-thirties, whom Derek recognized from the info pack as Chrissie Caley, one of the associate directors of the race, bustled up and excusing the interruption requested Aileen's attention on some urgent matter. Raising her brows in an expression of genial exasperation, the director excused herself, and the two women went off in the direction of the press room.

Seeing he'd get no more from either woman, at least for now, Derek walked out into the salted lot, with its fringe of deep, dirty snowdrift, keyed his snowmobile into action, and made his way slowly back along Front Street.

The town of Nome, Alaska, was larger and more developed than Kuujuaq, the remote Ellesmere Island settlement where Derek had lived most of his life, but it felt immediately familiar. Irrespective of their exact geography, tundra settlements seemed to share the same three or four characteristics: a desolate, disposable quality, almost but not quite like a lack of self-esteem, a sense of insignificance, of being dwarfed and outclassed by the landscape all around and a weird feeling of absolute licence, which persisted despite the fact that you could be in no doubt that news of your every splutter and fart was likely to be all around town before you'd had a chance to do so much as pull up your pants.

He passed the post office and a branch of Subway, and, on the opposite side, a fast-food place offering Japanese pizza. A handful of people trudged up and down the pavement but, for the most part, the street was pretty quiet. Everyone seemed to be in one of the five or six shabby-looking drinking hutches strewn along the street's shorefront side, establishments with cutesy names like 'The Northern Lights' and 'The Husky', their windows rivers of condensation through which you could see indistinct shapes swarming.

Derek turned down a side street and brought the snowmobile to a halt beside the cramped house of his old friend Zach Barefoot, with its scrapheap yard of old and broken kit, killed the engine and clambered up the steps into the house. Inside, the place had the feeling of some kind of home-grown museum, which had long outgrown its premises, the happy result, so Zach said, of his wife Megan's collecting habit. Everywhere there were shelves piled high with Inuit carvings, embroidery and bead and fur work. Elaborate

Russian dolls and meticulously painted wooden carvings lined the lower shelves and stacks of books were piled on the floor.

Zach was Inupiaq, originally out of Little Diomede in the Bering Strait. His wife had been born on Little Diomede's sister island, Big Diomede, just three miles but a whole world away. Back then, in the eighties, Little Diomede was officially part of the United States and Big Diomede belonged to the Soviet Union. From the fifties on, the Americans and the Soviets had constructed vast, intimidating military checkpoints on their respective islands and stopped local people from each island visiting one another. For the next forty years Inupiaq people found themselves unwitting pawns in this Cold War game, with families separated or displaced. In the nineties, when the borders opened you got a lot of Inupiaq families getting back together, Zach said. It was a good time, even though, for many, it was also when they discovered that their loved ones had died during their forced separation and they would never see them again.

Derek remembered Zach telling him that Inupiaq now came and went more or less freely but, after a brief flurry of interest over the border, *qalunaat* activity across the Bering Strait had tailed off. You got a few supply planes, some folk coming in for the Iditarod, one or two Russian scientific ships in the summer and that was more or less it.

There was a message from Zach fixed to the refrigerator suggesting the two men meet at the Anchor Bar after Zach's shift. The refrigerator itself was empty save for a block of what looked – and smelled – like seal fat. Derek fumbled around in the cupboards until he found a half-empty package of graham crackers. He made himself some sweet tea and sat down to a breakfast of crackers spread with chunks of fishy blubber.

He passed the day exploring along the coastline on the snowbie, familiarizing himself with the contours of the land. Every so often he stopped and pictured Sammy and his fifteen-dog team racing north towards him. Once in a while he thought about Edie, too, and hoped that when she'd dealt with Bonehead, she would decide to come up to Nome, at least for a few days. It wouldn't hurt to keep an eye on her. Despite all the bravado, he sensed his friend still blamed herself for her stepson's death and he didn't quite trust her not to get involved in the investigation into the death of the little boy as part of some misplaced attempt to redeem herself.

Later that evening, on his way by foot to the Anchor Bar (he intended to have a drink or two), he took a detour to the Glacier Inn to check on Sammy's progress. The musher had passed the Skwentna checkpoint and looked like he was through the marshes and heading up into the Shell Hills on his way to Finger Lake. Feeling cheered by his friend's progress, Derek trudged back along Front Street to the Anchor. A couple dozen raddled-looking *qalunaat*, faces beaten to red leather by Arctic winds, sat around a tatty, L-shaped bar. A few more perched at tables, hard-drinking and swapping shaggy dog stories. Of Zach there was no sign. He checked his watch. For the past fifteen years Zach had worked at D (North) Detachment as an Alaska Wildlife Trooper. His job was to police hunting and fishing permits and to assist the coastguard and he spent many of his days flying around his territory in his AWT PA-18 Super Cub. Most likely he'd been delayed out in the field. Derek wasn't bothered. In his experience, northern people had a more flexible attitude to time than their southern brothers. He ordered himself a brew then sauntered over to the pool table, where Aileen Logan was pocketing balls against a *qalunaat* man with the tattoo of a skull on his neck. The Iditarod director was a fine player, confident and steady-handed, more than a match for her opponent. In the couple of days he'd been in Nome, Aileen had impressed him more than anyone. He stood eyeballing the game.

After only a few minutes Aileen potted the final ball and high-fived the loser. Looking around, and winking to a couple of her fans, she spotted Derek.

'How's about a friendly?' She flapped a hand at the pool table.

He downed the remainder of his beer and stepped towards the table. Aileen was the kind of woman it was impossible to ignore. Up close, he saw that her face was laced with the spidery red web of a long-time drinker and wondered why he hadn't noticed that before.

Sometime after midnight, he made his excuses. He'd long since lost count of the number of drinks he'd consumed, but his unsteady gait and blurry thinking told him it had been several too many. The street outside was deserted. The icicle glockenspiels hanging from every roof and the squeal of the snow underfoot told their own story. The temperature had dropped dramatically since the early evening. It was proper cold, the kind of cold that always made him feel comforted even now, when he knew his senses were sufficiently blunted for temperatures like this to be dangerous. He tramped along the hard packed snow of the pavement. A low-lying frost smoke blurred the air directly in front of him, but the sky was brilliant dark, perforated with stars. For a while he just watched, his breath buffeting against the fur of his parka, then he set off up Front Street towards Zach Barefoot's house.

At the far side of the Tundra Inn, two men passed him, clasping on to someone smaller who stumbled along between them. He could just see the faces of the two men, one long-nosed and thick-jawed, like a moose, the other handsome and electric-blue-eyed. The smaller figure between them was hidden by their bodies. The two men were talking in low tones, the outline of their shapes unearthly in the frost smoke. He volunteered a greeting and, when no reply came, realized they weren't speaking English. The strange, buzzing cadences of the language suggested Russian, a language he had some grasp of, having for a couple of years had a Russian girl-friend, but they were speaking too quickly for him to be able to follow what they were saying. At Zach's street he stopped and hesitated. The Russians were no long visible, but he could hear three sets of footsteps, two heavy, the last lighter, in the snow. It was then he thought he heard whimpering.

The passers-by turned down a short side street. His curiosity aroused, Derek followed. As he reached the corner of the street, he saw all three figures illuminated in the thin, fluorescent sign for a run-down-looking boarding house, the Chukchi Motel. As the party headed up the steps towards the entrance, he could see that the small figure between the men was a young woman or, more likely, a girl. Moose-nose rang a bell. For an instant, it seemed that the girl knew he was watching her, then she was propelled inside and the door closed.

He waited at the corner for a few moments, then followed in the tracks of the passers-by until he reached the steps up to the motel. At the top, he rang the bell and waited. No response. He repeated the process but, again, nothing. A swooshing sound alerted him to a top floor window, where a blind quivered slightly in an unlit room, as though it had been opened then just as suddenly closed. The motel sign buzzed then clicked off. Derek stood watching the motel door in complete darkness until he began to feel the hairs in his nostrils freeze, then, deciding he was drunk and not functioning properly, he clambered down the stairs and made his way back to Zach's house.

There was a message waiting from him from Zach, apologizing for his no-show. There had been an illegal hunting incident he'd had to see through. He'd got back at 11 p.m. and gone to bed. Edie had been left a message on the answering machine, but she didn't seem to have anything particular to say. In the tiny spare room, Derek undressed and pulled on his pajamas. An image of the girl at the motel came to him suddenly and with force, as though it had been travelling at speed from some obscure corner of his mind. Going out into the kitchen and making some tea to clear his head, he tried to get his head to focus sufficiently to formulate a plan to go back to the motel. There had been something wrong about the scene. He knew it and in his inebriated state he'd tried to ignore it. There were many possible interpretations. The girl had been drunk, she'd had a row with her parents or she'd got herself into some trouble with a boy and her family were extricating her from the source of her woes. But he knew now that his conscience wouldn't allow him to sleep unless he went and satisfied himself that she was OK. He considered waking Zach then, thinking better of it, pulled on his outerwear and went back out into the night.

The wind had blown spindrift from the sea onto the street and the only footprints on the pavement were those of a raven and a dog. At the side street where the Russians had disappeared into the frost smoke, he stopped. The motel sign was flickering. Reaching the steps he walked up to the front door. A man with the face of an elderly walrus answered the bell and squinted at him.

'I'm looking for a skinny girl, fifteenish, pale-brown hair? She's with two men.' He checked himself. No point in coming over confrontational. 'Personal matter.'

The elderly walrus sucked his teeth and looked away, but Derek persisted, asking if the man would mind him checking around.

'Yes, since you're asking. It's late. You want a room that's a different thing, but we don't got any right now, so scoot.'

For a moment Derek stood his ground but his head told him that he was in no state to kick up a fuss. Without another word he turned and made his way back to Zach Barefoot's house. A light was on. Through the window he could see Zach in the kitchen fixing some coffee.

'I heard the door, but by the time I got up, you'd already gone. Where did you get to in the middle of the night?'

Derek told him what he'd seen.

'Probably nothing,' Zach said, pushing a mug of coffee towards him. 'I know the elder you spoke to. Name's Jimmy Aqtok. He's worked at that motel two or three years now. He's OK. If anything was going on, Megan or I would have heard about it.'

Derek nodded, nothing to add. The last thing he remembered was hitting the soft bulk of the mattress. Then the world disappeared and he was asleep.

# 7

Edie Kiglatuk popped five quarters into the newspaper bin, pulled out the morning *Courier*, swung into the Snowy Owl Café and passed by the sign reading 'Please Wait for Someone to Seat You'.

Stacey came over to her table. 'Hey there, Edie, how you doin'?'

Stacey opened her pad and made a show of being deep in thought. Despite all the black gear and piercings, she looked perky and bright. 'We got no reindeer chilli today. So what I'm thinking is one order of pancakes and reindeer sausage, hold the pancakes, a double side of crispy bacon and two cheeseburgers, with no buns, cheese or pickles. Am I right?'

'You missed out hot tea.'

While she waited, Edie turned to the newspaper. It was day three of the Iditarod and the front page was still dominated by race news. She thought of Sammy deep in the narrow mountain passes of the Arctic range with nothing but his sled and fifteen dogs, and felt a surge of affection and pride.

Stacey came over with the tea. She thanked her, added six tea-spoons of sugar to the mug and flipped through the remainder of the 'paper. No mention of TaniaLee or Lucas Littlefish. Things moved so fast in the city. She wondered if the girl and her baby would have received the same treatment if they'd been *qalunaat*. She wished then that she could speak with the mother of the boy, find out more about her, but it was clear that she wasn't going to get anymore about the young woman's whereabouts from Detective Truro.

From the corner of her eye, she could see Stacey coming towards her with a hot plate piled with meat.

'You OK?'

Edie raised a hand to her cheek, brushed off the wetness there and nodded but Stacey still hovered, wearing a worried look.

'I was thinking about that little boy, the one who was found dead in the woods.' She tailed off, aware, suddenly, that by even raising the topic she was putting herself at risk.

The last couple of days had given Edie the sense that the fewer people who were able to connect her to the death the better. She still hadn't got to the bottom of the young pregnant woman who seemed to have been waiting for her outside the cinema except in so far as she was pretty sure the girl was an Old Believer. What she'd wanted Edie still didn't know but she guessed that it was something to do with what she'd seen on that morning in the forest. Yet there was something about Stacey that made her feel she was on safe ground.

'I cross-country ski up that way sometimes. It could have been me who found him.' Clearly she'd heard the news without making the connection to Edie. 'God, what a thought. Can you imagine?'

Stacey went on, 'I think I saw that girl downtown a few times too, the mother.' She leaned in and added, 'They got some foreign girls down there, working girls, looked like she was with 'em, you know what I mean.' She let this lie for a moment. 'This town's a hard place for women, Edie. You have to be able to look after yourself. You see that girl's picture in the paper today?'

Stacey tucked her order pad into her pocket and turned to a page near the sports section at the back. There was a tiny image of Tania-Lee Littlefish wrapped around some text, easy to miss. The piece named her as the mother of the dead baby and noted that the body had been found on Old Believer land. She looked defiant, tough, Edie thought, but the uncertain curve of her mouth betrayed the vulnerability of her age.

'She's young enough it breaks your heart,' Stacey said. A group of women had come in and were settling themselves at the table next door.

Winking and drawing a finger across her lips, Stacey whispered: 'APD administrators.' Some unspoken confidence passed between the two women, then Stacey wheeled around to a group on a far table and Edie heard the perky voice asking if she could bring coffee.

For a while she sat and read the paper, and thought through her next steps. She figured that if the young Old Believer woman wanted to talk with her, she'd find a way without Edie having to go looking for her. In the middle of all this, she needed to keep her head in the Iditarod, make sure Sammy had the support he deserved. She pulled out her multi-tool, cut out the newspaper picture of TaniaLee and folded it into her pocket. As she rose to leave, she noticed that the table at which the women from the APD had sat was now empty but there was something lying on the floor under one of the chairs. She went over and, checking no one was watching, picked it up. The object was a plastic ID card clipped to a blue ribbon. The name of the woman on the ID was 'Patricia Gomez'. Above her name were the words 'Anchorage Police Department'. Edie closed her palm over the card and slid it into her pocket. As she stood to leave she saw that Stacey was watching her. There was a moment, no more than an instant, when the two women simply stood looking at one another, then Stacey moved over to the table, picked up the newspaper and held it up just enough to show Edie that she'd seen her cutting out the picture, then, folding the paper and sliding it into her apron pocket, she gave Edie a little nod and an approving wink. Edie acknowledged the look with a fragile smile, mouthed the words 'Thank you' and swung back out onto the street. Whatever Stacey knew or didn't know or had guessed at, it mattered less than the fact that the waitress had just signalled that she was on Edie's side.

# 8

Chuck Hillingberg was at the breakfast bar at home slurping down a third cup of coffee while his super-competent assistant April Montalo laid out the list of back-to-back meetings, public appearances and interviews that would make up his day in the mayoral office.

At some point in the middle of all this, he knew he'd have to find time to try to repair the damage caused by his reaction to the hysterical native woman up in Wasilla. His ducking behind Mayor Dillard had been pure reflex but, of course, he should have known, this being the twenty-first century, that the whole thing would have been captured on film and uploaded onto YouTube almost the moment it happened. It made him look like a fool. Worse, given the circumstances, a heartless fool. Then there were those new stats on sex crime. Rape and sexual assault were a perennial problem in the city, not something confined to Chuck's administration or the one before, more like part of the fabric of the place, but the Shippon campaign was bound to find a way to use the stats and the footage to appeal to native and women voters to vote against him. He'd asked Andy Foulsham, his comms director and campaign manager, to swing by. Once April had given him the day's calendar, he was planning to sit down with Andy and come up with a way to head off any bad press at the pass.

And here he was, head around the door, habitual grin on his face, right on time, as always.

'Morning, mayor, April.'

'C'mon on in, Andy,' Chuck said, 'grab some coffee and get me a refill while you're at it. Me and April were just finishing up.'

He took out his pen, signed a few of the papers April pressed on him, then motioned to his assistant to leave. Andy slid his mug over to him, took up the stool opposite. He blinked for a moment, gathering his thoughts. Chuck looked at the prematurely balding skull, the short body, thin, unmuscled arms settling in their preppy Oxford shirt. Andy was a big brain on a puny body, dressed like a Harvard postgrad. To get anywhere up here in politics you had to look like you could split logs and hunt moose for a living. However brainy they were, guys like Andy Foulsham would always be relegated to behind the scenes.

Sensing he was being scrutinized, Foulsham grasped his coffee firmly in one hand and gathered himself for his performance. So what if I'm not electable? he seemed to be saying. You aren't either without me.

'We've got a lot of opportunity here, boss. The native woman's not going anywhere. The moment Chief Mackenzie announces an arrest the Anchorage mayor picks up part of the glory for acting swiftly and the whole story is dead in the water. As for the sex crime thing, it's statewide. Shippon goes after you on that, we can turn it around so it looks like he's trying to duck his end.'

Chuck had to hand it to the man. Andy Foulsham was a human tornado. His campaign manager could spin Jesus Christ off his crucifix.

'Shippon's got a solid record on development and he was making some noise about it in an interview yesterday. Anyone you can think of who could endorse us development-wise who's not in Anchorage, I'd give them a call.'

Chuck thought of Tommy Schofield down in Homer, then decided it was probably best not to connect himself to the guy in public.

'We need to go in harder on Shippon's economic record. The economic stats for Anchorage are looking much brighter than the all-state figures, we can play on that. Cuts in state budgets are going to hit Juneau harder than Anchorage anyway. They've already started. Unemployment's rising higher statewide than in Anchorage and voters aren't gonna like the predictions about the size of the Alaska Permanent Fund dividend this year. All the polls suggest that a critical slice of the Alaska public remains undecided, so we just gotta help them make up their minds.'

'Fund a media campaign?'

Foulsham tipped him a 'you got it' finger.

'Which means money.'

Another finger.

Of course it meant money. Chuck felt his mouth go dry. Didn't it always mean money? And therein lay the problem.

A couple of weeks back Foulsham had averted what might have turned out to be a major scandal when the owner of Alaska's largest automobile franchise and one of the campaign's most generous sponsors had discovered one of the Hillingberg campaign team snorting coke while getting a blowjob from a hooker in the wash-room at the end of a $5000-plate dinner. Foulsham had persuaded the guy to retire on health grounds before anything got out. He'd called in every favour he possibly could to keep the thing out of the media and he'd succeeded. A couple of outlets had noted the retire-ment, but that was it. What Andy Foulsham hadn't been able to do was keep the owner of the car dealership on board. A week after the incident, the donor had quietly dammed the flow of funds and walked away.

What Chuck needed now was a money wonk to fill his place. But finding such a person at the last minute was no easy matter. He didn't have the range of contacts Shippon commanded and so far his powers of patronage had been confined to Anchorage. It was no good making promises to guys who weren't sure you had the power to deliver. In the medium term that just weakened you.

Marsha appeared, flushed and in her running gear. She greeted Chuck, then said 'Hey' to Foulsham, who acknowledged her with a nod. The two pretended to get on, but dig down a little deeper and you could see that their relationship was at best uneasy.

'You find my husband some funds, yet? We need those TV ads.'

'We were just talking about that,' Chuck said, in a tone designed to re-establish just who was in command here. Marsha's eyes narrowed but she kept quiet. If Andy Foulsham had dared, he would have smirked. You could see the smirk hovering there, somewhere in his eyes. It served Chuck to promote the tension so long as it continued to bubble below the surface.

'I just think we need to be more proactive here,' Marsha said.

Chuck held up a hand to stop her.

'We know what you think, hon.'

Marsha shot her husband a beady look. She hated him using the word 'hon', which he only ever did in public, said it was 'passive aggressive', whatever that meant. Right now he didn't care. She'd already made it plain that she wanted him to get on the phone directly to some of the bigger players in the state, ask them outright for funding. But he'd already contacted everyone who owed him anything and then some. He'd been in touch with old school friends, neighbourhood kids he'd grown up with and who had made good, his business contacts, fishing and hunting buddies, but the problem he came up against over and over again was that, by and large, his contacts were fewer and poorer than Shippon's, who only had to hold one of his governor's picnics to have every rich goon and his social-climbing wife in the state writing out a cheque. Chuck wasn't even very good at the schmooze. Something often seemed to go wrong; he asked for too much or too little, he was too grateful or not grateful enough or he offered sweeteners that ended up insulting people.

'I made a list,' Marsha said. 'Some new approaches.'

Andy Foulsham shot Chuck a regretful look, which said, *I'm as pissed as you are that she's right but it doesn't change the fact that she is right.* The election was in three weeks. If he was going to win the governorship, he needed to step up.

'We need to talk to developers, show them we're really on their side. Reassure them that we're going to be easing up on planning, cracking down on all those tree-hugging hippies who want to give this great state of ours back to the bears.'

This was a new thing for her, the pro-development cause, at least in its present, radical incarnation and, like any new convert, she liked to bang the drum as loud and as often as she thought she could get away with. These days, as far as Marsha was concerned, the sooner you ring-fenced a few parks and paved the rest of Alaska over the better. If the tree-huggers were so fond of trees, why didn't they take themselves off to Brazil or somewhere, stir up trouble there.

'Let's talk about it later,' he said, trying to sound emollient, but it was too late. He could see she felt that no one was really listening to her and if there was one thing Marsha couldn't tolerate it was to be ignored. She wouldn't attack Chuck in public, but she'd think nothing about going after Foulsham.

'We're exposed here. The dead boy. You understand the potential of that story to blow up in our faces, right?' There had been com-plaints about the Old Believers before. Chuck had never taken them seriously and, in retrospect, that had been a mistake.

'I got my team working on making that story go away,' Andy said.

So Foulsham had decided to stand up for himself, Chuck thought.

'Sure you do,' Marsha's voice was one small beat off full-scale sarcasm. 'I guess that's why the kid's name and the name of his mother were in the *Courier* yesterday morning.'

Chuck felt himself stiffen internally. He agreed with Andy that the story wasn't really going anywhere. So far as he could see, his wife was just trying to use it to stir things up.

'Marsh,' he said, softly. It was the name he called her when they were young, before everything went to shit. 'Let's not overreact here. It was a small paragraph right at the back of the paper. If anyone really cared there'd be press outside right now.'

'All the same, someone in the APD leaked the Old Believer con-nection. No one should have given that to the press at this stage.'

'We don't know that. Any cub reporter on his first day on the job could have found the body was on Old Believer land. Like Andy said, we're working on reining the story in.'

She cut him a savage look. 'You're underestimating this.'

He returned the look in kind. Sometimes she needed reminding just who had the power here, which one of them was running for governor. 'I already put in a call to Mac.' That much was true at least. He didn't mention that the APD chief hadn't yet returned from his fish camp. Mackenzie's wife said her husband intended to go direct to his office from the airstrip, but she'd have him call the mayor the moment he landed.

Marsha opened her mouth as if to speak, then, thinking better of it, tutted and shook her head and said she was going off to take a shower. Chuck's office cell phone buzzed. It was Mackenzie.

'What can I do for you, Mr Mayor?'

Andy got up and began to walk towards the door. Chuck caught his eye and he swung right around and went back to his stool at the breakfast bar.

'I'm gonna put you on speakerphone. Andy's here.'

Mackenzie and Foulsham greeted one another briefly, then Chuck took over once more.

'We're kinda concerned about the level of information that's getting out to the public on the dead boy case. Especially on the Old Believer stuff. You know how people love all that talk about satanists. We got a leaker we need to worry about?'

'No one inside, boss, that I guarantee you.'

'Apart from going ice fishing, what are you doing to shut the story down?'

'We've got the mother in the nut-shed under a fake name. There's the witness, some native from Buttsville, North Pole, knows no one within a thousand miles of Anchorage. She just got here for the Iditarod. Maybe she said something. I doubt it, though. I'll have Detective Truro keep an eye on her. He says she's kinda strange.'

Bob Truro. Chuck recalled the skinny-assed, pimple-faced Jesus freak he knew from Born Again summer camp. It wasn't his faith Chuck took exception to so much as his fanaticism. Back then Truro was just the kind of guy to think that people like the Old Believers should be run out of town on principle. Maybe he hadn't changed.

'Truro have issues with those Believer guys?'

'The Russians?' Mackenzie picked up on the insinuation. 'Nah. I mean, he don't like them much – who does? – but as to whether he would have set them up? Not a snowball's chance in hell. The guy's as straight as a moose's dick. The suspect, Peter Galloway, is a lone wolf. Anyway, we're close to being able to make an arrest.'

Chuck leaned in. Opposite him, Andy Foulsham gave a little grin of relief.

'How close?'

'We're hoping to move on it before we have to apply for an extension to hold him. We knew he was living at the Believer compound near Homer about a year ago but we got a tip-off that he had a connection to the mother of the dead kid. He was teaching literacy down there. He left around about the time the mother would have gotten pregnant. We're trying to establish whether he had sex with the girl, whether he might be the father of the dead boy. Plus we got that witness who found the body, she saw Galloway snowmachining in the area not long before and she's prepared to say so in court.'

'Hold on a second, Mac.'

Chuck gestured to Foulsham to leave the room and switched his cell phone back to normal. He waited for a minute after the door clicked shut then said softly.

'Wait five then call me on the private number.'

He put the phone down, walked out of the kitchen and up the stairs to his private study. He flipped the safe combination and took out a cell phone, which almost immediately began vibrating.

'Hey.' Mac's voice. The one thing Chuck couldn't stand about the guy was this perkiness, but it was precisely this perfectly executed smokescreen of cheerful amiability which gave Chuck confidence in him. The two men went all the way back to the same summer camp at which they'd both met Bob Truro. They'd bonded over a shared ambition, an interest in keeping fit and a deep-seated resentment of their respective parents. At the time they had both still believed that Jesus would sort out their problems but, as it turned out, their problems had outlasted their faith. At the U of Alaska they'd belonged to different sets, Chuck to the politicos, Mac to the outdoor nuts, but enough remained between the two young men to ensure they kept in touch. Twenty years later what they had wasn't a friendship exactly, but a confederacy of minds and tastes.

'I need a guarantee the dead kid's got nothing to do with us.' He'd already asked this, but he wanted to be absolutely sure.

'Like I said before, boss, we make the arrest, the whole thing's gonna go quiet,' Mackenzie said. 'Guaranteed.'

# 9

When Detective Bob Truro answered the phone he sounded slightly out of breath, as though he'd rushed to get the call. Edie had taken the precaution of calling from a booth downtown. The number, she knew, would show up on Truro's screen and this particular caller didn't want herself identified.

'Maggie Inukpuk.' Edie flexed her jaw to perfect the voice she'd been practising for the last ten minutes. 'I'm from the Ellesmere Island Police Detachment, here in Anchorage on some police business.'

'From *where?*' Truro said impatiently.

'Ellesmere. Up in Nunavut, Canada?'

'Oh.' Truro coughed, rapidly losing interest. 'So how can I help you, Maggie?'

'I believe you've been questioning TaniaLee Littlefish about her son.'

'We're not treating Ms Littlefish as a suspect at this time,' Truro said. Edie watched the cents on her phone card ticking down. The detective wasn't about to give anything away.

'I realize that.' Edie cleared her throat. 'Thing is, detective, we'd be glad to ask her a few questions.'

Truro said nothing.

'We're dealing with a case,' Edie went on. 'Cousin of Ms Littlefish. Petty insurance fraud, no big deal, we just need to clarify a couple of facts. A quick phone conversation would do fine.'

'I hate to disappoint, Officer . . .' searching for the name, failing to find it, 'but TaniaLee Littlefish is a dry river right now. We got her in a secure psych facility in the city under another name. At least until the case is cleared up. For her own protection.' The detective wanted to get off the phone.

'I see.' Edie made to sound breezy. 'Well, like I said, it's nothing urgent.' She didn't want Truro thinking there might be some connections he needed to pursue. 'Thank you for your time, detective.'

Edie put down the phone, felt for the photograph and swung out of the phone booth in search of a taxi rank. She found one down by the market along with a driver who knew the location of the psychiatric facilities in the city. Turned out cab drivers knew as much about nuthouses as they did about bars and brothels. In his day, her driver said, he'd taken dozens of lunatics in and out of various institutions, to say nothing of their families. She'd already concocted the cover story. She'd heard through a family about her distant relation but no one seemed to agree on which psychiatric facility was holding her. The driver didn't seem phased. He said he knew them all. They could drive around.

At the Anchorage Green Shoots Clinic a broad-beamed woman wearing an elaborate wig recognized TaniaLee's picture and, blinking at Patricia Gomez's ID, read off *Anchorage Police Department*, came to the conclusion Edie was hoping for and said:

'Sure. You'll find Terri Lightfoot in the Pinewood unit.'

She told Edie to buzz at the door to the unit then go right on in.

Terri Lightfoot aka TaniaLee Littlefish was sitting in the communal area of the unit leafing through a teen magazine. She was as young as her photograph suggested, certainly not more than fifteen, and brittle as all hell. The girl looked up and gave Edie a long, glazed stare. It was obvious she was heavily medicated. Her movements were about as lively as a dead seal's.

Edie flashed the ID. 'Mind if we have a little talk?'

TaniaLee said nothing and went back to her magazine. She wasn't really reading it, Edie could see, but scoping out the pictures. Her hand was trembling and there was a tangy, metallic smell about her. Edie had noticed that taint before among people whose spirits were disturbed. She'd smelled it once or twice up in Autisaq among women diagnosed with post-natal problems. An imbalance of hormones, the *qalunaat* doctors said, and maybe it was, but the elders had another explanation. They said that a mother has to voyage into the spirit world to lay claim to the spirit of her unborn baby. Every so often, on her way back to the visible world, a woman loses her way.

'TaniaLee.'

The girl looked up, but with the same faraway expression on her face.

'I'm not here to get you into trouble.'

TaniaLee's eyes narrowed a little and some thought played around her mind but did not reach her lips. Eventually she said: 'You Yupik?'

'My people are way up in the north,' Edie said.

'Do you work in Safeway?'

'No, TaniaLee. Why d'you ask?'

The girl ignored the question, flipped over the page in her magazine and pointed to the picture of some movie star.

'Are you a friend of hers?'

'Uh nuh. Are you?'

'Yes,' she said, 'I'm friends with everyone, even God.'

'Sure,' said Edie. She felt bad playing along with the girl but what was the alternative? 'Did God take your baby, TaniaLee?'

TaniaLee shook her head.

'The Believers took my baby. They came and took him away. I couldn't do anything about it.' Her voice was completely flat. Either it was the effect of the drugs or she had been coached. Maybe both.

'Why did they do that, TaniaLee?' As gently as she could.

'Because they are Devil worshippers.' The girl was staring into the middle distance now.

'TaniaLee, can you talk to me about Lucas?'

She said: 'Are you my sister?'

'No. But I understand what you're going through better than you might think.' Edie took the girl's hand. 'You have family? They visit you here?'

The girl looked at the floor, then turning her face to Edie said: 'I'm going to have lots of babies.' Edie smiled encouragingly. 'The Devil won't want all of them. Some of them I can keep.' Her face crumpled. 'They took him away.'

'Can you tell me what they looked like, the people who took your baby, can you describe them?'

TaniaLee frowned. 'I don't know, Fonseca said.'

'Fonseca told you the Old Believers had taken your baby?'

'Yes, it was them, they took him.'

Edie leaned in and picked up the girl's hands. They were small, the nails bitten to the quick, and trembling.

'Who's Fonseca, TaniaLee?'

A faint smile played across the girl's lips. 'My husband.'

At that moment a nurse came over. She gave Edie a cold, hard stare.

'Terri needs to rest now.'

Edie nodded, leaned over and pressed TaniaLee's hand.

At the locked door the nurse softened, and shot her a collegiate look. Fellow professionals, job to do, not always easy.

'You get what you needed?' she asked.

'She says she's married?'

'Terri says a great many things. At the moment, it's sometimes hard to tell what's true and when it's the illness talking. Most of them gradually settle. You come back in a few weeks' time, she'll probably be more able to talk.'

'Has her family visited?' Edie asked.

'The family isn't involved.' The nurse's eyes opened wider. The question had surprised her. 'I would have assumed you'd have known this is a police matter.' The receptionist must have buzzed through and told the unit to expect her.

'Of course.' Edie gave the woman a thin smile. 'Just routine questions.' She saw the nurse's expression relax. 'One more thing. Your professional opinion?'

'I'll do my best.'

'Could someone in Terri's condition harm their own child?'

The nurse glanced about to check that none of the patients was near the door, then swiped her pass key across the scanner.

'All kinds of people in all kinds of conditions see fit to hurt their kids, Officer Gomez,' she said.

# 10

From the Green Shoots Clinic, Edie asked the taxi driver to take her to the Anchorage Women's Correctional Facility. On arrival, she paid the fare, went up to the visitors' booth and explained her purpose. An officer took her details and asked her to wait. The waiting room was a windowless box painted cucumber green and littered with posters announcing prisoners' rights, security measures and the like. In one corner a woman in a business suit sat reading some papers. Edie took up the seat beside her. On the wall opposite, a vending machine throbbed away.

She tried to use the time to focus on her visit to TaniaLee but the atmosphere first at the secure unit and now here at the Pen scrambled her thoughts. She guessed that almost everyone else shared a horror of being shut away but the Inuit horror of being locked up had to be, if anything, even greater. All the Inuit she knew would say they'd rather die than spend even a night behind bars, and they meant it. In part, she thought, this was because they lived so much of their lives out on land which had no boundaries. It was also because Inuit knew they were obliged to act within a law based on principles they often found incomprehensible. It wasn't as though they wanted to break the law; it was more that they didn't feel it was their law in the first place.

She was sitting here waiting to pick up a dog she owned. But what did that really mean? Bonehead wasn't her possession. Anytime he wanted to wander out on the tundra and try to make his own way, he was welcome to do so. People couldn't own animals or things. Objects belonged to their spirits and, even then, only while the spirits chose to inhabit them. Rocks, land, sea; none of them could be held in perpetuity by inhabitants of the visible world because those inhabitants were themselves only temporary. Naturally, if you'd gone to the trouble of making a harpoon or flensing a seal, say, it was only fair that you got first dibs at its use, but to say that you owned that object was ridiculous.

The door opened and Bonehead detonated out through the gap. Behind him a red-faced guard emerged, white-knuckled and panting, only just managing to keep hold of the leash.

'Boy,' said the guard, relieved to be handing over responsibility. 'This animal is a rocket. You could use him to explore outer space. Might even make it as far as Jupiter.'

Edie wrinkled her nose. 'But then there'd be nothing to breathe but dog farts.'

'You're right,' the guard said ruefully. 'Pity.'

She led the dog outside, patted him, took off the leash and inspected his paw. He was barely limping; the veterinarian had bandaged the wound and tied a padded bootie onto the injured foot, and Bonehead gave no indication of being in pain. Traffic roared by and there was the same, all-pervasive smell of diesel in the air. As she walked along the icy pavement, she felt herself shiver. It was the relief that came from knowing she would never again have to visit the place they'd just left.

She thought: *I could do with somewhere to think.* And the dog needed to work off some of his pent-up energy. There was a path that wove between trees along the shoreline of Cook Inlet and she made her way down to it now. They went through a gate and she found herself instantly surrounded by forest, the only reminders of the big city a faint whiff of garlic and fuel and the sound of traffic. The dog bounded on ahead, turning circles through the snow. Edie walked along the path, allowing her mind to think back to the encounter with TaniaLee. The girl was very ill. Nothing she said could be taken at face value. But that didn't mean that none of it was true. She'd said she was married to Fonseca, but she was too young for marriage. If Fonseca was her boyfriend, why hadn't the police brought him in for questioning? But perhaps they had. She wondered if Fonseca was TaniaLee's name for the man on the snowmobile, the one suspected by the police? But if he'd had anything to do with Lucas's death, why would he have told TaniaLee that the Old Believers had taken him, effectively incriminating himself? And while it was true that elements of TaniaLee's story seemed to corroborate the version of events that Detective Truro was keen to promote, her version encountered the same problems. The whole Devil-worshippers angle sounded too ornate, somehow, and the way she had recited it rehearsed. She thought back to the Dark Believer websites. If the boy had been sacrificed in some satanic rite, why had his body been left in a place where, sooner or later, it was bound to be found? She was absolutely sure from the absence of prints in the snow and the level of snow cover on the roof of the spirit house that the couple on the scooter had not left the boy, leastwise, not on the morning she had discovered the body. Then why did Detective Truro think that they had? There was something about the broken ice crystals on the body itself which told a story, too, though she wasn't yet sure what.

Suddenly, the light opened up. Without realizing it she'd climbed up to an elevated section of the path where the trees gave way to a low cliff at the shoreline. She stood for a while, facing the city, watching the clouds scudding between the scattering of scruffy skyscrapers emblazoned with the names of oil companies, glancing backwards towards the sheeny ice slicked across Cook Inlet. How tiny and raw the city looked, how shakily scattered along the shore. Whistling for Bonehead, she turned back and began to make her way towards the city. It struck her then, looking at the clot of buildings from a distance, that, for all its unconvincing bravado, its shimmery glass and sparkle, its concrete-covered walkways and heated garages, Anchorage was fundamentally no different from Autisaq, or from any of the other tiny, frozen hamlets she was familiar with, human settlements hopelessly outclassed by surroundings that were forever threatening to swallow them up. The only real difference, she saw now, was that Anchorage had done a deal with itself to ignore the obvious. She guessed that maybe some people were fooled by its air of invincibility, and felt glad that she was not among them.

She reached the corner of her street and stopped, her breath catching in her throat, surprised to see the young woman with the long coat and braids who had been staring at her outside the cinema. As Edie approached, she backed off a little, her hand on her belly, wary of the dog and protective of her unborn cub, and Edie felt moved to grasp Bonehead's ruff and yank him to her side. The young woman gave a grateful, nervous smile. She was more delicate-looking than Edie had recalled, her skin more sallow and with dark, unhappy circles under her eyes.

Edie said, 'If I invite you in to warm up for a few minutes, will you stop following me?'

The young woman shifted about nervously, unable to make eye contact, but she did not make a move towards the apartment building.

'My name is Natalia.' The accent was American with some kind of other inflection, possibly Russian. She gave a small toss of her head towards a black Land Cruiser with privacy windows parked over the other side of the street. 'Please come with us.'

Edie felt herself stiffen. She looked over at the vehicle then at Natalia. The woman had serious back-up. This wasn't what she had expected at all.

'Are you crazy? I don't even know you.' Her voice sounded more hostile than she'd intended. Beside her, Bonehead picked up the tension and began to growl.

'You know what I am,' Natalia said simply.

Yes, that Edie knew. If the young woman's outfit hadn't been a giveaway, her archaic hairstyle and strange, hesitant mannerisms told their own story. She'd known it when she'd first seen her and this latest encounter only confirmed what she already knew. Natalia was Old Believer. Snippets of the Internet gossip she'd picked up, the sinister, paranoid descriptions of Dark Believer rituals, flashed through Edie's mind. Instinctively she felt for the hunting knife she always carried in the pocket of her parka. A part of her was shouting 'walk away'. She thought about making a dash into the building, but she had no idea who might be in the car and whether they carried weapons. She was a witness to a murder and now the people Detective Truro held responsible for the killing were begging her to get into their truck.

Natalia shifted on her feet.

'Please, we need your help,' she said, cradling her belly with her hand.

Edie met her gaze but her face was completely expressionless now, like new ice. She thought: *I owe these people nothing. Less than nothing.* They hadn't even been kind enough to give her a ride to the safety of her snowbie when she'd been lost in the forest. Then she thought about crazy TaniaLee and her baby son, Lucas, left out in the woods, and realized this wasn't about what she owed or didn't owe the Old Believers, that it wasn't about them at all. Edie thought about what Derek would say, the fuss he would make. Mostly, she thought about Sammy, about how by taking this on she was letting him down. All her focus should be on him right now. On the other hand, there was a limit to what she could actually do. She'd picked up Bonehead and there was nothing else outstanding right now. Besides, she wasn't going to be the woman who turned her back on Lucas Littlefish. She'd already learned that lesson. If she hadn't let Joe go out on his own with a man she knew to be irresponsible and a drinker, then he might still be here. She knew she couldn't live with letting another child down. Sammy wouldn't want that either. There was no bond she held more dear than her loyalty to the voiceless dead.

She said, 'How did you know where to find me?'

Natalia took a deep breath and looked away.

'OK,' Edie said finally, reluctantly. 'But the dog's coming too.'

A man was waiting in the driver's seat of the truck and popped open the front passenger door as they approached. Natalia introduced her father, Anatoly Medvedev, and waved Edie into the front seat.

'It's better I sit in the back with the dog,' Edie said. She was relieved to hear that Bonehead had stopped growling now. The animal was trained to scent out polar bears. He could smell fear and danger in equal measure. Right now, he was smelling neither.

Natalia nodded and got into the front. The truck drew away from the kerb and pulled into the flow of traffic heading north along N Street towards the Glenn Highway. While he drove, Edie inspected Medvedev in the rear-view mirror. He was difficult to age. His hair was the colour of two-year snow, grey-white and mottled. He wore it short on top but the sideburns were long and ungroomed, culminating in a flossy beard of the kind Edie associated with pictures of the old Victorian explorers after a long overwintering in the Arctic. A life spent outdoors in the northern winds had given his skin a rough, almost reptilian patina. The eyes were an unsettling colour, new iceberg blue with milky intrusions. Every so often they flicked up to the rear-view mirror. He was either one of those rare people who were possessed of a preternatural calm, she thought, or he was a psychopath.

They drove out of town and eventually turned onto a track road marked to the Hatcher Pass. The ice here, beyond the reach of the snowploughs that kept the main highway clear, was compacted and treacherous. Medvedev slipped the vehicle into four-wheel drive, but they skidded and slid along all the same. Soon, the trees closed in, shading the route ahead and they passed the curve in the road where Edie had first seen the spirit bear, then, a little further along, the spot where she'd emerged not far from where she found Lucas Littlefish's body. Her mind backtracked to the couple on the snow-mobile, looming out from the darkness of the trees. In her mind's eye she saw the man, large and frosty, the woman sitting mute behind him, her silver fox mitts tensed around his body, their red and green tassels swinging in the momentum from the snowbie.

Edie leaned forward ever so slightly and glanced in at the gap between the front seats. An identical pair of mitts lay in Natalia's lap, moving softly up and down in time with her breath. She felt the sound coming from her mouth before she heard it.

The young woman gave a faint smile. 'I wondered when you would notice,' she said. 'I watched you, I saw you taking us in. You don't miss much, do you, Edie Kiglatuk?'

It was all suddenly very obvious. Edie's gaze drifted down to Natalia's belly.

'Yes,' the young woman said simply. 'The man you saw on the

snowmachine, the man the police have taken away, he's my husband, Peter Galloway, and this' – she patted her belly – 'is his son.'

Edie breathed in hard. For an instant she cursed herself for getting into the car. She suddenly felt very vulnerable, the only witness to a horrendous crime which could see a man go down for life as a child-killer, in the middle of the forest with two of the people who had most to lose if he was convicted. Then she thought about the spirit bear and the instant passed.

They bumped along an unmade road, the snow chains gouging hard on the compacted snow, until at last they came to a break in the trees in the midst of which stood a large, ramshackle gate, gritty with rust. A young, thin man dressed in what Edie now knew to be the Old Believer costume of woollen overcoat and fur hat, with a rifle slung across his shoulder, opened the gate and waved them through. The truck swayed up a deeply rutted path, hemmed in on both sides by hemlock pines, before opening out into a clearing scattered with modest plank-built houses and, to one side, a school where children dressed in antiquated garb played with balls and hoops. Beside the school stood a clapboard church topped with an azure onion dome on which had been painted a thousand yellow stars.

At the far edge of the clearing they reached a house a little larger than most of the others, with a view out across the whole scene. Anatoly drew alongside the front door and switched off the engine. Natalia got out and, holding her belly, opened the back door. Bonehead burst from the car and immediately began smelling the dirt.

'We don't allow dogs inside,' Natalia said.

Edie followed her hosts up and into the house. Anatoly disappeared into the dim light of the passageway, his thick cotton shirt billowing out from under his jacket like a cloud on a windy day.

Natalia went after him, beckoning Edie to follow. They entered a panelled kitchen with a wooden table so large it virtually filled the space, and so polished with age that it dipped in the spots where generations of dinner plates had been laid. They sat in silence. They were alone now, Anatoly having slipped through a low door to one side of the kitchen and into another part of the house. The sound of distant voices leaked into the room. Shortly afterwards, Anatoly reappeared with a sallow-faced woman, dressed in some kind of housecoat edged with fur. Acknowledging them with a silent nod, the woman went to the counter and began to fiddle with what looked like an elaborate billy kettle.

Placing four small glasses filled with strong, sweet brew on the table, the woman pointed to herself and said: 'Natalia mother.'

There was a short exchange between Natalia and her father in Russian, then, turning to Edie, the young woman said: 'My husband, Peter Galloway, would never hurt children. He is a good Believer and a good husband.'

Beside her Anatoly finished his tea and wiped his mouth on his shirtsleeve. Edie saw him glance at Natalia and give an almost imperceptible nod.

'We will tell you,' Anatoly said. 'Then you will help us.'

It all started two years ago, he explained, when the Old Believers had been approached by a property developer called Tommy Schofield to sell a piece of shoreside property down near Homer. Galloway had been the point man for the Old Believers. Schofield wanted to develop the land into a resort for the cruise trade. The Old Believers weren't interested in selling – the whole point of coming to Alaska had been so they could live separately from worldly things and other people – but Schofield kept returning with new terms. He seemed determined to turn the whole coast down at Kenai into some kind of theme park. After a year or so of pestering them with new offers, Schofield began to get vindictive. A bridge they'd constructed across a creek got damaged, the road they'd built into the compound had been broken up with a jackhammer, their perimeter fencing was constantly being breached and they lost cattle as a result. The Believers dealt with all of this intimidation with equanimity, fixing the fence, rebuilding the bridge and filling in the potholes in the road. They were used to being persecuted, and in ways infinitely more creative than this.

'When none of that worked, he got really nasty,' Medvedev said. 'He had hired a group of Believers for a construction job in Meadow Lake. He went back to them and tried to turn them against the group in Homer, telling them that their brothers were blocking their way to a pile of money. He thought the group could be split, he thought we were just hillbillies.'

Medvedev gulped down another glass of tea and went on. Instead of fragmenting, the Meadow Lake group went direct to Galloway and told him what Schofield was trying to do.

'From then on, Schofield wanted to get Peter Galloway,' Natalia said. 'Peter was blocking the way to Schofield's dream. He called and threatened him. One time he found a dead wolf on his doorstep.'

'Did he report any of this?'

Natalia smiled and shook her head. Her father answered the question.

'We don't get involved.'

'But you're getting involved now.'

'Now we have no choice.'

Edie took a sip of her tea. It was bitter and at the same time syrupy sweet. 'So you think this Schofield guy pinned the boy's death on your husband?'

'Yes,' Natalia said. 'That's why we need to know exactly what you said to the police.'

Natalia cut a look at her father. Her eyes were large and fluid. Edie caught Natalia's gaze and sensed the young woman was holding something back.

Natalia swallowed hard. 'Mostly, we don't like to get involved with the Outside unless we have to, but Peter is different. He hasn't been a Believer all his life. He wanted to make up for . . .' She hesitated. '. . . for his life before. He volunteered at a literacy project when we were living down at the compound near Homer. He taught TaniaLee Littlefish to read.'

Edie felt Natalia's hand on her arm. She thought about the pattern of snowdrift around the spirit house, about the thin layering of iced snow on the roof. It hadn't been left at the same time as she'd encountered Peter and Natalia in the forest, but that didn't mean they couldn't have left it some other time.

'Think about it, Edie Kiglatuk. If we had left the baby there, would Peter have directed you to take the path right beside the body?'

Edie closed her eyes for a moment. Her mind was full of contradictory ideas. Part of her wanted to believe this young woman but nothing she had said proved anything. What if she and Galloway had wanted Edie to find the body? There was no way of knowing one way or another.

'I'm not going to lie to the police,' she said.

Natalia took her hand from Edie's arm.

'We're not asking you to lie,' she said. A coldness had crept into her voice.

Edie turned to the old man. 'I need you to take me back to Anchorage now,' she said.

Outside, it was already dark. Bonehead rose to greet her and flapped his tail. They passed the journey in silence. Anatoly Medvedev stopped the truck opposite her building. As she was about to get out, he reached out an arm to waylay her.

'Four hundred years we have been persecuted,' he said quietly and fixed Edie with a look which contained centuries of sadness. 'We came to Alaska and finally thought it had stopped. For forty years we have lived here, paying our taxes with no trouble.'

She got out of the car and let Bonehead out of the back.

Then she knocked on the driver's side window. There was a question in her mind that still needed answering but which she hadn't wanted to ask until she was safely back on her own ground.

'Who's Fonseca?'

'I have no idea,' he said. Nothing he'd done, no movement or change of expression on his face, suggested he was lying.

She stood back from the truck and watched him drive away. Tomorrow, she would go back to Detective Truro and tell him about the snowdrift around the spirit house. She would tell him about the absence of tracks, about the ice crystals on the baby's body, about the pattern of ice on the frozen skin.

And then she would never speak with anyone from the Old Believers again.

# 11

Edie got Derek out of bed.

'It's 4 a.m.' The policeman sounded hung-over.

Edie feigned surprise. 'I guess I was just having so much fun I forgot to go to bed.'

'Are you OK?'

'Yeah.' She didn't want to get into all that now. 'How's Sammy doing?'

'*What?* You rang at 4 a.m. to ask me that?' His voice had sobered up, now he just sounded rattled. 'Last I heard, he left McGrath. Why?'

'Because it's why we're here.'

'Congratulations.' He loaded the word with as much sarcasm as it would carry. 'You remembered.' She heard him yawn. There was a pause while he lit a cigarette and took a long toke. 'Sorry,' he said, 'you didn't deserve that. What you got?'

She filled him in on the visit to TaniaLee Littlefish and the Believer compound. He listened without interruption then, in an urgent voice, said: 'Edie, you found a boy in the snow and you told the APD what you saw. You did everything that could have been asked of you. We don't know anything about these people, we don't know how this place works. Let's just do what we came to do and get the hell out.'

It sounded good the way he said it. She only wished she could make it work that way.

'Listen, I need your advice. You think I can use my experience driving snowbies to rent a car?'

'Are you crazy?' he said, sounding stupefied. 'Edie, you don't have a licence.'

'I thought so.' She took a breath. 'OK, so here's what I need you to do.'

At 5 a.m. a bleary-eyed guy with a face full of old acne scars came along to open up the Anchorage branch of Pimp-my-Wreck. He looked admiringly at Bonehead.

'You hunt with that dog?'

'Yeah.'

The guy raised his eyebrows, impressed. He leaned down and patted Bonehead on the back, then, applying himself to opening up the premises, said, 'What, ducks, geese?'

'Polar bears.'

'Ha!' He shook his head and laughed, waving her into the office. 'You're funny.' Then, directing her to a seat in the waiting area, he added, 'I'm Arnaldo and I'll be right with you, funny lady.'

There was some coffee from the night before still sitting in the drip jug, but the place smelled like stale vomit. Edie leaned over, helped herself to the coffee, opened eight little sugar bags and dumped them in the Styrofoam cup. While Arnaldo flustered about she took a look around the office and found what she needed. Then Arnaldo settled in his swing seat on the other side of the counter and took in a deep breath.

'OK, Lady Polar Bear, so how can I help you today?'

She sipped at the cup, then spat back the contents and told him why she'd come.

'How're you spelling Palliser?' Arnaldo plugged the name into the keyboard and pulled up the emailed reservation.

'You the secondary driver?' He squinted at the screen, took a closer look. 'Oh, that's weird, we don't have a name for you.'

The reservation clerk looked up.

'We'll need Mr Palliser to sign off on the reservation.'

'No problem. It's Police Sergeant Palliser by the way.' She looked about, pretending to fix on a document pinned to the wall, then went nearer.

'Your fire safety certificate needs renewing. Technically, it's illegal, but I guess you know that.'

From the corner of her eye she saw him hesitate, unsure how to proceed. Then, with her hunter's instinct, stepping in for the kill, she flipped Patricia Gomez's ID onto the desk.

'Sergeant Palliser just got pulled away on a job but listen, we need that rental real quick, OK? Wish I could tell you more but it's sensitive. Operations.'

Arnaldo checked the time, trying to work out whether this was something he should wake his boss for, dithered for a few moments then decided to let it pass.

'Driver's licence?'

She flashed him an indulgent look. 'You heard of a police officer without a licence? That'd be kinda like a seal without a flipper. Wouldn't get too far.'

Arnaldo looked confused for a moment then saw that she was smiling at him and joined in the joke. Forgetting he hadn't actually seen the licence, he reached over and pulled the rental agreement papers out of the printer, got her to sign, passed her a set of keys and pointed to a beat-up dirty-white truck in the lot.

She let herself in, bundled Bonehead onto the back seat and sat for a while, inspecting the control panel. It looked more complicated than a snowbie, all right, but everyone south of Iqaluit did it, so how hard could it be? She turned the key in the ignition. Immediately, a loud rumbling started up from the engine. An inspection of the gear pattern seemed to suggest that R might be a good gear to try. She cranked into it and began to back out. The truck moved backwards, lurched, shuddered then quit. A repeat of the process was more successful, though this time she took off the side mirror of the vehicle next door. Changing gears, she turned the wheel, jackhammered down the driveway and slammed on the brake. The vehicle stopped but the engine cut out. She keyed it into action again, feeling proud of herself for being such a quick learner. As the truck creaked out of the parking lot, from out of the far corner of her eye she spotted Arnaldo holding the blinds apart and staring through the gap between, slack-jawed.

Edie had already done her research. She knew it was six hours' drive from Anchorage to Homer. She figured that this gave her three hundred and sixty minutes in which to practise her driving, by which time she'd be expert. The key, she realized pretty quickly, was to try to avoid crashing in the meantime.

In the city, the snowploughs had just finished their early morning route, so the roads were clear, the lights were on and there was very little traffic. The truck spluttered between signals. Each time it stalled she fired it up again and carried on. Pretty soon she had left the last of the southern suburbs behind and was driving south with the great expanse of Cook Inlet to her right, the ice lit up in the last fade of morning moonlight. At Bird she stopped to eat a breakfast of reindeer chilli at an Indian place just off the road. The truck went a little too far into a heap of snowdrift but the nice Indian guy who ran the breakfast place helped to tow her out and gave her a little lesson in avoiding drift. For a while after the going was slow. While she was used to driving in the semi-dark – in

Autisaq the sun set in mid-October and didn't rise again till mid-February – the depth of the snow and the height of the vehicle gave her the odd, disconcerting sensation of hovering above the ground. Once or twice the vehicle sheared to one side of the road or the other and ricocheted off deep drift, but Edie now understood to brake into the slide, rather than fight against it and, since there was no traffic coming the other way, there was no harm done. A couple of times she had to stop for a moose in the road and, once, for a lynx making its way home after a night of hunting. By seven the sun was fully up and she found herself driving along a river valley between mountains, with spruce and alder forest stretching up the slopes on either side.

At Cooper Landing she stopped and called the offices of Schofield Developments in Homer, told an executive assistant there her story, and was given an appointment with Schofield for 11.30. Her plan was to quiz Schofield about the coastal development, maybe even ask him about Galloway, but without him suspecting she had any interest in the death of Lucas Littlefish, or in Galloway's arrest. She filled her flask with hot sweet tea at a roadhouse and let Bonehead out while she checked her oil and snow chains. There was a moment, there, when she wondered what the hell she was doing, but it passed and she was on the road once more, heading south across the Kenai Peninsula to Homer.

Six and a half hours after she'd first started out, she found herself on a reveal overlooking the patchy ice of Kachemak Bay to the spectacular peaks of the Kenai Mountains with their toothy summits and milky glacial bowls. The sun was moving across the sea ice, lighting it up in a glow of magnesium flare. To the east, a long spit thrust out into the bay like an eagle claw.

Following instructions given to her by the woman she'd spoken to on the phone, she drove through the town, which was bigger than Autisaq, but not by all that much, and onto the Spit, where she found a parking spot beside a cheerful disarray of old-time berthings, fish sheds and chandleries. Leaving the dog in the car Edie wandered along the promenade shouldering the road, past souvenir shops selling everything from frozen halibut cheeks to adventure trips to the Kenai Fjords National Park across the bay, towards the ferry port with a large billboard advertising last year's summer schedule of sailings southwestwards to Kodiak and Dutch Harbor and northeast to Valdez. At the end of the Spit, so incongruous her head had somehow blanked them till now, stood a development of vacation condos, striking in their ugliness, which blocked the view out across the bay.

An old *qalunaat* guy with a huge wispy beard and bow legs shuffled by, stopped and turned back to talk to her.

'If you're looking for something, most likely I'll be able to tell you.'

'I'm looking for Tommy Schofield's office.'

The old man rounded on her. His eyes were so mean now she thought he might hit her. 'What you want see that moose turd for?' The index finger of his right hand came up and began pecking the air. He began to splutter with rage. 'I'll tell you something, missy,' he continued. 'Give that squirt of salmon spunk his head, this whole place . . .' he passed a hand in an arc over the Spit and out into the bay '. . . gonna look like freakin' Florida. Just one big golf course surrounded by condos about as gorgeous as them carbuncles up there, and trash stores selling plastic grizzlies made in goddammed Shanghai.' He snorted and closed his eyes, no doubt imagining the scene. 'Him and that cruise ship jerk-off.' He took a step towards her, so close now she could smell the chewing tobacco on his breath. The finger began pumping at her. 'What d'you freakin' think about that?'

She held her ground. 'Tell me where Tommy Schofield's office is, mister, I'll freakin' think whatever you freakin' want me to.'

He looked at her for a second, then burst into great peals of laughter, his gut trembling with the effort of his amusement. The finger slalomed around until it was pointing to a duck-egg coloured clapboard building on the other side of the road.

An old-fashioned brass bell tinkled above the door of the office of Tommy Schofield Developments. She waited a moment. From the other side of the road she could hear the old man shouting:

'No flies on you, missy, no flies at all!'

Pushing the door with her hand, she let herself in. The only associate currently present was an old moose head, which explained the sticky note on the front door reading 'Back Soon'. Edie took a seat in a small waiting area and brushed the creases out of a cheap business suit she'd bought in a thrift store on the outskirts of Anchorage. As it turned out, she didn't have long to wait. Two voices and three sets of footsteps approached on the boardwalk, then the door swung open and a short man with a shock of lustrous hair and chiselled features appeared. Beneath his Craghopper khakis Edie could see that one of his legs – the left – was bowed and shrivelled and he stood with his weight balanced on the one good leg. The short man scoped around the office then turned his attention to Edie. 'Where's Sharon?'

There was an awkward pause, which no one seemed to know how to fill. Eventually, Edie stuck out a hand.

'I'm your eleven-thirty,' she said. 'Maggie Inukpuk, Tourist Development Officer from the Nunavut Chamber of Commerce. The fact-finding mission to talk about waterside development tie-ins with the cruise industry?'

Schofield looked confused for a moment, then took a deep breath, clearly remembering and regretting saying yes.

A well-kept man in his sixties with faded movie-star looks and a tall, strikingly pretty blonde in her thirties appeared at the door.

'Byron, I'm real sorry.' Schofield shot his friend an apologetic look. 'I forgot.' The movie star's face darkened like he wasn't much used to memory lapses among his subordinates.

'Join you in ten minutes?'

Schofield watched the couple leave, still in their orbit, unable to speak till they'd gone.

'You want to talk to a real visionary, you talk to Byron Hallstrom,' Schofield said, pointing out of the door at the receding figure. 'He's already got a huge stretch of coast down near Sitka and he's looking to expand here. You should see it down there. He's cleared the top coat . . .'

'Top coat?'

'The trees, all that forest shit. He's put in spas, boutique retail, holiday condos, golf courses. Kept one or two specimen pines, set beautiful landscaping around them. The Cabo San Lucas of the north. Gorgeous. You should go there.' He cut a look at his watch again. Judging by the old man outside Schofield's offices there were people in Homer who didn't think of Byron Hallstrom as quite the local hero Tommy Schofield made him out to be. Edie made a note to remember the name and said nothing.

'Where'd you say you're from?' Now that he wasn't talking about Hallstrom, Schofield seemed distracted and uneasy.

'Nunavut.'

He stared blankly, then gathered himself. 'Well, I can only give you ten minutes.'

He showed her into an office crammed with papers and architectural plans. Across the walls were hung trophy salmon and pictures of Schofield demonstrating the size of his catch, but always, Edie noticed, with his bad leg out of view of the camera.

The developer sat down in a padded leatherette chair on the other side of his desk.

'So . . .'

'Actually, it's more your line I'm interested in, the land development end.' He nodded and seemed relieved to be asked something on which he, not Hallstrom, was the authority. She sat back while he rattled on for a bit, waiting for a natural break, then she said:

'I guess all that bad publicity must have hurt your plans some?'

Schofield's face clouded over. He glanced at the clock again, checked himself and assumed a look of bewilderment.

'I have no idea what you're talking about.'

'That poor boy, the one who got picked up in the forest. Wasn't the mother from round here, TaniaLee Littlefish, is it?'

Schofield's face set into a mask. His eyes scooted around the ceiling and he began shifting around in his seat. After what he judged to be a suitable interval he shook his head.

'No, no, I can't say I've been following that story. The name's not familiar to me, I'm afraid.' He smiled thinly and gestured towards the door. 'I guess that answers your question. Now, Miss Inukpuk, I'm a little pressed for time.'

'Name Fonseca mean anything to you?'

'Like I said, miss, I can't say I've been following that story.' He had risen from his chair now and was standing by the open door, his mouth clamped firmly shut.

# 12

Edie left Bonehead in the rental in the car park at the Homer Safeway and walked through the entrance turnstiles past a pile of local newspapers. TaniaLee had mentioned the store, and Edie wondered now if someone might remember her. She asked around among the shelf stackers and got a few 'No's and blank looks, but struck lucky with a woman at the deli. Yeah, TaniaLee had worked there one time when she was still at junior high, but she hadn't lasted long.

'That was a harsh thing happened to her.'

Edie said she thought it was.

The woman's eyes narrowed. 'You a reporter?'

Edie paused. It was difficult to say. 'I was the one who found TaniaLee's little boy.'

The woman flushed and looked flustered. 'Oh my.'

'Maybe you know where her parents live?'

'Oh I don't know about that.'

'I just wanted to tell them their grandson looked peaceful. Might help some, a time like this.'

The woman's eyes grew filmy. 'Oh yes, yes, of course.' She described a cabin on a ridge outside Homer, said Otis and Annalisa Littlefish had lived up there quietly for a long time, then gave Edie directions on how to get there.

———————

The Littlefishes' rough plank cabin was the kind of place that wouldn't have stood through a single winter in Autisaq. There were shingles missing from the roof and one of the windows was glazed with transparent plastic but here above Homer, nestling in the trees, it looked cosy in a rustic, rough-around-the-edges kind of a way. It seemed the Littlefishes were in. A chimney leaked smoke from its base and under a corrugated plastic carport sat a big old flatbed truck with a tarp over it. There was firewood piled either side and a splitting log with an axe buried in it and new cut marks. Beside the port, a pair of bald eagles sat in a spruce preening.

Edie swung open the door of the rental and jumped down. A huge native man with a hewn face and hair tied in a ratty pigtail appeared at the door of the cabin with a shotgun swinging from one giant, wind-whipped hand. Maybe Otis and Annalisa Littlefish didn't get too many visitors, Edie thought, or maybe the ones they did get they wished they didn't. She trudged up the steps and tried to look friendly. He stood and waited for her to speak. As she explained why she'd come she saw his expression soften. Immediately, she liked him.

'It's been hard for my wife,' Otis said, inviting her in. 'TaniaLee was wild. We hadn't seen her or our grandson for a while.' His voice was low and there was an edge of pain in it. 'The police got her locked away in some clinic, told us not to visit. Maybe that's easier for her, I don't know.'

He offered Edie a seat at the plank table beside the tiny kitchenette and went to fetch his wife in from the back where she was cleaning out the field-dressing shed. He came back with a tiny, plump woman with long braids, wearing rubber boots, a native like her husband. The woman held out a yellowed, arthritic hand, asked Edie if she'd like something to drink then went to heat some water.

Neither Otis nor Annalisa looked like they had any *qalunaat* blood. Since the little boy in the snow was mixed it stood to reason Edie thought that unless he'd been some kind of throwback, Lucas Littlefish had a white daddy. Maybe the guy TaniaLee claimed was her husband, Fonseca? She made a note to herself to find out.

While Annalisa fixed tea and a snack, Otis went out to the carport to fetch more wood. He walked with an odd rolling gait, favouring his right leg.

Annalisa said, 'Otis can't stand women's talk.'

She came over with a tray on which she'd balanced three steaming mugs and a plate of salmon jerky topped with frozen roe.

'I'm real sorry for your loss,' Edie said.

Annalisa wiped at her eyes with the back of her hand.

'The police said TaniaLee mentioned a man called Fonseca,' Edie went on. She wasn't going to say she'd visited their daughter at the clinic. 'I guess he's Lucas's father, right? Must be taking it pretty bad.'

Annalisa gave a stiff little shrug. 'We don't know any Fonseca.' Otis came back in and her face relaxed. He came and sat down in a chair opposite.

'I was just saying, I'm real sorry, Mr Littlefish,' Edie said. The old couple stared into the middle distance, their faces closed and tightened. Edie had seen that look before up in Autisaq. She'd gone too far in trying to make them talk about the dead. It was time to change the subject.

'You got a beautiful house here.'

Annalisa immediately perked up, a little smile of pride playing around her lips.

'Twenty years,' she said. 'Me and Otis built this place.' She offered round the snacks. Edie helped herself.

'Great salmon jerky,' she said. 'Thank you.'

'You Inupiaq?' Annalisa said.

Edie explained how she'd come to be in Alaska. 'What about you?'

The old woman seemed to have got over her initial reluctance to talk. They were full blood Dena'ina, originally from the hills around Eagle River. They'd moved up into the woods to get away from all the people and, even though their ancestors were buried elsewhere, they never regretted the move.

'Otis here works in construction and forestry when there's work going. We hunt, fish.'

'Is TaniaLee your only child?'

It was the wrong question. 'We have to get back to work now,' Otis said. He had an implacable look on his face.

Edie stood up and swung herself into her parka. As she was zipping up, she noticed some family pictures sitting on a console table just inside the door. Her attention was drawn to a photo of TaniaLee holding her son. Reaching out a hand she scooped it up. Mother and son were outdoors somewhere. There was a great deal of snow and from the shadows Edie could tell that the picture had been taken more or less at noon in full sunlight. TaniaLee was squinting, her pupils pinpricks. There was a dreamy look on her face, as though she was somewhere far away.

'That was Thanksgiving last year.' Annalisa spoke in a voice of barely disguised anguish.

There was a pause then, suddenly, she said: 'It's Lucas's funeral tomorrow at ten at the Orthodox Church up at Eagle River. We're having a potlatch in the hall afterwards, if you want to come.'

Edie smiled and returned to examining the picture. In it Lucas Littlefish was six weeks or maybe two months old. The body she'd found in the forest was that of a two-month-old baby. But now it was March and the picture had been taken at Thanksgiving, which could only mean that Lucas Littlefield had died sometime in

November or, at the latest, early December. Confirmation of what she'd already suspected, that for at least three months between his death and her discovery of his body, Lucas Littlefish must have lain frozen somewhere out of the reach of animals. In storage maybe. That would explain the profound freezing of the body, and the pattern of ice crystals across the skin. But why? And why had no one reported him dead before?

She returned the picture to the table, but her hand was shaky and as she replaced the frame she managed to knock over the one behind it. When she picked it up, she was shocked to see that it was an image of Otis shaking hands with a man who looked remarkably like Tommy Schofield.

'Oh, Mr Schofield,' she said, trying to sound casual. 'He's a big guy around here, isn't he?'

Otis nodded. He picked up the photograph and turned it so it faced the wall. 'He got a cabin ways up there, not far. Sometime I do maintenance work for him.' He was agitated, anxious for her to leave.

She drove back down to Tommy Schofield's offices on the Spit. Schofield's assistant had finished her break and was sitting at her desk staring at her computer screen. She was a perky-looking woman in her early twenties, somewhat over-groomed. Introducing herself as Sharon Steadman and explaining that the developer had gone to the airstrip. He often had to rush off to the capital at short notice – last-minute meetings with planners and financiers – and it was easier if he flew himself. He owned a Piper Super Cub he took to fish camp, Sharon explained, but when he was flying to Juneau he usually took his Cessna 180.

They heard the sound of a small-engined plane overhead.

'Oh, my gosh, I guess that's him.' She smiled indulgently. 'Mr Schofield just *loves* his planes.'

They waited for the sound to fade.

Sharon said, 'Sometimes I say to him, one day, Mr Schofield, you gonna fly clean away and never come back, but he always says, he says, how could I leave you, Sharon?' She flapped a hand in the air and giggled. 'Oh my gosh, he's always kidding around.'

Edie looked around and decided there was nothing more to be got from Schofield or his office today. She glanced at her watch and figured she may as well drive back to Anchorage.

'Mind if I just use your bathroom?'

The assistant waved both arms.

'You betcha! Right along there.'

Edie went through the door into the corridor. The door to the bathroom was in front of her. Opposite it, there was a photocopier and a small chest freezer, secured with a padlock.

Sharon was talking on the phone when she returned. The girl gestured for her to wait while she wound up the call.

'You get everything you need?'

'Sure,' Edie said.

# 13

Chuck sent April to the front door of the house to peek out between the slats of the venetian blind, clock the number of TV news trucks parked outside, and report back.

From the breakfast bar where he was sitting at his laptop reading his morning briefing, he could just about see Marsha doing her morning stretching exercises in the den.

'How's it looking?' This to April.

His assistant's voice came from the hallway. 'Four, maybe five.' April scrolled off the names on the OB trucks. 'KTYU, Channel Two, the usual local stations.' Andy Foulsham had invited them along yesterday, for an 'intimate personal interview' with the gubernatorial challenger in the mayor's backyard at 7.45 that morning.

In the den, Marsha began bobbing up and down, touching her toes, breathing faster. She was still fit but it made him a little sick to watch her all the same. The ageing skin, the relentlessness of her pursuit of a physical perfection she seemed unaware that she'd lost twenty years before. He guessed most men would still consider her attractive, but then they didn't know what he knew about her.

He'd been woken at four in the morning by Mackenzie, announcing that they now had enough evidence to charge the Old Believer Peter Galloway with the kidnap and ritual murder of Lucas Littlefish.

'What evidence?'

'Galloway's fingerprints on the grease used to draw the cross on the kid's body.'

'You didn't mention that before.'

'We were waiting for confirmation from forensics.' The APD would be feeding the story to the news outlets at 7.30 a.m. Chuck had immediately called Andy for advice. An arrest was what they wanted, but the Hillingberg campaign had also hoped to capitalize on the ongoing Iditarod story and fend off any negative campaigning Shippon might be throwing at them over those sex crime stats. Andy had got back to the police chief to ask him to hold off on the arrest story till the evening news, but Mackenzie seemed too wary of leaks to let it wait. So Foulsham had called Bob Morehouse, the owner of Channel Six, at 5.30 in the morning to offer him an exclusive interview with gubernatorial candidate Hillingberg on the understanding that he would guarantee to broadcast between seven and seven-thirty that morning. Six had always been good to the Hillingbergs. Morehouse had played high school football with Chuck, and his wife, Mindy, had cheerled from the sidelines with Marsha. More importantly, Six News had the biggest audience of all the local stations. A Channel Six reporter and crew had shown up at 6.00 a.m. to tape Chuck's segment. The interview had been a breeze; the reporter had given him seven minutes on the gubernatorial campaign with plenty of opportunities for sound bites and no tough questions. By 6.30 the tape was back at the Channel Six studio. A lightly edited version would go out as live at 7.15, just before the news hit of the arrest of Galloway. That way, Chuck would be the top morning story for fifteen minutes and would remain associated in people's minds with the arrest for the remainder of the day.

Timing is everything, Foulsham always said. A cliché, but nonetheless true.

Chuck checked his watch. It was 7.12 a.m. The TV was already on, muted. Reaching over, he grabbed the remote sitting on the breakfast bar and switched on the sound. Andy Foulsham appeared, April following behind him. Chuck hollered to Marsha, who came in breathing heavily from her exercise regimen. Six News went to commercial break.

Andy had already briefed the remainder of the networks waiting outside the Hillingberg mansion to expect him out at 7.45 for an eight o'clock start. This was supposed to be an 'at home' with Chuck, a chance for the voter to get to know the man himself. The personal approach had been designed to pull in women voters, with a promised tour of Chuck's trophy room at the end of the interview the lure for men. If it came up, Chuck would acknowledge the arrest of Peter Galloway and take as much credit as he could for it without seeming to be raining on Police Chief Mackenzie's parade, but he wouldn't bring up the issue himself. Andy had arranged for a vintage Iditarod sled to be displayed in the trophy room. Chuck would take them around his bear and moose trophies then he'd home in on the sled and use it to riff on his love for the Iditarod. Foulsham had advised him to express his admiration for Duncan Wright, the plucky challenger to Steve Nicols. The public was apt to draw parallels.

April poured coffee for everyone. The commercials segued directly into a sponsor's message, then a short intro for Chuck's segment, before cutting to the taped interview. The piece was a dream.

Six minutes later the whole room was applauding. Even Marsha broke into a smile. Chuck's performance had been flawless, his body language that of a governor-in-waiting.

They kept the TV on, waiting for news of the arrest to break at 7.30. At 7.32 Chuck's phone rang. It was Morehouse.

'Don't answer,' Andy said. 'I'll handle it.' Moments later, his phone began to peep. He flipped up the top and put on a smile.

Chuck could hear Morehouse screaming from over the other side of the room, Andy trying to calm him down. 'Well, see, Mr Morehouse, you need to be reasonable here, sir, the mayor wasn't informed about the arrest until after the Six interview had already gone out.' The man was an absolute pro. It didn't even sound like *he* had any idea he was lying.

Chuck went to his room, combed his hair, brushed his teeth, refreshed his make-up and ran a lint brush over himself. When he came back down Andy had come off his cell phone and it was ringing again. Someone was knocking on the door. Moments later, all the phones in the house started ringing simultaneously.

'Galloway?' Chuck said. *'Really?'*

Marsha lifted one eyebrow in a 'told you so' gesture.

'No sweat,' Andy said. 'We'll just do the "at home" interview like we planned and tell them they'll get a statement on the Galloway arrest at the end.'

'What's the line?'

Marsha looked up and made a scoffing sound and Foulsham cut in to rescue his boss.

'Just like we talked about, mayor. Terrible tragedy, fine police work, you're confident there are no implications beyond this one arrest blah blah, then draw a line under it.'

Marsha reached out and brushed some piece of carpet fluff off his shirt. 'Remember. You set the agenda.' She gave him one of her tiny nods of encouragement. 'Now go get 'em.'

Andy opened the door onto the backyard and Chuck walked out with Foulsham following. He sat down on the carefully placed chair, a rare Alaska antique made from Sitka spruce and moose antlers, and smiled vaguely in the direction of the press. There were more reporters than April had suggested and they seemed intense, even a little frantic. He took a deep breath and reminded himself of his brief. Andy Foulsham opened the interview for questions, then something unexpected happened. Instead of the gentle, lifestyle-orientated act of sharing he was expecting, reporters began jostling and shouting over one another and in the cacophony of sound there was only one question.

In the half hour since the official announcement of the arrest of Peter Galloway for the abduction and murder of Lucas Littlefish, it appeared that the men and women of the fourth estate had been seized by Dark Believer Fever. And Mayor Hillingberg, caught completely unawares, had laughed them off.

What seemed like a lifetime later, Andy Foulsham pushed Chuck back inside the house and locked the door. Chuck slid down the cedar panelling and sat on the thick shag carpet, head in hands.

What the hell happened?' It was Marsha.

'Gee,' Chuck said, 'I'm touched by your support.'

She picked up on his sarcasm but was in no mood to apologize. Throwing her arms around her body, she started pacing the entrance hall, and then swinging herself round with a voice of cold fury, she said:

'What did I say? I said you underestimated this, both of you.' She turned her ire on Andy, 'And you, his comms director, you fed my husband to the freakin' wolves.'

Foulsham's cell phone buzzed. He checked the screen and switched off.

'Hey, you know,' he began, trying to sound soothing, 'I don't think any of us could have anticipated that.'

'Uh, *wrong.*' Marsha unfolded her arms and pointed at herself. Her fingers were like fish hooks. '*I* anticipated it but none of you would listen to me.'

Andy adopted his smooth, damage limitation voice. 'We can come back from this.'

Marsha, who had started pacing again, whirled round and stood in front of them.

'You're darned right we can,' she said, pointing an accusatory finger at Foulsham. 'Because *you* are gonna remember who's employing you.' The finger moved across to Chuck. 'And *we* are going to work on a briefing document about the mayor's response to the arrest of Peter Galloway. Then we're going write a piece for tomorrow's *Courier* in which we are going to say that the mayor never suggested that Dark Believers don't exist, only that the evidence in this case so far did not prove that the sect had anything to do with the death of the boy. We're gonna say that despite Alaska's proud tradition of free speech Alaskans will not tolerate any kind of religious worship or ritual involving or advocating any form of violence against anyone, let alone children.' She sighed and closed her eyes for a moment. Her face bore a look somewhere between moral indignation and relief, as it always did when she felt in command. Turning to Andy, she asked for a moment of privacy with her husband.

When the comms director had gone, she said: 'You need to clear out the Lodge. Now. Everything.'

Chuck closed his eyes and sighed. He was already regretting the whole Lodge business. What a headache.

'And we should put in an appearance at that dead kid's funeral tomorrow. I'll have April make the arrangements.'

Chuck passed a hand over his forehead.

'Then there's someone we need to meet with about campaign funds. Someone we haven't asked yet. I got an idea he might be persuaded to fund some advertisements.'

Chuck sighed wearily. 'I'll need to check with Andy.'

Marsha drew closer, her arms tightly folded across her body.

'Screw Andy.'

# 14

Edie hadn't been back five minutes when the intercom buzzed.

'You went weird,' Derek said, voice tinny over the wire. 'I've been waiting for you at the coffee bar across the road, I figured Sammy can do without me for a coupla days.'

She smiled to herself. 'Come on up,' she said. 'I just got back from Homer.'

It was good to see a familiar face. His breath smelled of cigarette smoke. She reached out for his parka and pulled him in. 'You were right about driving. Trying to get that goddamned truck round those mountain roads was like rolling a greased seal across new ice.'

She told him about her visit to the Littlefishes, how Schofield had lied about knowing them and that when she'd asked him if he knew Fonseca he claimed that he hadn't been following the story of the boy's death, which seemed to suggest that he knew the two were connected – information that, so far as Edie knew, wasn't in the public domain.

'You think he knows who Fonseca is?'

'I don't know. It's possible he got flustered when I asked about the Littlefishes and just tripped up. In any case, if he does know Fonseca, he's not telling.'

'That was a big thing for the Littlefishes to invite you to the funeral. A trusting thing.' Like Edie, Derek had grown up around all the old taboos, was as familiar with them as he was with the whites of his fingernails. He'd travelled enough around the north to know that most indigenous people were reluctant to talk about the dead with outsiders. For the most part they kept burials and the rituals associated with them to themselves. Oftentimes, it brought bad luck even to mention the dead person's name after the burial. There were folk who thought it stirred up the spirits, made them unwilling to accept they were no longer among the living.

'Maybe they just want to put me off the scent,' she said.

Derek turned his head and gave a rasping laugh.

'That case, they have no idea who they're dealing with.'

'I think we should both go.' She told him about the confirmation of what she had suspected all that time, that Lucas Littlefish had been dead months before whoever it was laid his body out in the forest. 'We might meet someone at the funeral who can help us. And in any case, it doesn't hurt to go along, pay respects, show the Littlefishes that we care.'

'Because?'

Edie flashed Derek one of her exasperated looks.

'Because we do. Because I do, OK? I care a lot.'

He sighed and shook his head. 'Edie, I know you don't wanna hear this, but this stuff is beginning to stink. You need to tell Detective Truro what you know, let the right people deal with it.'

She waved a hand at him impatiently. 'He's gonna know about Lucas being long dead already from forensics. So, why was he working so hard to get me to say Galloway did it the day I found the body?'

'I don't know, Edie, but I know our business is with the Iditarod.'

Edie thought about Sammy, how much he needed the race. She

hadn't let him down yet, but the more she got wrapped up in the Lucas Littlefish case, the more likely she wouldn't be there when he most needed her.

'OK,' she said, with difficulty, 'let's go see Detective Truro. But that doesn't mean I'm giving up on Lucas Littlefish.'

Derek pulled the rental to the kerb outside the APD's offices in downtown Anchorage. She hauled herself out and made her way across the road without looking. The traffic slowed and veered around her, horns blowing. A man leaned out of his window and screamed, 'Dumbass bitch!' He gave her the finger.

She returned it with both hands. 'Put one of these aside for later.'

Entering the rotating doors, the motion feeling agreeably like rolling a kayak, she came out into the foyer of the trooper building. The receptionist told her to wait. A little while later the same woman with the clipboard who had first escorted her to Truro's workstation appeared. She searched for the name. Kathy.

'What can I do for you, Miss Kiglake?'

'It's Kiglatuk.' Kathy flashed her a mean smile. 'I need to talk to Detective Truro.'

The woman's mouth went tight.

'We're real busy today,' she said.

'I got more I need to tell Detective Truro about the boy. Lucas Littlefish. About what I know.'

'That's nice, Miss Kiglake.' Kathy took in a breath and pulled herself up to her full height, which wasn't high. 'Only Detective Truro got no need to hear it. We already made an arrest this morning and things are kinda getting busy here today.' She was about to turn away, when Edie reached out a hand and held her back.

'You charged Peter Galloway?'

Kathy made a low humming 'uh huh' and finished it off with a satisfied 'you betcha'.

Edie burst through the rotating doors out into the cold of the early evening and pulled open the passenger door of the rental.

'They charged Galloway already.'

'They did?'

'They didn't want to hear what I had to say. Something's not right. I don't know what and I don't know why, but it's like Detective Truro's got his story and he's sticking with it.'

Derek looked at her. His shoulders rose and fell and he sighed. She could see he understood then that she would go on with it regardless. She could also see that he was on her side.

'You in the mood for a drive?' She turned on the car radio.

'So long as I'm the one doing the driving.'

'I thought we might go for a spin to Meadow Lake,' she said. 'I hear it's lovely at night.'

As they left Anchorage behind them, a yellowish grey smear on a dark horizon, it was a relief to Edie not to be driving. At the fork in the road between the Glenn and George Parks Highways they turned west towards Wasilla. The ploughs had been out but the blacktop was already icing back over. Just outside of Wasilla, by Meadow Lake, an owl rose up and away from the truck and they came to the turn-off to the Hatcher Pass. The tyres whirled, searching for a purchase, then, finding it, swung the rental around onto the unmade, unploughed track. In the darkness, Edie could no longer be sure of the familiar curve in the road where she'd gone into the forest after the bear, or the place she'd come out after finding Lucas. Eventually they came to the gate of the Old Believer compound, picked out of the darkness by a lamp hanging in the trees above.

Derek pulled over and cut the engine.

'I sure hope this isn't about some bear.'

'No, not the bear.'

He turned in the seat to look at her. There was a resolute expression on his face, she thought. He didn't approve of what she was doing but he was going to do whatever he could to help her do it. She couldn't ask for more.

She got out of the car, sucking in the rush of cold, outside air, and felt strong. Being shut in anywhere, even inside a car, wrecked her confidence, made her feel weak. Right now she needed to be in the open.

Derek followed. They could hear sounds coming from the compound, a faint harmonium of voices. Clambering over the gate, they made their way in single file up the track. The sound of singing grew louder. Just before the clearing they stopped. The only light seemed to be coming from the church. Suddenly the singing stopped and a man began chanting. There was something raw about the sound that left a deep throb of disquiet in Edie's belly.

'My grandmother once told me that the missionaries made the Inuit women working for them wear skirts. Cotton skirts. In the High Arctic winter. They said God didn't want women wearing trousers.'

'People believe all kinds of crazy things, you give 'em half the chance,' Derek said.

'I had to witness that daub on the body of the little boy, Police. It was ugly and I don't mean walrus ugly. I mean some whole other universe of ugly. Truth is, I wanna see what they get up to, if any of the Satan stuff is true.'

Suddenly the chanting stopped and the sound of a single wailing voice found them. Men and women began to trickle out from the church.

'They're hardly going to be doing it now, with the police and the press all over them. You're tired, Edie, you're not thinking straight.'

They made it back to the car. The engine guttered into life. A blast of warm air coughed out from the ventilators.

'Turn around and drive back to that bend in the track.'

He did what she asked but this time he kept the engine running.

'Is this where you found the boy?'

She nodded, pointing into the great dark blank of forest.

'When I ran into them, Peter and Natalia Galloway were on their way back to the compound but they weren't out on the road here, they were cutting through the forest. It looked as though they'd been in town, shopping. I don't know how much I believe of what she said, but I believe that part. Lucas Littlefish was left on a route the Galloways must have regularly used, just outside the boundary of the Old Believer land. But I guess other people used that path, too.'

It had begun snowing, the flakes coming down until the windshield wipers could not move fast enough to keep the glass clear enough to see through. For an instant Edie felt as though she was being buried, the snow just one of many things, memories mostly, pressing down on her. She laid her fingers on the door handle.

'Edie, this is crazy.' But she was already jumping down into the snow.

He got out and came round to her side.

'It's dark and the snow's not letting up any time soon.'

'That's why we have to do it now,' she said. 'No one will see us and we can follow our tracks back to the car.'

As he went back around to the driver's side to switch off the engine, a figure suddenly loomed out from the spruces. The figure, a girl of about fifteen, stared, apparently dazed, and then just as suddenly as she had appeared, she evaporated into the trees like a startled deer. Derek swung round, bug-eyed. For a moment they were both paralysed. Beside them, the truck growled low.

'Dammit, Edie, I know that girl! She was being led into the Chukchi Motel in Nome a couple of days ago. I swear it is the same one. She was with a couple of much older men.' As Derek spoke, his eyes glittered.

Grabbing the flashlight from the trunk, they hurried down the track to where the girl had been. Edie felt her heart pound, the old thrill of the chase. Reaching the spot where the girl had been standing, she trained the flashlight on the trail of footprints and began to follow it through the trees and deeper into the forest. The snow cover was much sparser here and the prints more difficult to follow. It was dark as all hell too, the moonlight filtering through only occasionally in splashes and the proximity of the trees made Edie feel discomfortingly enclosed. The air smelled of electricity and spruce bark and somewhere distant she could detect the tang of human fear. Behind her sounded the faint purr of the car engine. It occurred to her suddenly that it might have been foolish to leave the engine running.

They reached a small clearing. Here the girl had tramped about, creating a confusing muddle of prints, some of which seemed to lead off in radials through the forest. The girl's intention was clear: she meant to buy time. There was nothing for it but to follow each spur of prints one by one until they found the one that led away from the clearing. This took several minutes and by then, they knew, the girl would almost certainly be too far away. There was no point in getting up a sweat. They slowed to a fast walk, following the steps as the girl's trail turned back on itself and headed once more towards the track and the car. They flashed one another an anxious glance. Reaching the edge of the woods, they scanned up the track. The car was about a hundred metres further up, right where they'd left it, the engine idling. She shone the flashlight along the ground. A single set of footprints led in the direction of the car. The girl had been running, fast now. They followed the prints, breaking into a jog up the hill to the vehicle, where they stopped before disappearing back off into the forest. Of the girl herself there was no sign.

Edie slumped over, hands on legs for a moment, her breath heavy from the effort of running. Beside her, Derek scoped the flashlight across the dark expanse of trees. For a moment she thought she heard a faint rustling coming from the woods but it might just as easily have come from an animal or snow falling from the spruce branches as anything produced by the girl. It might even be the sound of her own blood rushing through her veins. Quickly, she pulled open the door of the vehicle, lowered herself into the passenger seat, panting, trying to calm herself a little.

'Edie, look.' Derek was pointing at the windshield. Now it suddenly became clear why the girl had backtracked to the car. For a moment Edie sat back, taking it all in. Across the glass, the girl had carved a pattern in the snow with her fist; here and there, Edie could still see the knuckle marks. The lines and curves came into focus until a complex maze-like shape emerged. For a moment Edie just sat there with her eyes open, struggling to stave off an inexplicable urge to sob. Whatever was happening, she felt inextricably caught up in it now, trapped in a series of events whose sinister connections she was as yet unable to comprehend.

'What is it?'

Derek shrugged, his eye following the lines, a look of bewilderment on his face. His hand delved into his pocket and came out with a small hardcover reporter's pad and a pencil and sketched out the pattern of lines. On paper it remained as puzzling as ever.

'No,' she said. 'That's not exactly it.' She got out of the car and went around to the front. She closed her eyes and watched as patterns resolved themselves in deep red on the back of her retinas. Then she got back in the car, took the pad from Derek and made a couple of corrections to the sketch.

'Show me,' he said.

She held out the pad. шахта. It's Russian.' She'd forgotten he'd had a Russian girlfriend and spoke a little of the language.

'What does it mean?'

'It means "mine".'

# 15

The next morning, trouble starting the truck delayed Edie and Derek's departure from Anchorage. They'd hoped to get to Eagle River early before any of the mourners arrived, give themselves a chance to look around, but by the time they reached the church-yard, a few of Lucas Littlefish's relatives were already standing by the entrance to the onion-domed church in the cold morning sun-shine, some chatting, but most silent and watchful. A handful of reporters had stationed themselves at the gate into the churchyard. Otis and Annalisa Littlefish were at the church door with the priest. Under their fur parkas they were wearing elaborately embroidered buckskin clothing, on their feet exquisite, hand-sewn mukluks edged with fur and beads. There was no sign of TaniaLee. At the periphery, among the spirit house graves, stood Detective Truro in a dark grey suit.

A hearse rolled up, came to a slow stop. The photographers at the gate clustered round. There was a frantic clicking and the flash of lights. Beside the entrance, Edie saw Annalisa Littlefish blink back tears. Two pallbearers slid the tiny coffin from its fixings and began to proceed with it up the path towards the church. It struck Edie that there was something incongruous about this, something staged and fake. As the pallbearers passed, Annalisa Littlefish reached out a hand and for a moment laid it on the coffin, her lips moving in grief.

Edie and Derek waited until the last of the relatives had filed in behind the coffin, and then followed them in. At the entrance to the church, Edie felt a hand on her arm and turned.

'I didn't expect to see you here.' Detective Truro raised an eyebrow quizzically.

Evidently, Otis and Annalisa hadn't told the detective about her visit. She wondered if there was anything to be read into that.

'Your assistant, Kathy, told me,' she lied. 'I came to see you.'

His eyes opened a little then his face closed over again.

'It's been a busy time.'

During the service she thought about the boy, how he hadn't had time enough in the world to accumulate friends, lovers, memories. She considered all the things he'd missed out on: the dizzying delights of childhood, the shaping hurts. She thought about what lay ahead for TaniaLee. Edie knew that even if the girl recovered, she would, for the rest of her life, feel every birthday, each holiday and family gathering without her son, like a thorn working its way deeper into her flesh.

Filing out at the end of the service, she spotted the Anchorage mayor, Chuck Hillingberg, and his wife, Marsha, sitting neatly on the back pew. Uncertain as to whether or not he recognized her, the mayor flashed Edie a thin smile just in case. She saw his wife clock the smile and follow it with her gaze, then Marsha Hilling-berg leaned in and whispered something to her husband and the smile vanished.

Outside, in the sun, Detective Truro stood and watched the crowd filing out of the church. Leaving Derek, Edie went over.

'I came round to your office last night.' She leaned in to him and lowered her voice. 'Lucas Littlefish died a long while before I found his body.'

'Yes,' Truro said, blankly. 'We are aware of that. We already have a full forensics report and a post-mortem. The grandparents wanted Lucas buried as soon as possible.'

'I'm wondering, what you said about the mother. Could TaniaLee Littlefish have done this herself?'

Truro held up a hand.

'I've been investigating homicides for twelve years, Miss Kiglatuk.' He took trouble over the name. 'We appreciate your statement. All this must have been such a distraction from the Iditarod. You'll be wanting to get back to it. We might need your help when the case comes to court, but if we do we'll fly you back over as a witness.' She saw him glance at his watch then put on a thin imitation of a smile. 'For now, you've been real helpful and we're grateful.'

He turned and went up the path. Edie watched him taking his leave of the Littlefish couple. The pair seemed awkward, lost not so much in grief as in the effort of keeping it all in, she thought. She wondered if they knew what had happened to their grandson's body between the time he died and the time she found him more than three months later. If their daughter had kept herself away and they hadn't seen the body, there was no reason to suppose they did know. Then why was it their faces were so closed off? It was as though they were watching the whole event from an infinite distance.

Mayor Hillingberg approached and engaged Annalisa and the priest in conversation for a few minutes while his wife spoke with Otis. Hands were shaken and the Hillingbergs made a slow and dignified exit through the churchyard to their car, not stopping to comment to the waiting journalists. Not long afterwards, the Littlefishes followed them.

While the remaining guests filtered out of the churchyard and made their way towards the nearby hall where the funeral potlatch was being held, Edie snuck into the church and sat at the back and stared at the vast cross behind the altar. The hunter in her waited. The priest was laying a cloth over the altar. He was a thin man in his fifties with skin so white it was hard to imagine that blood ran through it.

The priest looked up, acknowledged her with a nod, and went back to his task.

'I'm the woman who found the baby's body,' she said.

For a moment he seemed transfixed, his hands suspended in mid-air. Then, gathering himself, he finished whatever it was he was doing with the cloth, and made his way towards her.

'They charged an Old Believer with the crime,' she said. 'You know that?'

The priest nodded.

She pointed to the crucifix above the altar. The same elaborate cross had been marked on the body of Lucas Littlefish.

'This is special to the Orthodox Church?'

'Yes,' he said. 'We use the Patriarchal Cross. In our tradition that short horizontal above the crossbar represents the monogram hung over Jesus as he was on the cross, the one that read "King of the Jews".'

For the first time he registered her ethnicity. 'You're Inupiaq?'

'No,' she said, 'I'm from the Eastern Arctic.'

'Far from home.'

'Very far,' she said. At that moment, she felt it. 'I'm wondering. Do the Old Believers use the same cross?' From the corner of her eye she could see he was intrigued by the question and wanted to know why she had asked. For some reason, he thought better of it.

'That short horizontal?' he said. 'No. It was one of the reasons they split from the true Orthodoxy; that, and other matters to do with priests, the signing of the cross. They call it the *raskol*. It means pulling apart.' He gave a little cough.

'It must have been tough for them, feeling exiled.' She knew how that felt too. To be an outsider in your own domain.

'They chose to leave,' the priest replied coldly.

There was a pause. She sensed there was more he wanted to say, but didn't dare.

Picking up on the mood she looked him directly in the eye.

'There are rumours that the Dark Believers took the boy.'

The priest's face took on a pained look, the eyes flickering from one side of the church to the other, as though anxious not to be overheard.

'Please,' she said, 'I need to know.'

The priest looked at her then said, in a low voice, 'Follow me outside the church.'

They stepped out into the light, their breath condensing into plumes before them.

'People say they've come from the Old Believers, that they're taking them over. They say this was bound to happen, that the date of the *raskol* is evidence of that.'

'When the Old Believers split from the Orthodoxy?'

He blinked as though this was painful for him to say: '1666.' He leaned towards her and said, very softly, 'Do you understand what that means?'

She nodded.

He wiped a hand across his face and gave her a look of such intensity, it was almost painful. 'Go carefully,' he said.

# 16

Chuck Hillingberg and Andy Foulsham were sitting at the table with the view out across Cook Inlet to the city, which the manager of the Skipper Seafood Shack always saved for the mayor, in case he came by, as he often did at lunchtime. From the funeral, Marsha had gone to one of her long-scheduled Pioneer Women's lunches, leaving Chuck and Andy to talk about damage limitation still to be done to repair the mayor's hopeless, stumbling performance in front of the cameras the previous morning.

The problem, in essence, was that he'd completely underestimated Dark Believer Fever. Unlike his wife, who really went in for all the accoutrements of a particular brand of conservative evangelism, Chuck was nothing if not practical in his professed beliefs. He was a hypocrite and knew himself to be. He'd made his peace with that. Marsha was different. Her belief in creationism, like her belief in the existence of Satan, was held in all sincerity. It made her private preferences all the more baffling to him. But it was as though she never questioned the contradictions. Who was it who said that it was a sign of a fine intelligence to be able to hold two contradictory positions in your head at the same time? Maybe Marsha was simply smarter than him.

The waitress came over. He checked her name – Janine – and was careful to use it as he ordered his usual reindeer steak. The business of eating reindeer, moose, salmon or halibut whenever he went out in public was about good PR and it was just one of the many things he wouldn't miss about Alaska. Sometimes he needed to remind himself why he was doing all this, and the dismal prospect of making his way through yet another salmon steak or reindeer burger was as good a memory jog as any.

Another was this view. Supporters would sit and lunch with him here and wax lyrical about the Anchorage skyline, little imagining that the mayor would be admiring it for other reasons entirely. For him, the skyline, like the reindeer, served only to reinforce his determination to get out, first to Juneau, which was even more of a dump, then to the lower 48. He liked to look out across the Inlet and imagine he was somewhere twice the size, Portland, Oregon say, then somewhere six times the size and so on all the way to Washington, DC.

In this too, he realized, he differed from his wife. Marsha's ambition seemed to begin and end at the state line. Alaska and Alaskans were, for her, everything and that kind of passionate conviction was the hardest thing to fake, in local politics especially. If he was the vaulter, she was the pole. He was well aware that, without her, he'd never have made it out of Wasilla.

He checked his watch. His afternoon was likely to consist of putting calls through to his friends at the larger media organizations in order to try to make amends for his radical lack of understanding of the Dark Believer story. He and Andy had already been through the routine. He would say how deeply he understood the public concern over satanists and it was precisely for this reason that he'd been so keen to focus in his press interviews on the arrest of Peter Galloway for the terrible crime of killing Lucas Littlefish. He'd sound contrite without admitting he'd been wrong. Words like missteps would be liberally sprinkled through his speech. Once that was done, he would put a private call through to Mac and make sure steps had now been taken to clear the Lodge. At three or thereabouts, he would fly out to whichever Iditarod checkpoint Steve Nicols had got to and have his picture taken with the favourite to win. He'd use his time on the plane to work on the piece he and Marsha had already drafted for the *Courier*. Then there was yet another fundraising dinner to get through. He hadn't yet decided whether to take up Marsha's advice to call a meeting with Byron Hallstrom. If tonight's pledges looked healthy, he'd hold off for a while. He had nothing against Hallstrom except that, first, he wasn't an Alaskan, was only just barely an American, having been naturalized only a year or two before and, secondly, he hadn't ever dealt with the man before. It wouldn't look good for him to be seen taking money from a man who was, to all intents and purposes, a foreigner and whose interest in Alaska was only very recent.

The waitress came by again. He was expecting to hear that the kitchen had run out of the venison, in which case he'd order the halibut, but Janine's message was altogether more surprising. Chief of Police Mackenzie had arrived, she explained, and was waiting for him in the parking lot.

Chuck pinched the napkin off his lap and slung it on the table. He felt his face darken. Where was Mackenzie at, ordering him around? Telling Andy to wait where he was, Chuck stood up, pushed back his chair and walked out into the lot. Chief Mackenzie was leaning up against his official vehicle, mouthing into a cell phone. Seeing Chuck approach, he cut his call short and came over to shake the mayor's hand.

'Sorry about this, Mr Mayor.' Chuck raised a brow. He and Mackenzie only called one another by their official titles when there were others listening. He looked around. There was a driver in the vehicle, but no one else.

'You mind if we talk in the vehicle?' Mackenzie was holding the door to the back seat open. The driver got out, flustered, and moved off to a discreet distance. Chuck went up to the vehicle and sat himself inside. Mackenzie opened up the other side and got in. He seemed explosively tense, his mouth an awkward tremble between fear and rage. Chuck gave the police chief an impatient, silent '*So?*'

'I just heard on my way here, that's why I didn't call before.' Mackenzie heaved in a huge breath, shut his eyes momentarily against the shit storm in his head. 'A couple of uniformed officers with dogs found another dead baby, same MO – body left in a spirit house, wrapped up, same whacked-out cross. Smothered probably. Looks like the boy was dead some time before he was dumped, just like the first one.'

Chuck slumped back. This was the last thing he'd been expecting. For a moment he couldn't think for the pounding in his head. His gut had knotted and his throat was dry. Keeping the first kid off the front pages had been hard enough, but a serial killer, that had the potential to capsize the Iditarod, and, more importantly, to completely overwhelm the gubernatorial campaign. In short, it was a fucking disaster. He chewed his lip, trying to focus.

'Any ID on the kid?'

The police chief shook his head. 'Jonny Doe. We're checking hospital records now. One thing, he had Down Syndrome.'

'Didn't I say keep this story low? Didn't I say exactly that?'

Chuck closed his eyes for a moment, trying to collect himself. He was thinking he needed to speak with Marsha.

'The uniforms just came across this kid?'

Mackenzie hesitated. 'They were searching the area. The dogs led them to the body.'

This put a whole new slant on it. 'You got dog teams up there? You telling me you authorized a *search*?' Surprised by the raised voice inside the car, the driver turned his head to check on the two men, saw there was nothing to be alarmed about, and then positioned himself with his back to them once more. Chuck told himself to calm down. He needed complete control over this. He stared ahead, willing himself to sound more measured. 'You actually *opened* this sewer and let the shit roll out all over us?'

Mackenzie sighed. 'Truro went up there with a team and some body dogs. If I'd known about this, it never would have happened, but I didn't. Seems like Truro did it off his own bat.'

Chuck closed his eyes to absorb this for a moment.

The police chief wore a look of shame. Chuck had to credit the man with one thing: he was in no doubt about the degree to which he'd fucked up. He felt an overwhelming urge to punch Mackenzie out. Instead, he grabbed one fist in another, working the fingernails into the skin to give himself some relief from the tension.

'The fella you got for the first one.'

'Peter Galloway.'

'When d'you bring him in?'

'Three days ago.' Mackenzie had a grim smile on his face to indicate he'd anticipated the question. It made him look damned smug, Chuck thought. Asshole. 'We don't got all the forensics in yet, but judging from the pattern of ice on the body it looks like this latest one's been out in the forest maybe around four or five days, though the preliminary findings suggest he's been dead longer than that. Seems like the first kid, the body was kept in storage before being put out. We're thinking he was dumped a day or maybe two days after the first.'

'You got any other babies reported missing?'

'Some old cases, parental abduction most likely. Nothing open that ties in.'

That was a relief. Chuck was already thinking about Marsha's reaction. He wanted to make sure he was in full possession of the facts before he spoke to her, or to anyone.

'Has anyone questioned Galloway about this one yet?'

'They're at the Pen now. He's denying it, naturally, but we dug up some prior on him in Canada and what with the witness testimony on the first killing and a little forensic help, I think we can nail the A-wipe.'

Mackenzie was perfectly capable of manipulating evidence to get a result. So long as he kept his old friend out of it, Chuck didn't care. From the sounds of things, this Galloway greaseball was guilty anyway.

'Has the governor taken any interest yet?'

Mackenzie gave a wolfish smile. 'Does the Pope shit in the woods?'

That much rang true. Governor Shippon spent so long sitting on his laurels in Juneau that most of the time he seemed content to forget the rest of the state existed. His record suggested that his complacency extended to electioneering, too. Shippon wasn't known for his proactive approach to winning votes. So far as he was concerned, the state apparatus and the family firm were more or less indivisible entities. His daddy had been governor before him, and his uncle Wright Shippon had been the senior state senator ever since Chuck was a boy. But however lazy and complacent Shippon might be, he wasn't stupid. He was unlikely to pass up an easy opportunity to stick in the knife and jigger it around some. The APD could pass this one over to the state police, but they'd look spineless and inept if they did and there would be more of a chance that Shippon would intervene. Since they were already associated with the first case, they would have more control over the situation by keeping this latest killing close. The mayor thought hard.

'Here's what you do,' he began. 'You put out a press release, stressing that you already got Galloway in jail and saying you aren't looking for anyone else in connection with this latest one. You don't say shit about the occult stuff, the Dark Believer stuff, OK? You keep the cross and all that completely under wraps. Then you talk to Truro and you make sure he understands no one's gonna be looking for any more bodies. No searches, no dogs. He's not happy with that, take him off the case, suspend him if you have to, but discreetly. We don't want press to think anyone's questioning his competence.'

'Sure, boss.' Mackenzie was wearing his trusty face. It made Chuck want to punch him all over again.

'And listen, if the Lodge isn't cleared out yet, you make sure it gets done before the end of the working day. I don't want to know anything about it, OK? Just get it done.'

# 17

Edie and Derek were at the studio watching KDTV's coverage of
the Iditarod on the TV with the sound turned down. They'd both
been subdued since the funeral.

'I guess one of us should be getting back up to Nome,' Derek
said. Pulling out his packet of Lucky Strikes he began tamping it
on the table distractedly. He had been calling in to the Iditarod HQ
in Nome for regular updates on Sammy's progress. Sammy himself
hadn't been in touch and nor did they expect him to be unless a
problem arose. There was no pressing reason for either Derek or
Edie to be up at HQ, except in so far as it was official race protocol.
He slid a cigarette from the packet and lit it.

Edie told him what the priest had said.

Derek was sceptical about the existence of the Dark Believers.
'It's got all the hallmarks of a conspiracy theory, like some kind of
urban legend,' he said. 'I mean, what's the evidence?' In the past
year, and especially since he'd had his research on lemmings published, he'd come over all empiricist. If there was no evidence for
something, he refused to believe in it. Maybe that was a good thing
in a policeman. It just wasn't very Inuit.

'If it *was* the Old Believers or this dark subset who took Lucas,
why would they use the wrong cross to mark him?' Edie said.

'Maybe whoever did it didn't know what the right one was?'

'In which case, he couldn't have been a Believer.'

'Exactly,' Derek said.

'Which brings us back to Tommy Schofield and the land deal. Could Schofield have set Peter Galloway up?'

'It's possible, but that would be pretty extreme, don't you think? You met Schofield. He seem like a baby killer to you?'

Edie shrugged. Derek's question only begged another. What does a baby killer look like? Edie knew the answer to that one better than most. *A baby killer is someone who looks like you or me.*

'Assuming Schofield actually killed Lucas Littlefish. We already know that Lucas had been dead weeks before he was put out in the snow. Maybe this was Schofield's way of disposing of the dead boy after someone else had already killed him, and getting Galloway out of the way at the same time.'

'But it doesn't explain why we saw the girl from Nome in the woods, or why she drew шахта on the windshield.'

'You know what?' Edie said, braiding and unbraiding her hair, 'until that day in the forest, I never once in my life felt lost. Not really, truly lost. Feeling lost happened to other people, to *qalunaat* people. But the last few days it's like it's become a permanent condition.'

Derek leaned in and switched off the TV. The phone was ringing. Edie picked up. It was Detective Truro.

Half an hour later, she was walking through a small group of protestors holding 'Ban the Believers' signs, and through the revolving doors of the APD building. This time Truro came out to greet her personally.

'It's good of you to come in at such short notice,' he said.

He flipped his ID on the reader and ushered Edie through an opening security gate. A light sweat sheened across his cheeks and his eyes were reddened by lack of sleep. 'I couldn't go into it on the phone.' He pressed the elevator button. A door slid open. Edie looked at the tiny tin interior. The scene from *The Bellboy* with Fatty Arbuckle trapping Buster Keaton inside the security gate sprang to mind.

'I'll walk,' she said.

He looked at her and decided not to argue.

'I'll be waiting for you on the eighth floor.'

He took her into a blank meeting room, kitted out with melamine office furniture and asked if he could get her anything. She sucked on her teeth.

Truro ignored the gesture. 'Miss Kiglatuk, we've found another body. A little boy like before, as yet unidentified. A Jonny Doe, you could say.'

Edie closed her eyes, hoping to find inside herself some sense in any of this, some means by which it could at least be partly understood, but there was only a bleak kind of horror and a hollowing feeling of repulsion.

Detective Truro had pulled a docket from his desk and was rooting around in it. Plucking out a file within the docket, he said, 'As you know, because you handled the body of Lucas Littlefish, Miss Kiglatuk, he was wrapped when you found him. We think the manner in which his body was wrapped is probably significant. Would you be able to look at a picture of this latest find and tell us if the wrapping is the same? I mean *exactly* the same?'

She looked at him through narrowed eyes. Didn't trust the fellow.

Sensing her reluctance, Truro pulled a print from the file and held it between his fingers, picture down.

'Let's just get on with this, shall we?'

She nodded, feeling vaguely ashamed, and he passed the photo. Her face felt hot.

'Whenever you're ready.'

She took a breath and turned the picture face up, sweeping her eyes across the image to reduce its power, in the hope that she might prevent whatever she saw from coming back to her in the years that followed. Truro watched her intently.

'That hot tea you offered?'

He blinked and nodded. 'Of course.' Then, scoping around for his assistant and, not seeing her, he got up to fetch the beverage himself.

She watched him from the corner of her eye. The moment she could no longer see him, she grabbed the file and pulled it towards her, willing herself to look hard. In among the photographs were images of a brightly painted spirit house very similar to the one in which she'd found the body of Lucas Littlefish. There were pictures of the baby's forehead just visible beneath the elaborate coverings, then there were images of the coverings themselves and, finally, of the baby's body, a sight so tender and peculiarly terrible that for a moment or two Edie had to fight for breath. The baby was perfect, his plump little body, still frozen, lying naked on what she supposed was the autopsy table, tiny fingers and toes curled in death. Edie's hunting experience told her that he must have been two to twelve hours dead, his body still in rigor when it was frozen. The length and thickness of the ice crystals suggested that, like Lucas Little-fish, Jonny Doe had been frozen and stored maybe weeks before he'd been put out in the forest.

She flipped over the pictures until she came to a series of close-ups. The baby's face seemed tenderly familiar. She ran her gaze over the tiny chin, the forehead, but it was his eyes that were the giveaway. She'd seen those eyes before in her cousin Tuviq's baby – perfect almonds, the lids occluded, smooth. Holding the picture away from her slightly she recognized the moonface.

One eye remained on the door through which Detective Truro

had left; with the other she flipped through the remaining close-ups, stopping at a side view of the baby's head. There was a faint blur on the skin, under the hairline, just above the ear. It might be nothing, but her instincts told her otherwise. The final photo was another profile of the same, left, side. There the faint blur appeared closer and clearer. If you hadn't seen it before, you might mistake the feature for nothing more sinister than a birthmark or, perhaps, a scar. If you had seen the shape before, it was absolutely unmistakable – шахта. *Mine.*

Truro returned with the tea. They spoke about the wrapping. So far as she could see from the photos, it was exactly the same as that which she'd found on Lucas Littlefish. She knew better now than to mention the tattoo. His reaction to her at Lucas's funeral had only convinced her further that he wasn't about to let anything get in the way of the story he'd already constructed in his mind. Maybe he knew about the tattoo. Maybe he thought it was some satanist mark.

And maybe he was right.


Leaving the APD as quickly as she could, she pushed through the now swollen ranks of protestors, returned to the studio and found Derek heating pizza.

'How d'you eat that stuff?' Anything other than meat or fish was just a waste of a chew.

She told him about the tattoo on the dead boy's head.

'You think the girl in the woods could be the mother?'

'That's what I'm thinking.'

Derek finished his pizza and licked his fingers.

'Why would anyone do that, tattoo a baby?'

'I'm not all that bright, as you know, Police, but my guess would be, to identify them, either as individuals or as part of a group, a kind of tribe if you like.'

She went to the kettle, checked the water and put it on the ring.

'Who would need to put identifying marks on a baby?'

'Who do you think? Someone who wanted to come back and claim him.'

Derek thought about this for a second. 'But why scrawl it in the snow on some stranger's windshield?'

'I don't know. Maybe we need to think about the mothers, what they have in common. Maybe that was why their babies wound up dead.'

'The girl we saw in the forest, the one I also saw in Nome, I'm pretty sure she was Russian.'

Edie fell silent, following a train of thought. 'Stacey told me she'd seen TaniaLee hanging around with some Russian prostitutes downtown. I didn't see any tattoo on Lucas Littlefish, though.'

'Who's Stacey?'

Edie ignored him. She was thinking.

'Misha,' she said.

At the mention of his ex-girlfriend, Derek coughed up his tea. Edie brought him a cloth to wipe himself with. 'Goddammit, Edie.' There was an expression of deep irritation etched across the policeman's face. 'What's Misha got to do with anything anyway? Misha's gone, finished, kaput.'

Edie rolled her eyes. 'Why is it I only have to mention that woman and your brain shrinks to the size of a lemming's and migrates south?'

The lines on his forehead cleared. He sighed.

'What I mean is, you speak Russian.'

'And . . .' he said, haltingly, relieved that she wasn't asking him to get back in touch with the woman who had ruined his life.

'And so if you wanted to find out about Russian working girls, where would you go?'

Derek's eyes narrowed. 'Strip joints, lap-dancing clubs, I guess.'
She winked at him.

'Holy walrus, Edie,' he said, with a weary sigh. 'I'm a cop, who's gonna talk to me?'

'Not on this trip you're not.'

'What then?' He looked momentarily flummoxed.

'Ordinary garden-variety sleaze.' She patted him on the shoulder. 'Play to your strengths, Derek. You'll do great, I feel it in my bones.'

He gave a bitter snort, checked his watch and, figuring there was no way out, rose from the table. 'And what exactly you gonna be doing while I'm risking my career pretending to be a scumbag?'

'What d'you think? I'm heading back up to Hatcher Pass. We got unfinished business, remember?'

# 18

The day's cool breeze was too soft to drive the spindrift up from yesterday's snow, and the ploughs had been out, so the drive north was pretty uneventful – a few slides, a couple of spins, but not bad considering. Bonehead sat in the back. She needed the expertise only a canine nose could bring to things.

Reaching the Hatcher Pass turn-off, Edie directed the truck down the track and began to swing to and fro, the tyres sliding through the icy ruts in the pavement. At the bend in the road where the path came out, she pulled to the side of the drift, switched off the engine, got out and let the dog out too.

She took a deep breath and stepped off the track into the forest. Immediately, the panicky feeling of being pressed upon set in and to steady herself she had to stretch out her hand and remind herself of the sky. The snow was crusty and a little dry, squealing as her boots punched holes in it. A pair of startled eagles scattered upwards, leaving the branches of spruce where they'd perched swinging softly and powdering the ground below them in snow. It became still. Edie found it unnatural, how still the forest world could be.

A raven whirred by and landed further along the path. She stopped then and listened. Bonehead whined, anxious to move. Not for the first time since she'd arrived in Alaska, Edie felt the raw, hollowing pull of homesickness. It was just under a week since she'd got lost in the woods following the bear. Just under a week since she'd unwrapped the body of Lucas Littlefish and held him in her arms. She wanted all this to stop, wanted to be allowed to finish the race and go back to Autisaq. She looked about for footprints, but of the girl who had appeared there was no sign. She wondered then who they were, the blond bear and the fragile, wide-eyed girl. Whether they had come from the same place, carrying the same message.

She tramped across dry, sandy snow through the aspens and descended into a hollow of swampy ice where there were moose tracks and up a short incline onto a narrow deeply rutted route running southwest to northeast between trees. It might be a logging track, she thought, or even a firebreak. Having had no experience of such things it was impossible to say. At the southwest end, Edie figured, this route would connect with the track where she'd left the rental, only somewhat further to the west, which made it likely that what she was looking for lay to the northeast. This was the way she turned, relieved to put at least a little space between herself and the sinister crumple of the surrounding trees. The track here was well used; it had been salted for vehicles and recently driven on, the tyre ruts were not completely frozen. She stopped for a moment, listened for the sound of vehicle engines but heard only the rustle of wind and the flapping of birds in the trees. The day had clouded over and it was beginning to spit sleet. Edie pulled up the hood of her parka and tromped on with Bonehead beside her, intently smelling the air. After a kilometre or so she came to a large gate topped with razor wire, marking the edge of some kind of compound. Two cameras sat atop the wire, watching the area around; there was also a large, expensive-looking video intercom.

Instinct told her to get out of the way of the cameras. This she did by ducking off the path into the trees, making her way through bushy alder to the compound fence where it cut through the forest. Here, too, the chain-link reached four or five metres and was topped with razor wire, but there were no cameras. Where she was from, the only places that had fences were the air force bases and the military installations. But this was neither. No uniforms, no official notices. Someone owned this place and whatever was going on behind that fence, the owners were in no hurry to sell tickets.

Her vantage point gave Edie a reasonable view across the interior. Inside the fencing were three large wooden cabins connected by covered walkways. Storm windows made it impossible to see inside the buildings, but there were two SUVs parked outside and the subtle shifts of light told her there was movement inside.

The girl had to have come from one of the cabins inside this fence. When they'd seen her, she'd been wearing a flimsy kind of dress, maybe a housecoat, but nothing you could survive a night outside in. This and the Old Believers compound were the only clusters of buildings for miles around. The way Edie reasoned, there were three possibilities. The girl had been moved, she was dead or she was still in there.

She lowered herself onto her haunches and waited.

When she was a kid, her mother had often scolded her for her impetuousness. It was a shadow on her spirit, Maggie would say. Up in Autisaq, impatience could lead you to make a move that could get you killed. Something about the scene in front of her told her that it was the same here.

Sit, watch and wait.

The minutes passed, then, after what seemed like a long time, the back door to the largest of the cabins opened and two men appeared. One, whom Edie didn't recognize, was about the same age as her, but three or four times her size. He was wearing hunting gear and he walked like an auk, the legs scooting sideways under the vast expanse of belly. As he sauntered towards the gate he held on to the Remington 700 slung over his shoulder. His companion, a lean man in his fifties, whose face was obscured by an Anchorage Bucs baseball cap, made his way along a gravel path towards the carport. Stopping at a late model Mercedes SUV parked there, he readjusted the cap by lifting it briefly from his head and in that instant Edie caught a glimpse of the features and realized where she'd seen him before. He'd been standing in uniform in the foyer at the APD headquarters, looking like he was waiting for his driver. He was a high-up, a top cop.

The SUV backed up, turned in the driveway and slid out of the gate. The auk gave a brief wave, then locked up and made once more for the back door. Edie watched the SUV crawl along the track out of sight. When she turned her attention back to the main building, the auk was at the doorway he'd come out of. A tall, reedy woman opened the door. Her face was obscured in shadow, but Edie could tell from the looseness of her posture that she was young. They exchanged a word or two, then the auk with the rifle stepped back inside, closing the door behind him.

For the longest time afterwards, Edie sat still on her haunches in the snow and watched.

# 19

Derek Palliser had never paid for sex, though, like most guys, he'd thought about it. Once, while on a training course in Yellowknife, he'd been offered a blowjob in a titty bar and would have taken it if he hadn't run out of cash buying the girl a glass of fake champagne, but that single time aside, need had never collided with opportunity. He'd revisited the Yellowknife moment many times in his mind, however, until it had become emblematic, somehow, of his inability to follow through, his general lily-liveredness, his apathy. The fact was, he could have made that blowjob happen. He could have got cash out of the ATM or traded his watch or used his police credentials either to borrow money from the bar owner, or to hustle the blowjob for free. Instead, he thanked the girl for the offer, gulped down the remains of his drink and got out of the bar as fast as his pride had allowed.

Driving around the streets of Anchorage now, he realized that he hadn't done any of those things for the same reason that he let so much in his life go: because he couldn't quite muster sufficient energy, erotic or otherwise, to make things happen. It wasn't laziness that held him back; it was a kind of lack of effect. His generalized sense of dissatisfaction never seemed to find a target. He was too apt to accommodate himself to the status quo. Time and time again he felt himself holding back. With the exception of Misha, his ex, and his research into lemmings, he couldn't actually recall the last occasion on which he'd wanted anything really badly.

Until now.

This realization had come to him, driving around the ill-lit, salty streets of Anchorage. It was an odd epiphany and he knew he'd have to give it some more thought before he could really get his head round it. Nonetheless, there it was. What he badly wanted, he realized, was to see Sammy Inukpuk through to the end of the Iditarod. Sure, he was fond of Sammy and he admired the guy's grit and determination, particularly after the horrors of the murder of his son. He was on Sammy's side. That said, there was something else, something about Sammy's endeavour Derek needed for himself. Something to do with follow-through.

He turned his rental into Spenard Road towards the airport. A quick look in the business directory told him he would probably find what he was after here. He was in a neighbourhood of strip malls, bars and lube shops. Up ahead, halfway along the next block, a neon sign reading 'Buddy's Bar' glowed beside a parking lot. He'd stop for a quick beer and ask around. If anyone knew where the cathouses were, he thought, it would be the clientele in somewhere like Buddy's Bar.

'You working the North Slope?' The barman slid a tankard of Hard Apple Ale across the bar. He was a thick-built man with a skinful of tattoos and a biker's beard, a booming voice, used to making himself heard above the din of thrash metal in the bar. Derek flipped open his roll, peeled off three twenties.

'Consultancy.'

He took a gulp of his beer and smacked his chops.

The barman nodded. 'Never known anyone not like Hard Apple.'

Derek pushed the twenties over. The barman cut a glance over at a broad-bellied biker sitting at the other side of the bar, then squeezed his lips together and took the money.

'What can I help you with?'

Derek explained what he was looking for. The barman listened without making eye contact, then, signalling to Derek, shouted over at the fat guy.

'Hey, Zoom, fella here looking for a Slope slut.'

Derek held out a hand. The fat guy didn't take it.

'What you out for?'

'Russian girl. Young.'

The fat guy turned ever so slightly and gave Derek a quick eyeball.

'Out of here, keep west on Spenard two blocks and you'll come to Mary-Jane's. T&A bar. Go past the APD substation, you've gone too far. Ask for Willis. Tall guy, biker. Tell him Zoom sent you.'

Derek finished up his beer, got back in the rental car and found Willis at Mary-Jane's. For another couple of twenties, the man sent him to an old, run-down house a few blocks down from the police substation at the western end of Spenard.

He rang on the front door. A short, plump woman in her fifties opened a door at the side of the building.

'We're not open for business right now.' She was speaking in English but her accent was unmistakably Russian. Derek felt a twinge of nostalgia, hearing it.

In Russian he said, 'Willis sent me. I only want to talk to you, just a few minutes.'

The woman frowned.

'We've got nothing to say,' she said in Russian. Then, switching back to English, 'Are you a cop?'

'Do I look like a cop?'

The woman gave him a haughty look. 'Like I said, we're not open for business.'

Whatever a john looked like, he thought, he wasn't it and the woman knew.

'Listen, I'm at the university.' He spoke in Russian again. 'A research project into the night economy. It's completely confidential.' He gave his widest smile. 'I can pay you.'

The woman looked up and down the street. Her face seemed sunken and exhausted. She opened the door a little wider and took a step back into the passageway. When he stepped inside she signalled for him to raise his arms, then patted him down, checking for weapons.

'Ten minutes, two hundred bucks,' she said, in English. Then in Russian she added, 'I keep a weapon. You try anything, I'll blow your balls off.'

She led him down a tiny corridor and into a small, self-contained living area at the back, where two women sat on a sofa, one dirty blond with eyes as blue as icebergs, the other younger, and delicate-looking, cradling a baby. The delicate one looked up when they entered, clasping the baby to her, an expression of fear on her face.

'Don't be so dramatic,' the older woman said. 'He just wants to talk to you for ten minutes.'

The two women exchanged anxious looks.

The older woman said something Derek didn't understand. By her body language he understood her to be reassuring the two women that he was clear of weapons. 'He's paying,' she added, turning to him and winking, 'a hundred and fifty bucks for ten minutes, more if he goes over.'

'It's a research project for the university,' he said, in his best Russian.

The two women sat back down.

Derek smiled at the baby.

'What's his name?'

The young woman clasped the infant more firmly to her breast. She looked afraid. From over the other side of the table, the older woman glared at him.

'It doesn't matter,' she said.

When Derek got back to the studio, Edie had a pot of blood soup on the burner, waiting. She poured off a bowl and placed it on the table. The soup smelled thick and wonderfully redolent of home. She saw he had no spoon and went over to the kitchenette, telling him about the compound with its heavy fortification, and the presence of the high-up cop.

'You think it's some secret facility?'

'Very possible,' she said. 'Something's going on there for sure.' She put a spoon down on the table. He picked it up, thanking her for going to the trouble of making the soup.

'I guessed you'd be needing a pick-me-up,' she said. 'I picked up some roadkill at the side of the highway, still warm.' She went to the refrigerator and opened the door. A skinned leg tumbled out. Bending down, she picked it up, brushed it off and pushed it back inside. 'Coyote. Rehomed him.'

Derek blew out air, chuckling grimly, then diving into the soup brought a spoonful to his mouth.

'So?' she said.

He closed his eyes, allowing the richness of the meal to make its way onto his taste buds. She let him finish the bowl in silence. When he looked up in expectation of a refill, she was staring expectantly at him.

'Slope sluts,' he said, 'not my phrase.' He called Bonehead over and began scratching his head. A dreamy, dog-heaven look spread across the animal's face. 'I spoke with a fella in a bar. He said they work the oilfield guys. The oilers come off a two-month rota up on the North Slope with cash in their pockets and an eight-week hard-on. He said the girls come in from all over. Russia mostly, or some part of the old Soviet bloc. Ukraine, Georgia, those kinda places. Four men to every woman in this state, so there's always a demand. He didn't seem to know how they got here.'

'Or didn't care.'

He raised a defensive hand. 'Hey, I'm just passing on what the fella said.' What was it with women, he thought to himself. Eyes like fists sometimes.

'He know why Russians particularly?'

'A lot of native girls left, big demand for them in the lower 48. They speak English, which makes things easier, but their pimps pass them off as Asian babes.'

'What are they thinking?' Native Americans and Asians were about as alike as walrus and moose.'

Derek shrugged. 'They're guys, Edie. At that point, they're not thinking,' he said. 'Not with their heads, anyways.' The conversation was about to go down a road he couldn't defend. 'Hey,' he said, 'I'm just the messenger here.'

'You speak with any of the women?'

He told her.

'The older of the two said they'd both come over from Russia of their own accord.' She'd given him a line about how they were just another kind of economic migrant. He'd mentioned TaniaLee Littlefish to them but they'd claimed not to know her.

'You think they were lying?'

'I dunno. The younger one looked real young,' he said. 'And kinda scared. She didn't really do any of the talking.' He thought about the baby in her arms. He'd tried to buy more time with them, but they wanted him gone. After he left the house, he'd gone into a bar and called Zach Barefoot.

'Zach said the state trafficking law is really weak. The whole sex industry is pretty much left to its own devices. You wanna bring a girl over from Russia, even a really young girl, it's not hard to do.'

'How young?'

'Thirteen, fourteen maybe.' He felt bad just saying it. Part of him wanted to forget the whole thing, return to Nome and do what he'd come to Alaska to do, help Sammy Inukpuk make it through the toughest dogsled race on the planet. The other part reminded himself that those girls were somebody's kids. 'You think they could be caught up in some kind of ring, working out of Nome and maybe at the compound at Meadow Lake?'

Edie was sitting at the table now, winding her braid around her fingers. She seemed to be lost in thought. The dog was back in the corner, chewing his balls.

'Maybe we need to find out what's going down at that compound. Like, who owns it.' She stared at him. There was a fierce kind of glow in her eyes. He'd seen it before but it never got any easier to look at.

# 20

Chuck Hillingberg's private cell phone had been peeping since they landed at Juneau airport an hour ago, but he'd not yet had a minute to check the log until now. For the first time since he and his team had left Anchorage early that morning, no one needed his immediate attention. He pulled out the phone, flipped it open and checked the screen, then excused himself to no one in particular and sidled into the bedroom of the executive suite at the Northern Palace Hotel.

With a sinking heart he dialled Mackenzie's number. He, Andy and Marsha had been up half the night, working out a press strategy for the mayor's office. They'd been in more or less continual touch with Mackenzie about whether to try to bury the story or come clean with whatever details they had in order to try to defuse it. It was important that the police chief and the mayor were singing the same tune. Towards dawn they'd agreed that Mackenzie should hold a morning press conference at the APD offices, going heavy on the fact that the chief suspect in the second death was already in police custody and the APD weren't looking for anyone else. They agreed that Mackenzie would announce a thorough 'fact-finding' investigation into the Old Believers living in Alaska and in particular into rumours that Galloway headed up a renegade splinter group, the Dark Believers. He would emphasize that there was no evidence at this stage to suggest that the Dark Believers were anything more than an urban legend, but would give his assurances that he would personally head the investigation. Andy had come up with a sound bite for him: 'In this rocky state, no stone will remain unturned.' That had even impressed Marsha.

The press call had proceeded smoothly, which was just as well. After the disaster of his appearance on yesterday's breakfast shows, the Hillingberg team couldn't afford another slip up. And that included Police Chief Mackenzie.

As the number was connecting, Marsha slipped in, pointing to a news item in that morning's *Juneau Globe* on her iPad and frowned. The Anchorage *Courier* had led with the second dead boy, the whole of the front top half a grim crime-scene picture complete with police tape and forensics in anti-contamination suits. In the normal run of things, the *Globe* went out of its way not to cover anything happening in Anchorage in an attempt to demonstrate that just because the city had all the population and most of the money, those living in the capital weren't obliged to sit up and take note of it. To the residents of Juneau, the happenings 600 miles to the northwest weren't usually of great interest on principle, but the possibility that a serial killer – and not just a serial killer but a child murderer – was on the loose was shocking enough to have cut through at least the *Globe*'s professional indifference. There it was, just underneath a lead about the sale of timber licences near Glacier Bay. *Second boy found dead on Old Believer land.* It wasn't a big spread but it was a mighty irritant, today of all days, when Chuck was due to give a major speech and appear in a prime time TV debate with Shippon.

He nodded and grimaced then held up five fingers to signal to his wife that he'd be with her shortly. She acknowledged him with a blink and slid back out into the living area of the suite.

Mackenzie picked up. 'Hey.'

'Tell me it's not about to implode out there.'

'Nothing's imploding yet.'

'You got any ID on the second kid, the Jonny Doe?'

'We've checked all the hospitals in the state for Down Syndrome babies born in the last year but until forensics are through we won't know how long they kept the body before leaving it out.'

'They? I thought we were only looking at Galloway for the killing?'

Mackenzie corrected himself.

'So did you formally charge that Believer asshole with the second kid's murder yet?'

Mackenzie took time to respond. 'Thing is, mayor, the evidence is trickier in this one, and we got no witnesses, but we're on it.'

'I don't want you *on* it; I want you on top of it. Move the guy to a quieter location, and then find the evidence to charge him. Shut this down.'

There was a pause. Chuck filled in the gap. '*What?*'

'The Lodge. One of the guards found footprints outside, along the perimeter. Said they were small, a woman's probably.'

Chuck's heart skipped a beat. 'Anyone missing?' In the three years since the Lodge had been just a regular old hunting spot, there had only been two they hadn't got back and it had been nearly a year since they'd gone. They both had really good reasons not to say anything and so far neither of them had.

'That girl who ran off?' They'd had a runaway a couple of days back, but so far as Chuck knew, they'd caught up with her.

'We got her back.'

He felt his chest loosen. He held the phone away from his brow, buying a little thinking time. His top teeth worked his lower lip.

'Any case,' Mackenzie said, 'they've all been moved out, like you wanted. Most probably it was nothing.'

Chuck felt the skin of his lower lip split open. He raised his fingers to his mouth and inspected the blood. 'Doesn't Galloway have a wife?'

Mackenzie cut in. 'She's about to drop a baby, don't see her struggling through the snow. In any case, it's not their style. Both Believer communities, the ones up at Meadow Lake and the ones outside Homer, have gone right into themselves. They're not gonna be giving us any trouble, I guarantee.'

'You checked the security tapes?'

'We're on that. The guard said there were dog prints. Ten to one it was just some native woman out hunting.'

There was a knock and Andy's head appeared around the door.

Chuck said, 'Listen, I gotta go,' and finished up the call.

Andy raised a finger to his lip. 'What did you do to your mouth, boss?'

Chuck waved the question away.

'You got something for me?'

'The Iditarod thing?'

Chuck moved out into the living room and shut the door into his bedroom. A couple of heads bobbed up from their phones and laptops, checked what was going on and returned to their work. Andy's two assistants had spent much of the morning anonymously discrediting the mothers of the two dead kids on Alaska parenting websites. The fact that no one yet knew the ID of the second baby, let alone his mother's, made their job easier. The goal was to convince enough people that the kids were the unfortunate offspring of deadbeat, crackhead mums so that the bloggers and lurkers would start to feel that, maybe, the kids were better off dead. Then they wouldn't care who'd killed them; they'd be secretly thinking, whoever committed the crime had kind of done those babies a favour.

At the same time as trying to cool down the story of the dead boys, the Hillingberg campaign needed to cook up some fast feel-good to shift the focus of the news agenda. He and Marsha and Andy had been talking about that, too. Negative stories were all very well but they never worked on their own. Alaskans were by nature good news people. The ones Chuck knew – and he knew a great many – weren't much given to navel gazing. Some time around dawn, they'd settled on a plan.

Chuck scoped around for his wife but Marsha had disappeared. From his spot in the wing-backed chair Andy said, 'She just went into the other room to make a phone call. Didn't want to be disturbed.'

Chuck, walked to the bedroom on the other side. He moved in close to the door and put his hand on the knob. He could distinctly hear his wife's voice.

'Have him call me urgently.' She was calm but clearly very angry. He made to turn the doorknob, then thought better of it. From the bedroom, he heard Marsha say, 'No, I don't care what time of the day or night. Just have him call.' The phone clicked off and he heard footsteps moving towards the door. He knocked. The door opened almost instantly.

'Oh,' she said, 'it's you.' She strode purposefully across the room and sat down on the sofa. For a moment she seemed to be resettling herself inside her skin. He sat down beside her. He couldn't tell what she was thinking about and her expression made it very clear she wouldn't take too well to being probed. Andy Foulsham pulled up the chair close enough so they could all three talk in low tones without being overheard.

'I had an associate bend Steve Nicol's ear at the checkpoint in Ophir.' They'd already discussed terms.

'Nothing traceable?' Marsha said.

'Woodward and Bernstein wouldn't get to this one. No paper trail, no electronic trail. We're talking the middle of fucking nowhere.'

Marsha frowned at the bad language. 'He's gonna play ball?'

'Looks like it,' Foulsham said.

Chuck said, 'What did you have to offer him?'

'Two and a half to lose and a few interviews. My associate said we'd get him an answer by the next checkpoint.'

Two hundred and fifty thousand dollars. This was some costly diversion. Chuck bit his lip. He wondered whether this wasn't all some kind of panic reaction; that Dark Believer Fever would drop off and people would forget about the dead kids.

'Tell him it's a deal,' Marsha said.

Chuck raised his eyebrows but she wasn't looking at him. Maybe she had some idea where they were going to get that kind of money. If she did, she hadn't told him about it.

There was a knock; the door to the suite opened and April came over.

'Marsha? *Alaska Woman* magazine is waiting downstairs.' Marsha tutted with irritation. 'You promised them ten minutes?' The first-lady-in-waiting took a breath and smoothed her hair. Chuck watched her glide across the room and out of the door.

He waited for Andy Foulsham to busy himself on the phone, then slid into the bedroom where his wife had just finished up. He went over to the phone and pressed last number recall.

A perky voice answered.

'Mr Schofield's office.'

For a while after he cut the connection he sat on the bed, staring into the middle distance, scrabbling for thoughts which seemed to tumble away from him like loose shale. Why had his wife been so insistent on speaking to Tommy Schofield? He could hardly ask her.

It didn't take a genius to see that she was trying to keep it from him. He looked around the room for clues but naturally there were none. His wife was never sloppy. She'd learned her lesson the hard way. He took a deep breath and went back out into the fray.

Andy had switched on the TV. The local Juneau news channel was showing a small protest by a group of mothers outside the APD building in Anchorage. Two or three had fashioned banners reading: 'NO DARK BELIEVERS IN THE LAND OF THE MIDNIGHT SUN'. Chuck Hillingberg sat back and closed his eyes. For some reason he felt as though he was about to step off a cliff.

# 21

The radio signal from the checkpoint flared, then Sammy Inukpuk's voice came back on.

'Say what?'

Derek Palliser cleared his throat and tried hard to enunciate. The comms centre at the Nome HQ was always so busy it was sometimes difficult for people at the other end to hear.

'The new dog booties you wanted? I got them dropped off on today's supply. They'll be at Anvik.'

'Huh.' Sammy sounded distracted.

'Something up?'

'No, no. Everything's fine. Team's running real well. I guess I'm just tired is all.'

There was a pause. Aileen Logan's deputy, Chrissie Caley, came by and tossed Derek a smile. Aileen was down in Anchorage for the day giving press briefings but Chrissie seemed admirably unflustered at having to take over. Derek waited for her to move on before returning to Sammy.

'You hear that?' Sammy's voice came in again, sounding thin. There was a pause while Derek searched for something to say. Since returning from his lowlights tour of Anchorage, he'd been distracted, finding it hard to get the young skinny girl out of his mind. Or, rather, her baby. He'd only spent ten minutes in their company, exactly ten, but those few minutes had been some of the most soul-destroying of his life. He thought about that little kid almost constantly. What chance did he have growing up in a box room listening to his mother being balled for money next door? Over the years he'd seen plenty of kinds of hell, but that kid, the life he had to look forward to, that was a whole new one on him.

'Sorry, Sammy, I missed it.' Doing his best to get himself together. Not making such a great job of it.

'I said I'm OK, just tired.' There was a pause while both parties swallowed thier disappointment, and then Sammy piped up, 'Has Nancy been in touch at all?' Nancy was Sammy's on-off girlfriend back in Autisaq. He'd wanted her to fly over to support him but she said she needed a new pair of snowshoes and couldn't spare the money. When he'd offered to pay for her out of the sponsorship kitty, she'd said she couldn't spare the time. Being quite the optimist, Sammy was convinced she was sulking about something and would come out of it soon enough. Derek suspected there were other, darker, reasons she hadn't called, reasons to do with Sammy's neighbour, Apiuk, whom he'd spotted sneaking out of Nancy's house the night before they left for Alaska.

'I'll bet she spoke to Edie,' Derek lied. 'And Edie forgot to pass on the message.' He was struck, once again, with a strong sense of wanting Sammy to get through the race, to be there when he and his team mushed over the finishing line. He certainly didn't see any point in undermining Sammy's morale by telling him the truth right now.

'She there? Edie I mean.'

'Uh nuh, she's in Anchorage, like we agreed,' he heard himself say. He knew he was being evasive, but didn't see that he had much choice. Last thing Sammy needed right now was a pile of worries. 'But hey,' he added in what he hoped was an encouraging tone, 'we're both psyched. You're doing real great. Think you'll make it inside two weeks?'

'Reckon so,' said Sammy. There was a slight pause, as though he was waiting for Derek to say something, then: 'OK, then, well I guess I'd better get back on the trail.'

Derek wished him good sledding. The moment the call ended, he was filled with the regret of having let his friend down, and wishing they could have the conversation over again. Sammy had travelled nearly 500 miles across some of the toughest terrain in the world with nothing more than a frame race sled, a tiny pack of supplies and sixteen – now fifteen – dogs for company. He'd been on the trail day and night, sleeping upright in his sled, if he'd got any sleep at all, eating on the fly; all his life focused on that thin, icy skein of the trail. Barring any emergency, the conversation they'd just had would be the last time Sammy would be in direct contact until he reached the Safety roadhouse a few miles outside Nome. From now on, Derek and Edie would have to make do with a sketchy outline of his progress drawn from his position on the GPS tracker and from whatever snippet might be emailed by the stewards at the various checkpoints.

After they'd finished their conversation, Derek wandered down to Zach Barefoot's place. At the top of the unnamed street in which the Chukchi Motel stood, he stopped. It wasn't yet dark and wouldn't be for a few hours, but the motel sign was lit up. As he stood and watched a big man with an elongated, snouted face strode out and down the steps, got onto a snowmobile and sped off. Not long afterwards, he noticed, the motel light went out. He thought about the young woman in the forest outside Meadow Lake who had carved шахта, *mine*, on the car windshield. Then, bracing himself, he strode down the street towards the unlit sign.

The same toothless Inupiaq man was at reception. He was whittling at a piece of walrus ivory with a knife.

'I'd like a room,' Derek said.

The man looked up at him. He had tundra skin: thick, brown and as hummocky as muskeg. His eyes, Derek noticed, were rheumy with cataracts. He could tell by the way the eyes blinked through him that the old man couldn't see much.

'We're all booked up,' the old man said.

Derek stood his ground, repeating himself. The old man nodded.

'You'll need to come back at nine,' he said, 'or maybe ten.'

Derek leaned in and picked up the piece of walrus ivory.

'You have trouble seeing or are you just paid to look the other way?'

'I seen all I need to see in this world,' the old man said, reaching out and taking back his carving.

The door to Zach's house was open. Derek called out and a woman's head appeared around the corner of one of the bedrooms. He recognized Megan Barefoot from the photos scattered around and was immediately struck, in a way he hadn't been before, by how much like Edie she looked. Same high forehead, arched brow, same look of barely constrained energy. She was holding a finger up in front of her mouth and looked as though she'd only just woken.

'Zoe's sleeping.'

Derek introduced himself in a whisper. Megan smiled and said Zach had already told her all about him. He thought about the baby in the next room, and the kid in Anchorage and felt a pulse start up in his temple.

He'd managed to get this far in Alaska without thinking too hard about his kid. Denial, Edie Kiglatuk would say, if she'd known he had one. Kept it to himself just so she wouldn't find out. How long had it been since he'd seen Serena? Nearly four years now. She'd be five. Her mother certainly wouldn't be keeping his memory alive. She was at least part of the reason he hadn't kept in touch, why he didn't talk about it. The woman had made it too difficult and painful and expensive. But that was no excuse really, and he knew it. He had a satellite connection to the Internet in the detachment office in Kuujuaq. It'd been connected for nearly two years. He didn't even know where Serena and her mother were living these days. He could have tracked her down and eaten whatever shit she wanted him to eat and begged to have contact with Serena again. He could have offered her mother regular money in return. Hell, he could be Skyping with his little girl right now. Instead, he didn't even know what she looked like.

Then the door swung open and Zach appeared with a six-pack in each hand. Seeing Megan, his face lit up like an ice crystal in the sun. He put the beer down, strode over to his wife and took her in his arms. Hand in hand they crept into the room where the baby was sleeping.

Derek went over to the sofa and cracked open a beer. A while later, he wasn't sure how long, Zach came back into the room alone, his face lit with the kind of love you didn't see enough of. He noticed the open can of beer. 'The man don't waste time,' he said, amiably. Fetching a beer for himself, he came and sat on the sofa and held up his can. 'I salute your style.'

Derek gave a low laugh and hoped it didn't sound too bitter. If it did, Zach didn't notice.

'They look so cute, lying there together, fast asleep,' he said. He gulped his beer, wiped the back of his hand across his lips and sighed contentedly.

'They sure do.' Derek lifted his hand to his mouth and bit hard down on his thumbnail. 'Zach, you doing anything around ten tonight?'

Zach sat up, intrigued, and reaching for another beer, said, 'Why, you got plans?'

'Yeah.'

Zach put down his can.

'Should I hold off on another beer?'

Derek grinned and gave him a pat on the shoulder.

'No sir,' he said, 'we're gonna need all the beer we can get.'

Five hundred miles away, in downtown Anchorage, Edie Kiglatuk was meeting Aileen Logan in a pioneer-themed drinking hole named Klondyke, east of downtown. Aileen had called her earlier in the day, saying she wanted to know more about the way folk trained their sled dogs up in Autisaq and suggesting they hook up. The place itself was a dank smelling room with a low ceiling and dim lighting which looked cheap rather than intimate. There were life-sized portraits of women on the walls. In fact, there were women everywhere.

A barmaid with elaborate facial piercings came over, greeted Aileen by name, and asked them what they'd like to drink. The clue was in the name of the place, Edie realized. Klon*dyke*.

'Jack Daniel's OK with you?' Aileen smiled.

'I had a coke in mind,' Edie said. She'd fallen off the wagon once too often, wasn't eager to repeat the process.

Aileen watched the waitress leave then said, 'So how long you been sober?'

Edie frowned. Hadn't Aileen asked her there to talk about sled dogs? 'Look,' she said, 'I'm a simple kind of a person. I like the old silent comedy greats, I like meat and I love my family. What I don't like is people I hardly know asking personal questions.'

Aileen lifted her palms in mock surrender.

'Phoowee,' she whistled, mockingly, 'I'd kill to see you when you're really angry.' With that she gave a great guffaw.

They talked for a while about the Iditarod, just chit-chat mostly.

'You got a good guy in the race, Sammy is it? Aileen said. 'I seen him at the start. He's got pluck.'

'Where we live, that kind of comes with the territory.'

'Tough up there on Ellesmere, huh? I guess Alaska must kinda feel like the south to you.'

'Furthest south I've ever been.'

The drinks showed up in glass tankards coated in a thin layer of rime frost. Aileen drank hers off. The woman could pack away some beer.

'We Alaskans like to think of anywhere out of state as the Outside,' Aileen said. 'We can be tough on Outsiders.' She said this in a way that left Edie in no doubt that she was sending some kind of message.

'Outsiders can be tough back.' she countered. Being an outsider had nothing to do with geography and everything to do with the landscape of the mind.

'Like your pal Sammy,' Aileen said. There was an edge to her voice.

'Yeah, like Sammy.' The two women glanced at one another. In that moment they acknowledged without having to say anything that Aileen was sending Edie a friendly warning not to get any further mixed up in investigations into the deaths of Lucas Littlefish and Jonny Doe. But why? What did any of it have to do with her?

The woman excused herself and went to the bathroom. While she was away, the waitress bustled up again. She said, 'Your first time here?' and when Edie nodded, she added, 'Like the decor? Most folks go crazy over the decor.'

'It's OK.'

The waitress continued as though she hadn't heard. 'This lady here'– she indicated a mural of a small woman with a regal face –

'this is Alaska Nellie. She was tiny, like five foot three, but she hunted big game. Can you believe that?'

Edie, five foot two, said, 'I'll try.'

After the waitress left, Edie allowed her mind to drift back to the old days. The old days! How uncomplicated everything seemed then. If she wanted a drink, or a meal or a fuck for that matter, she had one. When the spirit – or her belly – moved her, she went out onto the land and killed something. It seemed so simple then to take a life. You took a gun and a komatik, a sled, and a dozen dogs and you came back with some meat. She had thought of herself as liberating animals from their bodies so they could be born again. The act of killing had felt less like taking a life and more like releasing a spirit.

Thinking about herself now, it was hard to imagine that she once saw things in such black and white terms. Simplicity was the luxury of youth. The older you got, the more you realized nothing was that simple. Even death. *Especially* death.

Aileen returned and sat back in her seat.

Edie looked up. 'What you said, before? Do you have a reason to think I might be in trouble?'

Aileen flung her arms behind her head. The effect was one of absolute confidence. 'It's like I said, Edie. We can be tough on Outsiders.' She drained off her beer and signalled to the server to bring another. 'Now, about those huskies of yours. I take my hat off to you folks. You sure as hell breed a tough sled dog. If it's not a *personal question*, what's your secret?'

Edie shrugged. 'We say either the dogs have the right *ihuma*, like heart, for it or they don't. Same as people.' This, too, sounded simple. And yet *ihuma* made a labyrinth of even the most basic action.

Aileen laughed and leaned in, hands on the table. Her breath was wet and hoppy. She had the kind of hands you could kill kittens with.

'So what do you do with the bad dogs, Edie Kiglatuk? The ones with the wrong *ihuma*?'

Edie looked at the hands, then back at Aileen's face.

'We make them into hats.'

# 22

Derek Palliser crept up the stairs at the Chukchi Motel, with Megan Avuluq's police issue Glock 22 unholstered and at the ready. He reached the half landing, felt a lurch in his stomach and with his free hand held on to the handrail. Gathering himself, he glanced back to check on Zach's whereabouts, received an encouraging lift of the eyebrows and continued on down the corridor. What they were about to do was very probably ill-judged. It was certainly illegal. Plus they were drunk. In theory they still had the option to go back down the stairs right now, get a few hours' sleep and think things through more rationally in the morning. But who gave a shit about theory?

Zach had his own reasons for wanting to take action, reasons he'd explained over a few beers. Back in the late nineties just after the Bering border opened up he'd sprung a smuggling ring. Young native girls from Chukchi mostly. One of the girls got sent back to Russia, where the gangmasters caught up with her, raped her with a hunting knife and left her to bleed out. Her mother had sent an angry letter to the State Troopers in Anchorage, which had eventually found its way up north to Nome. The letter had played right into blue-shirt prejudices, that the Alaska Wildlife Troopers, the 'brownshirts', were aptly named: they couldn't get shit done without covering themselves in it.

Derek gripped the Glock, collected himself and moved forward till he was outside room number 26. He hadn't used a hand weapon for years. A rifle was different, more removed somehow. It felt odd to be so close to all that power, but exhilarating too. The old man at reception had a hard time remembering which room number to direct them to, but he'd recovered his memory the moment he saw they were packing. Folk never said no to a gun.

He put an ear to the door then nodded to signal to Zach that he'd heard noises inside. Zach took a deep breath and acknowledged him with a blink. The two men rested their shoulders on the door. Derek held up a three-finger count. On zero, they peeled back to gain force, then all at once thrust forward. In an instant, the lock caved, the door sprung open and the two men tumbled into the room.

Before he saw anything, he heard the girl screaming. When he steadied himself and looked up, he could see she was on her knees. Her hands were tied behind her back and she was wearing a blind. A middle-aged bald man stood facing her, grasping his cock in both hands. Blood trickled between the fingers. The skin on his face wasn't far off the same colour. He hadn't quite registered what had happened. His eyes were wide open and fixed, his mouth locked in an expression of amazement. Then something gave and he began to roar. The sound of his screams silenced the girl. For a second the four of them just froze as though wondering what to do next. Derek barked at the guy to show his hands, but the A-hole seemed unable to hear through the pain. He was clutching himself with both hands now, chanting the words 'She fucking bit me, the bitch fucking bit me' like a lucky tune. And then, just as suddenly, his brain clicked into gear. Derek saw him clock the two weapons aimed at his head. Immediately, he grew quiet. His eyes widened in terror. Slowly, he raised his hands in the air.

Looking at him now, his pants down around his ankles, cock tiny and red, made Derek want to laugh. It also made him want to make a clean sweep of it and shoot the asswipe in the balls.

He glanced at Zach.

'Police.'

The girl sat back, noisily spitting pink saliva on the cheap hotel carpet. Derek went over to her and removed the blind and hand ties. She sat for a moment blinking and rubbing her wrists where the ties had cut into the skin. She was very young. Derek didn't like to think how young. Then she stood up, went over to the man and spat.

The man screwed up his eyes, trying to block out his humiliation. His legs shifted about in an effort to reorganize his pain. He opened his eyes again and squinted, taking in first Derek then Zach.

'You gotta get me to a doctor.'

A dry smile flickered across Zach's face. 'What do you think, sergeant, do we?'

The man picked up on the word 'sergeant' and groaned some more.

Derek smiled and gave a little shrug. 'I'm in no hurry,' he said, then, looking round, 'hey, this is a nice room. Faces east too. I'll bet you get a great view of the sunrise in a room like this.'

'We could get room-service breakfast,' Zach said. He went over to where the man was standing, head bowed, clutching his groin and flipped his chin with his weapon so the man had no choice but to meet his eye. 'Or maybe that was what you already thought you were getting, you piece of shit.'

Derek looked over at the girl. She was still wiping her mouth with the back of her hand, but she caught his eye and gave a vague smile.

'What's your name?' The girl didn't answer.

The man said, 'She don't speak English,' trying to come over helpful.

Derek whirled round and waved his pistol at his bleeding member.

'She sure as hell said all she needed to say to you.'

He turned to the girl. 'We'll have you out of here any moment now.' She came towards him, moving slowly. Her face was a blank and it was hard to tell whether she had even registered that Derek had said anything. For a moment Derek thought she was making for the bathroom but, as she got closer, she sprang for the door and was gone. He heard her leaping down the stairs, three at a time. Zach shot him a look, which said, want me to follow? He countered it with a no. The girl had no use for men right now.

From the corner of his eye he saw the bald guy bracing himself, as if to make a play for the door. Zach must have seen the same thing. In a matter of a moment, the trooper lunged forward, flinging his back against the door, his pistol never leaving a direct line to its target. The bald guy's face fell. His whole body sagged forward. He knew he was beat.

Zach went over to him.

'What's your name, A-hole?'

'Harry Larsen.' The adrenaline rush caused by the bite was dissipating him now. His face was yellow and he looked scared. 'Look, cut me some slack here, fellas. I'm gonna cooperate, OK? I'm just the little fella. I'm not gonna hold out on you guys.'

Zach turned to Derek. 'Harry Larsen says he's just the little fella.'

'He's got that right,' Derek said, winking.

The man closed his eyes then took a deep breath.

'Do us a favour, little fella, tuck yourself away, then put your hands behind your back.'

Larsen did as he was told, gasping at the pain. Zach went over to him. 'You touch me with those hands, I'll kill you.' He threaded on a plastic cuff and tightened it around Larsen's wrists.

'I guess we really should be checking out now, trooper,' Derek said. He felt the beer he'd been drinking all night bubble up from his stomach and swallowed it back, hard. He turned to Larsen. 'Don't worry, we organized alternative accommodation for you. You'll get a bunk and a shared john. Safety locks on all the doors. Better still, we won't even charge.'

The road was familiar to her now and in the last few days she had picked up enough experience to be able to drive it without fear of turning the vehicle over or ending up on the verge. Still, she was cautious turning off the highway and onto the tiny track leading up to the Russian Orthodox church at Eagle River. It was the middle of the night and the road, which hadn't been properly ploughed since last snowfall, was well and truly iced over. The church wasn't the main focus of her journey – she'd decided to go back to the Old Believer compound and to the buildings surrounded by high wire beyond it to take a sniff around while everyone was asleep – but since the church was more or less on route she thought she would visit Lucas Littlefish's final resting place, and talk to the boy.

She parked alongside the church, took her flashlight and made her way through the garden of spirit houses to the Littlefish plot. Lucas's spirit house was blue, painted with geometric patterns most of which had been obscured by snow. Already, snow had piled on the roof then part-thawed, then piled again, leaving an odd crenellation of ice and new snow and giving the grave the look not so much of a house as of a tiny castle. The Littlefishes practised the version of the Russian Orthodoxy most common among their kind, a mix between the traditional church and native elements. She crouched down and shone her light through the window and saw there the blue and brown Athabascan weave shroud wrapped around the baby's body, where they had removed him from the *qalunaat* coffin, the one demanded, she supposed, by the municipality, and laid him to rest in the old way.

'Lucas,' she said. '*Qanulppit?* How are you? *Qiuviit?* Are you cold?' She spoke to him in her own language. It seemed more respectful. Somewhere above, an owl hooted. Startled by the sound, Edie strobed her flashlight up into the branches and caught a pair of bright, round eyes glinting out from a surround of pale feathers. The bird fell silent. Suddenly, she became aware of other noises; the rush of wind in the branches of the trees, the strangled bark of a fox nearby and, further off, the faint wail of a wolf. Then the owl rose from the tree, the burr of its wings like a death rattle.

She turned back to the boy in the snow. 'Whatever happened to you, Lucas, was wrong. And there are people here who are still not telling the truth about it and that compounds the wrong. I'm gonna do my best to find out what happened, kid. I'm gonna do it for you and I'm gonna do it for me. *Tukisivit?*' His spirit would understand this.

She pulled her parka tighter around her. The crowdedness of the night forest, the feeling of being spied on by creatures she couldn't even name, spooked her some.

She began to brush off the snow on the house, at first tenderly, then more urgently. Bit by bit, the spirit house emerged from under its wintery blanket. It looked cozier now, somehow, more loved. She swung the flashlight across the surface of the house, feeling better for unburying the boy. The shroud was fully visible from both sides. Above where the door might have been, she noticed a small, painted cross of the regular Orthodox Church, the kind the priest pointed out to her after Lucas's funeral, the same cross that had been etched in grease on Lucas Littlefish's body. The cross no Believer had used in 400 years.

She stood up and blew air through her nose in frustration. There was nothing unexpected on Lucas Littlefish's grave, no clues, no messages or signs. Back at the truck, she started the engine. While she'd been at the cemetery, a thick cloud had come over obscuring the moonlight. It was bitter dark, the kind of dark that seldom fell over Autisaq, where sea ice and glaciers reflected whatever little light the sky sent down. Halfway down the road in the direction of the Glenn Highway, she turned a corner and saw, in the distance, a thin, pulsing light which grew gradually brighter then took on a colour.

Blue.

Inside her chest the owl fluttered, beating its wings against bone. She braked hard, the metal tang of blood in her mouth from where she'd bitten her lip. The light swooshed across the windshield. Remembering Aileen's warning, she felt chilled and panicky. The forces of nature, ice, the raging of the winds, the rough heave of an ocean, a wounded bear or musk ox, all these things she knew how to deal with. But when it came to cops, Edie Kiglatuk was clueless.

She cut the engine and the lights. For what seemed like the longest time she just sat and watched the blue swish crossing her line of vision. Then, from in among the trees she saw a flashlight, heard the sound of male voices, footsteps crashing through the forest, the yelp of a dog.

Two men in uniform and a police dog burst from the trees. They both caught sight of the vehicle at the same time and immediately froze. The one who wasn't handling the dog drew his weapon. Beside him, the dog leapt on his leash, snarling and baring its teeth. She heard one of the men shouting at her to raise her hands and remain in her vehicle. Edie felt her breath catching in her throat. The police pistol was aimed right at her head. She did as she was told, slowly lifting her hands where the cops could see them. The one with the pistol advanced towards the vehicle. His partner stood in front of the car, with the dog at his side, his weapon glinting through the windshield.

The door flew open. She heard the first cop scream at her to get out of the car with her hands raised. Everything felt warped now. There was no way to tell how much time had passed. She felt herself clamber out. The first cop came up, frisked her out, and then commanded her to lie on her belly on the ground while they searched the vehicle. The ice felt hard, then soft. Freezing water started seeping through her parka and onto her skin. When she looked up, the dog was right beside her, its foul breath on her face. She buried the urge to punch it. The handler was speaking on his walkie-talkie while his partner went around inspecting the vehicle. She felt her skin begin to shiver. Someone was saying something to her. He repeated himself.

'Your *name*, lady.'

She answered. A hand squeezed in under her arm and she felt herself being lifted up onto her feet. She heard her name transmitted through the walkie-talkie.

'What are you doing here with your engine off? It's late.'

'Taking a nap.'

'Why are you travelling this late?'

She told them she'd come from Anchorage to visit the cemetery.

'I got a relative buried there.'

'You come see your relative in the middle of the night?'

She looked at the two men. Both were *qalunaat*.

'He keeps different hours now he's dead,' she said.

The two men glanced at one another, and then decided to let it drop. The first one said: 'How long you been asleep for?'

She shrugged.

'You see anyone along this route, ma'am? I mean, any other vehicle, a pedestrian, anyone at all?'

'I sleep with my eyes closed mostly. I guess I'm old-fashioned that way.'

The walkie-talkie clicked back into life. The two men seemed to relax. Both cops reholstered their weapons. The dog handler pulled his dog in to his side and got it to play nice. Edie wiped herself down.

'We got an escaped prisoner situation here.' She immediately thought of Galloway. The warning glance exchanged by the two officers was enough to confirm her suspicions. 'We gonna need you to drive on along back to Anchorage. You'll come to a police road-block just before you get there, but they'll let you through.'

For the first time, she became aware of the thrum of a helicopter.

The dog handler opened the car door for her. She clambered back in and he shut the door. He motioned to her to start the car and open the window. When she did as she was told, he leaned in with a superior kind of smile on his face.

'Next time you speak with that dead relative of yours, you might want to ask him to keep social hours.'

# 23

Back in Anchorage, Chuck Hillingberg was being called from his bed. It was Marsha and she sounded strained.

'You didn't hear the phone?' His wife's head appeared round the door.

He hadn't. His body, pushed to the limits by the past few days of stress, had skipped the doze stage and fallen directly into deep sleep. He felt groggy now, caught between competing demands for his attention, his conscious self awake already but some visceral part calling him back into unconsciousness.

Marsha came in and perched on the end of the bed. 'It's Mackenzie.'

He glanced at his watch, pushed the comforter aside and sat up, rubbing his hand over his forehead. It felt clammy; old sweat pooling in the furrows. He'd been on the phone to the police commissioner half the evening, then called Andy and hadn't got to bed till 1 a.m. It was just after 3.15, he'd had approximately two hours' sleep and it looked as though he wasn't going to get much more tonight.

He picked up the phone on the bedside table and pressed speakerphone.

'This better be an emergency.'

Mackenzie told it to him straight. As he spoke, Chuck felt some part of him fall away.

'Tell me I'm still in the middle of some fucking nightmare,' he said. His feeling of emptiness began to burn into a raw, red anger. 'Let me get this right. You let the guy *go*?' He had forgotten his part in setting up the Lodge, the savage, elemental pleasure he'd taken in the whole business, leastwise at the beginning, and felt a great rush of righteous rage towards Mackenzie and Schofield and all the other unimportant, small-minded, Alaska-bound men who had betrayed him, let him down.

'Like I said, boss, we were moving the guy up to the facility at Eagle River.' Mackenzie paused and changed tone before adding, 'Which is what you wanted.'

Chuck heard a yelp and realized it had come from his mouth. He took a deep breath and tried to quieten the pounding in his head. His voice, when it came, sounded like a rocket firing.

'. . . You so much as try to pin this on me, I swear I will fry your ass so crisp it's only fit for a bun and mayo.'

'Mr Mayor, right now I'm just trying to get this mess cleaned up.' He'd never heard Mackenzie sound so tortured or remorseful and never before considered how little he cared for the man or his feelings.

'What you doing to recapture Galloway?'

'I got the Highway Patrol sealing off roads; I got troopers sweeping the forest with dogs. One way or another, we gonna get that mofo back.' He sounded as though he was near to tears. Chuck hated him all the more for that. He checked himself. The last thing he needed was someone important to him freaking out at a time like this. He'd scared Mackenzie enough for now. Didn't want to tip the guy over the edge.

'Have you gotten to the bottom of how this happened yet?'

'Someone took their eye off the ball. It's a screw-up. The Bureau of Judicial Services is blaming the Highway Patrol, and vice versa. The driver needed to stop for a bathroom break. I don't know. It didn't help that some kind of ice fog came over the whole place and there was one big whiteout, no one could see further than—'

'Their overtime?'

There was a pause, while Mackenzie picked himself up off the floor.

'We got investigators in both Believer compounds, we got uniforms and body dogs out there and we've alerted the fugitive task force. There's nowhere for this A-wipe to go.'

'Except into the interior of the largest state in the Union.'

Marsha, who had been sitting quietly absorbing all this, suddenly piped up. 'You got the press on this contained, right? We got a two-time child murderer here, a serial killer. How you gonna make sure nothing gets out till you got this man back in custody?'

There was a groan. Marsha jumped on it. 'Say *what*?' Her face was like some kind of glittering stone. Without waiting for a reply, she stood up and swept out of the room, signalling that she'd be right back.

Quickly, Chuck flipped off the speakerphone. 'Listen, I *promised* Marsha that nothing's going to connect us to the Lodge. Ever.' He lowered his voice and put all the power he had into what he said next. 'I'm holding you responsible that the promise still stands.'

The door swung open and Marsha reappeared holding an iPad. The movement woke the screen, which glowed ice blue in the half-light of the bedside lamp.

'Hold on, Mac,' Chuck said. He flipped speakerphone back on.

Marsha clicked in a few keystrokes then let out a groan. 'Holy moly.' She slid the iPad towards him. He had to reach for his reading glasses to pick out any of the words then wished he hadn't. Marsha was on Mommabears, the most popular Alaska parenting site. News of Peter Galloway's escape was all over it. The Mommabears were going apeshit.

'I'm sorry.' Mackenzie's voice had completely broken now. 'Believe me, I'm sorry. We got every uni available hunting this fucker down.'

Marsha's snort of contempt sounded like the blood-lust bark of a wounded bear. 'Chief, We're *waaaay* past the ass-covering stage. Come the start of the breakfast news shows, you're gonna have every journalist in the entire state of Alaska looking right up your crack.' She pulled her BlackBerry out of the pocket of her robe and hit the speed dial.

'I'm aware it's *late*.' There was a look of absolute determination on her face. Chuck could tell from her tone she was talking to Andy Foulsham. 'Call your computer guy, you know the one I mean.' A short pause. 'Yes *now*.' She rolled her eyes. 'We need him to crash a website.'

Bonehead thumped his tail. Edie patted him on the head and ruffled his ears. Over in the corner by the sofa, the message light blinked. It was Derek.

'I think we've got something. Call me.'

She checked her watch. She was the only inuk she knew who wore one. Her stepson, Joe, used to tease her, saying because she was half-white she wore one on her *qalunaat* side. It was 5 a.m. Her first thought was: *Derek will still be in bed*. Her second: *So what*.

She dialled the number. He picked up. He'd been in bed twenty minutes and in the middle of one of his recurring dreams about a plane crash, he said. He sounded glad she was calling.

'Where you been?'

'You go first,' she said.

He didn't argue. She listened to him detailing the operation at the Chukchi Motel. This was all news to her, but she was glad to hear Derek Palliser was finally taking action.

Harry Larsen, the man Derek and Zach surprised with his pants down, was waiting in a cell at the Nome Police Department prior to being formally charged. Turned out, he was quite a squealer. Native of Wisconsin, he'd moved up to Nome five or six years before, taking up a position at a supplies company based out of the air terminal. He had prior for sexually assaulting a teenage girl down in Madison, and had spent three years in the pen down there and then got as far away as he could. He was cooperating, Derek said, out of a fear of being sent back to jail. He thought if he was a good boy the Nome police might just let him get away with a rap on the knuckles. At heart, he didn't really believe he'd done anything wrong. Zach, who'd had sat through the questioning, said the creep kept insisting he was only getting a lousy blowjob and hadn't fucked the girl, as though that made it any better.

He'd been given the contact through a guy who came through the airport occasionally, a bush pilot, by the name of Bolvan. Guy with a long nose. Once or twice this Bolvan had passed some small cargo he wanted ignored through Larsen, who let it go for a small consideration. To return the favour Bolvan had given him a number to call. Larsen claimed he'd lost the number and only called it when it resurfaced some weeks later. In any case, he hadn't seen Bolvan around for a while. He'd lost the number again and was unable to recall it.

'That walrus fart doesn't speak Russian or he'd know he was having his chain yanked,' Derek said. 'Bolvan is Russian for "moron".'

The girl had told Larsen her name was Peaches, but she couldn't pronounce it right. She had some kind of foreign accent, but Larsen, who had spent all his life first in Wisconsin then in Alaska, couldn't tell one foreigner from another.

'We have no trace on her as yet,' Derek said. The Nome PD had run a quick search in all the obvious places – cheap hotels, rental rooms, bars, even unoccupied buildings – but they hadn't turned anything up. Nome was surrounded by thousands of square miles of empty tundra dotted here and there with tiny settlements of native people who were generally pretty hostile to the police and would be likely to shelter anyone they thought might be vulnerable to interference from authority. Someone, in other words, exactly like 'Peaches'.

'But here's the punchline. Bolvan told Larsen that when he called the number Bolvan had given him, he should say Fonseca had recommended him.'

The name set Edie's heart rattling.

'Edie, you there?'

'Yeah, let me think a moment.'

'What we got?'

'Right now? One hell of a tangle, Derek, that's what we got.'

'Whoever Fonseca is, he's dirty. Sounds like he's running girls, really *young* girls, over the Bering Strait from Chukchi, first to Nome then who knows where, Anchorage, maybe, Meadow Lake for sure.

'He's the link to TaniaLee Littlefish too. She seemed to think Fonseca was her husband, remember? We find Fonseca, we're more than halfway there.'

Derek paused to light a cigarette. 'Didn't you say Peter Galloway knew TaniaLee?'

'So his wife said.'

'Everyone seems pretty fixed on the idea that Galloway killed those kids.' Derek toked too hard and coughed it out.

'Everyone? If the Dark Believers exist and those babies were murdered as part of some horrific sacrifice, either by Galloway or by any of his Dark Believer cohort, don't you think it's odd that they would mark the bodies with a cross they've spent 400 years resisting?'

'It's all weird, Edie.'

She said, 'It may be about to get even weirder.' She told him about Galloway's escape.

'When does someone with nothing to hide go into hiding?'

'When he knows he won't get justice, because of his beliefs, or because someone has something to gain by discrediting him and keeping him in jail, or because he's angered someone in power, or because he knows too much. Or all of those things.'

There was a pause while Derek registered the truth of what Edie had said.

'You think he'll go after Schofield?'

'I would. Leastwise if I'd been framed.'

Derek coughed again. 'Edie, you know there's a good chance we'll never get to the bottom of any of this.'

'The way I prefer to look at it, there's a good chance we will.' The tiredness had left her now. She checked her watch. 5.25 a.m. No point in trying to get any more sleep.

'I'm proud of you, Derek,' she said.

'You are?' For a moment he sounded inordinately pleased, then he checked himself.

'You didn't have to go and do that thing at the Chukchi Motel.'

There was a pause.

'You're wrong about that,' he said. His voice sounded exhausted.

'Get some sleep,' she said.

'What are you gonna do?'

She planned on dealing with the night's unfinished business, but, not wanting to alarm Derek, she said, 'I'm gonna get some breakfast.'

Afterwards, she slopped down the shared stairway onto the street, trudging along the icy pavement to the newspaper dump on the next block. It was the deep mauve of predawn, quiet, or as quiet as the city ever got, the street lights pouring grey light over the parade of cheap apartment blocks and shabby stores. A woman appeared up from a side street, then another. They appeared to be carrying placards. Edie watched them disappear into the gloom for a moment, wondering where they were off to, then picked up the morning's *Courier* and went down the street to the Snowy Owl Café which was just opening up for morning trade.

Stacey came over bringing her smile and the menu.

'You're early this morning. Decide to steal a march on the day?'

The word 'march' reminded her.

'Say, you see a couple of women with placards earlier, heading downtown direction?'

'Nope.' Stacey reached out to the next table, plucked up the condiment set and transferred it to Edie's table. 'Oh,' she said, as though the thought had only just occurred to her, 'yeah, there's supposed to be some kind of protest going on at the police department building today.'

'What kind of protest?'

Stacey shrugged. 'I guess maybe about that guy who escaped? The one who killed those kids. My sister's, like, a Mommabear? It's kind of this chat forum for Alaska moms. She sent me an email about it, some link, I don't know, I didn't get time this morning to follow it. She says they're pretty mad about that whole thing.' She took a breath. The smile returned. 'Now, what can I getcha this morning?'

# 24

At the bend in the road leading to the Old Believer compound there was another roadblock. A uniform – municipal police, State Troopers, she didn't know which and didn't care any – waved her down and asked what her business was. Searching around her head, quickly, the way a hunter has to when faced with a musk-ox stampede, then, thumbing behind, she said, 'Delivering a dog.'

The trooper raised his eyebrows. He was young, wouldn't know any better.

'Inupiaq huntin' dog.'

The trooper leaned in, gave Bonehead the eye.

'Careful,' she said, 'he can be real mean.'

The trooper offered up an uncomfortable little smile. 'I'm not really supposed to let anyone through. This whole area's a crime scene.' Then, as if not wanting to seem unfriendly, he added, 'Never heard of an Inupiaq hunting dog. That the same as a husky? He looks a lot like a husky.'

She gave an indulgent little laugh. 'This here is a special dog. That's why the Believers want him. Nothing this dog can't hunt. Not one thing. Wolverines, muskrat, moose. You want it, he'll get it. Hunt you a pretty girl if you need one.'

The trooper blushed and smiled.

'You got dogs?' she said.

'I got one, but my uncle keeps him up at his cabin.' He looked wistful, as if nostalgic for another life. 'We hunt with him sometimes.'

'I'm like you, come from dog people,' she said. 'My man is up running the Iditarod right now,' she said. She mentioned Sammy's competitor number. The trooper looked impressed.

'Expensive business. That's why we've gotta sell this old thing, pay the bills.' She spoke quickly so the trooper wouldn't have time to gather up his thoughts about not letting her through. 'Listen, I don't want to take any more of your time, you've got your job to do, so suppose I just go on by, drop off my delivery, then I'll be on my way.'

The young man thought about this for a moment, checked up and down the road, and hesitated.

'Ten minutes do it?'

'Fifteen and you got yourself a deal.' Edie stuck her arm out and shook the trooper's hand. When she glanced back in the rear-view mirror, he was standing where she'd left him, wondering what had just happened.

She found Anatoly and Natalia standing outside on the steps of their house, waiting for her. The Believer who routinely manned the gate had radioed in five minutes before, announcing her arrival.

'Police let you in? They're not letting anyone in. Our home has become a prison.' Anatoly flapped his hands impotently to indicate his irritation with the situation.

Natalia offered up a fragile smile. The young woman's face was puffy from crying.

'I thought you'd come back,' she said. 'We have someone to see you.'

They beckoned Edie inside to the kitchen, where the mother was sitting with a lean man with wind-tanned skin who could have been anything from thirty-five to sixty but was most likely the former while looking like the latter. Anatoly offered her a seat, and took one himself. Natalia followed. Edie looked around the table. Without exception the faces were rutted with worry. The mother rose from her chair and began to busy herself making tea.

Anatoly spoke a few words in Russian to Natalia, who stood up, flashed another little smile at Edie, and left.

He said, 'We are very private. For hundreds of years we have avoided worldliness and worldy people.' He checked the door to make sure his daughter was out of earshot, then added in a quieter voice, 'What is happening, God is telling us that we should not have accepted a worldly person among us.' He looked up, briefly, as though passing a thought to heaven, then said by way of explanation, 'But we are a very small community and it is difficult for us to find wives and husbands who aren't close relations. This man we took to us, Natalia's husband, he's an Outsider, a worldly person, but he's a good man.' He shrugged. 'Maybe God is testing us so we can prove that.'

The mother brought tea in the same delicately painted glasses as before. They all took a sip, and then Medvedev carried on. 'When the guard radioed to tell me you were here, I asked Gregor Nodgorov to come.'

The man nodded a greeting but didn't volunteer any words.

'He was out looking for hare the other day, he saw you running from the hunting lodge up by Hatcher Pass. He saw you before; he knew who you were. We don't get many visitors.'

Nodgorov nodded enthusiastically. Edie got the impression that he was only just following what was being said.

'Some of us work Outside. We do construction mostly.'

The Old Believers' reputation as builders sounded vaguely familiar. She tried to recall who had told her. The priest at the church in Eagle River maybe?

'Gregor and three of the other men worked as labourers on the hunting lodge, the one just up the road for a time, when it was being remodelled.'

Nodgorov nodded. He was very good at it, Edie thought, given that it was the only thing he seemed able to do. Maybe that was where he got his name from.

Edie was eager to know what Gregor had to say, but first she needed to understand what Anatoly had to gain by telling her.

'Why is this something of interest to me?' she said.

Anatoly gave her a little smile, an acknowledgement that he realized she was checking him out and was OK with it.

'The hunting lodge is owned by Tommy Schofield.' Edie opened her eyes wider, keen for him to go on. 'You will need to be a bit patient with Gregor's English, but he will tell you, Gregor will tell you.' The old man indicated to his younger companion to go ahead.

'We dig out basement,' the man began. His accent was thick but Edie had no trouble understanding him. 'We make big bedroom, many beds, not beautiful, cheap.'

'A dormitory,' Anatoly said.

Nodgorov nodded then went on. 'Then, at back, we make small rooms, very beautiful.' He hesitated. 'A cousin of me make beds from wood, very decorate, very expensive.'

Edie wondered where this was going.

'Later, we miss something on one bed, so we come back.' He looked at his hands. His face flared and twitched. 'There is girls, lots of girls very young . . .' He hesitated. 'In one part of big bedroom they are putting . . .' He made a slicing motion to indicate some kind of partition or screen, and then started laying out rectangles in the air with his right hand. 'For babies.'

Edie felt something compressing her chest. She drank a little tea to steady herself. A picture was forming in her mind.

'Why didn't you say any of this before?'

Immediately, Anatoly's expression darkened and he held up a hand.

'It's not Gregor's fault. They were threatening. And besides, we don't interfere with worldly matters.'

'But you've told the police now?'

He shook his head. 'Miss Kiglatuk, we have been persecuted for ever since—'

'1666.'

Anatoly looked startled.

'I know the date, and what people say about it.'

A great shadow moved across his face. His fingers worked at the tea glass in his hands. For a moment he could not make eye contact with her. He was trying to hold himself together so that he would not shout at her. His head began to shake violently from side to side.

'You see, you are the same as the worldly people who want to hate us,' he said, dismissing Edie with a hand. 'You want to believe there is such a thing as the Dark Believers, you will not believe us when we say the Dark Believers do not exist. You have seen how the police are, the newspapers, how everybody is. And now it is how you are, too.' He met her with his eyes. 'You judge us for not speaking out, but who can we trust to listen to us?'

'I will listen, but in return you need to tell me the truth. Do you know where Peter Galloway is?' She needed to be able to speak with him face to face to know if he was telling the truth. And if he was, he had information about Schofield which might be of interest to her investigation.

Anatoly shook his head. 'The police think we do, but that is because they don't understand the Believers. Peter would never have burdened us with this. So no, I don't know where Peter Galloway is, and neither does Natalia.' He cast his calm gaze on her face. He wanted to trust her with something, some confidence.

'You can trust me to listen,' she said. 'Beyond that, there are no guarantees.'

He acknowledged this with a little tip of his head. For a moment he sat thinking, then, making his decision, he began to describe their remote hunting hide, deep in the forest. It was possible Galloway might be holed up there.

'As you say, Miss Kiglatuk, beyond that there are no guarantees.'

From the Believers compound she drove up the winding track towards the Lodge. The ice was up now, and a few times the truck slalomed across the route and she toed the brakes and pulled it down a gear. As she drove she thought about the young girl who had been first up at the hotel in Nome then in the woods, trying to make sense of what she knew. The bodies of Lucas Littlefish and Jonny Doe had been meant to be found, she was sure of that. They had been so meticulously prepared, so carefully situated. Whoever had left Lucas out in the woods had kept the body frozen for more than three months before making his move. Perhaps the same was also true of Jonny Doe. If Anatoly Medvedev was right and Tommy Schofield *had* framed Galloway, then it seemed likely that Schofield had planned it, that he had either killed Lucas in order to frame Galloway or he was killing two birds with one stone so to speak and had concocted the frame-up as a convenient way of disposing of Lucas's body. Unless the death of the second baby was some sort of copycat killing, which was unlikely given what Edie knew about the way the bodies were identically wrapped, it followed that

Schofield must have known something about Jonny Doe's death, too. None of this proved that Schofield was the killer, only that he knew that the two boys were dead.

Edie thought about Sammy, battling his way along the Yukon River and hoped, when he found out, that her ex would understand.

She stopped at the bend in the track from where the footpath snaked off into the woods and eventually came out at the Lodge. Pulling the truck onto the verge, she emptied Bonehead from the back and swung a pair of binoculars over her shoulder. For a while, they trudged through thick snow into deep forest. At the clearing, where the young girl had doubled back, Edie and the dog carried on until they reached the boundary fence marking the perimeter of the Lodge. She stopped for a while, listening for the sounds of car engines or human voices, but the only noise was made by the wind calling through the spruce.

Bonehead lifted his nose, scenting the air. He stiffened and the hairs between his shoulder blades rose. He began a soft, low growl. Another dog. She took him by the collar, told him to be quiet. Once more there was no sound except the breeze. Most likely the strange dog was upwind, and hadn't scented either of them yet. Flipping his leash over a sapling, she ordered Bonehead to sit quietly and wait, then she went ahead, keeping low along the side of the fence. A few hundred yards further along she spotted movement among the trees inside the compound. A man in uniform was blowing on his gloved hands and stamping his feet. Beside him a German Shepherd shook snow off its coat. Edie waited for the pair to move away, then continued to pick her way along the boundary, making sure to keep herself downwind, until she had a good view of the Lodge. Then, crouching down, she sat and watched. The buildings gave all the appearance of being unoccupied. Shutters lay across the windows and from below one of the second-storey windows an alarm box blinked. A truck, marked Guardwell Security, sat under the carport. A single set of tyre marks led from the truck to the security gates.

The guard and his dog disappeared around the far side of the building then reappeared on the near side. The guard loaded the dog into the back of his truck then walked over to the front door and pushed the handle, as if testing the lock. He went back to the truck and flipped open the door on the driver's side, picked up what looked like a clipboard from the passenger's seat and began to make some notes. She saw him punch a few numbers into his cell phone, then back the truck out of the carport, his lips moving as he did so. She crept quickly round towards the gate, crouching low and sheltering behind an outcrop of alder. The gates clicked and began to open and the truck moved through and off up the track. There was another click and the gates began to close back up again. Edie waited until the truck was out of sight and darted out. The fence was razor-wired along its length. If she was going to enter, the only way out would be the way she went in. She yanked off her binocular strap, lurched towards the closing gates and jammed the instrument into the crack. There was a grinding sound but the gate panels stopped moving.

Edie thanked the spirits for making her small and squeezed herself through the gap. She followed the path the guard had taken, stepping inside his footprints. Though she couldn't see past the shutters everything told her that the place was empty. Round the back it was the same, closed up.

The footprints came to a halt beside a locked door. The guard had clearly been inside because there were slivers of hard-packed snow from where he'd stamped his boots on the step. The prints continued on to a row of trashcans hidden behind a wooden frame. Edie followed. One of the can lids had been cleared of snow. Inside the can was a small day pack. She opened up the zip, turned the pack over and shook its contents out onto the snow; several sanitary pads, some fancy underwear and a blue plastic pacifier, its rubber teat slightly withered. She picked out the dummy and put it in her pocket. As she was putting back the underwear she noticed on the inside of one of the bras a milky stain. Lifting it to her face, she sniffed. The sour, animal smell of human milk crept inside her nostrils. She felt her legs turn watery and had to steady herself on the trashcan. From somewhere inside her head she heard the faint voice of her stepson, Joe, calling her by the name he always used, reaching out to her from the spirit world. She closed her eyes to be nearer to him. Then she took a deep breath and, biting her lip, she wrapped the brassiere cups inside one another, folded them into her pocket and gave the bag a final vigorous shake. There was the sound of Velcro coming apart and something slipped out and onto the snow, a pink plastic My Kitty purse. She opened the zip, saw a wad of tissues and zipped it up, but through her gloves her fingers could feel something hard inside. Beneath the tissues, wrapped in cotton wool, was a small tin. Inside the tin were a series of thick needles, like those she and her mother Maggie and Maggie's mother and generations of Inuit women used to sew hide clothes. With the needles was a tiny bottle of inky black liquid and a scrap of paper onto which someone had written the word шахта, *Mine.*

She heard the sound of the guard's truck approaching and realized with the full force of a musk-ox charge that she must have set off some kind of alarm. She had no choice but to run for the gate, and quick. If the guard reached it before her, he'd find the binoculars and no doubt make another search of the compound. Wherever she hid, the dog would scent her out. Being careful only to tread in the guard's footsteps, she hurried around the front of the building, her heart banging like hail on a summer tent. The truck was close now. A light on a metal panel by the gate blinked red. She crouched low and ran with her knees bent to steady her, the way her grandfather had taught her, making sure each step landed in the footsteps the guard had left.

She reached the gate just as the bull bar of the truck became visible through the trees. As the truck slowed to take the bend in the trail, Edie squeezed through the gap in the gate, snatched the binoculars and ran into the trees, moving her feet in figures of eight to scatter the snow around the prints, stopping only to listen to the two halves of the gate clang into place. An engine purred and the guard barked instructions to his dog. Without waiting to see any more she took off. From the track came the rumble of the truck and then there was nothing but the wind.

Bonehead had managed to release himself from the leash and was waiting for her back at the vehicle. She opened the back door, ushered him in and got into the driver's seat. The engine started at the first turn and Edie let off the handbrake. As she did so, Bonehead began barking and as she turned around to shush him, she saw the security guard hurrying towards her, with his hand on his pistol. Her pulse thudding at her temples, she pulled up the handbrake and unwound her window.

When he saw it was a woman driving, the guard visibly relaxed. If he'd expected anybody, it hadn't been her. She felt her pulse slow a little. What remained was a lurching feeling familiar to her from her old hunting days. An adrenaline surge. Her body was preparing for fight or flight. Her job now was to control it. The guard looked back at the dog, then at the binos on the passenger seat. She noticed he had native blood.

'You been hunting?'

'If you could call it that.' She gave him a weary look but made sure her eyes were smiling. 'May as well have stayed at home and baked cookies for all the good it did me.'

'Not the right weather for it,' he said. 'Too windy. What kind of rifle you carry?'

She flipped her head back to the trunk. 'Regular Remmy 308. That's fine for what I go after. You hunt?'

The guard turned up the corners of his mouth just enough to acknowledge the remark while making clear he was done with small talk.

'You see anyone around here just now, ma'am?' he said. 'A man? Maybe on his own?'

She glanced up, pressed her lips together and shook her head.

'Just been me and the dog.' She looked the guard directly in the eyes and flashed him a smile. 'I may not be the sharpest tack in the box, but if someone came by, Bonehead would let me know about it.'

'Well, OK, then,' the guard said. He knew he'd messed up and didn't want anyone else to know it. 'Thank you for your time.'

She drove home in a state of fury. This was it, the confirmation she'd been looking for. Tommy Schofield was running underage girls, most likely trafficking them from Russia, the girls were having babies, and at least two of those babies had been killed.

# 25

At his breakfast meeting with the Mommabears at their down-town offices, Chuck Hillingberg had gone on an all-out charm offensive to reassure the mothers of Alaska that he sympathized with their issues and was absolutely on the case. He'd begun by expressing disgust at the hacking of the Mommabears' website. He shared their indignation. He couldn't imagine who might have a vested interest in depriving Alaska's hardworking mothers of a voice. What had happened represented nothing less than an attempt to do away with the constitutional right to free speech and, as their elected mayor, he would do everything in his power to support Police Chief Mackenzie in investigating the crime without in any way holding up or impeding the ongoing hunt for Peter Galloway, which, he assured them, was everyone's first priority.

He knew the Mommabears were beginning to soften when they started eating the breakfast muffins. Damn he was good! It was a secret source of pride to him that he'd been able to come to rely on the vote of a large swathe of the electorate he found physically repellent without them ever suspecting a thing. Over the years he'd made an art of being able to surround himself by all those sagging, maternal examples of the weakness of the flesh and have them imagine that there was nowhere else he'd rather be. He'd done it at the meeting this morning and by the time they were wrapping up, he'd had them purring like cats in front of a fire, feeling strong and heard and, most importantly, in control.

Not that they were, of course. Increasingly, it seemed to him that no one was really steering this thing in the way it needed to be steered. Mackenzie had proved himself completely inadequate for the job. If he'd kept a firm grip on Detective Truro right at the beginning, Jonny Doe would most likely never have been found and this whole thing could have been shut down long before it got to the stage of his having to step in to soft-soap a bunch of hysterical women who'd got it into their heads that their babies were about to be snatched up and sacrificed by satanists.

But they were where they were. Which, in Chuck's case, was now in the mayoral limo en route to the next firefight, an informal meeting over coffee at the mayor's office with a group of church leaders.

Personally, he thought all the talk about satanic rituals, the 'Dark Believer Fever', as it was already being labelled in the media, was a crock of shit. In his view, the Old Believers were pretty harmless as a group. He viewed the hysteria over the date of the *raskol* for what he knew it to be – the silly superstitions of a bunch of gullible people led by a group of opportunists who should know better. By his own reckoning, there had been one bad apple in the barrel. They'd identified him pretty quickly and, until yesterday at least, had him behind bars.

Naturally enough, that's not what he'd be saying at the church leaders' meeting. The challenge, as Chuck saw it, was to pretend to take the concerns of the interested parties seriously, allay their fears until such time as Peter Galloway could be located and then distract them away from the case altogether and back onto the gubernatorial campaign.

Once he'd mollified the church leaders, he was scheduled to

head over to the Seafood Shack for a lunch with Marsha and the new guy in town, Byron Hallstrom, and his young wife, Sandy. Just the four of them in the Shack's private function room overlooking Cook Inlet. He'd managed to overcome his previous reluctance to hustle Hallstrom when he heard how much money he was thinking of giving away. It was a lunch from which Chuck hoped to return with half a million dollars for the Hillingberg campaign. Exactly what Hallstrom would want in return, Chuck didn't yet know, but he was sure of one thing: the billionaire wasn't likely to be shy about asking.

The driver pulled up outside the mayor's office. As usual, Chuck opened his own door – to wait for the driver to do it would make him look like an East Coast preppy or, worse, some slick European – gave a nod to the two or three protestors outside the building, pushed his way through the doors into the foyer and waited for the elevator to take him to the sixth floor conference room.

The meeting turned out to be more challenging than he'd anticipated. Marsha had warned him that there would be some strong opinions in the room, but he'd radically underestimated how charged and resentful people felt about the presence of the Old Believers, even before their passions had been reignited by the deaths of the two kids. He quickly realized that all his planned entreaties for the group to remember the rights granted to Americans in the First Amendment would be seen as bleeding hearts claptrap so he shut up about it. However ridiculous he personally found the idea of there being a group of 'Dark Believers' practising what amounted to witchcraft in the forests around Meadow Lake and Homer, the churches really did seem exercised about it. In trying to defuse the situation at the start, rather than grabbing it by the balls, Chuck realized he'd completely misplayed his hand.

Coming out of the meeting bruised, he guessed he shouldn't

have been so surprised by the leaders' reactions. He didn't get the religious element but he didn't have to. For nearly half a century Alaska had been the Cold War frontier. Elsewhere, people might have moved on, but ordinary Alaskans had taken a lot longer to warm up. The Old Believers were still Russians and in many Alaskans' eyes, the Ruskies were still the enemy. It was a lesson to him that when it came to Alaska politics, his wife's instincts were usually better than his own.

The meeting had gone on longer than scheduled, which left him running late for lunch. To make matters worse, the limo got stuck behind a snowplough. By the time he was shown up to the private dining room, Marsha and the Hallstroms were already seated in front of glasses of chilled white wine, chatting animatedly about the view from the window across the ice. Byron Hallstrom immediately got up from the table and came round to shake his hand, on his face that expression of jovial, condescending bonhomie rich men adopt when meeting people less powerful than themselves. Chuck didn't know much about the man other than what Marsha had told him; that he was a newcomer and had a vision of Alaska's future which had nothing to do with salmon or oil and everything to do with cruise ships, theme parks and mass tourism. He certainly looked the billionaire part: hair slicked, shoes handmade, suit bespoke, the kind of uniform which might go down well in the boardrooms of Chicago or New York but didn't cut much ice up here in Alaska. Chuck Hillingberg clasped the giant hand held out to him and smiled to himself. Hallstrom was a hopeless outsider and he knew it.

'I've heard great things about your plans for Homer,' Hillingberg said, 'and I'm looking forward to seeing how I might be able to assist you with them.'

Hallstrom gave Chuck a penetrating, slightly anxious look that warmed his heart. The man was feeling ever so slightly vulnerable.

They took their seats. Without glancing at the menu, Chuck flung himself back in his chair and said, 'Why don't we order the ultimate Alaskan combo: snow crab and Alaskan steamed clams?'

Hallstrom nodded politely, aware that this was not a question.

Chuck raised his glass. 'Here's to ultimate Alaskan combos.' Everyone around the table laughed. Chuck felt his stomach relax. It was going to be OK. So long as nothing went terribly wrong Hallstrom would be serving up his half-million-dollar pledge somewhere between the snow crab and the brandy.

Afterwards, he and Marsha stayed behind to debrief.

'Well, that was easier than I thought,' he said, pushing his napkin away. 'Hallstrom's idea to turn southern Alaska into a new Dubai seems kinda whacked, but who cares?'

Marsha looked at him, cold. He didn't like being made to feel jumpy. It made him talk too much, 'I thought it was genius,' she said.

Chuck took this in. 'You're right. In any case, if that's what he wants, that's what he can have. There'll be objections from the tree-huggers but I don't think we'll have to worry about those.'

'Really?' Marsha raised an eyebrow. 'Maybe you've forgotten the northern spotted owl?'

He had, in fact, momentarily forgotten the owl. But he recalled the controversy now. The logging industry claimed that protection of the animal in the nineties, under both the Endangered Species Act and the National Forest Management Act, lost the Pacific Northwest timber industry 30,000 jobs. Environmentalists said the industry was on the decline anyway. The argument became a symbol of the fight between developers and conservationists, a fight that seemed to have deepened and become so personal and bitter in recent years that both parties often couched it in terms of the battle between good and evil.

'The optimum strategy would be to pitch the tree-huggers against the salmon fishery, watch them slug it out until they destroy one another,' Marsha said. 'Save us the trouble. It's not like either has a long-term future in Alaska. Quotas will continue to shrink the fishery and the environmentalists will soon find there aren't any jobs to be had that aren't in oil or resource development of one kind or another or construction. Outside entrepreneurs like Hallstrom might find it hard to get a toehold, but in ten years' time Alaskans are gonna be begging for the jobs men like Hallstrom bring in.'

Chuck's private phone began beeping. He checked the caller ID. Mackenzie. He was secretly relieved. Unlike the police chief, his wife made him feel outclassed.

Marsha took out her BlackBerry and slipped from the room to make a call of her own.

'Hey.' MacKenzie sounded rattled. 'We might have a problem. Maybe we got one.'

An involuntary rumble bubbled up from the mayor's gut. He held his hand to his belly, blinking slowly, letting his eyes close and flood a little, feeling tired as all hell. He made a mental note to get a check-up.

Mackenzie said, 'The bloods on Jonny Doe show likely origin in the Caucasus.'

'The what?'

'In Russia, boss.'

Chuck said, 'So?' then made the link before Mackenzie had time to answer: 'But we got rid of everything, right? You told me you checked this out.'

'Right.'

Chuck felt reassured. Half the kids in Alaska probably had Russian blood. Until 1867, the place *was* Russian.

'There's something else, just a small thing.' Mackenzie was hesitant, unwilling to say what he was about to say but knowing he had no choice. 'When they were clearing out the Lodge, they found one of the security cameras had no tape in it. Probably just an oversight.'

Chuck felt his spirit sink into his boots. It was as though someone had picked up his party balloon and used it to stub out their cigarette. He was tired of the whole business of the Lodge. When it started he'd been swept up in it, in the feeling of power it gave him. And the pleasure. But like most things, he'd become habituated. Now he was tired of all the code names and private phones and petty subterfuge. It no longer felt dangerous or forbidden, even though he knew it was. A slip now would not only put an end to his career, it might well put an end to his freedom.

'When were they last checked?'

A long pause.

'That's just it. They haven't been.'

'Dammit, that was Schofield's job.' The door opened and Marsha's face popped round the door.

'I'll call you back,' Chuck said.

'What was Schofield's job?' Marsha's voice was sharp with anxiety.

'They got a security tape missing from the Lodge.'

She looked at him wearily and rubbed her hand across her forehead. 'That place again.'

There was a knock on the door. It was Don Reynolds, the owner of the Seafood Shack, wanting to know if the meal had been up to par. April Montalo followed closely behind. Chuck had a budgetary committee meeting at city hall he was already late for and Marsha was due at a high school girls' soccer game photo op.

The meeting dragged on for hours. In the car on the way back to the scruffy room in the anonymous downtown office hutch that served as his campaign HQ, Chuck dialled Tommy Schofield's private cell. He hadn't forgotten the conversation he'd overheard between Schofield and his wife but her resentful outburst earlier made him wonder if there was something going on he didn't know about. He wasn't about to ask direct, but he had it in mind to poke around in Schofield's head, see what he could find there. The call went straight to voicemail and he didn't leave a message. Next he tried the man's office.

Schofield's assistant, Sharon, answered and, when he gave his name and asked to speak to the boss, she said, 'I'm real sorry, Mayor Hillingberg. Mr Schofield's not around. I think he may be at his cabin, but there's no phone reception there.'

Chuck thanked Sharon and hung up. He made up his mind that this one wasn't going away unless he made it do so. He dialled his wife's number and left a message for her to call him. In two hours he was due at a fundraiser at the Sheraton downtown, which gave him just enough time to draft some notes for a speech for his upcoming tour of the north, organized to coincide with the finish of the Iditarod. He'd hand them over to Andy in the morning. He set the alarm on his watch. For an hour and forty-five minutes he wrote, then, when his watch pinged, he went to the closet in his office and changed into his tux. At 6.55 p.m. precisely his driver called to remind him it was time to leave. It was only when he got out into the street and saw his wife sitting in the limo in her emerald-green gown that he remembered she hadn't called him back. He opened the door and clambered inside. She gave him a beady look.

'I was busy,' she said, anticipating his question. 'Tending to the lame.'

# 26

Edie decided to take breakfast at the Snowy Owl Café. But today it wasn't just the food she was after.

When Stacey bounded up with her usual busy smile, she said, 'Don't take this the wrong way, Stacey, I love my Snowy Owl breakfasts, but I've just got an urge to hunt me some meat today and I was kinda hoping you could recommend me an outfitter? I'm only looking to go after ducks, nothing fancy.'

For a moment the waitress looked taken aback, then the smile reappeared and, gathering herself, she said she could definitely help.

'Oh, no, sure, everyone hunts in Alaska. You know you can just buy your permit right from the outfitters.' She scribbled something down on her order pad and peeled off the page. 'My uncle Anthony's got a set-up just two blocks down the street. Here's the address and phone number. You just tell him Stacey sent you and he'll give you a good price.'

An hour later, Edie had the dog on the back seat and a rented Remington 308 in the trunk and she was heading up the Glenn Highway north again. The roadblocks had gone. She guessed the police figured that if Galloway was going to try to drive himself out of trouble, he'd have done it by now. At the turn to Wasilla, where she would normally have swung left, she kept right, following the signs to Palmer and Chickaloon. The journey up to the part of the forest where Galloway might or might not be hiding took longer than she'd anticipated. Several times she found herself struggling with Anatoly Medvedev's directions. Driving took your focus away from the land itself. The road signs were unhelpful and she was now on new terrain. Things were so different here. Back home, she was as familiar with the land as she was with the lines on her face. Everything had an Inuktitut name that made sense to her: rivers were called after the quality of the fishing or according to when the ice in them melted, cliffs were known for the birds nesting there. If you needed to find your bearings there were always high points from which you could get a view and the tundra was littered with inukshuks marking the route of hunting trails. Here in Alaska, low points or high points, all you could see were trees and more trees and it was hard to tell anything from names like McDougall or Sunshine or Palmer.

At Glennallen she made a left on the 4 north towards Sourdough, then another left there, bumping along on hunting and logging trails towards the Alphabet range until she reached a hollow dip in the land on the edge of a stream with a view of foothills, which fitted Medvedev's description. Parking up, she unloaded Bonehead, strapped on her snowshoes and plunged into the forest. The two of them brushed through thick alder and bitter-smelling hemlock pine into deep stands of dark spruce part buried in smooth snowdrift. She'd brought a compass with her, something she never needed on the tundra, and for a long time she followed Medvedev's instructions, heading north-north-west from the spot where he'd suggested she leave the car. Here and there they came across animal tracks in the snow which Bonehead had a hard time ignoring, but there were no signs of any human activity at all. They continued to dodge through the trees, straining for human sounds, stopping every so often for Edie to check the compass. She felt disoriented and light-headed, only the presence of the dog steadying her. After what seemed like the longest time, Bonehead began to whimper and shake, alternately sniffing the air and pressing his nose to the snow. She clipped on his leash, allowing him to lead and he took them along the bank of the stream, then back up through trees to a tiny clearing and there it was, the hide, a cube of two-by-fours simply roofed in corrugated iron and pinned with snow pegs and with a single plank door and a small window, the view through which was baffled by the way the sunlight fell onto it.

Edie crouched for a moment and let her breathing slow, then called out. No response. A shadow moved across the window of the hide. Again she called. Nothing. Reaching for the rifle, she let off a shot into the air. There was a silence broken by a rough voice saying, 'What do you want?'

'How's about an explanation?' she said. 'If I don't like it, I'm taking you in.' The biggest part of her didn't think Galloway had murdered Lucas Littlefish but she wanted to hear him deny it. His relationship with Schofield needed ironing out, too.

There was a pause, and then the door to the hide swung open and Peter Galloway emerged, holding up his hands in a gesture of surrender. His eyes widened. 'I know you,' he said.

'Sure you do. I'm the one you left in the forest a few days back, remember? Only on my way out I discovered your dirty little secret.'

He shook his head, caught her eye, and focused in on it. 'I didn't have nothing to do with that,' he said. The intensity of his gaze was unsettling. If he was lying, he was damned good at it. He'd probably already guessed who'd sent her, which meant he must know she was unlikely to shoot, or take him in for that matter. Still, he didn't know and it was his not knowing that put her in a stronger position.

She said, 'I know you and TaniaLee Littlefish were friends.'

'I taught her to read, and that's all I did,' he said. 'I saw her around town sometimes, when I was living in Homer. She worked at the supermarket for a while, but I hadn't come across her in something like a year when her baby was born.' He kept his voice low and his eyes straight, no sign of the rise or the small deflection which might indicate a lie. But he was scared, she could sense that, and it made him dangerous. 'I didn't kill that kid.'

'Which one?' she said, meaning to catch him out.

Peter Galloway stared at her, his face a blank. He appeared to have no idea what she was talking about. Edie glanced down at Bonehead but the dog remained alert and calm, his ears forward, eyes beady, tail relaxed down. He hadn't picked up any increased anxiety, the kind of subtle change in energy you might expect if someone were lying.

'Listen, I never touched TaniaLee. I'm very sorry for her troubles and I'm sad about the kid. But that girl will believe anything anyone tells her, they repeat it enough times. There ain't no Dark Believers so how can I be one of them? You think I'd kill a baby?' He let his arms fall to his sides.

'Put your hands where I can see them.'

He did as she asked.

'You gonna take me in or not?'

The dog let out a low growl. She clicked off the safety catch. He'd advanced a little as he'd been talking. He was near enough to her now that she could feel the warmth of his body.

'Watch yourself,' she said. Her fingers curled around the trigger. 'I've shot bigger and meaner.'

He stopped advancing and looked at her quizzically, like something had just fallen into place.

'You saw Schofield, didn't you? Natalia said you would. She said you were the nosy kind wouldn't be able to help yourself.'

When she didn't reply he sighed and paused for a while, thoughts moving on his face.

'Who's Fonseca?' Edie asked.

He shook his head.

'TaniaLee said Fonseca is the father of her baby.'

Galloway's hands began to move back towards his sides. 'Look, I have no idea what line you're pursuing here but I can tell you for sure it comes out at a dead end. There's powerful people wrapped up in this, more powerful than me or Tommy Schofield.' Watching her carefully, he took a step towards her without letting up his speech. 'I never killed any babies. How could I do that? C'mon, I got my own baby coming any time.'

Bonehead began to growl and she told him to be quiet. Then she felt the dog rush forward. There was the sensation of her legs disappearing from under her and a blur in front of her eyes as Galloway bounded for her gun.

Her first thought on waking was that a bear had got her. Then she remembered that the bears round this way were still in hibernation. Her arms windmilled out and caught Bonehead on the chops. The dog let out a yelp. She sat up and blinked. Her head hurt like a group toothache in a walrus pod. Her hand grazed across warm, sticky blood at the back of her skull. It was dark, her rifle was gone and she had no flashlight. Then she remembered Peter Galloway. In the moonlight she could just about pick out Galloway's tracks heading off into the forest. She got up and steadied herself and, ordering the dog to go ahead, she followed on. Before long they were back at her truck. Sitting in the driving seat with the locks fastened she felt safe enough to check the wound by tilting the rear-view mirror until it reflected the back of her head in the vanity on the passenger side sunshade. The blood was already beginning to dry up. She checked her face in the rear-view. Her pupils seemed uprooted and floaty. Or was that how she felt in general? It was hard to tell. She turned the radio on, screwing the dial to a heavy rock station and turning the volume up. In the back seat, Bonehead gave a pained whine. Thinking how best to keep herself awake, she settled on reciting the titles of Charlie Chaplin's short films in reverse chronological order, and pulled the truck out onto the road.

It wasn't until she reached the door of the studio and tried repeatedly, and failed, to connect the key to the lock that she realized how confused she was. Everything looked slightly off. Inside at last, she turned on all the lights and took a cold shower, standing in the water with her hair cascading from her shoulders like black rain. She stepped out of the shower and grabbed for a towel then everything suddenly went very, very fuzzy.

Some time later she thought she could hear voices in the studio. She opened her eyes. She was lying on the bathroom floor and someone was leaving a message on her voicemail. Using the basin, she pulled herself up and went for the door. Her head swam and she was as unsteady on her legs as a newborn pup. A woman's voice she didn't recognize was just signing off. By the time she reached the phone, the caller had hung up. She waited for the blinking light then pressed message play. The voice came back on again:

*'Miss Kiglatuk? I'm sorry to call so late. There's been a problem with Mr Inukpuk. Derek Palliser has already flown out to Unalakleet. We really need you to come up to Nome as soon as you can.'*

# 27

She struggled with contradictory impulses. Her head wound made her sleepy but she knew she could not afford to rest. She kept herself awake by watching Laurel and Hardy reruns on an old movie channel and drinking hot sweet tea. Every so often she called Zach Barefoot's and left a message. Calls to the Iditarod HQ went straight to voicemail. When she'd been phoning a few hours without getting any answer from anyone, she contacted the officer on night duty at the Nome PD, who promised to make some enquiries but never called back.

At 4.30 in the morning Edie pulled on her outerwear and went outside. The snowploughs and gritters hadn't yet got to work, so the walk from the apartment building was slow and treacherous, the street lights illuminating the ruts and gulleys of footprints made by the stamping feet of the Mommabear demonstrators, which had hardened and iced overnight. At 4.45 she was waiting outside the Snowy Owl, hoping to catch Stacey before she went on shift. At 4.50 a face she recognized appeared out of the gloom and came smiling towards her.

'Man, Edie, you ever sleep?' The young woman reached out for Edie's arm and gave it a squeeze. 'Come in and get warm. The cook doesn't get here till five, but I can make you some tea.' Opening the door, she walked through, turned on the lights and spotted the whorl of dried blood on Edie's head. In an instant, her expression changed.

'Hey, what happened?'

Edie squeezed the hand on her arm. 'Next time you got a week to listen, I'll explain.' She looked her directly in the eye. 'Right now, though, Stacey, I could really use some help.'

'Sure, whatever, you got it.' Stacey's eyes widened with worry and affection in equal measure. For a moment Edie was tempted to tell her the truth, about Sammy and the wounds, old and new, about everything that had brought her to this moment. But why burden the girl with it? There was nothing Stacey could do and there was in any case no time to explain. She needed to be on that first flight up to Nome.

'I need you to look after my dog,' Edie said. 'He's in my apartment.' She gave the address.

'Oh-kaaay,' Stacey said, waiting for the punchline.

'You'll need to give him plenty of exercise. He's not used to eating commercial dog food but you'll find a coyote in the refrigerator. I already portioned it up.'

She saw Stacey's composure give just a little but she took a beat and recovered. She took her wad of cash from her pocket, peeled off a couple of big bills and pressed them into Stacey's hand. 'You might need to buy more food. Meat, or whatever you got left over from the restaurant. He's real happy just to crunch on bones for a while. And it'll be best if you wear this when you go see him.' Edie handed over one of her old Arctic hare vests. 'Don't wash it.'

'Because?'

'If you smell of me he won't tear you to pieces.'

'When you put it like that, it's irresistible,' Stacey said. She took a breath. 'You know how long this might be for exactly?'

Edie shrugged. Why were southerners so stuck on timetables?

'If things go well, exactly for a couple of days. If they don't, I'm guessing exactly for ever.'

'Well, so now we've got that clear,' Stacey laughed, the anxiety still on her face. 'When do I start?'

Edie dug the apartment keys from her pocket.

At Anchorage airport she called Zach Barefoot's number again, but got no response. She went through the ID and baggage check in a daze, her mind fizzy with worry. Her ex must have had an accident. Why hadn't Derek called her himself? Once on the plane, she waved aside the Air Alaska breakfast and tried to focus her mind on the soft purple early morning light creeping over Mount Denali, but it was hopeless. Her head throbbed from the rifle butt and her heart ached for Sammy. They continued on, over the Kuskokwims and the Kaiyuhs, over the Iditarod trail, then moved out across Norton Sound and into the barrens. As they left the treeline behind, she felt herself expand into the tundra. It was fully light now, a few high clouds throwing shadows on the Seward Peninsula. The plane began its descent. She felt a sudden pain and realized she'd been biting her lip to distract herself from the catastrophic thoughts crowding her brain.

At the terminal in Nome, she called Zach's number, and getting no response, decided to head directly to the Iditarod HQ in the centre of town. When she explained her predicament, the volunteer at the info desk seemed out of her depth. She didn't know anything about any message. Unfortunately, Aileen Logan was in the field all day, inspecting checkpoints, the volunteer said, but she would call Logan's deputy, Chrissie Caley, who would probably be able to help.

After what seemed like for ever a pert businesslike woman with hair the colour of spring run-off came over, introducing herself as

Chrissie Caley and giving Edie a sympathetic look. She listened to Edie then said she'd go and check the records and be right back. Ten minutes later (Edie counted them in) Caley took a seat in the waiting area. She wondered if whoever had left the message had given her name.

'Uh nuh.' Edie shook her head, and then, feeling her brain shaking in its box, regretted it. She lifted her hand to the wound. Caley shot her a concerned look.

'Do you need to see a doctor for that?'

'Please, I just need to see Sammy.'

Caley nodded but her eyes remained anxious. She explained that the reason for the delay had been that she'd checked in the records and the last communication the team had had with Sammy Inukpuk was at the checkpoint at Eagle Island. She'd asked around in the back office but no one seemed to know anything about a message. An added mystery was the fact that Sammy Inukpuk's GPS tracker was indicating he was still on the move and due to arrive at the Kaltag checkpoint within the next few hours.

'But the message said my teammate had flown out to Unalakleet?'

Caley knitted her brow. She gave a tiny glance at the wall clock, keen to get on with the business of the day.

'Please re-check.'

Caley's eyes flared impatiently but she went off nevertheless. Not long afterwards she returned looking steely-faced and somewhat put out.

'I just went through all our records real well, Miss Kiglatuk. No one has any recollection of making a call to you and there's nothing in the books to suggest anyone did. I understand your concern, but your sledder is doing just fine. Like I said before, we're expecting Sammy Inukpuk at Kaltag early this evening. If you want, we can give you a call when he arrives or you could come back around six and wait. That way, when he calls in, you'll be there to speak to him in person.'

Edie tried to recall the phone message. Part of her wondered if, in her current state, she'd misinterpreted something, but every time she replayed the message in her mind, it seemed perfectly clear.

'Did you locate Derek at Unalakleet?'

Caley gave a peevish snort. 'Maybe you need to look harder at your team communications, ma'am. Mister Palliser,' she emphasized the 'Mister', 'went over to Council with his hosts last night, said he'd be back before lunch. We got a snowmachine going there in a couple minutes, if you want a ride over.'

Edie rubbed her forehead, trying to get something to make sense. Caley coughed. She was nearly out of patience. 'Thank you,' Edie said, 'that would be great.'

About five miles out, past the sink marking the workings from the old gold mines, past the Cold War remnants of the nuclear weapons facility on the Council Road, the driver of the snowmachine turned his head and shouted: 'Up ahead!'

Bobbing along the road towards them were two snowmobiles. On one sat a man, with a woman riding pillion behind. In her *amaut* there was a baby. A lone man was riding along beside them. She shouted into the ear of the driver and he began to signal the travellers up ahead. They slowed down until all three vehicles were stationary in the roadway, their engines idling.

Edie pulled off the hood of her parka. Derek looked at Zach in surprise before swinging from his machine and heading over, stamping the snow out of his boots as he came. She felt a great wave of relief crest, then flecks of white anger foaming off it.

She thanked her ride and tumbled out, trudging across to meet him.

'Edie, what the hell?' He looked worried.

'I could ask you the same question.'

There was a look of puzzlement on his face. He obviously didn't know what she was talking about.

'Zach got some time off so we drove over to Council to see some friends. We were going to stay for lunch but Zach got radioed. Someone found a dead musk-ox calf just outside Nome. A lot of blood. Looks like it was cut out of the mother. Most likely there's some hunters out there shooting off-season without permits. What's the big deal anyway? What are you doing here?'

When she told him about the message, his look of bewilderment deepened. 'We've got some kind of miscommunication. I told the folks at the Iditarod HQ where I'd be, left them a number. No one called.'

The driver tooted his horn, wanting to proceed.

Derek waved him on. He suggested they go directly back to Zach's house, try to sort out what had happened from there.

It was Megan who first noticed Edie's head. They were sitting in the living room, warming up with some hot sweet tea. While Megan applied seal oil to the wound, Edie told them what had happened to her. Derek listened, an expression between worry and anger on his face.

'Edie, you're crazy, you know that? Whether Galloway is guilty of killing those boys or not, this is a desperate man.'

'You don't say?'

Derek cut her an angry look. He was used to her taking chances. Last year, after she'd flown off to Greenland to confront a couple of geologists she thought knew something about the death of her stepson, he'd made her promise not to do anything so rash again. She'd warned him then that people didn't always keep their promises.

'Look, Police, I don't blame Galloway for running, I don't even blame him for thumping me on the head, though leaving me to the wolves wasn't too friendly. I needed to find out what he knew and now that I do, I'm not at all sure that Galloway did it.'

'Why are you so obsessed with this?'

Edie grimaced. The oil felt hot on her scalp. 'I found that little boy in the snow. That kid's got no one who wants to uncover the truth about how and why he died.'

'Except you, his knight in shining armour.' Derek wiped the back of his hand across his mouth. 'Maybe his kin already know the truth, Edie, they just aren't telling you. You think about that?'

Megan gave him a disapproving look. He raised his palms in response.

'Any idea where Galloway might be heading?' His tone was neutral now, the voice of an investigator.

'Anatoly told me he came from Canada originally. Maybe there?'

The door opened and Zach came in, stamping out the cold. Megan set the baby in her bouncer, greeted him then went to the kitchen to heat some water for tea. He sat down and rubbed his hands warm, then reached out and took his daughter into his lap.

'You find out who left the calf?' Derek asked.

Zach shook his head.

'Tourists come in for the Iditarod most likely. It happens. I put out a request to the hotels to let me know if they get anyone asking the kitchen to fry up musk-ox steaks.'

Zach bounced the baby up and down in his lap. When Megan arrived with hot tea, he passed her over and, turning to Derek, asked if he'd had any luck with the call.

'Nope.'

A thought came into Edie's head.

'Did the police department here get any further with their investigation into that Larsen guy's connections?'

Zach gave her a sorry look. 'We got the airport looking out for the scumbag pilot who flies the girls but he's probably just the gofer.'

'Larsen said Fonseca was the guy at the top.'

'Right,' Zach said. 'The same guy the Littlefish girl says fathered her son. Derek filled us in.'

'Did Larsen have any more information on Fonseca?'

'We got almost nothing useful out of that pissant. It wasn't like he wouldn't talk. By the time me and Derek here was done with him he was ready to betray his grandma. He just didn't know anything.'

'What about the girl, Larsen's . . .' she couldn't bring herself to say it '. . . whatever? She give out any leads, any other names?'

'We never found her and I don't think the Nome PD or any of the agencies looked too hard. A foreign national, probably got no papers, no records in this country, not someone people around here are gonna miss too much.'

'That stinks worse than a dog fart.'

Zach's brows moved up in a pained shrug. 'Welcome to my world. If the Nome PD had pressed it, they'd have had an investigative unit from Anchorage crawling all over them. Last thing they want. Why do you ask?'

'I'm just thinking maybe whoever made that call telling me to get up here must have been trying to distract me, get me to leave Anchorage.'

'You saying the Nome PD's behind that?'

'Uh nuh, no.'

Zach had started making funny faces at his daughter. The little girl was laughing and reaching out for his face. Maybe he was signalling that he didn't want to get too involved. Edie could see he was in a difficult position, caught between her and Derek and the Nome PD and she didn't want to push him. He had his kid to think about.

She remembered Aileen's warning in the Klondyke bar. The voice on the phone message hadn't sounded like Aileen's but voicemail could be distorting, so it was possible. Then there was Kathy, Detective Truro's assistant. The investigative unit down in Anchorage had behaved weirdly towards her from the start, trying to sculpt her testimony, get her to pump up the connection between the Believers and Lucas Littlefish's spirit house coffin. She considered other candidates. Natalia? Annalisa Littlefish? Then there was Schofield's assistant Sharon. Truth was, she just didn't know.

Breaking off from her thoughts she saw Derek coming towards her with a piece of paper in his hand.

'I thought to ring Stevie, get him to check if Galloway had any history in Canada.' Constable Steve Killik was Derek's subordinate up on Ellesmere Island, the only constable in a detachment of two, serving an area the size of Great Britain. He was holding the fort while Derek was away, which most of the time meant doing nothing because nothing happened in Kuujuaq. Steve was loyal and totally without ambition; both qualities, Edie always thought, which made him perfect for the job.

'The fella's more than he's giving out. He's Canadian, all right, out of Quebec City. Got himself involved in some biker gang about fifteen years ago, got done for a string of misdemeanours, passing bad cheques, that kind of thing. Twelve years ago there was some kind of feud between gangs and Galloway ended up breaking a rival gang member's legs with a baseball bat. He did three years, got out for good behaviour and was rearrested for cooking up meth. When the Mounties searched his house, just routine, they found a bunch of pornography featuring underage girls. He said it was his room-mate's, his roommate said it was his, nobody could prove anything either way, so he was done for the meth and cautioned for the other stuff. This is not a good guy.'

'Like I need reminding.' Edie's hand went to the sore spot on her head. A thought suddenly occurred to her, as though brought to the surface by the pain. When she'd asked Tommy Schofield if he knew Fonseca, he'd said he hadn't been following the story but the name Fonseca hadn't been mentioned in the press coverage of the story. No one apart from herself, TaniaLee and the investigators on the case had any reason to connect the name to Lucas Littlefish's death. Unless they had some inside information.

She said: 'What's the quickest way to Homer from here?'

Zach looked up. Edie saw his face stiffen, a moment of resolve come across it. From out of the corner of one eye she just caught Megan wrinkle her nose in silent agreement.

'In my Piper,' he said.

# 28

As they buffeted through a cloud wall, Zach dropped the plane a couple of hundred feet and in the seat behind, Derek tensed and went silent. His fists were balled and his mouth was a streak of pure tension. Zach checked in his rear mirror and chuckled. 'Hey, Edie, looks like we got ourselves a fly-baby.'

They'd come up with a plan on the ground in Nome. Edie had put in a call to Schofield's office as tourist development officer Maggie Inukpuk. Schofield's assistant Sharon had answered the phone and said that the developer was away on business for an indeterminate time and couldn't be contacted. It was beginning to look as though that was just a polite way of saying the man had gone into hiding. The plan was for Edie to head over to Schofield's offices anyway. But if they couldn't hunt down the man himself, they might find something among his papers. After that, Edie and Derek intended to rent a truck and head over to his cabin in the woods above the town. If the man himself wasn't there, then evidence of his activities might well be.

Beneath them the land slid by, green etched in white. They were crossing over Lake Clark wilderness now, heading southeast towards Homer. Ahead of them the frozen expanse of Cook Inlet dazzled. Zach pulled up his headphones, tuned in to the radio frequency for the flight control at Homer airstrip and announced himself. She saw his face brace, his nostrils flaring, a ticking start up in the muscle of his jaw. He flashed a look at Derek, and then took a longer look at Edie in his mirror. His voice sounded tinny against the whine of the engine.

'There's been some kind of incident down at Homer, they got the coastguard and the police out there. We're gonna have to land on the ice, but we might have to do a few circuits before we get cleared.' He sounded calm but you could see from the pulse in his forehead that he wasn't. Break-up was only a couple of weeks away. To land on the ice this late in the season was horribly risky but to turn back to the landing strip at Kalifornsky or risk landing across the bay at Seldovia would put them miles away from Homer and with no way of getting to the town. For a moment all three caught each other's gaze. They were all thinking the same thing.

*What the hell are we doing?*

For fifteen minutes, the Piper circled high above Kachemak Bay, banking over the glaciated bowls of the Kenai Mountains, scooping over Halibut Cove to the neck of the bay at Razdolna. They needed to land on a patch of smooth ice in the channel, clear of the pressure ridges where the shore-fast ice met the moving pack nearer to the coast. The plane lost altitude, Zach scanning the ice and waiting for permission for the final descent into the area. When the call came through, Zach turned the little plane in towards the long needle of Homer Spit and they began dropping through cloud. On the ground at Homer Spit they could see the flashing lights of the police and coastguard. Below them, the Kachemak ice pan stared.

Zach shouted over the engine buzz, 'It's gonna be a bumpy landing.'

They were parallel to the ice now, moments from touching down. In the passenger seat, Derek was rapid-blinking, trying to control his breath. Then the skis hit and the frame gave an almighty groan and they were bouncing at speed across the sea ice. Zach pulled in the engine and the plane shuddered and slowed and they came to a gradual stop. Zach leaned in to Derek and slapped him on the back.

'How's our fly-baby doing?'

Derek returned the slap with the kind of shoulder punch that wasn't as jokey as it might seem. 'Never been better.'

'Copy that,' said Zach.

They waited beside the plane for transport and not long afterwards a snow coach in coastguard livery came bobbing along the ice towards them. A man got out and peeled off his snow goggles. Zach gave a little whoop.

'Chris Taluak, you old dog. They didn't tell me.'

Taluak said, 'So now you got a nice surprise.' Laughing, he grabbed Zach's arm with both hands and shook the hell out of it. He was a native man, deeply wind-burned, with spiked hair and teeth that looked like they'd been chipped from a berg. 'That there was a landing. You got lucky. A couple of minutes later, they'd have sent you back to Soldotna or someplace. It's a mess back there.' He strode around the back of the snow coach and opened up the luggage hold. Taluak showed them into the coach, keyed the ignition and as they began to bump along the ice he told them what had happened.

Sometime in the predawn, around 4.15, a chartered Fairchild had taken off from Homer for Sitka on what had gone down in the flight logs as a routine cargo flight. Twenty minutes out of Homer the pilot made a distress call to say that the plane had run into a flock of geese, the engines had stalled, they were losing altitude and he was going to try to make an emergency landing at Chenega Bay. The airport official in turn contacted the coastguard, who requested details of the cargo. Routine procedure, to make sure there was nothing dangerous on board. The plane checked out as having been leased to Aurora Logistics, a subsidiary of Hallstrom Enterprises, for a cargo of wood veneer. Coastguard assumed it was material to be used in refurbing Hallstrom's cruise liners when they came up to Sitka in May and duly sent out a Jayhawk to pick up the pilot and co-pilot. Taluak had been cage operator.

When the coastguard reached the site, they were startled to see, along with the pilot and co-pilot, a man and a woman huddled together. Neither the pilot nor the manifest had mentioned passengers. Taluak's colleague, Don Harrington, a Homer native and sixteen-year veteran of the coastguard search and rescue, winched down to assess the situation and to evacuate what appeared to be two crew and two passengers. As he neared he radioed up to say the woman was holding a baby in her arms trying to protect it from the up-draught with her body.

There was something about this story that was beginning to make Edie's spine prickle. She threw a look at Derek, who returned it.

Taluak went on.

'We thought better of questioning anyone until we were safely back in Homer but in the meantime neither Don nor me could get any of those folk we'd just rescued to make eye contact, which we thought was pretty weird given that we'd just saved their lives.'

Pulling up at the airport terminus, Taluak now cut the engine and came round to the luggage portal.

Tod, the pilot, had taken the precaution of radioing in to request police attend the helicopter's arrival. 'It seemed like the woman overheard the request and began to panic. She was shoutin' and screamin' that they'd done nothing wrong. By the time we got to Homer she was near hysterical. When the Homer PD approached her she tried to run out of the terminal building clutching the baby.

Police thought it was better not to try to move her. They're still in here questioning them.'

Edie and Derek exchanged glances once more. Taluak handed Edie her pack. Outside in the parking lot there were three patrol cars and a coastguard truck. A few troopers were standing around waiting for something to happen. The coastguard helicopter was parked a way off near the runway.

'You folks down here for some recreation?'

'Thought I'd show 'em some of our famous Alaskan hospitality,' Zach said.

Taluak tipped his hat and gave a little grimace.

'Sorry to say, you folks aren't getting the best of us right now.'

They walked up the steps into the terminal building and were met by a uniform, who asked them for ID, then seemed to lose interest and waved them through.

They waited for Zach to sign off on his flight forms. Taluak grinned. 'What's Zach got in mind for ya? Glacier skiing? Cross-country? We got great ice-fishing round here.'

Edie cut a glance to either side. The terminal building was built in an L shape, the short arm being given over to luggage facilities and a waiting room, and the longer arm comprising offices. Excusing herself to use the bathroom, she made directly for the administrative section. The doors had glass peepholes. In the first two offices senior airport officials sat at their desks talking on phones. The third was empty but in the fourth there was a short, wiry-haired woman in her mid-forties turning her parka string over and over in her hands. She looked like she'd been doing a lot of crying. There was no one else in the corridor. Plucking Patricia Gomez's ID from her pocket, Edie knocked on the door and went in.

The woman looked up. In a voice thick with sorrow, she said, 'Where have you put my baby?'

Edie flashed the ID. She didn't even have to introduce herself. The woman showed no sign of caring who she was.

'We're taking good care of the baby,' Edie said. 'You want to tell me what happened?'

The woman looked up wearily.

'I've been through this a dozen times already.'

Edie pulled up a chair across the table from her. They were in some kind of meeting room, with a long board table and matching plastic chairs. A screen in the corner was silently playing the weather channel.

'In that case, I guess one more time won't make much difference to you. I'm sorry, Mrs . . .' Edie rubbed her eyes, as though exhausted from the morning's events. 'How d'you spell your name again?'

The woman looked tired and irritated. 'Which. Darlie or Stegner?' On Edie's prompting, she spelled out her last name.

'And your husband . . . ?'

'Morris.' She spelled out the letters. 'Like I said, he runs a franchise of farm equipment stores out of Heartland.'

Edie smiled encouragingly.

'It was all arranged on the phone.' She hesitated. 'Morris arranged it. We were told to buy a regular fly-drive package in Anchorage over the period of the Iditarod. They told us to drive down to Homer and gave us a location to go to.'

'Which was?'

'I already told you guys, some place in the boonies. They said the baby'd be there.'

'They?'

'I don't know any names. There was one guy who spoke regular and another who had some kind of foreign accent.' She leaned forward. Her eyes had a pleading look. 'Look, they said the little boy was an orphan, that we were doing him a favour taking him.'

'I'm guessing this was the kind of favour you pay for.'

The woman drew a hand over her face and looked away.

She said, simply, 'My husband dealt with the money side. If I'd have known there was something wrong about it . . .' She tailed off. Her eyes watered with tears then brimmed over. For a moment, Edie just allowed her to sob. 'You have no idea how hard we've tried. The endless fertility treatment, then the adoption agencies. There was always something. You're too white-collar, you're too old.'

Edie said, 'I heard India and China were the places to go for people like you. Maybe Central America too.' She'd seen a TV show about it.

Darlie Stegner was shaking her head.

'We didn't want that.'

Edie's brow wrinkled up involuntarily. 'Because you wanted a white kid?'

The woman took in a deep breath, but she did not look at Edie. 'Because we wanted a kid who could have passed for ours.'

Edie tutted. 'Hard to come by, nice, perfect little white babies.'

Darlie Stegner looked down at her hands. 'It's not what you think.'

'No,' Edie said, 'it never is.'

A man in coastguard uniform came by the door, peered in and, without acknowledging them, checked his watch. Edie sensed he was waiting for someone.

'You notice anything unusual on the kid when you picked him up? A tattoo?'

Darlie Stegner looked up, surprised.

'I just assumed it was something the orphanage put there.'

'The orphanage?'

The woman nodded.

'Yeah,' she said, as though this all made perfect sense. 'The orphanage where he came from. In Russia.'

'Right.' Edie couldn't tell if the woman was lying just to her, or to herself too. She dived in her pack and brought out a notebook and pencil and drew the tattoo.

'Did it look something like this?'

Darlie Stegner hesitated.

Edie said, 'You're in a lot of trouble, lady. It's best you cooperate.'

Stegner reached for the pad, nodded and handed it back.

'You know what it means?'

'It means "mine," Edie said, 'that's as in *not yours.*'

Edie put the pad back in her pack then walked to the door, peeped out of the glass to make sure no one was coming and reached out for the handle.

'Thanks, Mrs Stegner. You've been real helpful.'

She walked back along the corridor. Zach Barefoot and Chris Taluak had disappeared and Derek was waiting on his own. He smiled thinly at her.

'I just remembered something I didn't tell you before. One of the girls I met in Anchorage, the sex workers? She had a kid, a baby actually. It was like she was hiding him, like she was scared someone would take him away.'

Edie gave him a beady look. 'Your brain fall off the cliff the same time as your precious lemmings?'

Derek held up his hands in a gesture of surrender.

Edie said, 'You think you could find her again when we get back to Anchorage?'

# 29

Chris Taluak opened the door to his garage. Sitting inside in the gloom was an old-style Land Rover. Derek and Edie peered in.

'There you go.' Taluak slapped his hand on the hood. 'Marriage material. What she ain't got in looks she makes up for in low maintenance. We been together fifteen years and she still runs like a young 'un.' Chuckling at his own joke he held out the key and turning to Edie said, 'You driving, lady?'

Derek stepped up and swiped the keys from Taluak's hand.

'Edie doesn't drive. She bulldozes.'

Derek drove. They turned along the main drag, past the museum on one side, the gas station and Safeway on the other.

Derek said, 'You think Schofield was running the Lodge in Meadow Lake as an underage brothel?'

'We've pretty much established that.'

They looked at one another. There was a look of disgust on Derek's face. He wiped a hand over his forehead and across his hair. 'What I'm thinking is too fucked up.' He pulled into the verge and pulled up the handbrake. 'It wasn't just an underage brothel, was it?'

Edie took in a deep breath which expanded in her chest like water turning to ice. 'You know what I think? I think the girls had kids and Schofield sold them to infertile couples desperate for perfect white babies.' It was an unbearable thought. Children raped to produce more children, human beings sold like farm animals. But if nowhere else, within its own frame of reference, it made sense. 'The word the girl drew on our windshield, the little tattoo template I found in the trash at the Lodge, the one that was on Jonny Doe was also on the infant the Stegners were trying to buy when they got caught this morning.'

It all seemed clear now. Edie had seen Tommy Schofield's particular brand of ruthless opportunism before. He was the kind of man who flourished in places with few controls and almost limitless opportunities, a man who had made the step from thinking he could own land to imagining he could do the same with human beings, the kind of frontiersman whose psychopathic tendencies had for years been tolerated because they brought results.

Like any business, this one depended on supply and demand. There would be a network of men and women whose perverted sexual needs or warped sense of entitlement to parenthood only he could satisfy. Edie guessed Schofield's clients would be wide-ranging and diverse, but they would have one thing in common: their willingness to turn a blind eye.

Derek started the engine again and turned onto the road that led to the Spit. They drove up the Spit past the souvenir stores and chandleries towards the offices of Schofield Developments. Derek jammed on the brakes and slowed. A man in uniform appeared to be loitering outside.

'You see that?'

Edie peered out. 'They already got an alarm in there. Control panel's inside. He's using the same security detail up at the Lodge.' She gave him a quizzical look. 'What does he need extra security there for?'

'We're about to find out,' Derek said.

The security guard standing outside the blue clapboard building looked like the mean kind. He was a huge, hard-bodied guy in his late twenties, some Indian blood, a surly expression on his face. Edie watched Derek paste on his best friendly smile, introduce himself and pull his police badge from his pocket. While the guard scrutinized it, squinting in the cool wind, Derek checked his name tag. Eric Fleetfoot.

Fleetfoot's eyes narrowed. 'Where you come from? I ain't never heard of Ellesmere Island.'

Derek had already anticipated this. His eyes widened and he smiled indulgently.

'For real?'

Fleetfoot flashed him a look. It wasn't pretty.

'That thing that happened this morning, they seconded me in on the investigations team.'

Eric Fleetfoot looked off into the distance, shrugged. 'You gonna need a warrant to search Mr Schofield's office.'

Derek laughed. It sounded phony but Fleetfoot didn't seem to notice.

'We're not interested in your boss. But that alarm he's got in there? Something's tripped it. It's not sounding out here, but it keeps flashing at the alarm company. They called the PD. I was on my way over the Spit anyway, said I'd give you a heads-up. Either you got a loose circuit in there, bud, or someone's been in.'

Fleetfoot looked sceptical for a second, then relieved. He pulled a ring of keys from a chain stashed in the pocket of his parka, swung around to the front door of Schofield's office and let himself in. Derek moved forward.

'I'm gonna help you here.' He reached out and took the door from Fleetfoot, stepped inside. 'You want I stay up front to keep an eye on things while you check the control panel?' Fleetfoot turned and sized him up, then grunted a yes.

Derek went to the door and signalled with his finger. A second or two later, Edie's face appeared around the door. She slid inside and into the corridor leading to Schofield's office. Moments later she reappeared carrying a stack of files. Derek waited until she was back inside the Land Rover, then he shouted out to Fleetfoot from the front door, 'Oh hey, you know what?'

Fleetfoot appeared around the door. 'What? I ain't finished yet.'

'That's just too bad, bud, because I am.'

# 30

Sitting in Taluak's truck as they wound up the hill towards the forested ridge above Homer, Edie read the estimate she'd pulled out of Schofield's drawer. The paper bore the name Meadow Lake Construction and was addressed to Schofield Developments. It referred to 'Improvements to Lodge at Meadow Lake'. The signature at the bottom belonged to Gregor Nodgorov.

'The man was going to have a dorm built for trafficked girls. You'd think he'd have done it on the wink,' Edie said.

'Tax write-off. The fella's a businessman, remember?'

He pulled the wheel around a pile of drift. A pair of loons flew across the road, calling to each other with a haunting *ha-oo*. 'It's documentary proof he owns the Lodge, even if it doesn't prove he knew what was going on there.'

They came to a row of mailboxes. Edie said, 'Turn left here.' Derek slowed and took the turn. She thought back to the moment she'd felt the ghostly presence of the spirit bear. She could smell him now. A warm, musky scent at odds with the crisp, medicinal odour of pine resin. 'A week ago I wouldn't have been able to do this.'

'Do what?'

'*This.* Direct us through the forest.'

The contours of the land no longer looked the same to her. From among the spruce she could now pick out alder, western hemlock, aspen, cottonwood and feltleaf willow. Without warning, an image of Lucas Littlefish's frozen body sprang into her mind and an odd, choking sound bubbled up from her belly so that she had to blink hard and swallow in order to gather herself.

'There was an itemized phone bill on Schofield's desk.'

Derek's gaze briefly left the road. He shot her an expectant look.

'My number was on it.'

Derek made a clicking sound in his throat. 'You gave the guy your *phone number*?' His tone of voice said *just one more crazy*.

'I guess I must have done when I went to see him. Either that, or he got it from the Iditarod office.'

There was a pause, then Derek said, 'Edie, Schofield didn't know you had any connection to the Iditarod.'

This was true.

He carried on, 'He must know something's up, or there wouldn't be a security detail outside his office.' Derek reached over and checked the glove compartment for Megan Avuluq's service pistol then flipped his head to indicate the Remington 308 hunting rifle they'd borrowed from Taluak lying on the seat behind. 'We may be needing these two.'

They drove on awhile. Otis Littlefish had said the developer's cabin was on a dog-leg bend in the road at the top of the hill a couple of miles from them. Edie was pretty confident she could find it. At a smaller track branching off to the right, she told Derek to keep driving straight. They soon came to a hollow covered in crab apple and dogwood. A buck moose burst from the undergrowth and lumbered across the track. Edie reached around for the rifle and felt Derek's hand on her arm.

'Sorry, old habits.'

The moose stared at them for an instant then disappeared back into the forest. The track rose on a soft incline. At its apex, they found what had to be Tommy Schofield's cabin. They drove past then pulled the Land Rover into the verge a little way along, took up their weapons and tromped back in deep drift through the trees around the side of the property.

The cabin was a fancier, uglier affair than the Littlefishes', made not of uncut logs caulked together in the traditional way but from some kind of treated cinder block, a style more suited to the suburbs of Anchorage than the middle of the forest. A garage sat beside the cabin and behind it was what looked like a meat cache and field-dressing shed. Fresh footprints led from the cabin to the garage and there were tyre tracks on the driveway leading out but no sign that anyone was still inside. Evidently, the Homer PD hadn't yet made the connection between Schofield and the Stegners, which wasn't altogether surprising since Schofield had been canny enough to use an intermediary while the Stegners seemed unable to recall any real names of the people they dealt with.

From their position in among the trees they could see through the French windows at the back of the property. They moved cautiously forward in hunter's gait, low and with their knees bent until they got to the edge of the trees, then slipped across the cleared area and flattened themselves against the side of the cabin. To the right of where Edie was standing there was a small window. She cupped her hand around her face and peered in to a simple bathroom. From the brand of shampoo in the shower and the shaving foam on the wooden shelf beneath the mirror, it was clear that a man lived here alone.

They slipped around to the back of the property, then reaching the French windows they peered in. There was a bottle of Scotch on the coffee table and a single glass. Edie sensed that the room had been recently occupied. Next to the Scotch sat a recent photograph of Schofield beside a halibut almost as tall as himself. To one side, towering over Schofield, stood Byron Hallstrom.

They retraced their steps. As they were about to turn to the front of the property, Edie caught a flash of yellow out of the corner of her eye. She turned her head and went over to the field-dressing shed. On a shelf under the window stood a can of bright yellow paint. She went over to the log splitter, pulled out the axe and went back over to the door of the shed. Hearing the sound, Derek came running up.

'What are you doing?'

She raised the axe, chopped the padlock and popped the twisted metal in his hand. Then she yanked open the door. The raw, ferrous smell of old blood hit her nostrils like a bad clam hits the belly. Inside, a tangle of meat hooks hung from the ceiling. On a shelf to one side, a line of assorted animal skulls stared out, their pelts hanging companionably to one side. A series of knives clung to a magnetic strip above the stained dressing table. In a corner were an empty blood bucket and several pairs of gloves. The floor and walls had recently been wiped down, the swooshes made by the cloth still visible.

A paintbrush rested on top of the yellow paint can, still smelling of turpentine. Below the shelf was a work table. Edie crouched until her eye line was level with the wood. The table had been scrubbed and smelled like the paintbrush.

'Sex trafficker, baby smuggler and spirit-house carpenter,' Derek said darkly. 'Is there anything our man can't do?'

Edie pressed her lips together and swallowed hard. 'Get away with it.'

They went around to the front door of the main cabin. It was locked, but there was no deadbolt and the lock gave way easily.

Edie took a deep breath and drew herself up. A look passed between them.

Derek said, 'I'll start in the bedroom.' She flashed him a smile of thanks. From what she already knew of Tommy Schofield, the man's bedroom wasn't somewhere she wanted to be.

She began at the back of the living room, near the tiny kitchenette, turning over everything lying on the floor, then pulling out drawers and cupboards, peering under chairs and running her fingers along the rough plank floor, feeling for something, anything, that might turn out to be of significance and finding nothing. She worked her way methodically round the room until coming to an old battered leather easy chair in the corner. Lying to one side of the chair was a souvenir ashtray from Kodiak Island and inside it the abandoned stub of a cigar. She picked up the ashtray. Beneath lay the cigar wrappers. Sammy had smoked all through their marriage and she'd become used to clearing away the leavings. Checking herself she put it down again.

Derek emerged with something in his hand and passed it to her. It was a yearbook picture of freshmen students at Homer High School. Edie cast her eye along the rows of young faces until she came to one she recognized.

TaniaLee Littlefish.

All of a sudden, it was as though she had moved beyond the treeline and could see out across the tundra. Her heart quickened, her throat closed and she felt a sweat break out on her brow. Going back to the ashtray she removed a cigar wrapper and checked a small, diamond-shaped paper label attached to it.

'Derek, I think I got something.'

The policeman came over and took the wrapper from her hands.

'Well I'll be damned.' In red writing stamped onto a gold background was the word 'Fonseca'.

'Cuban,' he said. 'Pretty rare.'

The light was beginning to fade as they drove back into Homer. The remains of the sun sat rosy on the hill to the west of the town and an easterly breeze blew spruce branches briefly into the orange motes from the street lamps. Across Kachemak, they could see the odd sparkle at Halibut Cove and Jakolof Bay and the lights along Homer Spit dazzled off the sea ice and gave the thin fang of land a glow all its own.

Chris Taluak was waiting for them back at his house with a bowl of sticky salmon roe and bottles of ice-cold beer and cans of soda. The coastguard's house was modest but cosy. Logs smouldered in the stove. Taluak had built it himself from cedar way back when Homer was just a tiny pioneer town with a halibut fishery attached.

'How was the hunting?'

'We got what we came for,' Edie said.

Derek shot her a warning look and rapidly changed the subject. 'That business this morning sorted out?'

Taluak shrugged. 'We handed it over to the PD.' There was a pause, which Taluak filled by slapping his knees and asking if anyone wanted another drink. He came back in a few minutes later with a new set of frosted tankards, which he put down in front of them.

'I don't know what happened to my manners,' Taluak said. Edie dumped her soda into a tankard, then curled her right hand over the glass, enjoying the burn of the ice crystals as they melted on her fingers.

'You guys heading back up to Nome tomorrow?'

'Guess so,' Derek replied.

A log spat sparks on the hearth. Taluak went over and poked at it.

'Pretty exciting Iditarod this year,' he said, by way of making conversation. 'I was just watching on the TV. I got twenty bucks on Steve Nicols. A couple of days back I thought he couldn't lose. Nicols was steamin' ahead. But now, I don't know. He seems to have lost his edge. He's not careful, Duncan Wright's gonna lick him.'

He rattled on. Edie had stopped listening. She picked up the frosted tankard and turned it slowly in her hand. The surface was smooth, the light coating of frost crisp and matt under the fingers like frozen whale skin. Her mind flashed back to the pattern of ice crystals on Lucas Littlefish's skin where it had been crushed from contact with the embroidered cloth. She remembered the freezer in Schofield's office. Then she thought about Sharon. Her focus turned outwards. She blinked. Chris Taluak was saying something to her, his face so close to hers that she could smell the warm scent of beer from his breath.

'Oh I forgot,' she said, over him. 'A friend of mine in Anchorage gave me something to give to her pal, Sharon, and I haven't done it.'

Taluak looked peeved at the interruption. Edie caught his eye and tried to rustle up a calming smile.

'I can't remember her last name, but our friend told me she's an executive assistant. Works for a man named Tommy Schofield. You wouldn't know?'

Taluak thought for a moment. Something clicked and he held up the index finger of his right hand. 'I'm guessing that'll be Sharon Steadman,' he said. 'Used to work as a beautician with my wife.' He checked himself with a bitter little laugh. 'Ex-wife.' He pressed his spoon into the salmon roe, brought up a heaped spoonload, jammed it into his mouth and began chewing. 'Small town. Everyone here knows pretty much everyone else. They got heavy snow forecast for tonight, but we can go visit Sharon in the morning, no problem.'

Edie smiled. 'Nothing like now. In any case, Sharon's not the morning type.'

Sharon Steadman lived in an apartment in an undistinguished building just down from the Homer Museum. It wasn't yet 9 p.m. but she came to the door in a pink bathrobe and pink slippers.

Behind her, Edie could see she had a pink thing going on all over her apartment.

'Hey,' Edie said simply.

Sharon squinted first at Edie then at Derek, then back at Edie again. Recognition began to dawn on her face. She reached out and grasped the door lintel, blocking entry.

'I have nothing to say to you.'

'I have nothing to say to you either.' Edie paused, glanced at Derek. 'But we both have plenty to say to your boss. I guess you realize he's in danger.'

Sharon glanced at her feet. Her skin flushed and she bit her lower lip. When she looked up, Edie could see there were tears in her eyes.

'Honestly? He asked me to leave that message on your phone. I have no idea what's going on. I haven't seen Mr Schofield in three days.'

Derek took a step forward. Sharon tensed. For a moment she looked afraid. He brought out his Ellesmere Island police ID. She scrutinized it but didn't ask any questions.

'We need to get inside Schofield's office. We're not interested in any of his papers, we just want to look inside the building.'

Sharon looked up at Derek. 'Mr Schofield gave me the number of a security firm to call, asked me to set up a guard.'

'You think you can persuade the guard to let us through?'

She looked at her slippers again and nodded. He was good, Edie thought, just the right mix of gentleness and authority.

'How's about you put on some clothes and we'll just go right on over?'

Sharon bit her lip, her eyes wide and watery. She looked so lost and terrified that for a moment Edie felt sorry for her. Then she remembered Lucas Littlefish and Jonny Doe and the feeling went away.

The fluorescent overhead light flickered on in the offices of Schofield Developments. Edie walked through the door and into the corridor where the freezer stood. She opened up her Leatherman and flipped open the pick. Within seconds she had the padlock open. Pushing up the lid she felt the sudden suck then the hard pulse of air at −20C on human skin. A light shone up, illuminating the icy layer around the freezer walls. She glanced over at Sharon. The girl was clueless: this part of Schofield's activities she knew nothing about.

As Edie expected, the freezer was empty. The appliance hadn't been defrosted in a long while. Her eyes scoped across the surface of the interior, clear now what she was looking for. The ice was evenly encrusted, suggesting that the chest hadn't been full for a long time, maybe ever. Nonetheless, when you looked closer there were places here and there, small indentations, where the surface of the ice had been disturbed, the crystals compressed or crushed. She switched on her flashlight and began meticulously scanning her eye in the Inuit way, in ever-decreasing circles, around each indentation until she found what she was looking for – a tiny, almost invisible, tuft of superfine black hair. Baby hair. She closed the freezer back up and refitted the padlock. Nothing she didn't already know, but it was good to get confirmation.

Sharon was staring anxiously at her. She seemed drifty and dissociated, as though she was in a state of shock. Edie reached out and clasped her arm. It was an old Inuit custom she had picked up as a child from her mother. When it really mattered that someone answered a question honestly, you made sure you were in contact with them before you asked it. Made it tougher for people to lie.

'Sharon, what do you know about Lucas Littlefish?'

The girl's brow furrowed. She shrank back.

'You need to go see the Littlefishes,' was all she said.

# 31

The moon bathed the ice across Kachemak Bay in soft, silver light. Edie stared at it in the side-view mirror of the Land Rover as they ground their way back up onto the forested ridge where the Littlefishes' cabin stood.

Annalisa Littlefish came to the door with her sleeves rolled up, smelling of meat. There was blood on her oilcloth apron and her hands looked like two raw steaks. Her upper lip was beaded with sweat. For a moment or two she just stood there, resting her hands on her apron and gave no sign of recognizing Edie.

'Mrs Littlefish?' Edie held out her hand. Annalisa Littlefish squinted a little. Bad eyesight, Edie thought. She wiped her right hand on her apron, as if she was about to take Edie's, then thought better of the idea.

'Yeah, I remember you.'

Derek got out of the truck and stood smiling.

'This is my friend, Derek Palliser.'

'Mr Littlefish in?'

Annalisa maintained her impassive stare. Her jaw set tight and there was hurt in her eyes.

'Nope, he been hunting. Goes off to the bar afterwards to brag about it. I'm out at the back kitchen, field dressing.'

'What you got?' Edie said. A little of the old hunting fire coursed around her blood.

'You come round at ten at night to ask me that?' She flashed Edie an indignant look. 'Blacktail, since you're asking.'

Edie swung round to Derek. 'You need a hand? Me and Derek can have it all butchered up in no time.'

Annalisa shook her head. She'd already played friendly with Edie once and didn't seem willing to repeat the experience. There was nothing for it except to get right to the point.

'Mrs Littlefish, I saw the picture of Lucas at Thanksgiving. I saw his body. I know your grandson had already been dead months before I found him.'

Annalisa gulped. Her head snapped back. The skin on her face looked grey-green in the moonlight.

'Please, Mrs Littlefish.'

Annalisa was breathing heavily now. She was shaking. All of a sudden her legs seemed to go from under her. Derek leapt forward and caught her as she fell. She came to on the sofa. Her eyes were vacant for a second, then they filled with fear.

'I knew this would get out eventually. I told Otis it would.' Rocking slightly to and fro she brushed her hands across her apron. 'That Detective Truro came and talked to us, right at the beginning, but he didn't ask about Lucas's birthday and we didn't tell him. I guess he got the hospital records so maybe he knew, but whichever, he didn't say nothing about it. A while later he left a message for us to call him back. We didn't get back to him but no one never followed up on it.'

'Detective Truro is off the case,' Derek said.

'Off?'

Edie jumped in. 'We think maybe he stopped doing what he was told and got himself suspended.'

There was a rustling sound from outside. Annalisa looked up. Derek went to check. The two women heard the truck door slam.

A couple of minutes later, Derek was back, carrying Taluak's Remington. Annalisa looked up and registered the weapon. She gave Derek a sideways look.

'I shut up the shed for you. It was just an old porcupine out there.'

Annalisa grunted.

Edie said, 'Mrs Littlefish, you told me when we first met that you didn't know who Lucas's father was. We're pretty sure now it was Tommy Schofield.'

Annalisa looked up suddenly, eyes flashing. 'You think I don't know that.' Her mouth formed a tight, angry line. 'I know that.' She began to cry, then, picking herself up, she leaned forward, resting on her elbows, her voice lowered. 'Now you listen to me, no one killed anyone. My grandson died a cot death. TaniaLee discovered the body and it drove her crazy. She was crazy with grief.' Annalisa's face seemed to swell then. The rims of her eyes reddened. She looked down at her hands, trying to steady herself. 'Why would you understand?' Her tone was despairing.

Edie closed her eyes. 'I understand, Mrs Littlefish, believe me.'

But Annalisa wasn't listening. She carried on. 'Tommy took Lucas away. He said they would blame TaniaLee, say she did it in one of her crazy spells. I don't know, maybe he didn't want an investigation, didn't want anyone finding out he was the father.'

'Did you know your daughter was seeing Tommy, Mrs Littlefish?' Annalisa bowed her head. It was answer enough.

Derek said, 'Your daughter was thirteen years old.' His voice was full of disgust.

Annalisa whirled round to face him, her eyes flashing.

'Mister, I was thirteen years old when I married Otis Littlefish. Might not have been official according to them folks down in Juneau, but if you'd asked me I woulda said me and Otis was married.' Her face took on a softer expression. 'He might look like some old cripple to you and me, but TaniaLee loved that man. Pass any judgement you like, but I know my grandson was born out of love.' She sighed. 'Any case, we wouldna been able to say nothing even if we'd had a mind to. Otis gets work from Mr Schofield and we need the money.'

'Mr Schofield ever tell you what else he was up to, Mrs Littlefish?' Derek snorted. 'Aside from love, I mean.'

He's a developer, that's all he said and all I knew. He had some crazy scheme to put buildings all over Kachemak Bay.'

Edie flashed Derek a warning look not to go any further. Some things the family didn't need to know right now. They'd find out soon enough.

Annalisa went on. 'It was Tommy paid for TaniaLee to go to that place she's in first time. She got out a couple of times, one time around the same period you found Lucas. The police picked her up and she told them that story about her boy. I don't know whether she cooked that up with Tommy or where she got it.' She looked Edie directly in the eye, her expression almost infinitely sad.

'Did you know what happened to Lucas's body between the time Tommy Schofield took him away and the time I found him?'

Annalisa shook her head. Edie leaned in and took her hand, but Annalisa moved it off. A faraway look came into her face. 'His spirit went to heaven, that's all I know.'

Derek said, 'Mrs Littlefish, you know where Tommy Schofield might be right now?'

Her face hardened. 'Don't know, not so sure as I care,' she said. 'Caused us enough trouble.'

In the silence that followed, Edie and Derek both stood to leave.

Edie said, 'You want us to stop off wherever Otis is, tell him we had this conversation?'

Annalisa shook her head. 'I don't need the trouble. Otis asks about the tyre marks, I'll say it was a couple of duck hunters stopped for directions.'

She waited for them to leave, then they heard the door lock.

Back on the track, the wind whirled little eddies of ice but by the time they reached the top of the ridge the air had cleared some. Below them, the lights of Homer blinked and sparkled and beyond these the broad arm of Kachemak Bay stretched out silver in the moonlight all the way to the ocean.

'Let me get out,' Edie said. She felt bruised, as though something was inside her trying to punch its way out. 'I need to be in the open for a moment.'

She jumped from the truck and landed in the hard, compacted drift at the side of the road. Steadying herself, she reached out to the ground and it was then that she saw it, dark grey in the moonlight. A tyre track, made within the last few hours, and from the same model of vehicle as had driven out of Tommy Schofield's cabin earlier that day.

It might be coincidence. Then again, it might not. She called to Derek who got down from the truck and inspected the tracks.

'Won't hurt to follow. One of us will have to stay down here on the ground, though,' Derek said, volunteering himself as the tracker. It was cold and the wind made it feel colder. 'Can't see zip from up there in the driver's seat.'

Edie followed the tracks with her eyes. 'You know the way I drive, Derek. I'd like to get out of this with at least one of us still alive.'

They followed the tracks her way, with Edie walking along the side of the road, pausing every so often to make sure they were still chasing the same set, Derek idling the truck up behind her. They turned a blind bend and just ahead, in a break in the forest, the tracks appeared to veer off the main road between the trees.

Signalling for Derek to pull over, she swung open the passenger door and pulled out the rifle borrowed from Taluak. Derek went first, diving confidently into the forest with a flashlight in one hand, the other resting on Megan Avuluq's service pistol. From the state of the thin new ice, which had gathered around the edges of the tracks where the heat from the truck had melted the snow, Edie guessed the truck had made its way up the path around 6 or 7 p.m. They crept along among the spruce, the path so narrow now that they could see where the sides of the truck had brushed snow off branches, or snapped them altogether. Whoever had driven up the path had been careless or else in a big hurry.

After a while, the path widened and came to an end in a tiny clearing. To one side of the clearing stood a hunting hide and there was a fire ring poking out of the snow beside it but neither the hide nor fire had been used in a good while. From here, the tyre tracks plunged directly back into the forest, swerving crazily between the spruce, leaving broken branches and pine cones scattered all around. Whoever had been driving the truck then had either been in one hell of a panic or in some other way out of his mind. Not far into the trees, they caught a glimpse of the outline of the truck itself, picked out in dappled moonlight, leaning at a strange angle where the front wheel on the passenger side had caught in some kind of gulley.

They approached with care, hands on weapons. A few metres from the vehicle Derek called out, but there was no answer. The area around the truck had been cleared of snow in a hurry. Or maybe there had been some kind of scuffle. Either way, the snow had been kicked about and it was impossible to discern any discrete footprints in it. Derek called out again. Once more, nothing. He turned to Edie and whispered,

'You ready for this?'

They moved forward slowly, tensed, weapons drawn and ready. Derek swung his flashlight through the interior of the vehicle. The air inside seemed milky but there was no one there. The door on the driver's side was unlocked. As Edie opened it she was hit by the smell of stale cigar smoke. In the ashtray the nub of a cigar lay, extinguished. She scoped around and found nothing else until she opened the glove compartment. Inside was a key on a ring. She pulled it out, turned the tab of the ring over in her hand. The word Cessna was printed on it in raised letters. She ducked out of the vehicle and dangled the key for Derek to see.

'He wanted to get far away, you would have thought he would have gone in his plane.'

'Maybe there was nowhere his plane could take him that would have been far enough.' Derek looked puzzled.

Edie went on, 'You want to get away from everything you ever thought or knew or were, where do you go?'

He looked at her and picked up her meaning.

They moved forward to the edge of the clearing, where the trees began. A single set of footprints snaked away. They agreed that Derek should stay and watch the vehicle in case anyone came back for it. Following the prints Edie came suddenly to a place where the spruce and hemlock pine gave out onto a wide frozen lake, brilliantly lit in moonlight. She stopped and looked. The footprints stretched out to the water's edge of the lake then onto the surface of the ice, where they became much fainter. The only other prints visible were those of a moose a little way away, its hoofmarks snaking back away from the shoreline. Edie bent down and inspected the human prints. They were small and the pattern matched that of the prints leading from the front door of Schofield's cabin to the carport. There was a heaviness on the left side consistent with Schofield's limp. The right footprint seemed to swing out a little as though the hip was a little stiff. She hadn't noticed anything on Schofield's right side, but she'd only seen him walk briefly.

Pulling her hare-skin bafflers onto her boots for grip, Edie moved cautiously out onto the lake, feeling the surface shiver, checking with each step the movement and solidity of the ice. A few clouds had collected, and began dropping snow in large, open flakes which caught the air currents above the ice. For a moment Edie could see nothing, then as her eyes accustomed to the light, it appeared in her field of vision, a warp, some dark imperfection which resolved itself into an ice-fishing hole and, beside it, the ice saw that had been used to carve the hole out.

She went over and knelt a few feet from the hole, where the ice would still be stable. The footprints went direct to the edge of the hole but there was nothing leading away. She flipped on her flashlight to get a better look. The cut edge of the ice was clean with no sign of struggle and, oddly, she thought, no splash marks from the lake water. Whoever had gone into that hole hadn't splashed around to try to save themselves. And they hadn't got out.

# 32

Chuck and Marsha Hillingberg watched Police Chief Mackenzie detailing the facts surrounding the death of Peter Galloway on the breakfast news in the privacy of their den at home. The body had been found in remote forest in the Chugach wilderness, about thirty miles from where he had escaped. There was no sign of foul play and all the indications were that the man had died of exposure while evading recapture. The corpse had been badly damaged by animals, Mackenzie said, but tests had proved conclusively that this was Galloway's. As a result of the find, Mackenzie went on, the Anchorage police were now considering the investigations into the deaths of Lucas Littlefish and Jonny Doe closed.

The anchor signed off on the story and headlined an insert about a rogue bear in Fairbanks. There was a trailer for an update on the Iditarod race, then the news cut to a break. Chuck muted the TV, relishing the feeling of relief settling into the muscles of his face. Marsha yawned and poured herself some more coffee. It seemed that they wouldn't be following up the Galloway story. The whole business of the Dark Believers would die away, too. They were free and clear.

The phone rang. It was Andy Foulsham reminding the Hillingbergs to check out the new campaign commercial, which was debuting right after the Iditarod insert. Chuck had already seen the tape a half dozen times, but there was nothing like watching it for the first time broadcast live.

The Iditarod insert started and Chuck unmuted the TV. Strictly speaking, he guessed, events had overtaken them and they'd wasted their money on Nicols. Now that they'd managed to draw a line under the deaths of the two boys and secured funding for the new TV spots, it didn't matter to the campaign who won the Iditarod, only that Mayor Hillingberg be there to hand over the championship trophy. Since the organizers had introduced the compulsory eight-hour rest stop 70 miles out of Nome at White Mountain, the timing of the finish had become much more predictable. This, of course, was exactly the intention. A predictable finish time made life much easier for the organizers, the dignitaries and the media. Chuck was planning on flying himself up in his private plane. He wanted to be on camera, cheering at the finish line when Wright came in.

The Iditarod insert cut to a break. He sat back, preparing to enjoy his performance. Hallstrom's money had got them some hotshot director out of Seattle who'd made him look amazing: smooth-skinned and vigorous without seeming too youthful, a man absolutely in his prime. He clicked up the volume. The sound of his own voice made him feel calmer, anticipatory. He'd healed what he realized now was a long term sore in the Lodge, diverted a crisis, and was back in command of the news agenda once more. Today was going to be the turning point the campaign needed.

Then why was he hit with a sudden needling feeling that something, somewhere was wrong?

He waited for the TV spot to finish, then turned to Marsha.

'Tell me we haven't forgotten about anything, anyone.'

His wife swung round and gave him one of her looks. 'We've been through it over and over already.'

'Humour me. Go through it again one more time.'

She paused, pursed her lips and gave a little sigh of irritation.

'There was only one wild card in this whole thing, and he's gone.'

'What about the Eskimo?'

'The one who found the first boy? She doesn't know anything. A couple of days she'll be back at the North Pole, or wherever the heck she comes from.'

He switched off the TV. Marsha went to do her morning exercises. He helped himself to more coffee and went through it all again in his own mind, trying to focus on what might be causing his uneasiness. He took out his phone and pressed speed-dial. Maybe Andy could put his mind at rest.

The comms director's voice came on. Chuck heard him saying something about positive feedback on Twitter, but his mind was elsewhere.

'Andy, is the Schofield announcement out yet?'

There was a pause while Foulsham shifted gear. 'At ten.' He sounded disappointed that his boss didn't want to chat about feedback on the TV spot.

'Bring it forward.'

Chuck Hillingberg ended the call. He leaned into the soft upholstery of the sofa, closed his eyes and imagined the editor and sole employee of the Homer Community website arriving at work and scrolling down his emails, selecting the one Foulsham had drafted and sent on to a tame attorney to send and reading the only official acknowledgement of the death of Tommy Schofield, a one-line announcement issued exclusively to a tiny local website of the suicide by drowning of the head of Schofield Developments.

# 33

Edie flashed Patricia Gomez's ID and asked to see Terri Lightfoot.

The receptionist at the Green Shoots Clinic peered over at the pile of teen magazines Edie had bought at a mall a block down, saw there was nothing for her among them and waved Edie on through. Something about the meeting with Annalisa up at the Littlefishes' cabin hadn't felt right. Annalisa hadn't met her eye. That was usually a bad sign.

The girl was sitting in the same chair, only now she was staring at the TV. Edie went right over and sat down beside her.

'You remember me, TaniaLee?'

TaniaLee's hands curled and uncurled in her lap but she made no attempt to make eye contact.

Edie put the pile of magazines down on the table between them. 'I got these for you.'

A light came on in the girl's eyes. She pulled the magazines onto her lap and began flipping through them.

'You recall our conversation from before?' TaniaLee stared fixedly at the magazine she was holding and shook her head. Her hands were trembling and Edie noticed a certain stiffness in the way she was sitting. They had her on some strong meds.

'TaniaLee, did Mr Schofield ever hurt you?'

The girl dropped the magazine into her lap. A flash of pain streaked across her face. Edie wondered whether TaniaLee knew

the man she called her husband was dead. Most likely they protected you from that kind of stuff when you were as sick as Tania-
Lee was.

'Fonseca never hurt me,' she said. Her voice was peeved, shrill.
'He was my husband.'

'Who did hurt you, TaniaLee?' On an impulse, she added, 'Was
it Tommy?'

The girl nodded.

Edie wondered if it was possible for someone to split a person
they knew into two halves, one they liked and the other they didn't.
Maybe that's what TaniaLee had done. There was the good aspect,
the man she called Fonseca and the bad one. They were both parts
of the same Tommy Schofield.

'Did Tommy ever do anything to Lucas, TaniaLee?'

The girl looked up. Her eyes were glazed but Edie could see that
something of what she'd just said had gone in.

'He said he wanted Lucas to have a good life. He said Lucas
needed a new mom, someone better than me.'

Edie leaned in to the girl now. She felt how near she was to giving
something up.

'Did Tommy say he was going to take Lucas away from you?'

The girl's eyes swelled with tears. Mucus baubled from her left
nostril. Edie glanced about to make sure an orderly wasn't watching, then reached out for TaniaLee's arm and gave it a squeeze.

'It's OK, TaniaLee.'

The girl turned her face to meet Edie's eye.

'No,' she said. She shook her head. 'It's not.' She looked crumpled,
infinitely vulnerable. Edie pulled out the piece of hare pelt she carried around to rub her face warm and began to stroke TaniaLee's
temples with the soft fur. The girl kept her eyes closed. Her cheeks
flushed slightly and a tentative expression of pleasure appeared on

her face. Edie stroked her for a while, until she sensed she was calm
again.

'Did Tommy ever let anyone else have sex with you? No one's
gonna be mad at you if he did, it wasn't your fault.'

'I don't know,' she said. 'I guess one guy a few times.'

'Do you remember his name?'

She shook her head, then said, 'He had a big nose.' She opened
her eyes and stared at the TV again. Her pupils suddenly went
glassy. Edie figured she didn't have a lot of time left for questions.

'Have they told you why you're sick?'

'Uh huh. Because of the baby.'

Edie recalled her cousin. It had taken a year to get a diagnosis
of post-natal psychosis. For the first few months her family assumed
she was suffering from *pitoq*, polar madness, brought on by four
months of perpetual dark, but when spring came and the sun rose
again and she did not get any better, they said the *pitoq* had sent
her spirit to the bottom of the ocean where it became tangled up
in seaweed and they chanted songs to Sedna, the sea spirit, so that
she would send walruses down to the seabed to eat the weed. They
made her a snow house and her mother moved into it with her. By
the time the diagnosis came she was already on her way to getting
better, but the *qalunaat* doctor insisted on treating her. He gave
her drugs which made her tremble and forget her name. She was
unwell for a long time after that.

'TaniaLee, this is just between us, you understand? Just between
us. Was it Tommy who told you to say the Old Believers had taken
your son?'

The girl's face crumpled again.

'Fonseca told me. He said I had to say that so they wouldn't put
me in prison.'

'Did Fonseca tell you you'd go to prison?'

'Yes.'

Edie sat back, momentarily floored. A sense of thwarted rage shot through her. She wished for an instant that Schofield were alive and in front of her, just to give her the pleasure of killing him. A nurse walked by, smiled a query, and Edie retrieved the part of herself that was able to give a reassuring smile in response.

After the nurse had gone, TaniaLee said, 'And Annalisa.'

For an instant, Edie thought she'd misheard, but when she played what TaniaLee had said in her mind again, she knew she hadn't. She leaned towards the girl and took her hand. It was by turns limp and shaking, like something newly dead.

'Your mother said you'd go to prison?'

A nod.

'Listen, your baby died, TaniaLee. Lucas died. It's a terrible thing but it's no one's fault.'

TaniaLee sucked on her teeth and shook her head. 'It's my fault.'

'No, TaniaLee, cot death isn't anyone's fault.' Edie thought of the desperation of a sick girl breaking free from the unit and wandering the streets of Anchorage, and felt a swell of admiration for the girl's toughness, a stab of pain at her vulnerability. Then other, less bearable thoughts came into her head and she had to fight hard to push them away.

'Why do you think Annalisa said that?'

From the corner of her eye Edie saw a nurse approaching, with a look on her face that meant business. She was about to be asked to leave. There were only a few seconds left to uncover the truth.

'Why, TaniaLee, why did your mother say you were going to prison?' She tried to catch the girl's eye but TaniaLee was evasive. She began to jig compulsively up and down. The nurse was nearly upon them now. Edie had one more shot. She desperately tried to put herself in the mind of the sick girl. A thought came to her, a terrible, wrenching thought but she knew she had to give voice to it.

'Did you do something to stop Tommy finding Lucas another mom? Did you, TaniaLee?'

The girl looked up briefly and noticed the nurse coming towards her.

'Yes,' she said blankly. 'I wanted to stop him having another mom so I put a pillow over him. I put a pillow over Lucas so no other mom or dad would want him.' Her fingers began working in her lap again. 'So his spirit would always stay with me.'

The nurse reached them and stood expectantly.

Edie flashed her a look.

'It's OK,' she said, 'I was just leaving.'

She stood up. Without warning, TaniaLee whirled round and grabbed her sleeve. Her face was wild, distress piled high in the creases in her brow, the corners of her mouth trembling. When she spoke it was almost in a scream.

'Only I can't find him. I can't find my little boy,' she said.

Edie looked at the girl's face, the soft, unblemished skin and felt something rise up out of her belly. Reaching down and gently squeezing TaniaLee's hands, she said, 'It wasn't your fault, Tania-Lee. Don't ever think any of it was your fault.'

Back at the studio, Derek was pacing the floor, anxiously waiting for her. He'd packed a few of her things into a bag and left it by the front door.

'I can see from your face you found something. Tell me on the plane up to Nome,' he said. 'Can Bonehead stay with Stacey again? If not, Aileen said she'd have someone pick him up. We gotta go.'

He was pulling her by the hand now, trying to chivvy her along. She shook him off angrily.

'What happened?'

'You have to promise not to go crazy.' His voice was firm, a little defensive. He held his hands out, palms upwards like stop signs. 'They called in from the checkpoint at Koyuk. Sammy's had an accident. And this time it's for real.'

# 34

It was already getting dark when the Piper Super Cub bumped onto the landing strip outside Koyuk and Edie Kiglatuk walked down the steps. Behind her, looking rather ashen, came Derek Palliser.

Two stewards picked them up and drove them on snowmobiles to the school building, which served as the checkpoint. Inside, competitors and stewards and pilots sat on makeshift tables either warming themselves with soup and hot coffee or catching a quick nap before getting back to the trail. They found Sammy sitting on a hay bale in his indoor gear a way off from the throng, turning something over in his hand.

He hadn't looked this desolate since his son Joe died nine months ago. Seeing him like that, so alone, made Edie wonder for just a second why she'd left him. But you couldn't stay with someone out of pity, and you couldn't stay if staying meant staying drunk. He was bent over now, elbows on his thighs, sucking air in through his teeth and shaking his head. There were scratches on his face, a swelling starting up on his forehead which would probably become a mighty bruise and maybe a black eye later on, but worst was his expression. No whipped dog ever looked so dejected.

She went over, put her arm around him and gave him a hug.

'You OK? A doctor see you?'

'I got a mild concussion and a few bruises is all. Doc said it's nothing to worry about.' His hand went to the egg on his forehead. 'I was more worried for the dogs.'

Edie said, 'You want to tell us what happened?'

'Just a freak accident, I guess, but, aw, nothing like this has ever happened before.' Sammy looked up, his face screwed into a ball of frustration.

The team had just crested a low but steep-sided bluff a few kilometres outside Koyuk and were about to head down a steep slope ending in a sharp turn through the trees. The dogs were energized having made it up the hill and as they came over the top Sammy lowered the drag mat to give the sled some torque and slow it a little, send a message to the dogs to control their pace.

'But they'd been growing a little crazy in the last couple of days. Maybe the feed mix was too rich or maybe they were missing Bonehead or maybe they knew they were kinda on the home stretch. Unpredictable anyways. I don't know why, but at least half a dozen of the team paced up, forcing the others to increase their speed, then the whole team got themselves into a kind of feedback loop. They were hurtlin' down the slope like the devil was on their tails.'

'At that point, it was just chaos. I got dogs cartwheeling over one another, getting all tangled up in harness, panicking and the ones who could were pulling even harder.'

By the time the sled had come to a halt at the bottom of the slope, four of the dogs were seriously injured and five more had bruises, minor rib cracks or concussion. With only six dogs remaining, Sammy had no choice but to bow out.

'You had to have the veterinarian euthanize any?'

Sammy took a breath. 'Uh nuh. Vet's done what needed to be done. They'll heal. They're with a family in the village, they're looking after 'em. We'll fly 'em out to Anchorage tomorrow, get them looked after in the Pen till we're ready to send them back to Autisaq.'

He held up an object in his hand, a U-bend of toughened aluminum tubing fitted with titanium spikes that had split and failed to hold. 'Cause of all the trouble's right here.' Turning the thing around, trying to understand just what it was that made the brake bar crack like that. Edie patted his shoulder and he pulled her hand down and kissed it, sat with the palm set against his face for a moment. She couldn't see his face now but she could feel the damp collecting on her hand. In the whole of their six years together, she'd never known him to cry. In the years after, it had only happened once, after Joe died. She got the impression that last night's accident had somehow bled into their earlier calamity, that he was feeling the kind of pain he hadn't felt since that dreadful time last year.

He wiped his hand over his eyes. 'I'm finished,' he said. 'The rules say I have to keep with the same dogs, can't substitute in any fresh ones, and I only got six left that even can walk, let alone run along in harness.'

There was a pause in which nothing was said but an awful lot communicated.

'I gotta stay here until the dogs fly out, tomorrow maybe. I need a favour?' He tipped his head round and shot Edie an awkward look, went rosy around the cheeks. 'Would you mind calling Nancy, tell her what happened?'

At the name Edie tried not to look surprised or, worse still, disappointed. This was something she hadn't anticipated, but she had no right to complain. Whatever she felt about Sammy now, she had to remind herself that it was she who'd left him. 'I thought you guys had broken up.'

Sammy gave a sheepish little chuckle.

'You know how it is.'

Edie knew exactly how it was.

'One thing I just can't figure out,' Sammy said, 'is how that damn brake bar cracked. The only weak point was at the bolt where it joined onto the mainframe of the sled but the darnedest thing is, the metal fractured on a straight section of tubing about ten centimetres from the joint, exactly where the stress to the metal should have been the weakest.'

A thought went through Edie's head. Derek was cutting her a look. The same thought was going through his head too.

Trying to make it sound casual, Edie said, 'Hey, Sammy, I guess no one coulda handled the sled when you weren't around?'

'Man, Edie,' Sammy gave her a searching look. He tried and failed to disguise his disgust. 'These people are my friends,' he said in a defensive tone. Any case, why would anyone want to trip me up? I'm a rookie here, just a bit player. I was never even a prospect for the top ten.' He lowered his eyes and tutted quietly. 'Which you'd know if you'd come out to the course more, met up with me at a couple of the checkpoints maybe.'

Edie felt herself getting hot. She went to open her mouth then saw Derek giving her the eye and thought better of it. He was right. You don't kick a man when he's down unless it's your intention to see him bleed.

Sammy went on, 'I had this crazy idea, that I could bring Autisaq back some good news. But that's gone now too.'

A man walked by with a husky pup under his arm and gave Edie an idea.

'Hey, when did we ever care about *qalunaat* rules?' she said.

Derek raised his eyebrows.

'OK, OK, so it's Derek's job to care just a little bit. But me and you, Sammy, we never gave a ptarmigan's ass, did we?'

Sammy's eyes narrowed and he gave Edie a sideways glance. Edie returned it with one of the looks she reserved for Sammy alone.

'What you cookin' up, Edie Kiglatuk?'

'You can't complete the race officially, so what? Who in Autisaq's gonna know the difference, or care for that matter? They gotta have dogs out there in Koyuk they'll rent us. You ask me, won't take us more than a coupla hours to put together another team. You could be on the trail again by sundown.' She chin-flicked to his injuries. 'Think you could manage that?'

Sammy's face lightened and he began to smile. He looked at Derek and thumbed towards Edie.

'*Pikkaniqtuq.*' She's a clever one.

# 35

'That's a pretty big thing you're alleging. You sure of your facts?'

Aileen Logan picked up the bleeping cell phone sitting on the table, checked the caller ID and pressed the off switch. Around them, Iditarod volunteers buzzed to and fro, preparing for the race finish.

Derek pulled the brake bar from Sammy's sled out of his pack and laid it on the table.

'Here's the evidence, Aileen. See this? He pointed to the fracture in the tubing. This is no fatigue break. If it had been down to wear and tear, the surface here would have been rough. This is smooth, more like a typical crack fracture. But the point is, see, the bar cracked at the point of least stress.'

Aileen glanced at the bar but seemed more interested in the volunteers. Derek flashed Edie a look of exasperation. She returned it with what she hoped was a sign of encouragement. Derek went in for a second time, holding out the bar so that Aileen could get a better look and running his finger along the cracked edge.

'We think someone took a chisel to this bar. What you're looking at right here is a crack fracture begun by someone deliberately introducing a stress line.'

Aileen gave a sympathetic little smile. She was leaning on her elbows with her hands curled around her chin in a gesture of motherly concern. 'You know, guys, you've been under a lot of stress yourselves. I'm just wondering if you're not making too much of this?'

Edie had been leaving the talking to Derek. But now she couldn't help herself. 'What we're saying is, there's no way this could have happened accidentally. Sammy Inukpuk got off light. He could have gotten killed out there.'

'The Iditarod's always been a dangerous race,' Aileen replied defensively. 'Folks are aware of that when they apply. Leastwise they should be.'

'You're missing the point.'

Derek followed up. 'Ms Logan, we've received warnings, threats,' he said.

Edie glared at him. Since one of the warnings had been from Aileen herself, it seemed to her they were heading into tricky territory. But if Aileen took Derek's remark as aimed at her, she didn't show it.

'About what?' she asked, impassively.

Edie said, 'We're just saying, it seems like there's stuff going on and we don't feel comfortable about it.'

Aileen glanced between Edie and Derek until something seemed to give. She sighed and rolled her eyes. 'You want me to set up an investigation?'

Derek leaned forward and stretched a hand out over his knee. 'Don't you think that would be the most appropriate response? If this kind of thing's allowed to go by, how can people be expected to trust the Iditarod is clean?'

'You find anything cleaner than this race in Alaska, sergeant, you come let me know and I'll raise a hallelujah chorus.' Aileen's face tightened and a hard light came from her eyes. 'You want some input on this, we can give you input, but the first person we gotta interview is Sammy which is kinda hard to do while he's still out there on the trail. I have to tell you, we don't encourage that. We don't encourage it at all. Some will say Sammy's not playing clean himself.'

Edie took this for what it was, an attempt at deflection. But Aileen wasn't going to get off that easy. 'We can wait.'

'Till after what? Week from now we'll all be back in our day jobs. You want an investigation, you can have an investigation, but you'll need to pull Sammy off the route. Officially, he's out of the race anyway. Now, if you'll excuse me . . .' She glanced at her watch, then at the crowd of reporters and cameramen jostling for their finish line accreditation up by the desk. 'I have a busy morning preparing for Mrs Hillingberg's speech at the Pioneer Women's Lunch.' And with that, she gave a little nod, turned and disappeared in among the crowd.

Edie and Derek trudged back along Front Street in thin sleet to Zach Barefoot's house and found him sitting on the floor of the main room playing with his daughter. He and Megan had been asleep when Edie and Derek had finally got back from Koyuk this morning and they hadn't yet had a chance to catch up.

'How's Sammy?' Zach said, raising his eyes from his daughter just long enough to cut them a worried look.

'Unofficially back in the race.'

Zach's expression relaxed. 'I'm real glad to hear that.' He held out the index finger of each hand and let Zoe make a grab for them. 'Hey, you guys eat yet?' He picked up the baby and handed her to Edie. Without waiting for an answer, he said, 'I'll go fetch you something.'

They watched him disappear into the kitchen. The little girl grabbed for one of Edie's braids and jammed the end into her mouth. Edie set a kiss on the top of her head. Her skin was as soft as a hare. She held the tiny body close to her heart. The baby smelled fresh and true, like a tundra summer.

Zach came back a moment later, carrying two bowls of meaty-smelling soup. His put down the bowls and reached out for Zoe.

Edie said: 'You mind if I hold her a bit longer?'

While Edie stayed with the baby, Derek filled Zach in on last night's events and this morning's conversation with Aileen Logan. He then pulled out the sled bar.

Barefoot's eyes moved over it and he pulled it towards him and began inspecting the break.

'A crack fracture. That's weird, wouldn't you say?' Derek observed.

'I don't know, you guys,' Barefoot said. 'What would someone get from putting Sammy out of the race? It's not like the man was ever gonna place.'

Edie said, 'You remember that false alarm I got a few day's back?'

Barefoot blinked, then gave a little nod.

'Tommy Schofield's assistant, Sharon, admitted to making the call.'

The front door opened and there was the sound of boots being taken off. Megan Avuluq appeared through the door to the snow porch, shaking out the cold.

'Hey, Edie, Derek,' she said, scooping her daughter from Edie's hands. Burying her face in the baby's, she rubbed noses and plastered the baby's face with tiny kisses. 'That's just too bad about Sammy. How is he?'

'Back in the race.'

She sat down, dandling the baby in her lap. After a few moments she looked up, distracted. 'Remind me why I go to that Pioneer Women's Lunch every year.' She shook her head, smiled at Zoe, and said, 'Mamma's getting sick of hearin' 'bout Helen Callaghan and Nellie Trosper and all those white ladies who made Alaska what it is today.' She looked up. 'Alaska Nellie this, Alaska Nellie that. You'd think Mrs Marsha Hillingberg sprung clear from Alaska Nellie's belly. All that down-home, field-dressing hokey. Ask me, the only thing that woman ever field dresses is her gym bunny body.' She was running a finger along the baby's chest. 'You and me and your daddy, baby, we're the real Alaska people.'

She looked up suddenly and blushed.

'I'm sorry, did I interrupt something?'

Barefoot reached out and squeezed her hand.

'Derek and Edie think Sammy's sled was sabotaged.'

Megan gave everybody a quizzical look. There was a moment of silence while everyone wondered how much to fill Megan in on, then Edie broke it.

'You remember that girl in the Chukchi Motel? Her "client" . . .' Edie laced the word with the irony it deserved, 'told Zach and Derek here that the guy at the top was called Fonseca. Me and Derek went down to Homer, found out that Fonseca is the cover name for Tommy Schofield, a developer based down there. Schofield is also the father of Lucas Littlefish.'

'The kid you found?'

Edie pursed her lips in a yes.

'Schofield was smuggling underage girls in from Chukchi, through Nome. We think he took them to a hunting lodge down near Meadow Lake. He had a dorm specially built, with some fancy rooms for servicing "clients"' – the heavy irony again – 'and a nursery.'

Megan's eyes grew wide.

'A *nursery?*'

'Seems he was letting the girls get pregnant then selling their babies to couples who wanted a nice new white baby more than they wanted to examine their consciences.'

Megan had stopped stroking the baby's hair now. Her face bore an expression of disgust. 'That's awful,' she said simply.

Edie nodded and went on. 'One of those babies belonged to TaniaLee Littlefish.'

'Schofield tried to sell his own *son*?'

'Seems that way,' Derek said.

Megan pinched her eyes together hard.

Edie carried on. 'TaniaLee couldn't bear the idea of losing Lucas so she smothered him to stop it happening. Schofield put the body in the fish freezer at his office.'

Megan looked at Edie uncomprehending. 'Why would he do that?'

Edie shrugged. 'Lucas died shortly after Thanksgiving. Ground's pretty frozen then. Maybe he knew he wouldn't be able to dig a hole to dump the body in. Maybe he was just buying himself some time. We don't know. He wasn't in any hurry. Didn't have to be. TaniaLee Littlefish couldn't stand what she'd done . . .'

'. . . so she went crazy,' Megan finished. She held Zoe in close.

'No one had any reason to tell the truth,' Derek chipped in. 'If Lucas was traced back to his father, it would have been easy enough to indict him as an accessory after the fact and charge him with statutory rape. TaniaLee Littlefish was thirteen years old when Tommy Schofield got her pregnant. Plus Schofield didn't want his smuggling operation rumbled and the Littlefishes were trying to protect their daughter from going to prison.'

'So he pinned it on those Russian folk?'

Derek said, 'Schofield was trying to get the Believers to sell him a strip of prime shoreline in Kachemak Bay. We think he probably already had a buyer for the land, some cruise-liner operator named Byron Hallstrom, quite a hustler. Maybe Schofield had been over-confident, thought the Believers would be easier to persuade than they turned out to be. Got himself into trouble with Hallstrom as a result.'

'I'm tearing up,' Edie said drily.

'I think he's smart enough to know that the Old Believer story would stick.' Derek finished off the last of his soup and pushed the bowl away. 'Those folks are outsiders. People're wary of 'em.' It all kinda came together. He needed to get rid of the body of Lucas Littlefish in a way that was unlikely to be traced back to himself.'

'And he caught a lucky break when Detective Truro was assigned to investigate the death. Man's a dedicated evangelical. He had the Believers down as some kind of satanic group right from the start.'

Zoe was fast asleep in her mother's arms now. Megan tucked a blanket around the baby. 'Didn't they find another little boy not long after Lucas? How does he fit into all this?'

'Edie found a home-made tattoo kit at the Lodge. A Russian word, шахта,' Derek said. 'It means "mine".'

'I saw the same word tattooed behind the ear of the second baby, Jonny Doe. It wasn't completely clear in the pictures, but I'm sure that's what it said.'

Edie and Derek exchanged a look. Edie felt a swell of something in her belly, a wave of nausea bubbled up. Someone had to say it, she thought. However awful it was, someone had to say what needed to be said. 'It's possible that Jonny Doe was a product of the sick kind of breeding programme.'

She saw Zach Barefoot's mouth fall open. Beside him, on the sofa, Megan groaned.

'That girl Derek saw outside the Chukchi Motel resurfaced in the forest near the Lodge. We tried to follow her, but we didn't know about the Lodge then and we lost her tracks. She wrote out the word шахта in the snow on the windshield of our truck.'

Megan looked up. An idea went through her mind. She turned her head toward her husband. Zach's face tightened into an expression of disgust.

'Thing makes me sick to my stomach,' he said.

'That kid, the second one, didn't he have Down Syndrome?' Megan's eyes began to fill with tears. 'Tell me that's not why they killed him. Tell me that didn't happen.'

'But it did,' Edie said.

They sat for a moment taking this in, then Zach said, 'You mean that fella they found dead this morning in the Chugach never did anything?'

Edie swung a wild look at Derek, who returned it. Her pulse began to rise. She had to hold in her voice until she could trust it to come out and make sense.

'Which dead fella?'

'The guy whose body they found outside this morning, the Old Believer dude, the prime suspect.' His gaze slalomed between Edie and Derek, then something clicked. He jumped up from the sofa, tapped into his laptop and brought up the front page of the *Anchorage Courier.*

### Baby horror suspect found dead in Chugach forest.

The article reported that Peter Galloway's body had been found on the forest floor by a hunter. The body had been substantially compromised by animals, but preliminary forensics suggested Galloway had died only hours after escaping from a prison vehicle while being transported from a correctional facility in Anchorage to one in Eagle River. It had been cold, even for March, and Galloway had been dressed only in regulation overalls. The police were not treating the death as suspicious.

Edie went over to the laptop and reread the piece.

'That doesn't add up. I saw Galloway up in the Alphabet Hills two days after his escape. He was wearing proper outerwear.' She prowled around her mind for a moment, looking for ideas. 'Zach, mind if I google something?'

Zach got up from the chair beside the laptop. 'Go ahead.'

Edie sat. 'Me and Derek found an ice hole down in Homer, Tommy Schofield's truck parked nearby. There were footprints leading to the hole and none leading back.' She keyed in the letters then scrolled through the search results and found a single reference to Tommy Schofield's death on a Homer community website.

'Suicide?' Zach said.

'That's what it says here. Only there was something not quite right about the prints. And there was no splash around the hole. A guy falls through a hole in the ice, even a guy who wants to fall through that hole, even a guy whose aim is to die in the water, he's gonna make a splash.'

'What are you thinking?'

'I'm thinking maybe no body ever actually fell through that ice. I'm thinking it's weird that Galloway and Schofield apparently die on the same day, no one finds Schofield's body, and Galloway's body is apparently so messed up by animals it has to be ID'd from DNA.'

The phone rang. Zach picked up, nodded a couple of times, saying *uh huh*, then passed the phone across to Edie. She took it and mouthed 'Who is it?' Zach shrugged. She flipped the mic to speakerphone and answered.

A heavily accented voice said, 'This is Lena, friend of Olga.' Edie sucked in air, trying to recall. From the corner of her eye, she saw Derek look up in surprise then start gesticulating for the phone. She passed it over and he introduced himself, then she saw his expression fade.

'She wants to talk to you,' he said.

'Who's Olga?'

'The girl in Anchorage. The one who was hiding her baby. Lena's her friend. I gave them the number here.'

'But she asked for me.'

'I might have mentioned you.' Derek gave her a sheepish look. 'I thought she'd be more likely to call a woman.'

Edie took the phone back and spoke into it. 'Lena, are you in trouble?'

'Not yet, but soon maybe. We have CCTV tape. For your research. Maybe you get something done. You should see it.'

'Where are you?'

There was a pause. Edie thought she could hear a baby crying in the background, then Lena said, 'The man, your friend, he knows.'

# 36

'Edie.' Stacey's smile beamed from the service entrance. She was dressed in black, as usual, but she'd partly dyed her hair white now, and shaved a swathe down one side of her skull. In spite of all this, or maybe because of it, she looked dazzlingly pretty. In one hand she was holding a box. This she offered up to Edie.

'Some ribs, a coupla orders of reindeer chilli, figured you'd be hungry. It's on me.'

Edie thanked her. 'Why did you switch to late shift?'

Stacey pulled a face. 'Half the staff called in sick. I guess they wanted to watch the Iditarod finish on the TV. I decided I could use the extra money.' They moved across to a door in the back of the building. There were some kids taking turns with a pair of stilts in the parking lot. Stacey gave them a wave.

'Those guys make me laugh. They're always here,' she said, drawing a set of keys from a chain in her apron pocket. 'I sneak 'em out some food sometimes.' One of the kids took a tumble from the stilts, got right back on, laughing.

Edie turned the key in the door and Bonehead came bounding out, his sinuous body snaking joyously back and forth. She bent down. 'Look at you, big guy. Thanks for keeping him.'

Stacey caught her bottom lip with her teeth. 'I'm glad you're back but I'm gonna miss this old hound. We had such fun together. Boy, that dog likes to walk!' She took a breath and, thumbing the back entrance to the cafe, said, 'I guess I should be getting back.' Then she added, 'Old Bonehead and me, we're pals. Bring him back any time.' Her eyebrows went up into a pleading expression. 'Please?'

Edie waited till the waitress was back inside, then she clipped on Bonehead's lead and they began to make their way in the boys' direction through the parking lot. The surface had been ploughed but a thin layer of snow had fallen since then and wolf tracks ran all the way through it.

'Hey, kids.' They dropped their stilts and came over. There were three, all boys, probably around eleven, dressed in the Alaska uniform of jeans and down parkas with bobble hats. Good-looking kids, well cared for. One of them reached out and began patting Bonehead.

'You see those prints?' She pointed to the litter of wolf prints on the lot. 'There's wolves come around this way. Heading for the trash cans maybe. Most likely they won't bother you, but maybe you wanna think about getting back home?'

The three boys burst out laughing and kept on bellowing so hard they had to clutch their stomachs. That set Bonehead off.

Edie felt herself redden. 'Aw, kids, c'mon, wha'd I say?' But this only set the boys off all over again. Edie bent down and looked at the prints. There was no doubt in her mind they belonged to wolves, but now she could see not only that there was no gait in them, no order, and they were all of front paws. She walked over and picked up the stilts. On the base was stamped the classic lupine four elongated toes spread wide. One of the boys came running over.

'Hey! They're ours!'

She handed the stilts to the boy. 'They got other types like this in the store?'

'Sure,' the boy said, giving her the kind of disdainful look kids reserve for stupid adults. 'Lynx, moose, whatever.'

A bigger thought had begun taking shape in her mind. The moose tracks on the shoreline of the lake. She loaded Bonehead into the back of the truck and reached for the nature guide she kept in the glovebox. The tracks of everything living on Ellesmere Island were as familiar to her as the sound of a northeast wind blowing across the ice, but the first time she'd seen moose tracks was only a few days ago. From the guide it appeared that the front and back footprints were strikingly similar, but she could see straight away now that the distance between the prints on the lake was slightly off. Which could only mean that the prints up at the lake had been faked. Someone had walked onto that ice in shoes and come back off it wearing stilts.

She turned off McRae onto Spenard Road and headed south. The strip malls and buildings on either side of the street began looking distinctly seedy. Eventually, she came to the row of old houses Derek had described, and pulled off the road. In front of her were steps up to a shabby door. She climbed the rises slowly, listening out for voices or movement coming from inside the building. Her instincts told her there was no one home. After waiting a few moments she knocked. Again, nothing. The thought occurred to her that maybe she'd got the wrong place, the world of blocks and grids being so unfamiliar to someone brought up in a two-street settlement in the midst of thousands of miles of tundra that she'd just mistaken one spot for another. She pulled out Derek's written instructions and in her mind retraced the drive but every reworking brought her back here. She knocked again and when no amount of stamping could keep out the cold any longer, she turned and went back down the steps.

Back at the studio she called Derek and gave him the news. He sounded relieved to hear her voice.

'I'll go back over there again later.'

'Can't it wait till the morning? I don't like the thought of you around that place after dark.'

She laughed.

'I been handling polar bears half my life, I think I can handle this.'

Derek said, 'Polar bears aren't motivated by money.'

'That's 'cause polar bears are smart.'

'Listen, Edie, I know you better than you think. Seems to me you got some reason to be chasing this thing, I mean something you're not talking about. I haven't asked you about it—'

'Because you know I won't tell you,' she interrupted.

He gave a sigh, long and full of irritation, and tinged with something else, too.

'I may be dumb but I got a good nose and I don't like the way this smells,' she said. 'I sensed at the time there was something wrong with those prints but I couldn't put my finger on it. It was the gait. Whoever left those prints had problems with his right hip. Could have been Schofield, I guess, but then there was the lack of splash ice.' She told Derek about the kids in the parking lot behind the Snowy Owl.

'You think Schofield faked his own death?'

'If he just intended to disappear, why would he have put a guard outside his office? You ask me, Tommy Schofield was intending to lie low for a few days until the thing with the Stegners blew over, then he was planning on coming back.'

Derek paused, gathering his thoughts. 'Instead of which . . .'

Edie said, 'I'm thinking that field-dressing shed we looked in on at the back of Tommy Schofield's cabin, that'd be an ideal place to kill a man. There'd be blood all over that shed. Animal blood or Tommy Schofield's blood, hard to tell which, particularly if you clean up afterwards. I'm saying someone had scrubbed that shed very recently and fixed on a new padlock.'

'Who?' Derek said.

'Take your pick.' They ran through the list of possibilities. Of the clients of the Lodge the only one they had identified was Police Chief Mackenzie but any one of them might have had reason to do away with Schofield. There were the Schofield's associates, the two Russian men Derek had seen at the Chukchi Motel. Then there was Galloway.

'Why would Galloway stage Schofield's suicide? He's already got a two-murder tag on him. What's another in the bag?'

'I think we can count Galloway out.'

They fell silent for a while, lost in thought. Then Edie said, 'But say Mackenzie, or whoever else at the Lodge, needed Galloway and Schofield off the scene, only they couldn't find Galloway.'

'So . . .'

'So how's about that person, or people, get rid of Schofield, make it look like a suicide, release the body to the Old Believers as Galloway and make a big song and dance in the media of closing the case.'

'What do the Believers get out of it?'

'Exactly what they need. They get the APD off Galloway's back.'

Derek thought about this for a moment. 'Then they get their man the hell out of Alaska.'

'Which can't be all that difficult to do when you got a vast, unpoliced international border on either side.'

'But how would you ever prove that's what happened?'

'According to the Orthodoxy, the body of a deceased Christian must be returned to the earth. The Old Believers have some issues with the Orthodox Church but on that they agree. They won't cremate their dead. I read that when I was doing research. All you'd have to do to prove it would be to dig up the body of "Peter Galloway" and I'd be prepared to bet that you'd find someone remarkably like Tommy Schofield.'

Derek paused. 'The Believers would never agree to a disinterment.'

'They wouldn't have to. You forget, Derek, that even in Alaska there's a thing called the law.'

'I thought you didn't believe in the law?'

'I don't. I believe in justice.'

In the background Edie could hear the sound of Zach's voice and some high-pitched baby noises. Good noises, she thought, the best.

After the call, Edie made some hot tea and sat on the sofa thinking. Then, on a whim, she got up, went over to the small chest where she'd stashed the papers she'd removed from Tommy Schofield's office and checked through them once again, stopping when she came to notepaper headed 'Kachemak Properties'. Director: *Tommy R Schofield*. On the paper were some scribbled notes, what looked like points of discussion, and clipped underneath was what seemed to be an agreement between Kachemak and someone with the unusual name of Tryggve.

She wondered how much Schofield's assistant, Sharon Steadman, might be able to tell her. Now that her boss was presumed dead, she might be more willing to talk.

Sharon answered on the second ring. Edie didn't have to introduce herself.

'So, we took your advice, went to see Annalisa Littlefish.' Edie imagined Sharon sitting on her pink chair in her pink bathrobe. It made it easier to do what she was about to do.

'Like I said before, I don't know much.' Sharon's tone seemed a good deal less perky now.

'Let's see. We got human trafficking, procurement of children for sex, statutory rape.'

'I don't know about any of that.'

'You know enough to go down as an accessory after the fact.' The term came from the TV cop shows Edie watched with Sammy sometimes, on a dark night, for want of anything better to do.

There was a pause down the line, then Sharon said, 'What d'you want?'

'You ever want another job in Homer, Sharon, you better start talking.'

'I already told you what I know.' Sharon meant to sound authoritative but came across as both resentful and terrified.

'Kachemak Properties mean anything to you?'

'Sure. It was some kind of shell company Tommy, Mr Schofield, set up to deal with Mr Hallstrom.'

'Byron Hallstrom?'

'Yeah. Tommy never had the kind of money you'd need to buy the shoreline land and develop it. He was only ever acting as an agent.'

'But the Old Believers didn't want to sell. Tommy Schofield was trying to blackmail Peter Galloway and the other Believers into selling that land?'

Sharon fell silent. Finally, she said, 'I think Mr Schofield would have thought of it more in the way of persuasion.'

'Tell me about Trygvve. That Hallstrom's outfit?'

'Yes.'

'Anyone else involved?'

There was a pause, then Sharon came back on. 'At one point, Mrs Hillingberg tried to muscle in on it somehow. But she and Tommy had a fight about it.'

'What do you mean, they had a fight about it?'

'I heard Tommy, like, going apeshit on the phone. Mr Schofield never much liked Mrs Hillingberg.'

'They have some history together?'

'I guess they were at high school at the same time.' Sharon hesitated.

'And?'

'My parents once told me there was this rumour that he kinda fell for her but she was mean to him.'

'She was *mean*?'

'It wasn't like that,' Sharon said, defensively. 'Tommy had some sort of a breakdown, my parents said, he had to leave school. It was because of that he didn't go to college.'

'Because she was *mean*?'

'Mr Schofield was a loner. He got teased a lot about his legs. But he had a dog. My parents said Marsha paid some local psycho to take a baseball bat to the dog's legs. They left the dog on Tommy's porch with a note calling him a cripple and told him to stick to his own kind.'

Edie left Bonehead in the studio and drove south to the old, run-down house at the end of Spenard Road. The lot was empty and a light covering of snow had obliterated her earlier tracks. Newer, fresher tracks led into the house. She felt her pulse quicken. Lena was in. Reaching the small platform outside the door, she paused for a moment, knocked and heard the sound of footsteps approaching. No light came on inside, but the door opened and someone stood just inside the doorway.

'Come in,' a female voice said.

Even as she stepped inside, Edie Kiglatuk knew she'd been a fool. An instant later, too short a time for her to turn around, she felt a rush of air and heard a cracking sound. Then nothing.

# 37

He was in the car going east towards Merrill Field when his personal BlackBerry buzzed and Marsha's ID came up.

'Hey,' he said, 'how's the Slope?' For the past twenty-four hours his wife had been on a whistle-stop tour of the north, basing herself in Nome and from there making visits out to Kotzebue, Barrow and the North Slope oilfields. Chuck was intending to fly up there in a couple of days' time. It was important for the Hillingberg campaign to be seen to be supportive of the oil business in general, given how much of Alaska's wealth depended on it.

Marsha said the Slope was looking good. 'They're as pissed with Shippon as we are. All on message. Too old, too set in his ways, Alaska needs a new broom. ' She let out a little laugh. 'Well heck, they're about to get one.'

They were passing the headquarters of the APD now. Chuck peered out the window, pleased not to see any demonstrators. His work BlackBerry buzzed. An email from April to say that all the arrangements were in place and she'd meet him at the terminal building in Nome. Andy, April and the rest of his team had flown up there on the morning's scheduled flight out of Anchorage. Chuck had decided to fly himself up later in his Cessna Stationair. It was a good way to present himself as an independent, all-Alaska kind of a guy, cut a bit of a dash.

'I gotta go,' he said. 'See you at the hotel in Nome in about three hours?'

'Take your time,' Marsha said.

Being driven through the familiar streets, blank and icy in their late winter garb, Chuck thought what a relief it would be to get away from Anchorage. He hadn't been a bad mayor in the circumstances, but it was time to leave the role to someone who really loved the city. The Alaska state motto 'North to the Future' didn't include him or his future. The way Chuck saw it, oil and politics had polluted the state without making it powerful. For him, the years ahead all lay to the south, first as Governor of Alaska in Juneau, then in Washington DC. As the driver pulled into the public zone at the airstrip, then rolled on into the VIP area, he could feel a new start making its way inexorably toward him like spindrift rushing in off the sea.

His maintenance engineer, Foggy Banks, had the Stationair's sidepanel off and was checking the hardware around the elevator bell crank. Chuck was fond of the guy. Banks was one of those increasingly rare men, an old-time sourdough Alaskan who loved hunting and the outdoors, could turn his hand to more or less anything from house-building to salmon-smoking, and took pride in his work. He was always grimy and never seemed to have a woman around long enough to make him take a wash, but that didn't bother Chuck. Foggy Banks and his ilk were the blood and guts of the North Star State. He'd often thought that if Alaska had been populated with men like Foggy, he wouldn't be so keen to leave. It was all the others, the petty bureaucrats, the strutting oilmen, the tree-huggers, the hydroponics nuts, the libertarians, East Coast environmentalists and the pseudo-sophisticates, who made Alaska intolerable.

He strolled over with what he hoped was a big, generous-hearted smile on his face.

'Good to see ya, boss,' Banks said, wiping his hands on an oily cloth and slapping a huge, greasy palm into Chuck's cleaner, more tender one. 'Real sorry, but I got called away a while for an emergency, so I'm running a little behind.'

Chuck tried hard to keep up his smile. He knew he should ask about the emergency, but couldn't get up the energy for it.

'Give me twenty minutes?' Banks said.

Chuck nodded, went round to the office side, glad-handed all the folk he needed to keep sweet, dropped off his flight plan and checked the latest weather forecast. Looked like it was going to stay partly cloudy with a variable force 3 wind. No precipitation expected. Pretty perfect flying weather for the end of March.

He asked permission to take over an empty desk and began to check through the speech he was due to make at the Iditarod champion's dinner but he soon found his thoughts distracted by the events of the past few days. He saw the Lodge now as a bizarre aberration that he'd allowed himself to get sucked into, a monstrous hydra-headed thing at the centre of which lurked Tommy Schofield. It was a relief, at least, to know that the man was dead. Schofield had always been a hustler, a loser with pretensions. He thought himself back to the time, it seemed so distant now, when he'd made a play for Marsha. Ha! He allowed himself the luxury of examining the shiny, luxurious heft of the power he'd held over Schofield in the years that followed. Something jolted him out of his reverie, an uncomfortable little reminder of how rapidly and with what utter ruthlessness Marsha had decided Schofield's fate. He stood up, took a deep breath and tried to turn the feeling around, reminding himself how much he'd benefited from that. Never had his path to power been clearer.

He checked his watch. Banks would most likely have finished by now. Walking back to the plane, he managed to recover his sense of a wide future opening up. A tall guy in navy-blue overalls stood tightening up the nuts in the Stationair's side panel. He flashed Chuck a broad smile and held out a clean hand.

'Mayor Hillingberg, it's such an honour to meet you. You got my vote for governor, sir. Foggy got called away again, so he put me onto the last few bits and pieces, just clean-up stuff. He didn't want to delay you any more.'

Chuck felt himself relax. Right now, that wide future felt like it was only a short flight away. Tonight he'd be on camera shaking up the champagne with the winner of the toughest, most prestigious dogsled race in the world, and making what was almost certainly the most important speech of his career, so far. He opened up the cabin door, slung his papers inside and gave the thumbs up to Foggy Banks's friend.

Thirty minutes later, he was up at 15,000 feet flying in good weather over Talkeetna. Before him, the outline of Denali dazzled in the sun. For the first time in his life he felt as though he and the mountain were one of a kind, kindred spirits. He laughed at himself. OK, so that sounded kinda tree-huggy. What he meant was he felt solid, impressive, open to the sun. The plane bumped over some loose air. Up ahead, a large cumulus hung at the plane's altitude. Chuck checked the altimeter and decided he could afford to dip a little, get himself out of the way. The plane dropped, skimmed the bottom edge of the cloud and burst out into sun on the other side. He pulled on the elevator to correct the altitude but nothing happened. The lining of his stomach curled up, as though someone had poured bleach into it. He shook the feeling off and told himself to calm down. The plane buffeted into another cloud and began to roll a little. He straightened up, but still found himself descending, the nose still refusing to lift. His heart began to pound now, the blood draining from his brain, making him light-headed. He knew he was in trouble but his previous feelings of invincibility still lingered, like some old unwanted habit. He thought to himself: this isn't happening, whilst knowing simultaneously that it was. And then he knew. This *was* happening. Foggy Banks's friend had made sure of that.

The Stationair was dropping rapidly now. He figured he only had a few more minutes before he would cease to be able to stabilize the wings. At that point, the plane would start to spin before plummeting to the ground. Thoughts flashed before him like shooting stars. The pressure of the adrenaline racing through his veins was almost unbearable. He started to feel dazed, as removed from the situation as he would have been if he were looking at it on a TV screen. He adjusted the ailerons and the plane began to roll as though it were a boat in a high storm. For some reason, he found the movement momentarily calming. He thought back to himself as a baby when his mother used gently to rock him in a cot made by his father. Below him the mountains dazzled. He closed his eyes for a second, trying to regain the feeling of communality he'd felt with Denali only moments before. The plane began to list, then spin, and he became vaguely aware of desperately flipping switches. But it was all too late. He could hear the rush of the air on either side of him. He raised his arms and unbuckled his seat belt. Being free of it suddenly there was a moment in which he felt he was flying and wondered if he had already died. But then he saw the mountains looming at vast speed towards him and knew that the impact was yet to come. He tried to will himself into unconsciousness but the terror of his situation only came more fully into relief.

The last thing Mayor Chuck Hillingberg remembered in this life was what his wife had said to him. *Take your time*. He heard himself give a bitter little laugh. She knew. Marsha knew. In spite of everything he felt himself smile. I'm taking my time now, Marsha, he thought. I'm taking all the time in the world.

# 38

She woke cold and with the sense that she had left her body. She could see that she was lying on what seemed to be a concrete floor, but the feeling she had was that every part of her had liquefied and was swirling and cresting, uncontained by anything. There was a rich, sharp smell which was familiar but which she could not identify. Her mind felt as fluid as her body, like a blob of oil floating on a swelling sea.

A woman's voice percolated into her consciousness. She opened her eyes but nothing happened. The voice continued, soft, insistent. She tried to imagine a snow house and put herself inside it. This seemed to help her focus. Turning her head in the direction of the voice, she gazed through a screen of metal mesh. A pale face loomed, topped with a mess of dirty blonde hair.

'Where am I?'

'It's OK.' The woman's voice sounded like it was coming up from under the waves. 'She gave you Nembie, why you feel weird.'

Edie didn't know what Nembie was but it didn't seem to matter. She tried to blink away the pain at the side of her head. Reaching up with a hand her fingers came back rusty-coloured and sour smelling. A word popped into her mind. Ammonia. That was it. There was a pervasive smell of piss. The voice broke her train of thought.

'You got thump on head, Edie. On top of another one, looks like.'

The voice waited while this sunk in. So the woman knew who she was.

'It's Lena. I called, remember? You came to my house.' She broke off suddenly. Edie blinked some more and pictured herself sitting safe inside that snow house again.

A door opened and a second voice broke in from outside the cage.

'You're dumber than I thought. This isn't your fight, hell, this isn't even your country!'

This voice she knew immediately. It went on, insistent:

'I played nice, I even gave you a warning, but you got the hide of a freakin' walrus. You brought this on yourself. You should have stopped when I took your ex out of the race, but you were too dumb to get the message. This is the worst possible time. I should be up at the race now and you've put me out.' Aileen Logan sucked on her teeth. Her face loomed huge behind the wire mesh. 'Get this message. *You've put me out.*'

A door opened, they heard the sound of a lock and Aileen was gone. Edie sat up, leaned against the mesh and scrabbled around in her mind.

'Nembie?'

'Nembutol. Aileen say she uses to euthanize dogs,' Lena whispered, 'but listen, stay awake, you can fight it.'

Edie focused her eyes first on the mesh then on the figure of Lena. She heard her breath come long and slow, pinched herself hard to quicken it. Before long, she could see both the mesh and Lena. It was then she understood they were in two wire pens, like those in a dog kennel. They were boxed in, their front gates secured by padlocks. The pens gave onto an internal boardwalk lit by two windows under high eaves. Clearly, the building hadn't always been a kennel. The high roof suggested some other, earlier use. Aside from a small meshed viewing window, the external door looked solid and locked from the outside.

'Has this got something to do with the CCTV tape you told me about on the phone?'

'Uh huh.'

This took a while for Edie to process. Then she said, 'How's Aileen even know about it?'

'Marsha Hillingberg,' Lena hissed. 'Aileen and Marsha speaking on the phone when Aileen was bringing me here in car. I think they have relationship. Aileen say "darling".'

Edie wondered for a moment whether she'd heard right. Aileen Logan and Marsha Hillingberg lovers? That sounded crazy. In any case, it probably didn't matter so much who was screwing who, as to how they were going to get themselves out of the mess they were in.

'We must find way out very quick,' Lena said.

Edie felt herself going. In her mind, she saw Sedna, the sea spirit, how she held men and women captive in great forests of seaweed, drowned men and women, on the seabed, in order not to be alone. A memory bubbled up of her as a girl, being dragged under the water by a seal, being taken to Sedna. She saw a face under the water but it was not Sedna's face. It was her murdered ex-stepson Joe's face and he was calling out the name he used for her. *Kigga, Kigga.* And then she was a bird and flying and she flew up and found herself on the back of the spirit bear and the spirit bear was clambering up rocks and out of the forest and then she was on the tundra again and all around she could see the frozen rocks and sparse, tufted vegetation, the brilliant yellow and red lichens, the frozen sea and green-blue icebergs of her home on Ellesmere Island.

Then she blinked and felt the water and remembered that she wasn't in the sea at all and she opened her eyes fully and put her hand to her face and felt a cool liquid and saw that, in the next pen, Lena was dipping her fingers in a bowl and flicking them in her direction, keeping her from sleeping and for an instant she felt her eyelids droop and a wave of resentment came over her because all she wanted to do was rest but she kept blinking and shaking her head and the wave crested over her and died away.

And that was when the only thing she knew about padlocks came to her. She knew how to pick them. The thought seemed to rouse her. As though from somewhere far distant she felt a tiny spike of adrenaline. The pain in her mind flew away suddenly and a pocket of clarity opened up, like a splash of sun on a cloudy day.

'Lena,' she hissed, 'look for something sharp, something like a toothpick or a hook.'

Edie pressed her teeth into her lip and felt the blood trickle, the warm, metallic taste in her mouth. Taking six deep breaths in, hoping the oxygen would clear her head, she blinked herself back into focus and began to scour the pen, looking for anything she might use as a pick. The pens had been swept and cleaned and they were screened off by two layers of wire mesh, secured to supports with what looked like solder. Aside from the dog bowl full of water, there was nothing inside. She tried to focus on the wire mesh itself, looking for a loose end, a fracture or stress line she could try to exploit, but the mesh was heavy grade and looked new.

After a long while, she heard a hissing noise. Lena was pressed up against the side of the pen closest to her. She'd managed to wedge her fingers part way through the mesh.

'What you got?'

'Hairpin.'

'Show me.' She leaned into the mesh and focused on the hand. The fingers moved and a slim two-pronged object appeared.

'Was stuck in the middle of my hair,' Lena said. 'Aileen pulled my bun but this was left.'

Edie looked at the pin, then at the padlock. This was as good as it was going to get. She shuffled forward. Her eyes swam. She pushed her finger through the mesh but the gauge wasn't wide enough to accommodate her whole hand. Her fingertips made contact with the padlock but it slipped away. What she needed, she knew, was focus. She closed her eyes and thought about the scene in *Safety Last!* with Harold Lloyd swinging unprotected from the moving hands of the clock high up above the city. For a moment she put herself on those hands until it felt as though her head might dissolve into a tiny ball of fierce, white light, then, without opening her eyes, she pushed her fingers through the mesh, hooked the two outermost fingers of her right hand around the padlock to hold it in place and using her index finger and thumb inserted the hairpin into the lock and pressed each pin in turn until the lock gave and she was free.

In the neighbouring dog pen Lena had begun panting. Feeling unsteady on her legs, Edie staggered over and grabbed the padlock. Lena was shaking now, her breath heavy in her throat. It was hard to say whether it was the effects of the drugs she'd been given or a panic attack. Either way, it didn't make Edie's job any easier. She closed her eyes and pictured the clock scene again, steadied her breath, inserted the hairpin and felt it suddenly snap. She pulled it out, broken. The two women looked at it for a second. Lena's face scrunched. She took a deep breath in and opened her eyes. Her jawline was tight now and a new light blazed from her eyes.

'You go,' she said.

'Lena, I'm going to get you out of here.'

Lena was shaking her head. She raised a hand to her hair and pulled out a skein from the side.

'Take this to Detective Truro. He's a good man, Edie. A bit of a religion fanatic, but good to working girls.'

Edie looked at the lock of hair but she did not take it.

'We'll go together, Lena.'

Lena shook her head sadly. 'If Aileen does not kill me, they will deport me anyway. Listen, Edie. I want you to know this. Jonny Doe, this baby, he was son of me. His name Vasilly Chuchin. This hair prove. Another thing. Olga know where is tape. She run away, protect her baby. She will let you have.' Lena was crying now. 'Please, for Vasilly.'

Edie's head began to throb and a wave of nausea overtook her. She stood bent over for a moment then took a deep breath.

'Lena, tell me this once we're out of here.'

She edged up to the door. It was locked from the outside. Going slowly, she peeped through the viewing window. The door to the yard had been padlocked from the outside. The lock itself was a simple pin construction, easy to pick, but she could see an iron bar fixed to the wall on the other side with a large padlock which held in the door frame. And the door faced directly onto Aileen's house. Inside the house she could see Aileen juggling phones. From the looks of things she wasn't coming back any time soon. Once she'd got Lena out of her pen, they'd have to find a way to clamber up to the windows and squeeze through. She looked about for something with which to break the padlock. Just in front of her feet she noticed a dog's dewclaw. She picked it up. It was curled and dry, sharp as a tack. Perfect. Moments later, the padlock gave and Lena was standing on the boardwalk.

They scanned the room for something to climb, then Edie had an idea. 'Lena, you wearing thermal liners?'

'Of course,' Lena said, 'is March in Alaska.'

'Can you strip?'

Lena shot her a bitter smile. 'I'm professional.'

Moments later Edie had two pairs of long johns in her hands and was busy knotting them together and making a loop at one end. 'One of us is going to give the other a leg-up. Whoever's on top will have to lasso this loop over the latch there and haul herself up and out.'

Lena looked up, following Edie's gaze.

'I don't know is secure,' she said.

'You see any other way we can do this?'

'No.'

'OK, then, you're going to have to lean your shoulder against the wall and brace your hands like this.'

On the fourth attempt the loop hooked over the latch. Edie quickly pulled it tight and hung on. The effort had sent blood to the wound in her head and she had to wait for the pain to subside. Using the wall, she clambered upwards, swung a leg up to the window ledge to give herself some leverage and, using all the force of her arms, pushed herself out and onto the roof. She lay flat in the snow against the shingles for a moment, catching her breath, feet balanced on nearby snow hooks. She was at the back of the kennel building, but most likely visible from the house, should Aileen look up. Untying the loop from the latch, she attached it to a snow hook and took a few tugs. She leaned back inside the window and signalled for Lena to begin to climb. The rope of liners grew taught. Halfway up the snow hook squealed and bent, but held. Then, from the house, a clatter came. For an instant Edie froze. In her peripheral vision she could just see the back door fly open and Aileen emerge, striding down the path towards the kennel. Edie snaked her way up to the window and leaned in. Lena was three-quarters of the way up now.

'Hurry, hurry, Aileen is coming.'

Lena stopped climbing and looked up. There was resignation in her eyes.

'Don't you do this, Lena, don't give up.' Edie stretched out a hand. The woman was only a metre from the window and freedom. Edie saw her look down, then look up, uncertain as to what to do.

'Lena, look at me.'

The young woman looked up, her hair tumbling down her back as she did so. At that moment a phone rang. Edie heard Aileen's voice. She had stopped on the path. Another wave of nausea spread up from Edie's belly. She took a deep breath.

'You can lose a child and life can still be worth living. Believe me, Lena. Climb up, climb out of the window.'

She saw the woman's lips form a hard line and her jaw tighten. Her hand reached out, then she was manoeuvring herself up onto the roof. Edie put a hand around her mouth to stop her talking and gestured to her to keep low. Aileen was still on the phone, with her back turned to them. Edie frantically snatched up the rope of thermal liners. Lena grabbed it and began rappelling down. Reaching the end of the rope, she looked down at the ground a couple of metres below. Then she let go. Edie dropped down after her but as she did so, her foot slipped on ice and bent under, twisting her ankle. Aileen was finishing up her conversation. Edie pointed to a thicket of alder beside the kennel and they ran, their footsteps soft in the snow. They heard Aileen fiddling with the padlock and they turned and fled further into the thicket, Edie biting her lip so that she would not cry out in pain. Not long after, they came to a deer fence electrified at the top. Edie began to climb, instructing Lena to follow. At the top, Edie wrapped her hands in her fleece then she reached out and, bracing herself, grasped the fence wire. A pulse raced across her palms and sent a burning sensation into her wrists and up her arms but she knew the voltage wasn't sufficient to kill her, so she clung on until Lena clambered over then released her grip and followed. They jumped and found themselves on a suburban highway with the skyscrapers of downtown Anchorage a few miles distant. Behind them they could hear the sound of an engine firing up.

Aileen was coming for them.

# 39

Derek had been trying to reach Edie all night and was now feeling very anxious. When he'd spoken to her, she'd seemed intent on going back for the tape, which he'd thought was probably a bad idea, but that was over eight hours ago and he'd heard nothing from her since.

No one in Nome had slept much that night. News of a plane crash had come in around five, a couple of hours before Duncan Wright was due to cross the Iditarod finishing line. What little information was available seemed to suggest that this was the plane belonging to Mayor Hillingberg and began to seem more and more likely as Wright's finishing time drew nearer and the mayor had still not made an appearance. Things weren't made any easier by Aileen Logan's sudden departure that afternoon for what she described as a 'personal health emergency'. The woman wasn't even answering her phone. Gossip suggested that she'd had some kind of breakdown. One or two of her colleagues speculated that she'd left the country altogether. Aileen's deputy, Chrissie Caley, had been doing a good job of reducing the inevitable chaos to a minimum, but amidst all the rumour and counter-rumour, it was difficult to work out where the truth lay.

While Wright was checking in at Safety, only an hour or so from the finish line, confirmation came through that the plane which residents at Rainy Pass had reported to be in trouble was indeed

Chuck Hillingberg's and that wreckage had been seen burning just a few miles north of Rainy, not far from the landing strip at Farewell. A search and rescue helicopter hadn't been able to reach the site on account of some localized weather but the S&R team was able to corroborate the testimony of the residents of Rainy Pass that the downed plane was a Cessna Stationair and to further report that there were no signs of life either at the crash site or nearby.

The Champions Dinner had long since been cancelled and Marsha Hillingberg was reported to be getting ready to return to Anchorage. Governor Shippon had issued a statement of support and condolence to the Hillingberg family, which had been duplicated by the mayors of Alaska's other major population centres at Fairbanks and Juneau. By the time Duncan Wright spun across the finish line, the Iditarod had come to seem like a distraction.

Amid such turbulence and uncertainty, Edie Kiglatuk's failure to get in touch was of no consequence to anyone but Derek. Sammy, of course, didn't know. He was making his way along the Yukon River, with a couple of days still to go before reaching Nome.

The door from the bedroom swung open and Zach blundered in and went directly to the coffee pot.

'You get any sleep at all?'

'Not much.' Derek mentioned not hearing from Edie. 'I tried Olga's number, Edie's, nothing.'

'You know anyone else who could go round and check on her?' Zach sat himself down on the sofa, stretched his legs a little, yawned. 'You need to get back down there, man. I can keep an eye on Sammy at the checkpoints.' He took a gulp from his coffee and picked the sleep out of his eyes. 'I don't need to tell him anything he don't need to know. Just say you got some police business from home to attend to.'

Derek checked his watch. The first flight out of Nome bound for

Anchorage would be leaving in a couple of hours' time. He thought about calling the APD in the city but when he remembered Galloway and Schofield he decided against it. An idea came to him.

'Mind if I use your laptop?'

Zach waved in the direction of the little table in the corner of the room.

Derek waited for the machine to boot then tapped in Snowy Owl Café, got up the phone number and called. A man answered, said Stacey was filling the breakfast shift and would be too busy to talk. When Derek said it was an emergency, the man reluctantly agreed to bring her to the phone so long as whatever Derek had to say was quick.

Stacey immediately offered to go round to Edie's studio. She sounded genuinely worried. Derek gave her the Spenard Road address but told her not to knock on the door.

'You see anything there, don't get involved, just call me, OK.'

He promised to wait by the phone until she called back.

Megan appeared. She, too, looked wrecked. When Zach explained the situation, she soon gathered herself and went off to the kitchen to make breakfast so Derek wouldn't have to fly on an empty stomach. While he was waiting for Stacey to get back to him, he put his mind to thinking about where Edie might have got to. Homer was one obvious possibility, the other was the Old Believer compound up at Meadow Lake. He just had to hope something hadn't happened, either at the studio or at Lena and Olga's place.

When the phone rang, it startled him. The number at the studio flipped onto the caller ID. For a tiny moment he allowed himself to think that it was Edie calling, then Stacey's voice came on.

'Derek, I'm real worried. Bonehead's here. He's had an accident on the floor and he's real hungry. I don't think anyone's been here at all since last night. I went down to that big old house you said?

Edie's truck was parked outside, but there's no one in and no sign of her. No message, nothing.'

He told her he'd be down just as soon as he could. He didn't have to ask about Bonehead; she volunteered to take him.

At the airport he remembered Detective Truro. Lena and Olga had mentioned him. He called Zach from the phone booth and, remembering that Truro had been suspended, asked him for Truro's home number and address. He dialled but got a blank tone. Thinking he'd misdialled, he repeated the call and got the same tone. He spent the flight making lists of the possibilities on his beverage napkin.

At the airport in Anchorage he went straight out onto the concourse, picked up a cab and gave the driver Bob Truro's address.

# 40

An old model, beat-up SUV came bowling around the corner. Edie stepped into its path, waving her arms, and it slowed to a halt just ahead. A woman leaned out.

'You all in trouble?'

Lena opened her mouth to speak but Edie flashed her a warning look.

'Our truck broke down is all.'

The woman scanned the road for the breakdown.

'It's just up that path a little.' Edie waved in a vague direction behind her. 'The axle hit something hard, a rock most like.'

The woman hesitated, then waved them up.

'Well, OK then,' she said, glancing at her watch. 'I guess I could give you all a ride to the next tow-truck place. C'mon in then, before you all catch your death of cold.'

Edie clambered in the front passenger seat, Lena got in the back. The woman introduced herself as Toni. She'd just been to see her elderly mother in her care home and was heading to her shift at work in a yard selling construction materials on the other side of the city.

'What brought you all out here?'

'Dogs,' Edie said. 'Malamutes and huskies, mostly. There's a kennel . . .' she tailed off.

The woman glanced at Edie and reached for the radio. The car filled with the sound of golden oldies.

'I guess you people have a natural ability around huskies.'

'I guess,' Edie said. She glanced into the rear-view mirror to check whether Aileen was following. The road was empty.

They came to the junction of Bragaw and Debarr and stopped at a red. On the opposite corner was a gas station which doubled as a tow, repair and tyre shop and she let them out. Lena made a call from the gas station phone.

Now the immediate danger was over, Edie allowed herself to feel the full force of the Nembutal comedown. A taxi drew into the forecourt and a man with a crooked mouth honked his horn. Lena went over and had a word with him then came back.

'His name is Jeton. He's Albanian. He knows me as Nina. He looks after me when I'm working. I've told him you are a friend and your name is Sacha.'

They got in. The car smelled heavily of cheap air freshener. Jeton had laid lacy antimacassars across the seats. He smiled and nodded a friendly greeting to Edie. It wasn't just his mouth that was crooked, his teeth looked like scree.

They drove through the suburbs of Anchorage, past the pretty houses of professionals lying in the shadow of the Chugach Mountains, north and westward until the houses got smaller and less spaced, then gave way completely to sullen strip malls and drive-throughs selling unbranded fast food. Jeton finally dropped them in the parking lot outside what looked to Edie like a strip club.

They went in the back door, through a series of ill-lit and smelly corridors to a room full of women dressing and undressing. Lena asked Edie to wait and disappeared into the throng. Not long afterwards she returned holding a key ring which unlocked a battered-looking Chevrolet crouched in a far corner of the parking lot. They got in and Lena drove between heaps of dirty snowdrift, through the poor, unlit streets of the city. They turned into the parking lot of a cheap motel on the northern outskirts of downtown with a broken neon sign over the entranceway which once read 'Bear Motel'. Lena led them around the back to the service area then through a yard to a small concrete cabin divided into two apartments, with steps leading to the upper floor. The blinds were closed but the light was on. She knocked and said something in Russian. The door flew open. Olga glanced outside, briefly checked up and down, then closed the door and threw her arms around her friend.

Waiting for them inside were Derek Palliser and Bob Truro. It was such a relief to see them there that Edie felt her legs give way, but Derek leapt forward, grabbed her by the arms and pulled her in to him. He held her like that until she felt herself soften, then she pulled away.

'Kiglatuk, you disappear like that again, I'm going to have to kill you.' He noticed the fresh wound on her head. 'How did this happen?'

She pushed his hand away. The wound was throbbing but she didn't want to have to think about it just now.

She said, 'How did you find us?'

Derek flipped his head in Truro's direction. Truro gave a tiny nod but Edie didn't feel in the mood to acknowledge it.

They were in the kind of place you wouldn't want your mother to know you knew about. Thinly painted drywall, pitted and stained where the damp had come through. In the centre of the room a low-hanging plastic light fixture dimly illuminated whatever action took place on the sagging bed. The carpet tiles were brown, but they hadn't started out that way. On one side of the bed were stacked a small pile of clothes. On the other a baby was sleeping in a carrycot.

While Edie told the men what had happened, Lena went over and cooed at the baby. As he listened, Bob Truro crumpled into a chair at his side with his head in his hands. When she was finished the detective took a deep breath.

'Miss Kiglatuk, Edie, believe me, I'm more sorry than I can say for the way this has played out. I had no idea how far it had reached until they took me off the case.'

Edie felt a wave of nausea rise up. Most of it was anger, directed at the balding zealot on the other side of the room. The rest was Nembutal.

'I don't need your apology, detective. But Lucas Littlefish and Jonny Doe do.'

Truro bristled a little. 'That's why I'm here.'

The truth was on the point of bursting out of her. She wanted to tell Truro that Jonny Doe had a name, that he was Vasilly Chuchin, and that he was loved and that his mother, Lena, was standing right there, in the room, and that she and Vasilly deserved justice, just as Lucas and TaniaLee Littlefish deserved justice. She felt Derek's hand on her shoulder, pressing, squeezing and checked herself. Right now they needed Detective Truro on their side. In any case, if anyone was going to tell Truro about Vasilly, it had to be Lena herself. She sat down and flashed Derek a look of gratitude, which he returned with a wink.

'We went round to the old house, where I first met Lena and Olga, but there was no sign of anyone, so we drove to Aileen Logan's place. We thought you might have contacted her. There was no one in and no vehicle in the driveway,' Derek explained.

'Because . . . she was out looking for us.' Edie suddenly felt sick again. 'Is there any chance?' She checked the two men and saw they were both armed.

Derek shook his head. 'Aileen Logan has no idea about this place. We only found Olga here because Bob knew who to ask.' Edie noted the familiar. Bob. So, she guessed, Derek and Bob were a team now. 'We were just figuring out what to do next when you showed up.'

Lena and Olga had been hunched over the baby, talking animatedly in Russian. Lena came over now and placed a kiss on Edie's cheek. Edie patted the woman's arm. In the other corner of the room she saw Derek bite his lip.

'When I called, I was scared,' Lena said. 'A few days ago, friend of me at the club say a woman came in, asking for me. I wanted someone to help.' She took a breath and started to tremble. 'You risk your life, Edie,' Lena said. 'And maybe you save mine.' She ran a hand over Edie's hair and gave a nervous laugh. 'Small lady, but not so small here.' She pressed her palm over her heart.

'I want justice for Vasilly Chuchin, Lena, same as you.' At the name, Olga looked up anxiously.

Derek said, 'Who's Vasilly Chuchin?'

Edie looked to Lena. The woman closed her eyes and took a deep breath. She was sweating slightly and the cords on her neck stood out like parcel string.

'Jonny Doe is Vasilly Chuchin. He was son of me.'

Edie got up from the chair and went over to Olga's baby. She reached out and stroked the downy head. There on the right side, where she had imagined it would be, was the word шахта. Alarm suddenly signalled on Olga's face. Seeing it, Lena laid a hand on her arm and spoke to her softly in Russian.

Edie sighed. "Mine," she said. 'I've seen this word before.'

'On Vasilly you see it?'

'Yes, on Vasilly,' Edie said. She explained she'd seen the picture on Truro's desk. 'And on a baby down in Homer. You see that word, detective, when you were investigating the death of Vasilly Chuchin?'

Truro ran a hand over his face. There was a pause, then he nodded, shamefaced.

'I assumed it was part of the Dark Believer ritual, the sacrifice
element.'

Edie said, 'Is assumption usually part of your investigative
method, Detective Truro?'

Derek grimaced and she backed off.

Turning to Lena, Derek said, 'When we met, you told me you
came from near Moscow.'

Lena shook her head. She began to tremble again.

Edie said, 'Lena, please, for Vasilly.'

The young woman shot a glance at the baby, then at Olga. Then
she began her story. She'd been trafficked from Bilibino, a remote
and depressed gold mining town in the Chukotka Autonomous
Region through the Chukot capital, Anadyr, to Nome, by two men,
on the promise of a job in a hotel in Anchorage. It was the Russian
dream, she said, a chance to escape from the poverty of her surroundings, to earn some money, to become American. She was
fifteen, from a small, remote town, and she didn't know any better.
One of the men flew her to Nome. He took her to a hotel and told
her she would be flown to her ultimate destination the following
day. That destination turned out to be the Lodge.

For three winters she worked at the Lodge. Initially, she was
expected to service the men who came. Only one man never
touched her, the cripple. The men never gave their names and for
the first year her English was very poor and she could not speak to
them. She was afraid all the time. Once she reached seventeen the
men seemed to stop being interested in her. She earned her keep
cleaning and they told her they would fly her back to Chukotka
eventually, but a year passed, and it did not happen. A security
guard promised to allow her to escape if she had sex with him, so

she did. He went back on his promise, though not before making her pregnant.

'Then I am more afraid because they are taking babies away.'

It was during that period she made friends with Olga, who was pregnant too. They both dreamed of escaping but they had nowhere to go.

'When Vasilly born special boy, not ordinary boy, I thought they let me keep.' An odd, animal noise bubbled up from her. Olga came forward and held her.

Olga gestured to a bag lying under the desk. 'Watch film,' she said. Edie went over to the bag and pulled out a memory card. Detective Truro pulled a laptop from his case and fired it up.

The blank screen was replaced by a grainy black-and-white image of the Lodge, illuminated by security cameras. It was winter, at least it seemed that way to Edie. The centre of the driveway had been cleared but there were deep drifts around the periphery. Before long, the figure of a woman emerged from one of the side doors holding a baby. Beside Edie, Lena began shaking. The woman passed close enough to the camera to be identifiable as Marsha Hillingberg. The baby who lay asleep in her arms was part covered and Edie would not have been able to say for sure that this was Vasilly, though the shape of the face suggested an infant with Down Syndrome. As the woman in the film turned to walk along the side of the snow bank, Olga leaned in and pressed on the keyboard until the picture stopped. Lena's eyelids were drawn tightly together. She held her fist to her mouth, biting the fingers to stop from crying out. Then she managed to gather herself.

'The mentality is very dark in that place. We mark the children. We think, one day, we can find our children this way. Three babies we mark: Vasilly, Olga daughter and a boy.'

'The Stegner baby,' Edie said.

Lena looked at her blankly.

Edie described the girl she had seen in the woods. The writing on the windshield. 'Was she the mother of the third child you tattooed?'

Lena looked at the floor. Her face expressed such infinite weariness, it was as if the spirit in her had been swapped for another.

'Yes, Katerina, maybe.'

For the first time since she'd sat beside Lena, Edie looked away. Bob Truro was still sitting in the chair with his head in his hands. Next to him, Derek was biting his fingernails and staring at the brown carpet.

'This girl, Katerina . . . the baby father is Police Mackenzie,' Lena said. 'I seen his picture on TV.'

From over on the other side of the room, Bob Truro groaned.

Olga called for someone to fast-forward the footage. Truro got up and made himself busy. He stopped the film just as Marsha Hillingberg reappeared down the path, this time without the baby.

Lena said, 'They told me in the morning. They said he was gone to new home, but later I hear Tommy Schofield, the Hillingberg woman fighting. She told Tommy Schofield she gave my baby back to Nature. She call Vasilly "God's Little Error". When Tommy Schofield left, he was crying. He didn't want Vasilly to die. Maybe Tommy thinks he is God's Little Error too. I saw him go out into the forest. I think he collect Vasilly body. Later, I go out into the yard, I see footprints but I cannot get through, past guard. In the next night, I climb snow bank and I took out camera memory card and I hid this. Then I say Olga, we are leaving now. If they kill us, it will be nothing. Without our children, we are dead anyway. I wait for security guard, Vasilly father. I tell him, the Hillingberg woman kill your son. Two days he doesn't care, he doesn't do anything. Then he signal to me and in the night he let us out of the gate.'

Once more her eyes welled with tears.

'We come to Anchorage near two months, we clean in club, sometime we do' – her features bunched up in disgust – 'other things. But we are trapped. We cannot leave because we have no papers. Since Vasilly body found, I am afraid they will say I kill him. When the Logan woman come looking for me, I call you because I am very frightened she will find me and kill me before I can get justice for my Vasilly.'

Edie jumped off the bed, kneeled down beside Lena and took her hands in hers.

'She'd have to kill us first,' she said.

# 41

Edie woke with a fluttering heart, looked around at the unfamiliar surroundings, heard Derek Palliser breathing heavily in the bed beside her and remembered where she was. They had taken a room at the front of the Bear Motel from where they could watch vehicles enter the property, the idea being to take shifts through the night. Edie had fallen asleep on her watch, which had ruined the plan somewhat. Blinking away the remnants of sleep now, she realized she'd been dreaming about drinking. An enormous desire came over her, as strong and ineluctable as a spring blizzard. There was a twenty-four-hour bar only a block away from the motel. She had already registered its presence, which made her wonder how far a recovering alcoholic ever recovered. Softly, doing her best not to wake Derek, she unpeeled the bedcover, went to the window and pulled back the drape just enough to see out. It was nearly dawn. The lot was quiet. In a back room, Olga, Lena and the baby would be asleep, with Bob Truro propped up in the chair, on guard.

Derek's voice, as drowsy as a late summer bee, drifted from over the other side of the room.

'Edie?' The bedside light went on. Derek was sitting up on his elbows, blinking. 'My shift?'

'Go back to sleep,' she said.

He checked his watch. 'I'm done with sleeping.'

Edie turned from the window. 'Sammy's due in when exactly?'

'Last time I spoke with Zach, he said Sammy was at Elim. They'll still make him wait the statutory eight hours at White Mountain, so I'm guessing he'll be shooting over the finish line in just under twenty-four hours from now.'

'OK, then, so that's how long we got.'

Derek rubbed his hand across his face. 'Got for what exactly? Aileen Logan's disappeared and I don't think she's gonna be making an appearance any time soon.'

Edie moved away from the window and sat on Derek's bed.

'I'm talking about Marsha Hillingberg.'

'*What?*' He looked irritated. 'Edie, I'm not gonna be the one to give the news to Lena, but that CCTV footage doesn't prove anything.'

'It connects her to a place that was trafficking underage girls, then selling their babies.'

'Marsha would have a hard time coming up squeaky clean but you want justice for Vasilly, you won't get that from the CCTV footage. It's not like we can even go to the APD. Mackenzie's up to his neck in this.'

Derek was up now, dressed in only a pair of boxers, fiddling with the ancient coffee percolator on the table. She thought about how it would be to lead him back to bed.

'Right now Marsha Hillingberg is bombproof. She's enjoying a widow's premium.' The TV news had shown scenes of a sombre-looking Marsha accompanying her husband's coffin off the plane at Anchorage airport, surrounded by emoting fans. 'I wouldn't be surprised if she announces her candidacy for governor any time now.'

He poured out the coffee, threw six spoonfuls of sugar in Edie's and passed it over to her. She drank down the bitter fluid and remembered how much she preferred tea. An idea suddenly came to her.

She said, 'The black widow's forgotten something.'

'That so?'

'The spirit world.'

Derek let out a sour, dismissive laugh. 'Or maybe the spirit world's forgotten us,' he said. He thought of himself as a rationalist. But his blood was Cree and Inuit and that kind of blood, blood thick with ancient stories, that was just the kind of blood the spirits kept close. 'What we got? Some CCTV footage doesn't prove anything and the testimony of a couple of hookers, only one of whom speaks English, a girl in a nut bin, and a few whacked-out Jesus-heads in old-time robes.'

'Maybe you're forgetting where we are, Derek. Hookers, lunatics, religious freaks, garden variety Alaskans. This state is on the migratory path for every lame duck and dodo who can't settle anywhere else. The bats out of hell, the flying pigs, they all come here to roost.'

'Just your kind of place,' Derek said drily.

'My ma always used to say that bad things happen when good people do nothing.'

'I hate to be the one to break this to you, but your ma was wrong. Bad things happen *whatever* good people do. You wanna know why? *Because it's not the good people who are doing the bad things.*' He flashed her a look of exasperation, then went over to the bed and lit a cigarette. For a moment he just sat with his head in his hands, smoking. 'Here's what we're *supposed* to be doing, you and me. What we're *supposed* to be doing is helping out an old friend who's had some bad times. Instead we're talking about nailing some woman we don't even know in a country we don't even live in.'

'You even *hear* yourself, Police?' Her former notion of taking Derek to bed had disappeared as swiftly as a hard-on dipped in icy water. She now felt more like punching him out.

Instead, she moved away from him, closing her eyes and

summoning the image of the spirit bear leading her through the forest on a morning which already seemed so distant. Derek would scoff, but in Edie's mind she had no doubt that the animal had come with a message. What could the bear tell her? What was he *trying* to tell her? An idea bubbled up.

She said, 'Why would the Old Believers suddenly decide to sell their land?'

Beside her Derek took a breath. 'Because they're under pressure?'

'From who? Tommy Schofield's dead.'

Edie and Derek looked at one another, thinking the same thing. Byron Hallstrom. Edie went over to the wardrobe, pulled her outerwear off the hanger and began to throw it on. Derek reached out a hand and grabbed her arm.

'Promise me, after twenty-four hours, if we don't get what we need, we'll let Detective Truro take this one.'

She shrugged him off.

'I can promise, Police, but you should know that people break promises all the time.'

They made their way up the Glenn Highway for what they both hoped would be the last time. Edie drove, the route so familiar now it seemed to her like something out of a recurring dream. Two weeks in Alaska had taught her how to drive a truck without stalling the engine or bouncing off the verge. It had also taught her that she preferred to be in places where there were no roads or trucks or verges. Her longing to return home to Autisaq was a hollow hunger in her belly. This was the reason they called it homesickness. *Angirraqsirniq*. A griping feeling of nausea. She yearned for the horizons, for the great sweep of ice and rock and for the people she loved there. But she also missed the fact that things were simpler there, too, that there was an acknowledgement of the smallness and frailty of human life which, for her, was part of what made it worth living.

Turning onto the Hatcher Pass, she imagined Natalia, not knowing whether she would ever see the father of her baby. Though Edie could never share it, there was nevertheless something wondrous about the young woman's faith, not so much in God as in Galloway himself. No human being, except perhaps for her darling Joe, had ever engendered such confidence in Edie. As they rolled and bumped along the rugged track through the forest, she thought about Lucas and Vasilly and felt a deep mournfulness for those two newly minted lives which would never now grow old or wise or fully comprehend, even as spirits, the riches they had been forced to leave behind.

The truck rounded a corner where the large spruce stood and they came before long to the gate fronting the Old Believer property. Edie pulled up and they both got out and went over to the guard standing there in his thick, old-fashioned overcoat and fur hat.

She said, 'We've come to see Natalia or Anatoly Medvedev.'

The guard nodded an acknowledgement, pulled a walkie-talkie from his coat pocket and began talking into it in Russian.

'He coming, you wait.'

They stood on the far side of the gate, stamping their feet against the cold while the guard stamped on the other side, neither party speaking. After what seemed like the longest time there was a light and Medvedev came striding down the path.

'Edie Kiglatuk,' he said. She introduced Derek Palliser. The old man eyed him wearily. 'Why are you here?'

'We know Peter Galloway is alive.' She caught his eye in hers and gave him no opportunity to look away. His face clouded over, then he frowned and swung his head about, as though checking that they hadn't been overheard. This was not news to him. What had taken him aback was the fact that Edie knew.

'How can I trust you, Edie Kiglatuk?'

She turned and squinted through the light at him. 'Right now, I'm about the only Outsider you *can* trust.'

He took this in. 'What about this man?'

'My name is Palliser. I am a police sergeant, from the Ellesmere Island Native Police,' Derek said, in Russian. For a moment Medvedev froze, then, when Derek added that he was not here on official business but as a friend of Edie's, the Believer seemed to relax.

'We'll go back to the house in your truck. You can have some hot tea.'

He climbed into the front passenger side. Edie got in beside him and took up the steering wheel. Derek clambered into the back. They drove to the house at the far corner of the compound, but instead of asking them to park up, Medvedev waved Edie on towards a narrow track winding through spruce. 'Through there.' She pulled the steering wheel around and did as he suggested. The truck rocked along deep ruts leading into the forest for half a kilometre or so, to a small clearing at the back of which stood a small cabin.

They got out and Medvedev led them towards it. Derek waited until they were behind him, then, placing his hand on the weapon he was carrying, he flashed Edie a warning look, which she returned with a nod. The Old Believer held the door for them and they went into the cabin's only room. There were thick drapes at the window. Medvedev took out a lighter, lit an oil lamp and drew the drapes. He pulled aside a large, knotted rug to reveal a small hatch, from around whose edges a thin light shone. He knocked twice then opened the hatch. Natalia's face appeared, and when she saw Edie standing above her she broke into a wide smile, grabbing at the steps and launching herself up and into the room. Seeing

Derek, she hesitated, glancing anxiously towards the hatch. Medvedev said something to her in Russian and she softened, went back over to the hatch and spoke down into the hole. A pair of hands appeared, then two burly arms and Peter Galloway stepped up into the room.

He held out a hand then, and when Edie did not take it, he let it go slack at his side.

'Edie Kiglatuk, I used you very badly.'

Her eyes narrowed to take him in. He seemed thinner than from a few days ago. 'I guess you're now going to give me your excuse.' In her peripheral vision she saw Natalia run a hand over her belly.

'No excuse,' Galloway said. 'I'm not proud of what I did to you. Anatoly thought I would want to see you, but he was wrong. I had to get away.'

Natalia cut in then. 'Edie, my husband had nothing to do with the death of those children.'

Derek stepped forward. 'I guess you know this man's history?'

Natalia dropped her gaze to the floor, allowed herself an instant of shame, then took in a deep breath and raised her head so that she was looking directly at Derek.

'I know that God made all men capable of redemption.'

Derek gave a little cough. 'Even Tommy Schofield?'

Galloway shifted on his feet. 'I didn't kill those babies and whatever you think I didn't murder Tommy Schofield.'

Edie said, 'I'd like to shake the hand of the man who did.'

Galloway gave a low, sorry laugh.

Medvedev coughed. 'Natalia, do we have tea?'

She nodded and made for a little gas burner on one side of the room. There were four rustic-looking chairs and a worn leather pouf. Edie sat down. Derek continued to stand. Galloway glared at him.

'Why have you sold your land?' Edie asked.

Natalia brought over a teapot and some tiny glasses. Medvedev allowed her to pour the rusty-coloured liquid. When she was done, he leaned forward and said:

'We decided to leave. We have sold everything, this land too. No one wants us here. The moment something happens, then people will start talking about Dark Believers again. There are no Dark Believers here, Edie Kiglatuk, you will not find any. The dark people, the ones in league with Satan, are those who will not allow us to lead decent lives following the word of God.' He stroked his beard, then put the glass of tea to his mouth and took a sip. 'There's a place in Brazil we can go back to.'

Edie turned to Natalia. 'You too?'

Natalia shook her head. 'It's too dangerous. Even though he's officially dead, every port and airport in Alaska will have had Peter's picture – in any case' – she folded her palm around her belly again – 'I am too far gone to fly now.' She darted a look at her husband. There was anxiety in it, Edie saw, but love too. He reached out and took her hand. 'The border between Alaska and the Yukon Territory is very long. A lot of it is not guarded.'

A look passed between them.

'So you sold to Tryggve.'

Medvedev raised his eyebrows. His eyes shifted to Galloway, who signalled to him that it was OK to talk.

Tommy Schofield had been pressuring the Believers to sell their waterfront land near Homer for years, but in the last months he'd begun to make threats, saying that if they didn't sell, he had the funding to build a condominium complex on adjoining land and divert the sewage outpipe onto Believer territory until it was no longer fit for cattle or agriculture. He kept hinting, Medvedev explained, that someone much bigger and more powerful was interested in the land now, and that this person wouldn't stop until he had it.

'He never said a name, but we knew it was Byron Hallstrom,' Galloway added.

'We didn't want to sell the land,' the old man said, 'it was our home. When we heard Tommy Schofield had killed himself, God forgive us, we were glad. But then the troopers came. They said they had identified Peter Galloway's body.'

'My body was released for burial in a closed casket,' Galloway said bitterly.

Medvedev took over again. 'But even allowing for animals, Peter is a large man and Schofield was a small man, and besides we have rituals. We saw immediately this was not Peter and they had given us Thomas Schofield's body.'

'Well, what's a body among friends?' Derek's voice was thick with irony.

Medvedev glared at him then turned away and shrugged.

'You judge us but you have not suffered like us.'

Edie put her head in her hands. Us and them. Them and us. How many times had she heard it, repeated over and over as if it was something ineluctable and impossible to overcome. The differences usually started off so inconspicuously. For the Old Believers, it had been the insistence on that extra plank of wood on a cross, one more stroke in genuflection over four hundred years ago. Small differences, between groups of people who were, in essence, the same.

'Please,' Natalia said, holding up a hand. She gave Edie the look women give one another when they both agree their men are ridiculous.

Everyone settled down. Natalia poured more tea.

'Maybe you can make this clear to me,' Derek said. 'You buried Schofield?'

Medvedev shook his head. 'We made a grave for Peter, but we burned the body. We have a brick kiln. It gives a very intense heat. It didn't matter to us, Schofield is from the Outside.'

'But it *did* matter,' Edie said. 'When you burn a body, no one can ever dig it up.'

'Or learn the truth,' Derek added.

Medvedev placed his hands on his knees. 'The ultimate truth is God,' he said simply.

'How's about we settle for the intermediate truth right now?' Derek retorted.

Medvedev acknowledged the joke with an almost-smile. 'I've told you everything.'

Edie shook her head. 'You owe us, me, more than that. You held out on Hallstrom. Why give in to him now?'

There was silence. In the chair opposite Natalia bit her lip. She looked at the floor then at Edie, then finally took a breath in and, directing herself to her father, she spoke very quietly.

'For us, this is over, but for the parents of the babies who died it won't ever be over.'

'Which is why you need to finish the story,' Edie pressed.

Natalia's eyes swelled with tears. She swallowed hard and nodded. 'The day Schofield's body was found, my father had a call from Marsha Hillingberg. She said that she knew Peter Galloway was still alive and that if my father didn't sign the land over to Tryggve, she would have every trooper in the state out looking for him. It was then we understood that God no longer wants us to be in this place. And so we signed.'

Edie and Derek swapped glances. It didn't surprise Edie to know that Schofield had been Hallstrom's puppet all along. She'd witnessed firsthand his fan-like adoration of the Norwegian. But once Marsha Hillingberg had got herself involved in the action, Schofield was doomed and he must have known it. If his old playground wound hadn't opened up then, Marsha's casual disposal of Vasilly Chuchin must have brought the blood to the surface all over again. Edie could only imagine how much Schofield hated Marsha Hillingberg and how powerless he was to do anything about it. They were so tied that the only way to denounce her would have been to go down with her. Marsha had boxed him in so that his life was no longer his own. Edie wouldn't have been surprised to discover he had contemplated suicide. And yet, if she knew anything, it was that footprints in the snow never lied.

'That's it,' Natalia said. 'You have the story.'

Edie rose from her chair and went over to where Derek was standing. 'We're done here.' At the door, she turned and wished Natalia good luck.

# 42

They picked up Edie's things at the studio and called round at the Bear Motel. A man in a thick blue parka was standing in the walkway just in front of Olga and Lena's room. Derek flashed Edie a warning look to stay back and went ahead, clutching his weapon, but catching sight of them, the man waved and shouted over, 'It's OK, I'm with Bob.'

The man was Tom Brokovich, an old friend of Truro's. They'd met at the Alaska Investigative Bureau in Anchorage. He owed Truro a favour and this was his way of helping out.

Inside the room the two women were sitting on the bed playing with the baby. Detective Truro sat in the chair beside the bathroom talking on his cell phone. He stuck a finger in the air to indicate he wouldn't be long, then pointed to the chair on the other side of the table. Derek plucked his Lucky Strikes from his pocket and made a sign to indicate that he was going out for a smoke, while Edie asked the two women on the bed if they'd slept.

Lena said, 'A lot better than in dog cage.'

'You get some breakfast?'

Lena smiled and pointed to a half-full Dunkin' Donuts bag. 'Bob treat us like Empress of Russia.'

'Don't get any big ideas,' Edie said, chucking the baby under the chin, 'this little one's a Republican, I can tell.'

Lena laughed and explained the joke to Olga, who cracked a little smile. Oblivious to all the trouble, the baby lay on her back doing her best to remove her socks.

'Bob say if we cooperate, agree to testify, maybe we get leave to stay.' Lena gently lifted the baby up and, clucking, said, 'You American baby.'

Derek came back in, looked inside the doughnut bag then put it down just as Truro was finishing off his conversation.

'The house of cards has a brick missing.'

Edie raised her brows and gave him a quizzical look.

Truro shot her a sheepish grin. 'OK, so I'd make a lousy contractor, but you wanna hear some good news or not?' The women stopped playing with the baby and went quiet. 'That was an old bud of mine at the APD. Seems like Police Chief Mackenzie's taking early retirement with immediate effect. Grounds of ill health.'

'The rats are running for cover,' Derek said.

'They got Harry O'Brien flying in from Juneau as Acting Chief. We go way back. He's a straight-up guy.'

'What if Mackenzie goes public with what he knows?' Edie said. 'Wouldn't that lead directly to Marsha?'

'What's his incentive? That way, all he does is incriminate himself. He was at the Lodge too and, presumably, DNA tests can prove that he fathered the Stegner baby. Besides, what could he prove even if he wanted to? Unless he's got something we don't know about, there's nothing to connect Marsha Hillingberg to the Lodge except the tape. And even the tape's no proof that she knew what was going on or that she had anything to do with Vasilly's death. Mrs Hillingberg's real smart. Right now we got a suicide, a plane crash, a dead baby everyone thinks got sacrificed by a satanist nut, plus a bunch of circumstantial stuff but nothing definitive.'

Lena suddenly let out a choking sob. She'd risked her life to get the CCTV tape and this was the first time she'd heard it wouldn't be enough. She sank back and put her face in her hands.

Bob Truro said, 'I apologize, Lena, for my tactlessness. That was low cop-talk. I should have phrased myself better.'

Lena looked up through eyes punched with grief. 'You think phrase hurts me? Everyone betray my son. No justice for God's Little Error. That hurts.' Olga reached out her arms and held Lena on the bed. For a moment no one knew what to say.

Derek waited until he thought no one was looking, then checked his watch. Lemming brain, Edie thought, glancing at him. Bob Truro had picked up on it too.

'Derek, you'd make a lousy undercover cop,' he said. Derek's head snapped up. He looked guilty, then grateful.

'Sammy doesn't know about any of this and I wouldn't want to let him down.'

He was right, Edie thought. Her ex had been through a lot. He deserved this. She sucked on her teeth.

'Lena, I'm sorry,' she said, 'our fella lost his son last year. Running this race means the world to him.'

''s OK,' Lena said, digging her thumbnail into the pad of her index finger. 'I know how is, losing child. You go.'

'Thank you,' Edie said simply.

'Don't worry about Lena and Olga or the baby,' Bob added, as much for Lena's benefit, Edie thought, as for her own. 'They'll be fine. Tom's gonna stay here until we can get 'em to a safe house. Alaska's full of places to hide.'

Edie opened her mouth to speak. Truro tried to wave her off, but she ignored him.

Turning to Lena, she said, 'Lena, we're gonna get Marsha Hillingberg. I guarantee it.'

From the other side of the room, she saw Derek Palliser bite his lip.

# 43

At the Iditarod HQ in Nome, people were shifting to and fro packing things up. Chrissie Caley let out a disappointed sigh. There were dark moons under her eyes and her skin was sallow, a nerve twitching in her left cheek. Ever since Aileen Logan's quick exit and the mayor's tragic death the atmosphere had been muted.

'It's such a shame what's gone on. At one point it was looking so exciting.' A TV news crew came up waving their accreditation passes. She waved them off. 'I'm tellin' ya, I was Aileen's biggest fan but, boy oh boy, did she leave a stink behind when she baled.'

The room was being used as the communications hub for Marsha Hillingberg's visit. The mayor's widow was due to lay a wreath at the site of her husband's plane crash, then make a speech this evening at the Glacier Inn. In the circumstances, the gubernatorial election had been postponed, but all the buzz suggested that Mrs Hillingberg was going to use tonight's event to announce her candidacy. She seemed to be riding high in the political blogs.

Derek said, 'You think she's got a chance?'

'People are ready for a change,' Caley said. 'They were ready to vote her husband in, why not her?'

Derek flipped a cigarette from the carton and lit it. 'Democracy, dontcha love it.'

Caley gave a wry smile. 'Not a fan, huh? Me neither. Even less so since Aileen debunked. My ex-boss was crazy about Mrs Hillingberg, almost convinced me at one time, but these past days, I've kinda come to question Aileen Logan's judgement.'

The film crew moved away. Edie waited till they were out of earshot then said in a low voice, 'Look, Chrissie, tell you the truth, the reason we came is we're kinda anxious for news about Sammy.'

Caley looked uncomfortable. 'He's officially off the race, guys, so I don't have any more information than you. We've said he can use the trail so long as he does the stopover at Safety. We don't want the animal welfare folks on our backs, but he's not on our GPS tracker any more.'

Derek put the cigarette out on his boot and threw the stub in the trash. He looked at Zach.

Zach said, 'Last time I saw him, he'd just rested up at White Mountain and was heading for the Safety roadhouse.'

Caley went on. 'Like I said, I don't have any more accurate intel on that than you. We had a call from White Mountain a couple of hours ago. They're shutting up right now, but they mentioned Sammy had been through. Said he looked real tired. My guess is he should be reaching Safety any time around now.' Her phone rang. 'You might wanna go down there yourselves. It's only twenty miles or so.' She answered the phone, listened for a moment, then, placing her hand over the receiver, she furrowed her brow and said apologetically, 'Sorry, guys, I gotta take this.'

As they tromped back to the house, Zach made the plans.

'Actually, that's not a bad idea of Chrissie's, you meet Sammy up at Safety. Megan and Zoe are at some mom and baby programme at the school most of the day and I gotta go on shift so you'd be welcome to take our snowmachines.'

Later, when they were out checking over the snowmobiles, Derek said, 'Things seem to have worked out pretty good for Marsha Hillingberg. No one has been able to link her to any of this.'

Edie looked up and pulled off her snow goggles. She remembered her mother's saying that great hunters were fashioned out of patience. 'Not yet,' she said.

Derek keyed up Zach's vehicle, then let the engine run idle.

Edie followed suit. 'What say we ask her about it?'

Derek swung around. His eyes were full of light. 'Tonight?'

'Why not?'

Derek laughed. 'Hell, yeah,' he said.

Someone had ploughed a track from the drift leading out of Nome along the shoreline towards Safety, but they chose instead to take the snowbies out over the pressure ice onto the flat pan, where the going was smoother. On the way out, Edie tried to erase the investigation from her mind. She wanted to meet Sammy clean, unimpeded. Partly, it was being on the move that made her feel that way. There would be time to fill him in on the story later. The sun appeared, briefly, and it was bitter cold, the kind of hard crisp freeze you could do business with. Heading east on the sea ice with the land spread low and rocky to her left, the great expanse of Norton Sound to the right, she felt more at home than she had since she'd arrived in Alaska. Home. It felt as if it was just over the horizon, right up ahead.

They made landfall a few miles shy of what was a speck of a building on the horizon, and carried on along the track. The wind had picked up alarmingly now, stirring up drift like a great brush sweeping a dusty yard. Six feet up, the air was clear, but look down and you couldn't see your own foot. Up ahead a pair of snowmobile lights appeared out of the gloom, followed by the machine itself. The driver slowed and stopped. He was a large man, a *qalunaat*, wearing the uniform of an Iditarod steward.

'You folks heading for Safety? We're just packing up there. Last musher left about two hours ago.' He was shouting against the wind.

Edie said, 'Sammy Inukpuk?'

The man cupped a mittened hand around his ear to indicate that he hadn't heard. When she repeated herself, he shook his head slowly.

'Can't say that name's familiar, but we've been real busy with the stragglers today. If you wanna go up to the roadhouse there's still a coupla folks there can help you out.'

The roadhouse was the only structure in Safety, a large, wooden building surrounded by a handful of outbuildings and fishing shacks, all shabby around the edges and oddly out of keeping with the grand sweep of tundra and low hummocky slopes and wide, salt-ridden ice lakes about. A pair of ravens clung to the snow hooks, buffeted into green-black bouffants by the wind. All around were sled tracks, but no sleds.

Edie and Derek exchanged worried looks. They went into the snow porch, tamped the ice off their boots and removed their three layers of mittens and gloves, their snow goggles, hats and parkas. A woman and a man bustled around inside tidying up equipment. The woman whirled round, said her name was Laurie and asked how she could help.

'We've come for Sammy Inukpuk. Chrissie Caley down in Nome said he'd be here by now.'

Laurie looked surprised. 'He a musher?' She dived into a bag, pulled out a list and began checking it. She was the kind of *qalunaat* woman Edie had seen a lot around Alaska – well-intentioned in a flinty sort of a way, can-do and unflappable. The kind Edie always took to.

'I'm real sorry but he's not on our list,' she said, looking up. Her face took on a sympathetic air.

'He dropped out of the official race at Koyuk.'

Laurie let the paper fall back into her bag. 'Well, that explains it right there. He should have flown out of Koyuk then.'

Edie continued. 'No, he wanted to carry on. They said he could still use the trail.'

Laurie raised an eyebrow. She was still sympathetic, only perhaps a little less patient. 'I'm real sorry, Miss, but we can't fully support competitors who've dropped out. Last musher on my list passed by here two hours back. We're packing up and getting ready to leave, before that old blizzard gets going.' Just then there was a loud clanging sound from outside as the wind whipped up something metallic and threw it around a little. 'Look, there's fresh water and some cans and plenty of fuel if you want to stay here and wait for your friend. I guess he should be along any minute, right?'

The man hurried by carrying a box, acknowledged them with a nod, and addressed himself to the woman.

'We gotta go, hon.'

'Love, honour and obey!' Laurie let out an ironic but affectionate little laugh. 'You guys staying?'

Edie nodded.

'OK, then. Good luck with your friend. Looks like the wind's whippin' up. When he shows it'd be best if you all keep in here till it's passed over.' And with a wave of her hand, she was out of the door.

Edie and Derek heard two snowmobiles start up then fade into the screeching of the wind. They dumped their packs on a table to the left of the front door, pulled off their outerwear and looked about. The place was cosy at least. A large dark wood bar curved around at the back. Someone had tacked postcards and foreign banknotes up on the supporting pillars. Edie went over and cast an eye over them. Nowhere she'd rather be right now than at home in Autisaq. Derek pulled off his fleece and lit up a cigarette, a worried expression on his face.

Edie said, 'You think something's happened to Sammy?'

'You think it hasn't?' He sucked on his smoke, anxiously squeezing the fingers of one hand with another.

'It could just be the weather. Or maybe the dog team. Some of those dogs we picked up at Koyuk weren't as fit as the ones he left behind.'

Derek wasn't so easily reassured. 'The fella already got sabotaged.' He shook his head. 'We should have told him what was going on. We should have pulled him off the race.' His voice was full of anger and regret.

Edie bit on her lip. 'Derek, this was the only thing in his life he always wanted to do. Run the Iditarod. You crush a man's dreams, he's dead already.' As she said the word 'dead' a bolt of terror shot up her spine and made her light-headed. If something *had* happened to Sammy then it was because of her, because she had just kept going on and on picking at the old sore. Justice for Lucas Littlefish and Vasilly Chuchin. Who was she kidding? Wasn't this all just another Edie Kiglatuk production?

She sat down on a barstool and took a deep breath. They would just have to go out and look for him. The trail was still marked, if not by official flags, then by the runner lines of dozens of sleds. Sure there was a blizzard coming up, but they had snowmobiles and emergency supplies. If he'd been at White Mountain earlier in the day, he couldn't be that far away.

'We need to go find Sammy,' she said. 'You got your service pistol?'

'What kind of question's that?'

Edie started pulling on her outerwear. She was putting her hat back on when she heard the door swing open. For a second she thought it was Derek going out to the snowmobiles. Then she knew it wasn't. She moved her head round slowly. There, standing in the doorway were two large *qalunaat*. The one with the ice-blue eyes was pointing a handgun at her. The other, moose-nosed, held his weapon against Sammy Inukpuk's forehead.

# 44

The two men took them outside the roadhouse at gunpoint, forced them to remove their outerwear then hog-tied each. For what seemed like an age they waited outside in the gusting snowdrift while the two men hitched Zach's and Megan's snowmobiles behind their own, laughing and bickering in a combination of Russian and broken English. Edie picked out the words 'Ice Row Truckers'.

'Ice *Road*, dipshit,' moose nose said, in English. 'How they gonna truck down Ice *row* for chrissakes?'

'Man, that's what I said,' his companion said. 'You listen one time, you know this.'

Their work with the snowmobiles done, they hauled Sammy and Derek to their feet and got one man on each of the towed snow-mobiles so that he was sitting upright with his hands tied around the steering column. For some reason, perhaps because they saw her as less of a threat, the man with the moose nose untied Edie's ankles and instructed her to ride pillion behind him.

She looked back at Derek and Sammy. If they were afraid for what was to come, none of that showed on their faces. Say what you liked about Inuit men, when it came down to it they were tough as walrus hide. Women, too. She worried about Derek in particular. He had taken his fleece off inside the Safety roadhouse and what he had on was nothing sufficient for the weather. Tough he might be, but even Police was still human.

They started up along the beach towards the sea ice. She could feel the body warmth of her captor ahead of her, his broad back giving her at least some protection from the wind.

Swivelling her head about, she tried desperately to get a bearing on the Safety roadhouse as it disappeared into the spindrift but it was hard to keep her balance with her hands tied behind her back and the sky was a formless white and the selvedge where the land pressed up into it almost invisible. Behind her, she could see Sammy and Derek, with their legs clamped to the snowbies, struggling to stay seated as the vehicles bumped along. If either of them fell, she knew the men would leave them there and she sensed that Sammy and Derek knew this too.

As their captors picked their way through the pressure ridge where the shore-fast ice met the pack ice out onto the smooth pan of the middle of Norton Sound, the thought suddenly occurred to Edie that all three of them were going to be taken out into the middle of the Sound and left to die. She felt herself liquefying, a rush of terrorizing adrenaline course around her veins. She bit down hard on her lip, willing herself to keep her head. If she did not, how could she expect Sammy or Derek to keep theirs?

The men picked up speed now, racing south and west into the swirling drift. With no outerwear, each gust of wind felt like a new assault, the cold slamming into the face, tearing at the ears, forcing the eyes to close. She wanted to turn her body in, to protect herself with her shoulders, but with her arms tied behind her back she could not. She began to shiver uncontrollably, the spasms coming like the waves on a stony beach. She took a deep breath then, and forced herself to take her mind on a trip around her body, tightening and releasing the muscles. This she did over and over until the heat had stopped the shivering, then she jammed her head around. Behind her, Derek was still bouncing in the saddle, his body hunched and rigid, eyes shut tight against the formidable cold. The ropes held him without providing any support. Off to one side, she could just about see Sammy through the spindrift. It was probably −28 on the sea ice, −35 if you included wind-chill. Unprotected from the wind, and without outerwear, they would soon begin lapsing into a disorientated state of hypothermia.

Whatever their destination, Edie was in no doubt now that this was a one-way trip.

She began to lose control of the muscles in her limbs. However much she tried, she could no longer waylay the agitation of her body. She was shaking violently, her fingers, nose and ears throbbed with frostnip and though she kept her eyes closed, she could feel her tear ducts forming little boulders of ice. Soon, she knew, she would stop feeling the pain. Then her mind would begin to wander and she would hallucinate. Finally, an overwhelming urge to sleep would come over her and then it would all be over.

She had no idea how much later it was when she began to feel the snowmobile slowing, then sliding gradually to a halt. She tried to open her eyes but the lashes were firmly frozen together now. The driver got down from the snowmobile and she felt herself being heaved off the saddle. Then she fell and landed on her side in wind-dry snow. She still could not open her eyes but she knew she was lying close to the vehicle from the loud roar of the engine and the stench of exhaust fumes. Something was thrown off the vehicle onto the snow, and she felt a knife sawing at the ties on her wrists. Her two captors shouted to one another, there was the sound of the snowmobiles accelerating, then a swoosh in the snow as the vehicle beside her turned. The snowmobile roared off, kicking snow in her face. She listened to the sound of the engines. Then there was only the shriek of the wind and they were alone.

Suddenly, she realized that her body was no longer shaking.

Forcing herself to sit, she shouted out and, with a bolt of relief, heard Derek and Sammy respond.

She screamed, 'Don't move, I can walk. I'm coming for you.' Her eyes were still held fast with ice. Though it felt as though the sockets were full of sand, she began to screw them up hard, then release, until she thought she would faint from pain, but she could feel the tips of the eyelashes gradually begin to soften, then she began to force the lids apart, feeling the tearing as, one by one, the lashes popped out at the root. She looked about. They were out on the sea ice in very low visibility. The wind was coming in from the east-north-east now, whipping snow into her ears, her mouth, her nostrils. In the distance she thought she could see a slight darkening on the ice and hoped it was Sammy or Derek. She knew she had to get to them fast and willing her legs to move she tried to lift herself from the ice but nothing happened. She tried again, harder this time, but still her legs did not move. Yet in spite of this, a kind of calm had come over her. These were the conditions she had been born into, this is what she knew.

No longer able to feel her fingers, she used her elbows to rub her legs until a fierce pain came back into them, and then she stood, wobbly at first, but gradually gaining her balance against the scooping action of the wind which threatened at any moment to lay her back down on the ice. Though her eyes felt as though they were being scoured, she could see a few feet ahead. Step by step she made her way through the whipping drift towards the dark patch on the ice some way away. It was Derek. He was lying on his side in the snow. She put her arm on him. His eyes were partly open but he could not see. The telltale hard white waxiness of frostbite had settled on his face. The ties around his hands had been cut. He was moaning softly. She stood up and looked about but could see nothing except driving snow. Derek made a coughing sound. She looked down and saw that he was trying to point with his finger but his fingers had frozen together and what he was holding out looked like a stump of a hand, its edges already swelling with frostbite.

She knelt down and shouted into his ear, 'Are you trying to tell me where Sammy is?'

He nodded.

She shouted Sammy's name and heard a faint sound. Using all her strength to pull Derek up by the shoulders into a sitting position, she began to rub his body with her elbows. 'Keep on rubbing your skin till I come back. Think about lemmings,' she said. 'All the different types of lemmings and all the research you still need to do on them.'

Derek give a little nod and what would have passed for a smile if his lips weren't iced together.

She found Sammy nearby, doubled over on the ice, his arms tucked between his chest and knees. He was shaking violently. His eyebrows and nose were white with frost but he looked up as Edie approached and blinked an acknowledgement. She bent down and rubbed him hard. His skin had frozen but the flesh was still soft below. He had frostbite, but it wasn't yet deep. Hunter's response, that mysterious opening of capillaries in the hands and feet, the adaptive flushing of warm blood unique to those who worked constantly in frigid conditions, had protected both Sammy and his ex. Derek, who had fewer clothes on, was past all that.

'Can you stand?'

He nodded. A look of deep concentration came over his face. She reached out a hand to help him, but he pushed it aside. He wanted to feel the limits of his own capabilities. He rose slowly, first elevating his knees, then pushed off first with the left foot, then with the right. At the top, he caught Edie's arm briefly to steady himself and they began to walk like that, arm in arm, towards the spot where Derek was sitting.

For a moment they huddled together, each enjoying the warmth of the others' breath on their frozen eyes, on the frozen hairs inside their nostrils.

'We went over a pressure ridge not far back. I felt it.'

Sammy grunted an affirmation. He'd felt it too. In a world where she could no longer be sure where the lines between reality and her own confused state lay, this was good, this suggested that she was right, that there was a pressure ridge and that they might reach it. She didn't have to explain that the wind would have piled snow there and they might be able to make a shelter. They would all know that was the only hope they had.

Derek groaned again. She could feel the force of him, trying to move his legs, but it came out as nothing more than a momentary tightening.

Edie said, 'That's OK, Police, we'll pull you.'

She and Sammy helped each other up, then, looping their arms under Derek's shoulders, Sammy and Edie began to drag the policeman like a sled behind them. It was slow going, he was heavy and they were weak and had to be careful not to bring on a sweat that could make their hypothermia worse. All the same, step by step they retraced their path, following the snowmobile tracks that were growing ever fainter as the wind frisbeed snow across the ice. Then, after who knew how long, Sammy pointed out the band of grey marking the place where the ridge began. They came to where the two ice floes had raised up at their edges. Right here the ridge was small, too small to act as a wall for a shelter, and it was at the wrong angle for either side to be in the lee of the storm, but it would make a suitable foundation.

Sammy was by now becoming unsteady on his feet. Edie left the two men huddled together and set off along the line of the ridge to find deeper snow, making sure to move downwind from them so she could hear Sammy's voice. Her footprints might be sufficient, but every couple of minutes Sammy would shout to keep her orientated. She'd come back for them when she'd found a drift.

It didn't take long. A little way further, the ridge grew taller where the floes had been forced up high against one another and the wind had already driven loose piles against the pressure ridge. What snow lay in drift was dry and the wind had not yet had a chance to compact the layers. It would be too frail for a snow house. She made her way back to them. Where her footprints had been rubbed out, she waited for the sound of Sammy's voice to come to her over the roar of the wind. The fear that had terrorized her earlier had gone. Her only feeling now was the absolute focused determination that, whatever happened to her, Sammy and Derek would get through this. She could feel herself weakening now, her hands hardening already, but she would not allow them to die here. Quickly, scoping about, she decided that the three of them working together might be able to mound up the snowdrift into a temporary snow cave in which they could at least take some shelter from the blizzard.

She found them where she had left them, Sammy keeping Derek warm with his body.

She said, 'We need to drag him a little further. Can you do it?'

Sammy flashed her a look of absolute conviction. She gave him a wink back. The old team.

All three found the walk to the pressure ridge exhausting, but they had no time to acknowledge their throbbing arms, their stiffening skin, their increasingly muddled thinking. And yet they all knew, could see from one another's faces, that they were all suffering, all becoming too weak to think about anything but conserving their resources for the job of survival.

They left Derek sitting on top of the pressure ridge, clambered down and kicked up the snow around, pressing down with numbed feet to pack it a little so that it would not collapse when they started scooping out the hole. When they had a good-sized mound, they fetched Derek, dragging him down the slope and installed him on one side of the mound. While they built it up around the sides, Derek went to it with his elbows, hollowing out a shallow shelter in the snow. The effort of concentration seemed to perk their spirits and get their adrenaline circulating. Sammy began to sing, old songs, songs about spirits and hunters, and though they could hardly hear one another above the yelling of the wind, just knowing they were singing together gave them a renewed sense of hope.

They clambered into their newly fashioned shelter, and pulled in snow around the entrance. They were bunched together, knees up against their chins, their arms around one another to hold in the heat. None was shivering now, none could feel their extremities and yet they were full of the greatest affection for one another. If they went like this, in one another's arms, then each would know there were many worse ways to die.

For hours they sat singing in the dark of the snow cave, the strength of their voices gradually ebbing with their life force until a violent, katabatic gust, twisting its way towards the pressure ridge, spun off the makeshift entrance to the shelter, allowing the driving snow to cover them. Without hesitation, Sammy made his way forward on his knees to the broken entrance.

'I'm going to make some repairs,' he said.

Derek and Edie looked at one another, weak and nearing death. They both understood what Sammy had just volunteered to do and it humbled them.

Outside the blizzard sang its own raucous, anarchic tune. Moments passed and they heard Sammy's shouts. Shuffling to the entrance of the snow cave, Edie peered out. The sunset wasn't far off and the snow was now deep grey. She squinted. In front of her she thought she could make out something blue. Sammy's clothing? No, she remembered. Sammy never wore blue. It was a kind of cloth though, or perhaps a sheet. The wind was pressing it into whatever was behind it. She slid from the cave, stumbled in the wind towards it then saw that it was pressing into the contours of a human body. Sammy. She went towards it now, walking bent, in a hunter's attitude, against the worst of the wind.

Sammy was trying to handle a blue tarpaulin, which was flapping crazily in the blizzard and threatened to take off in the wind. She went towards him and, using her arms, because her own hands were by now quite useless, helped to manhandle the tarp into a twist they could then carry through the snow and back to the cave. They did not speak – the roar of the wind was too loud for them to make themselves heard – but immediately got down to what needed to be done, the collecting and heaping of snow around the tarp to make an entrance. Finally, they rolled back inside, and tamped up the entrance with more snow.

Sammy shouted, 'It's the one from my sled. Must have torn off in the wind. I found it flapping from an ice boulder just along the pressure ridge.' The skin on his lips peeled open and began to bleed and he put a hand up to it. The flesh beneath wasn't frozen yet. Another sign of hope.

The tarpaulin flapped and billowed in the wind but it remained firm.

'I guess the team didn't make it,' Sammy said.

Edie reached out and squeezed his arm. 'But we will,' she said. Snow began to accumulate at the base of the tarp. They could hear the tap tapping then nothing, as the layers piled higher. The snow cave began to warm from their body heat. They started to feel sleepy, but knew they must not sleep. There were three things Inuit did in these circumstances. They sang the old songs, they played the old games and they told the old stories.

About halfway through the night, when they had told the stories and sung the songs and as sure as they could be that they would make it at least to the next day, Sammy said,

'Maybe one or other of you can tell me what this is all about?'

And so there, in the snow cave surrounded by a howling blizzard and not knowing how they were going to get out of it, with frostbite already creeping like a shadow across their limbs and faces, Derek and Edie took it in turns to tell him the story, from the moment Edie found the body of Lucas Littlefish to their last, disastrous, trip to the Safety roadhouse in the hope of finding their friend.

# 45

Edie did not hear the snowmobiles but she felt the sound as a vibration coming up from the ice beneath her feet. The heft of the air gave her the sense that a great deal of new snow had piled around the snow cave and that they were under it. It was impossible to know for sure who might be heading towards them. But there were only two people who knew where they were. And she was pretty sure she didn't want to see *them* again.

Sammy felt it next, then Derek.

Derek said, 'Holy walrus.'

Sammy looked up. His face had swollen so badly in the night that it looked like some kind of red tuber. It alternately hurt and itched, he said, and he would have had a hard time not scratching it were it not for the fact that he'd grown up knowing that this was the worst thing you could possibly do for frostbite. Besides, he had nothing to scratch it with since his hands were in the same condition.

'It's not like there will be any footprints. It's not like we're visible. It's not like they can even hear us.'

Sammy said, 'So what we'll do is . . . ?'

'Hope and pray they're gonna ride right by us,' Edie said. She was whispering now, though she only realized this when she heard her voice.

'Pray,' said Derek, with what his lips could manage of a scoff.

'Late in the day for that, isn't it?' Of the three of them, he had suffered most on the journey. On the snowmobile, Sammy had managed at least to stick his hands down his trousers, which had probably saved his fingers, though it had led to an agonizing patch of frostbite on his lower back. No such luck for Derek. He had been wearing less than the other two and nothing at all on his hands, which were still frozen, the skin billowing off them like sails in a stiff breeze. Underneath the skin, the flesh was already blackening. His sight had partly returned, or at least he imagined it had. It was too dark in the snow cave to know for sure. Maybe the strange swirls in front of him were the effects of the frostbite. Maybe, he said, they were just what blind people always saw.

The trembling grew stronger and was accompanied now by the burr of engines, the sound coming up from the ice. Edie put her ear to the ice beneath them.

'Definitely two,' she said. 'Not far away now.'

They sat bundled together, barely daring to breathe. Then the sound seemed to dim.

With her ear to the ice again, Edie said, 'They've passed us.' A moment later she said, 'They've stopped.'

Gradually, the sound grew louder once more, then died.

Whoever it was had pulled up right beside them.

All of a sudden, they heard something else. Edie felt herself take a deep breath. A methodical thump started up, coming from somewhere above them. She tipped an ear to the ceiling of their tiny shelter. The sound was at shoulder height.

Someone was using an ice axe.

She wasn't afraid to die, she realized then. She was only afraid of the pain that would come before.

Little particles of ice, fragments of snow which had melted with their breath and crystallized, began to crumble off the section of snow wall nearest to the sound.

Sammy said, 'They're gonna bury us.'

'Uh nuh,' Edie said. She felt oddly calm now. 'If they wanted to do that, they'd have dug in from the top. Whoever it is, they know what they're doing. They want us out alive.'

They could hear the rhythmic chopping of the axe now, slicing its way through the compacted snow. After what seemed like an age, a thin blade of light shone grey through the wall.

Then a voice said, 'Hey, is anyone in there?'

It was Megan Avuluq.

The relief Edie felt passed through her chest and into her face like an electric storm, fizzing as it went. She heard herself gasp, then Sammy's voice booming, 'We're here, we're here!'

A minute later a gap opened up in the snow. The light shone briefly then dimmed as Zach Barefoot's face appeared through the hole. There was a loud whoop.

'You folks down there ready for breakfast?'

They were less cheerful when they saw what a state Sammy and Derek were in, and stunned into anxious silence when Edie explained how they'd got there. Once they were out of the snow, Zach threw up a bivvy shelter, hustled them inside and lit the oil stove. He wrapped them in survival blankets while Megan inspected their frostbite and administered hot sweet tea. There would be time to explain how they'd found them later. For now the priority was to get them back to Nome and into the clinic.

Zach dialled the satphone and immediately got through to the Alaska State Troopers' dispatcher who promised to send the helicopter and a doctor right away. They talked about what to do with the frostbite and agreed it would be best to wait for the doctor. They could try to unfreeze the tissue slowly in warm water but while there was still even the faintest possibility that the helicopter might be weathered out and the flesh refrozen, they decided it was just too risky to begin thawing them out.

The 'copter arrived shortly afterwards. Edie's own hands, only mildly frostbitten, were already beginning to thaw, the pain coming on strongly now. Sammy and Derek were still too numb to feel much from the frostbite and from the looks Zach and Megan were exchanging Edie understood that things were worse for them than even she had realized.

They loaded up. Zach hitched the two snowmobiles together and started back to Nome alone while Megan came with them in the helicopter. She was in uniform, and she was armed.

In the air, Megan said, 'When you didn't come back we called Chrissie Caley. She said two of the race stewards at the Safety roadhouse had left you and Derek waiting for Sammy.' A while later Caley called her back. Sammy's dog team had come limping into White Mountain. They were still dragging the sled but the tarpaulin was missing.

'We called the AST but they just blanked us. Zach said that stuff with Harry Larsen got their backs up. They kinda thought we were muscling in on their territory. Whatever. They just said they were tied up with Marsha Hillingberg's visit right now, but they'd send out the search helicopter when the weather had cleared.'

Marsha Hillingberg. In all the circus of the past twenty-four hours, Edie had forgotten. Megan saw the look on Edie's face.

'Listen, Edie.' Megan turned away from the men and, leaning in to Edie so far that their noses almost touched, she spoke in a grave voice. 'You can't go on with this. Whatever you think Marsha Hillingberg did or didn't do, you've got no proof at all.'

'I've got Detective Truro.'

'You honestly think that Truro's gonna be able to rock the boat? Edie, you don't understand how things are here. For half a century Alaska's been run by the same bunch of old sourdoughs, bankrolling each other, glad-handing, swapping jobs, pushing their agenda and keeping anyone new out. Marsha Hillingberg is the first real opportunity for political change Alaskans have been offered since they became Alaskans. Believe me, they aren't gonna turn away from her because you have some grainy tape with her holding a baby, even a baby who was subsequently found dead. You won't persuade them to connect the two events because they don't want to and because *there's no proof.*' She laid a hand on Edie's knee. 'The moment Derek and Sammy are fit to travel, you have to leave. You have to go back to Autisaq. We can't protect you, Edie. Neither can Detective Truro.'

Most of her knew Megan was right. It was the other part Edie was worried about.

An ambulance with two gurneys was waiting for them on the landing strip in Nome. They bundled Sammy and Derek inside. The paramedic went in after them. Edie and Megan squeezed in last and they moved off towards the airport road. From out of the tiny back windows, Edie could see something out of the ordinary seemed to be happening in the terminal building. There were troopers everywhere and men in fancy outerwear over city suits talking into headsets. Over in the parking lot, a couple of TV crews were stationed. The whole thing screamed 'dignitary'.

They waited for a moment at the exit to the lot as a black SUV drew up to the airport entrance. The driver went around to the passenger side and opened the door.

Edie could feel the adrenaline rise up inside her like some tundra weed at the first summer sun. Megan saw her, shouted, 'No, Edie!'

but it was too late. She had grabbed the handle of the ambulance, pushed open the door and was already running towards where Marsha Hillingberg was settling herself in front of the TV news cameras, Andy Foulsham beside her, with a phony grin on his face. The only thing going through her head right then was the hunter's overwhelming need to bring down her prey.

Others had seen her running now. A tall man wearing a headset came up and made a grab for her, but she managed to shrug him off. Another filled his place, but she dived under his arms and escaped. It seemed that Marsha Hillingberg hadn't yet seen her. She was talking into the TV cameras. Edie ran forward, her heart pounding, aware of a uniformed trooper, a young guy, tall, approaching her from the side. There was a moment when Marsha spotted her and time ground to a halt and in that moment Edie was driven by some wild energy that seemed not to belong to her. The trooper was nearly on her now, she knew she didn't have much time. There was no rational explanation for what happened next. She leaned down and with her puffy frostbitten hands, she scooped up a handful of snow and threw it as hard as she possibly could, watching, as if in slomo, the snowball rising up and over the heads of the security detail, the TV news crews, and in one instant she felt hands bundle her arms to her sides and saw Marsha Hillingberg's face, the eyes screwed into blank slits, her mouth a gasp of horror as the snowball detonated on her face.

As the gubernatorial candidate just stood there, stupefied, Edie heard herself scream, 'You'll trip up, Marsha Hillingberg. God's Little Error will turn out to be your biggest.'

A large mittened hand went over her mouth and she felt herself being whirled around and the trooper's face was in hers, shouting something she could not hear. And then it was all over. From the extreme edge of her field of vision, she saw Andy Foulsham brushing Marsha Hillingberg down. Her eyes snapped about. Megan was pushing through the crowd towards her, shouting something she couldn't hear.

The young trooper brought out his cuffs. She held out her hands and noticed him reel back a little. The hands were like blown rubber gloves, puffed, raw and sinister, the wrists swollen and purple.

'Cuff *those*, sonny.' Her lips widened into a wry smile.

Megan bustled in, panting. She threw the trooper an apologetic look.

'I'm sorry, officer, the lady's just come off a S&R. She's a bit, you know, rattled. Hypothermia and all. We're trying to get her to the clinic right now.'

The trooper hesitated, looked at those hands again, then gave a little nod.

'You make sure they keep her inside till she's . . .' He searched for the right phrase. '. . . till she's *all* better.'

Megan looped an arm through Edie's and escorted her away. When they reached the ambulance, she frowned and said, 'What *the hell* was that?'

Edie clambered back up into the vehicle and cracked Megan a smile. 'Just one woman giving another a heads-up.'

# 46

The sound of the phone woke her. She blinked and saw her hands, huge and bandaged, lying on the counterpane and remembered where she was. Then the pain kicked in.

The phone continued to trill. She wondered how long she'd been asleep, glanced through the chink in the blinds, saw that it was still dark and realized that it couldn't have been more than a couple of hours. She hoped Sammy and Derek were managing to get some rest at the clinic. The phone stopped ringing and a woman's voice came drifting through from the next door room. There was a knock on the door, then the sound of the handle turning. She saw Megan's face, then heard her voice, still thick with sleep, saying:

'Hey, Edie, it's Sharon on the phone. She says it's urgent.'

Edie took a breath and tried to bring the name to mind and the only one she could think of was Sharon Steadman, Tommy Schofield's assistant. She checked the alarm clock beside the bed. It wasn't far off midnight.

'OK,' she said, scrambling to get out of bed, 'I'm coming.'

Megan came into the room and switched on the bedside lamp. 'I got the phone.'

Edie sat up. They both looked at her bandaged hands and swapped sad smiles.

Megan said, 'You want me to put her on speaker?'

'Sure. Then we can both hear.'

Megan gave a sorry shake of the head. Her eyes shifted back to the doorway. 'I'm sorry, Edie, but, you know, I gotta go feed Zoe.'

Edie watched her leave the room. She knew that Megan was trying to tell her that she was drawing the line, that she had a daughter to think about, and that was OK. She took a breath and leaned forward towards the phone.

'Sharon?'

'That you, Edie?' Sharon Steadman's voice for sure. The girl sounded as though she'd been crying.

'What's up?'

'Edie, you near a laptop? I'd like for you to go online.'

There was a laptop on the small table in the living room. She'd seen Zach using it. Lifting herself from the bed, she went to the door and peeked out. The laptop was where she had last seen it. She went back inside and bent down so her mouth was as close to the phone as she could make it. The throbbing in her hands had become an all-out burn now.

'Sharon, I got some stuff going on right now. Maybe you could tell me what this is about?'

The voice just said, 'Please.'

'OK, but be patient, right?' As she said the words, Edie heard her mother, Maggie, asking the same thing of her when she was small. Right now, that seemed impossibly distant. Grasping the phone between her wrists, she shuffled to the door and into the living room. The laptop lid was down, but she managed to work the top loose with her teeth. Strong teeth, she thought. Maggie would have approved. A woman with strong teeth could chew many pelts and a woman who could soften pelts could make clothes for many children. That's what Maggie would have said.

She found a pen and, holding it awkwardly between her bandaged hands, pressed down the On button. The screen lit up and a chord sounded.

'OK, so what now?' she said.

'Type "MoFo Eskimo" into Google.'

Edie felt her heart sink right there.

'Sharon, it's midnight, I'm in pain and I don't have any fingers available, so maybe you just want to tell me why you called?'

The door to Megan's room cracked open. She looked like she wanted to get back to Zoe then get some sleep. But not yet. 'Seems like you could use some help,' she said.

Edie gave a reluctant nod. Into the phone, she said, 'Sharon, my friend Megan's here. Anything you want to say to me you can say to her.'

The voice on the phone sounded frayed. Perky Sharon had left the building. 'So, like I said, what I want you to do is to type "MoFo Eskimo" into Google.'

Megan's eyebrows rose. She typed in the words and followed the link to a YouTube page with a blank screen and the legend 'Eskimo gets hot under the collar with would-be-governor Marsha Hillingberg'. The clip had 187,945 plays. Megan groaned and put her hands over her face.

'This MoFo Eskimo says bring it on,' said Edie. She was thrilled that nearly two hundred thousand people had seen Marsha Hillingberg getting snowballed.

Megan raised her eyes and pressed play. Whoever had taken the footage had captured Edie throwing the snowball, then spun round and picked up Marsha Hillingberg's reaction. Edie's voice played through the laptop's microphone, muffled but still audible:

*You'll trip up, Marsha Hillingberg. God's Little Error will turn out to be your biggest.*

The clip faded out.

'What do you know, Sharon?' Edie asked quietly.

There was a pause, then what sounded like a single sob.

' "God's Little Error", you said that.' Sharon blew her nose.

Megan mouthed, 'Drunk?'

Edie shrugged a 'maybe', then in the kindest voice she could muster, she said, 'Look, Sharon, it's late, why don't you get some sleep? You can always call me in the morning.'

'You think I can sleep knowing what I know?' Sharon's voice screeched up an octave.

'At this point, that's hard for me to say.' Edie's hands were on fire now and she was struggling hard not to lose her temper.

'I gotta tell you, but I'm scared.'

Edie gave a long sigh. 'Scared? We're all *scared*. Get this straight, Sharon. The only folk who aren't scared are the dead ones, and even they get a little nervous sometimes.'

There was a pause. 'I know what you thought about Tommy Schofield.'

'We don't need to discuss it, then.' She cleared her throat. 'You know, seeing as it's midnight.'

'I felt bad about making that call to you, Edie. But you shouldna come to Tommy's office pretending you were someone you weren't.'

'Who would you like me to pretend to be?'

'You don't like Marsha Hillingberg much, do you?'

'If I had a Christmas card list she wouldn't be on it.'

'Tommy hated her. He called her Hellingberg.'

'A wit too,' Edie said drily.

Sharon went on. 'I knew something was wrong when Otis and Annalisa Littlefish kept coming into the office some time after Thanksgiving. Mr Schofield seemed fine for a while, but after Christmas he started to get kinda agitated. He would come in yawning like he hadn't slept and he was kinda ornery with me. One time I thought I heard him crying in his office but then he came out all smiley like nothing happened. I heard him shouting on the phone a lot too. First I knew he'd, you know, killed himself, was through my neighbour Diane who read it on the Homer web page. Afterwards, I had to clean out the office. I found the combination for the safe.' Edie leaned forward. Now they were getting somewhere. 'Maybe I shouldn't have peeked in. There was a pile of stuff, just papers. None of it meant anything to me. There were so many files, so much crap, you know, I didn't know what to think of it. But there was this one file, with "God's Little Error" written on it in Tommy's handwriting.'

Edie and Megan exchanged glances. This was beginning to feel like something now. Sharon had seen the YouTube clip and heard Edie use the same phrase. She'd made the connection.

'I went and got the file out of the storage facility.' She was a bit breathless now, replaying the scene over in her mind. 'Edie, the file had one of those cards in, you know, those memory cards, like the ones you put in a camera? I'm not good at all with that technological stuff, so I took it over to this friend of mine.'

'Pictures?'

'Uh nuh. It was a recording of a phone conversation.'

Edie felt her breath quicken. Her eyes shifted briefly to Megan. Her face wore an expression of intense concentration.

Sharon said tentatively, 'Does that make me a bad person?'

Megan leaned forward.

'Sharon, this is Megan. You tell us what was on the recording.'

'Yeah.' There was another sniff and a pause. 'It was Tommy and Marsha Hillingberg and they were fighting. I don't think Marsha knew she was being recorded.'

In the brief silence that followed Edie could hear her own blood rushing through her veins.

'What were they talking about?'

Silence. There was a gasp on the other end of the line then Sharon Steadman burst into wracking sobbing. For a few impossible minutes all they could hear was the sound of anguished weeping. Then, gathering herself, Sharon said:

'They were fighting about what she did to "God's Little Error".'

# 47

'I'm sure gonna miss that hound!' Stacey laid a mug of hot tea on Edie's usual table at the Snowy Owl Café. 'Bonehead and me, we're like this.' She crossed the first two fingers of her right hand and scanned the table. 'Now, can I getcha anything else or you gonna wait for your guest?'

'I'll wait, thanks,' Edie said, pouring sugar into her tea. The bandages had come off her hands now but they were still red and leathery and exquisitely sensitive to temperature. She wrapped some napkins around the handle of the mug and took a sip.

Two weeks had passed since Megan Avuluq and Zach Barefoot had dug Edie, Derek and Sammy out of their snow cave. The doctors in Nome had discharged Derek and Sammy only yesterday morning. Sammy's left hand was still in bandages, and Derek's frostbite was likely to take a few months to heal, but right now it looked as though they'd both avoided any amputations. All three of them had flown back to Anchorage. They'd checked into a bland hotel in the middle of downtown and were expecting to board the evening plane to Vancouver, from where they'd take the red-eye to Ottawa. So long as the weather held off, they could expect to land in Autisaq in a couple of days. It felt good to finally be going home.

Meantime, though, there was business to attend to. First off, Detective Truro had asked to see her. After that, she intended to fetch Bonehead and make her way back to the hotel where she was meeting Annalisa and Otis Littlefish. The Littlefishes were picking up their daughter from the Green Shoots Clinic. TaniaLee had put in a particular request that Edie be there so she could say goodbye.

She flipped open the morning's *Courier*. The front page was dominated by a picture of a grizzly making his way through a crate of garbage, under the headline 'Humans Encroaching On Bear Territory'. Beneath the bear story there was a piece about whether or not it was possible to predict the amount of the Alaska Permanent Fund Dividend into the future and a link to an Iditarod competitor's training programme for next year's race. It was almost as though the extraordinary events of the past month – the deaths of Lucas Littlefish and Vasilly Chuchin, Dark Believer Fever and the protests of the Mommabears, the 'suicide' of Tommy Schofield, the stalled sale of land to Byron Hallstrom—which was a fraud investigation still pending—even the fatal plane crash of the most popular gubernatorial challenger for years – none of that had ever happened. It had snowed and the landscape was clean once more. North to the Future. Who cared about the past?

She felt a presence to her left and looked up to see Detective Truro taking a seat at her table.

'Howdy.'

He asked after Derek and Sammy and commiserated with her on the state of her hands. He seemed larger, she thought, or maybe it was just that he took up more space now. He'd allowed his hair to grow out a little and was no longer wearing his Christian pin.

'You give up on God?' she said.

'No,' he said, smiling, 'I'm just more relaxed about God not giving up on me.'

The Alaska Investigations Bureau had acknowledged his contribution to the indictment of Marsha Hillingberg and hired him at senior investigator grade with the possibility of a promotion in six months. Hillingberg, meanwhile, was at the Anchorage Women's Penitentiary, spending her supervised work hours looking after the residents at the Pen's dog pound.

Stacey came bundling up with coffee and a tea refill for Edie and they ordered breakfast: pancakes for Truro, reindeer sausages for Edie, with double bacon on the side.

'DA says we got all the evidence we need on the death of Vasilly Chuchin. The forensics on Chuck Hillingberg's airplane crash came in inconclusive. And without a body or any other evidence the bureau will decide to close the Tommy Schofield case before too long.'

'What happened to the girls, Lena and Olga?'

'Lena's application for leave to remain is being fast-tracked. Olga has a daughter born here. She's gonna be OK.'

'And the Stegner kid?'

'Social services is still trying to trace the mother. Lena's been pretty helpful with leads. She and Katerina talked a lot when they were at the Lodge. They think they know which town the girl came from in Russia. They've talked about putting up posters of the kid's tattoo.'

'I guess there's no chance of Mackenzie getting a guided tour of the wrong side of the law?'

Truro washed down the last of his pancakes with some coffee.

'Last I heard he'd retired to Panama.'

'I guess there are some things no one can fix.'

'No one but God,' Truro said. He gave her a smile.

She let it pass. God, the spirit world, nature, truth, whatever you liked to call it, there had to be some order somewhere. If you didn't believe that, you really *were* lost.

Truro wiped his mouth on his napkin and rose to leave. He stuck out his hand, gave a brisk laugh at the reddened, distorted fingers held up sheepishly in return and instead, leaning in, he placed a solitary kiss on Edie's cheek.

'I'll see you at the trial.'

She watched him leave. Moments later, Stacey reappeared to clear away the plates.

'You about set to pick up that cute old canine o' yours? I got him in the staff locker room at the back.'

Edie gave her a warm smile.

'When you're ready.'

Stacey wiped her hands on her apron. Her eyes were shiny with tears. She took Edie along a narrow corridor, past the kitchen and a storage area, until they reached a grey fire door. The dog had already scented them and was scrabbling at the other side and squealing like a chased pig.

'He's pleased to see you,' Stacey said quietly.

In fact, the dog seemed more thrilled by his reunion with Stacey, leaping and twirling about her like a puppy, Stacey laughing and patting him on the flanks. Bonehead came to rest leaning up against her legs, his muzzle on her thigh, the lower part of his body still snaking joyously to and fro.

'I'm gonna miss this great hunk of dogmeat,' she said sadly, scratching the dog's head. 'The walks we've been on. He has a sixth sense, you know, he can find his way back from anywhere.'

Bonehead's wild youth tracking polar bears out on the tundra was behind him and Edie thought about how his life might be back in Autisaq. She'd sled him for a few more years, then, when he began to slow, she'd have to shoot him. That was just the way things were up there. Everything had to earn its keep. No back-ups, no spares, no second chances.

'I guess maybe I could leave him,' she said.

The waitress's face lit up like the first sunrise of the year.

'Straight up?'

'Only if you want.'

She turned to the dog, grasped his head in both hands, and kissed him. 'Looks like you and me just got it together.' The dog's tail spun like a helicopter blade.

Edie gave him a pat goodbye. 'Lucky dog,' she said. She meant it.

Outside, the ice was beginning to break up. Where the piles from the ploughs lay, the edges were already rotting away, the seepage twisting in salty liquid ropes along the street. Spring was coming to Anchorage, though Edie wouldn't be there to see it. Beneath the persistent aroma of gasoline, the smell of the air had changed. It was piney now, and something spicy came in off the ice on Cook Inlet.

Otis and Annalisa Littlefish were already in the hotel lobby, waiting for her. Annalisa had oiled her hair and put on a pair of beaded earrings and greeted Edie nervously. The two women exchanged a few awkward pleasantries. Otis was exactly as she'd remembered him: craggy and internal, his stiff hip reflecting something, she thought, about the workings of his heart. They'd come early for a reason. Annalisa needed to say one or two things that needed to be said, straighten a few things up. No wonder she was nervous.

They took a corner cluster of chairs at one end of the lobby and ordered coffee. While they were waiting for it to arrive, Annalisa messed about with her earrings. A server came and put a large French press and some cups and saucers on the table, then left them. Annalisa took up one of the cups and passed it to Edie. Her hand was trembling.

'I'm a plain-talking type,' Edie said, as much to put Annalisa out of her misery as anything, 'so why don't you just say what you need to say?'

'I guess we want to say sorry and also thank you.' Annalisa Little-fish's eyes flicked to her husband for affirmation. Otis Littlefish blinked.

'Let's start with the regrets, then we can end on a high.'

Annalisa closed her eyes. The pain on her face was just awful to see. When she opened her eyes, there were tears in them.

'I'm sorry I lied to you about how Lucas died.'

Edie couldn't quite bring herself to forgive just yet. If Annalisa had been more honest, it could have saved her a great deal of trouble. Still, the woman was protecting her daughter. Any mother would have done the same thing.

'Understood,' she said. 'Now, about that gratitude part?'

Annalisa cracked a smile.

'Thank you for trying to get justice for our grandson. And thank you for keeping the truth to yourself.'

Edie sat back and sucked that in for a moment. It felt about as good as a bath in a summer lake to hear it.

'Let's go see TaniaLee,' she said.

The girl was in the visiting room at the Pinewood unit. She was still fragile, but her eyes were bright and engaged and she had a new kind of presence. Edie could tell TaniaLee had re-entered the world and it was clear she had detected this change in herself, too. She'd woven strips of decorative fur through her braid and put on a bead necklace. She embraced her parents then came over to where Edie was standing. Her smile suddenly vanished.

'What happened to your hands?'

'It's a long story,' Edie said. 'I'll tell you some other time.' She'd given a lot of thought to the version of events she wanted to tell TaniaLee, and the events of the past few weeks didn't figure in it.

'I know Tommy Schofield – Fonseca – is dead,' TaniaLee said.

'That's OK. When I was sick, a lot of things went through my head which had no place there.'

Annalisa was smiling at her daughter, a look of pride in her eyes. Even Otis had split his lips a little.

Edie turned to the parents. 'You mind if me and TaniaLee have ten minutes together?' She sat on the sofa in the visiting room and motioned for TaniaLee to come and sit beside her.

'I want to tell you a story,' Edie said. 'I've never told this story to anyone before, and I don't know if it'll be helpful or not, but I have a hunch that maybe, later on, much later, it will be, so I want you to remember it.'

TaniaLee sat silent and expectant, her eyes solemn.

Edie started quietly. 'It's about a woman, not as young as you, but young all the same. She got together with someone she loved, but they shouldn't ever have been together because the two of them drank, and each encouraged the other. Because they drank, they didn't take enough care of the kids he already had. Why would they? They were too busy drinking.'

Edie shifted her position.

'The woman got pregnant, but she didn't tell anyone. She didn't know what she felt about the responsibility of having a baby, didn't want to face up to the prospect of having to give up her drinking. No one noticed her belly swelling because she lived in a place where they wore lots of clothes. Her husband didn't notice. At night, he was usually just passed out on the sofa anyway. And then, one day, when the woman was about five months gone, she took herself off fishing. It was summer, so she went by boat and camped along the shoreline. Leastwise, she told everyone she was going fishing. But she kept her real motivation a secret, even from herself.

'The first night the woman was away, she put up camp, but she didn't bother to eat, didn't bother to do anything much but drink. She'd got her hands on some hooch. You know what that is?'

TaniaLee shrugged. 'Alcohol, I guess.'

'Homebrew. Bad, bad stuff. Real strong and nasty. But that didn't matter to the woman. She just drank that stuff down till she passed out, then she was woken by an awful pain. It was like someone had stuck a knife in her belly and pulled out her guts. Really, it was an agony. The pain went on for a long time, cramps, spasms, and when it was gone, so was the baby. Passed right through her, just like the liquor.'

It was odd to say it now, for the first time, as though the words had only just come to Edie on the wind.

'What did you do?' TaniaLee said quietly.

'I buried her. I dug into the tundra and I left my daughter there.'

'I'm sorry,' TaniaLee said.

'Yeah, me too. But you know what? For years I hated myself for what I did so I drank to try and forget, and that made me hate myself more. But in the last few weeks, since I found Lucas's body in the forest, I've stopped hating myself. What I'm thinking now, some people go out of their way to do awful things. They plot and plan. A few of them even get pleasure from it. But most of us, we just stumble through making mistakes. Sometimes the mistakes we make are terrible, but they're still mistakes.'

TaniaLee looked at her gently, then she said, 'Will you come visit?'

Edie looked at her straight. 'No. But there's a part of me that will never leave.'

TaniaLee took this in. It seemed to make sense to her. 'You mind if I talk to that part every now and then?'

'I'd be offended if you didn't.' Edie leaned in. 'Bye, TaniaLee Littlefish.'

'Bye, Edie.'

---

TaniaLee's parents saw her outside. There had been some unexpected heavy snow in the hour or so they'd been inside and it lay on the ground thick and untrodden.

'I'll give you a ride back,' Otis said, heading towards their truck, his bad hip lending him a kind of pimp roll. She followed his footsteps. For such a large man he had surprisingly dainty feet. She had a sudden flashback to the churchyard in Eagle River, to Otis Littlefish and Marsha Hillingberg deep in conversation.

And then she knew.

It was Otis Littlefish who had killed Tommy Schofield. Maybe Marsha Hillingberg put him up to it, but he'd had reason enough on his own. He must have parked up along the main road and made his way through the woods to Tommy's cabin, then hollered for him. When Tommy came out, he must have pulled his hunting rifle and marched his employer around to the field-dressing shed and killed him right there and then. All the blood in the world in that shed. Tommy's wouldn't make any difference. The way she could see it now, he laced on Tommy's shoes, then he'd driven up to the lake, and he'd gone out onto the ice, carved out a hole, slid back along the ice on his ass so as not to leave any prints, and clambered onto a pair of kids' stilts and made his way back to the road, leaving only moose prints behind. He and Marsha must have already agreed that she would arrange to pick up the body, take it up to Meadow Lake and try to pass it off as Peter Galloway.

Frontier justice. A lifetime of being underpaid and undervalued, an abused daughter and a dead grandson, avenged in the killing of one man. And everyone looking the other way.

Otis Littlefish had just pulled off the perfect crime.

She smiled to herself. 'You know what, Otis? Don't worry about the ride. I'll call for a cab.'

He looked surprised, then grateful. 'Well, OK then.'

'I'd like to shake your hand before I go,' she said. 'And I would if my own weren't so beat up.'

He tipped his hat. 'Goodbye, Edie Kiglatuk.'

'Goodbye, Otis Littlefish.'

She watched him walk back into the clinic to fetch his daughter home.

The taxi dropped her back at the hotel where Derek and Sammy were already in the lobby, waiting for her.

'We're all settled up,' Derek said, 'ready to go.'

They followed the bellhop with the luggage cart past the reception desk and towards the exit. As Edie strode past the gift shop, she caught something from the corner of her eye, a white bear standing alone on a shelf just inside the door.

Whistling to Derek and Sammy, who were already ahead, she yelled, 'I'll catch up!' and went into the store.

The assistant was a young *qalunaat* girl with short, glossy moose-coloured hair and a pleasant, freckled complexion. She got the bear down from the shelf and handed it to Edie. It was a tacky souvenir, made of stuffed rabbit fur, stitched up crudely, and with tiny beads sewn in a collar around the neck.

'I guess it's supposed to be a polar bear,' the assistant said.

'Maybe.' Edie smiled, pulled out her purse and handed over the money.

'Is it a gift?'

Edie thought about this. 'Yeah, that's exactly it. A gift.' She thanked the assistant, jammed the bear into her day pack and went out into the cool Alaska spring air where Derek and Sammy were waiting for her. Then she threaded her arms through the arms of her two friends and said:

'Let's go home.'

# Acknowledgments

Alaska writer Nancy Lord made my trip to her glorious home state both possible and fruitful. Thanks also to Ken Lord, Pam and Larry Brodie in Homer and to Kristine Rawert and family in Nome for their hospitality and for their generosity in sharing their very deep knowledge of, and love for, Alaska.

I owe a great debt of gratitude, as ever, to Simon Booker and Dr. Tai Bridgeman for seeing me through various drafts of the manuscript.

Thanks to Peter Robinson, Stephen Edwards, Margaret Halton, Alex Goodwin and the staff of Rogers, Coleridge and White and to Kim Witherspoon, William Callahan and the staff of Inkwell Management. Very many thanks are also due to Maria Rejt, Sophie Orme, Eli Dryden, Chloe Healy and the team at Mantle and to Kathryn Court, Tara Singh and the team at Penguin USA.

Any errors are mine.